Published by
Passion & Pleasure Books
8939 S. Sepulveda Blvd., Suite 110 #259
Los Angeles, CA 90045

Printed in the USA.

Cover Design and Interior Format

LIES YOU TELL

 LIES BOOK 2

Jacki Renée

As always, I dedicate this to my daughters, Jai'Lauren and Jos'Lynne.
Sometimes you have to just step out on faith.

ACKNOWLEDGEMENTS

I AM FORTUNATE TO HAVE THE love and encouragement of family and friends who understand my pleasure for writing. Without the support of two incredible women, Jacqueline Miller and Joan Goldman, the release of this book would be more than a month behind. Thank you for your critiques, input, and keen eyes for detail. I couldn't ask for better beta-readers.

A big thank you to The Killion Group, Inc. for all you do to make me feel as if I'm your only client even though I know I'm not.

A special thank you to my friends and colleagues at IUSD who coordinated a surprise Congratulations/Book Signing party after the release of my first book, Necessary Lies. I cannot put into words how much I appreciate your support.

My deepest gratitude to iProofread And More for your insight and services.

IAMJACKIRENEE.COM is maintained by the very talented Kenward Romero. Thank you for your continued generosity and the one-on-one consultation.

Finally, I want to thank the readers for purchasing, sharing, or recommending my books. Yes, I love to keep you guessing, and the method to my madness is for you to see the story through the eyes of the characters. I strive to create a portal to a different reality. Thank you for traveling this road with me and experiencing the peaks and valleys and the walk with Bryan and Danielle into the arms of a "Happily Ever After."

CHAPTER ONE

"WHERE'S MY WIFE?" I SPEAK into my vest mic.

"Mama Hawk's running through the East Wing with Edwards," Porter reports.

"I've got the lobby doors covered." Ricci's voice comes through the earpiece in my ear.

"Since they're in the east side of the hospital, I'm heading to Mobile Command." Paul's voice crackles.

I take out the earpiece, make an adjustment, and put it back in.

"MC's sitting at the loading dock," Barrett says.

"Porter, did you get that tracker on the ambulance still parked in the emergency room lot?"

"Affirmative, sir," he replies.

"We're ready for anything he throws at us." Acosta secures his weapon in the thigh holster.

They know I'm uncomfortable with Dani being with Edwards.

"Chen, you set?" I speak into my mic.

"Phantom Secret Service have freeway exits blocked. And I've got eyes on the Baby Hawks," he replies.

The elevator doors open.

Acosta and I jog to the midnight-black, semi idling at the loading dock in the back of the hospital. The eighteen-wheeler Phantom Bullet is our Mobile Command. Paul's already activated the hidden fold-down steps. He's climbing inside the trailer.

We follow. I push the button to retract the steps and bring down the door. Porter's sitting at a station viewing multiple screens at one time.

Paul's boots pound the metal floor as he jogs to the front of the trailer. A hidden door slides open, he walks onto the customized step attached to the tractor unit and through the passage of the sleeper to take his seat in the cab next to Barrett.

Paul designed and helped build this rig. It's bigger and better than the Milk Man truck Langford had when he was Second Command. I hated riding in that thing.

"We're picking up Ricci at the exit," I say as I plop down in the chair in front of my station, buckle the seat belt, and let the scanner read my palm. My computer comes online.

"Smoke bomb detonated in the lobby. I'm right behind Mama Hawk," Ricci reports. His mic rustles from the movement of his body.

I quickly access Riley to dispatch a backup team to retrieve the remains of the bomb and the device that caused the blackout.

On the monitor, I watch as Edwards presses a keycard on a sensor. Porter allows the emergency room doors to open and holds them until Ricci clears them.

Porter pulls up the satellite tracking as the ambulance flees from the hospital.

Our rig slowly rolls out of the loading zone.

The gears on the roll-up door hum. Ricci climbs into the trailer. He pats my shoulder and takes his seat.

Acosta turns up the volume on the speakers at his station. Since we're not on a seek-and-destroy mission, he's playing hip hop from one of his favorite artists, Lil' Wil.

On the outside, our Mobile Command looks like a regular semi. But the detachable trailer is armored, and inside the cargo haul is a state of the art military setup.

The ambulance is heading north toward Old Towne Arvada. We're traveling the parallel streets so we don't spook Edwards.

Paul does a city search and comes up with five possible locations where Edwards might ditch the ambulance. In all the years I've known him, Paul's always been on the money when predicting hiding spots.

Porter types in the locations and watches the map on the screen, directing Barrett on the parallel streets.

Dani knows about the black Suburbans. At this point, I don't know if she'd warn Edwards to be on the lookout or distract him from noticing.

The orange dot disappears. Porter is still learning, so I verbally tell him how to relocate the signal while I do it on my computer. He's too green for me to wait and see if it works. Hopefully his memory is as good as his file says it is.

On the central monitor, the image of the ambulance's last location comes up. The unit is engulfed in flames yet still in motion. It's on a collision course with the playground equipment.

I dispatch the closest fire station and send a message to Riley to transfer ten grand from my business account to the City of Arvada's Parks and Recreations funds along with an email to the mayor from Hawkeye Personal Protection.

I give Porter the code to activate the tracking chip in Dani's engagement ring. The green dot is heading south. Barrett makes the block; we change direction. The satellite view shows Dani and Edwards jogging up a dark street. I hope all this running doesn't harm the baby. Especially since I blocked her from strenuous workouts.

The car they dive into takes the highway entrance heading toward Boulder.

Having modified tandem axles makes it possible for Barrett to pick up speed once we're on the highway. Paul went to great lengths to ensure the frame and axles could withstand the weight of the trailer and still move at maximum speed with ease.

Edwards has been bouncing from hotel to hotel since he got to Boulder three weeks ago. With certain highway exits blocked, he has no choice but to go to the one off Baseline Road. It seems to be his favorite anyway. I breathe a little easier knowing he's heading to a location I can control.

Earlier, Marine Guards evacuated the hotel, planted remote-controlled toy cars in every room, and are posing as hotel staff.

Ricci starts cussing in Italian, then throws his phone across the cab. He *was* on a conference call with his division leaders. They must not have given him the answers he wanted. He's been barking at them since he sat at his station. This is Porter's first ride-along with the Elite team. The magnitude of Ricci's anger can be nerve-racking. He'll get used to it.

The Bullet exits the highway seven minutes after Edwards, and Barrett parks a block away from the hotel. Paul is using the remote-controlled cars to do a visual search of the rooms. The first thing we notice are the black duffle bags on the floor of Edwards's room and the room above his. Paul tries an infrared scan of the closest bag, but can't get a reading.

The rest of us get ready to set up a secondary command center in the hotel and bring in Edwards in—alive.

After a back and forth debate, I pull rank. Acosta helps me into the full torso armor vest. No one is stopping me from getting my wife out of here safely.

I disengage the magazine in my weapon and check the ammunition. "Vin, give me a live mag." No emotion in my voice. I toss the one filled with blanks back to him. "If I were going to kill him, I would have done it in the courtyard."

He tosses me a new mag. And four more.

Engaging the clip, I take the safety off and rack the slide, then put the safety back on and holster my weapon.

This time Edwards didn't search the room for electronic bugs. Paul's had to get creative with surveillance.

"Someone's trying to tap into our surveillance," Porter shouts.

The camera feed goes in and out. Wavy lines and static.

The monitors go black.

I rush to my station and start typing in a series of codes while watching the screens.

Nothing.

Don't panic, Hawk. Stay focused or Dani and the baby could get hurt.

Inhale.

Exhale.

"Riley?"

"Yes, sir."

"On my mark, shut down all IP addresses worldwide for sixty seconds," I command.

"Roger that."

"Porter, you have forty-five seconds to get the U.S. military back online before some serious shit happens. Chen, find the bastard trying to access our feed, block his ass, and send a team to the address."

"Roger that," both men respond.

I type a quick message to POTUS while watching the clock on the monitor. "And"—it hits the hour—"mark."

Porter's fingers punch the keyboard at his station. In the earpiece, I hear the keys of Chen's keyboard. Right away the gear of the roll-up door hums. One by one the Elite Team jumps out of the trailer. I'm always the last to exit.

Like the ghosts we are, we keep to the shadows and silently make our way to the back parking lot. I deactivate the fire alarm on the emergency exit and we infiltrate the building, going up the stairs to the second floor.

Even though Porter's already told me the camera is back online and Danielle is okay, the minute we get into a hotel room a few doors down from Edwards's, I log on to my laptop to see for myself.

I check the military's systems as an afterthought. If Langford were here, he'd ride my ass for putting my country second.

Ricci pulls up an area map and we plot our next move based on Edwards's only exit routes.

Acosta assembles a makeshift lab.

Paul is keeping an eye on Danielle. "Hey. Check this out." Using the controller, he gives us a close-up of her. She's blushing.

If I were an insecure man, I'd kick in the door and beat that traitor's ass for dropping his drawz in front of my wife.

While Edwards is walking around ass naked, I tell the Marine Guards posing as diner workers, to stall him when he comes in and places an order. We need time to search the room.

Barrett informs us our backup driver is here with an ambulance. I like that he anticipates our transportation needs and makes decisions without me telling him to. He's the best in his field and an asset to the team.

The guys and I wait until Danielle's in the shower to sneak into the room.

Paul scans the duffle bags, finding explosives. Using sign language, he assures me the explosives can't detonate and he'll examine them once we have Edwards in custody.

Ricci searches the room for weapons, finding several stored in the box spring. Porter's taking notes for whoever I assign to sweep the room once we leave.

Acosta collects samples of Edwards's DNA from the bloody gauze pads.

After I check out the equipment on the table and in the backpack, I have Riley block all Wi-Fi signals and cell phone towers within a hundred-mile radius. It's excessive but necessary.

The water in the shower stops. We quietly leave, going back to our secondary command center.

Acosta tests Edwards's blood samples so he'll know how much of the tranquilizing solution to fill in each plastic bullet. We want Edwards to appear dead, not actually be dead. At least not today.

We double-check each other's gear, then form a circle.

Heads bowed, we stretch our arms around each other's shoulders. Paul recites our team prayer.

Ricci starts the fight chant.

The ritual started as a way to relax us before our first official mission as the Phantom Elite Special Operations Team. Since none of us was killed or injured that day, we continued to do it before every operation, big or small. It's been our thing for nine years.

"I'll take him out if it comes down to it," Acosta tells me before he follows the others out the door.

Alone in the hotel room, Edwards and Danielle eat from take-out containers. I watch. Her nostrils are flared. Something's bothering her. I didn't peg her as a good liar, but she's convinced Edwards she's seen his laptop. Actually, she has. She used it back in December to research home spa stuff. I'd purposely left it out.

"Edwards knows the Wi-Fi is down. He has a gun in his right hand and one tucked in his back waistband," I say into my mic.

"Copy that," Acosta confirms.

Edwards's hotel room door opens and they creep into the corridor.

"Stairs," I tell my team, then shut down my laptop.

Ricci's on the rooftop of the adjacent building. He's the sniper. Paul will cover the exit.

I pull my weapon, take the safety off, and open the door, quietly stepping into the hallway. My steps are light as I come up behind Edwards.

We get to the door at the stairwell. I tap him on the shoulder. Edwards spins around, switches the gun from his right hand to his left and pulls the weapon from behind him aiming it at my chest.

"So, we're at an impasse, Hawk?"

"I guess we are, Edwards."

"You enjoy fucking my wife?"

Which wife are you referring to? The one you actually married or the one you got all dressed up for and pretended to marry? If you're talking about the real Mrs. Edwards, I wasn't the one who fucked her. But I was told she's a boring lay.

"Every *fucking* minute of it." I laugh to get a reaction out of him. *Yeah, I know you want to kill me, but you don't have the balls to do it.*

"My brother didn't deserve to die."

Danielle gasps. Guess he still hasn't told her he had a twin.

"You shouldn't have played this game with him."

"I knew you followed Kimberly to Canada."

I didn't hide the fact that I controlled your every move. I wanted you to come after me.

"You knew because I wanted you to know. Just like you found Danielle because I wanted you to find her."

"Bullshit!" he sneers.

"You got what I wanted you to have, when I wanted you to have it."

"I'm good at what I do."

"I'm better."

Oops, maybe I need to take it from a ten to a two on the confidence level. I don't like the look Dani just gave me.

Playtime is over. It's late. Mama Hawk needs to be in the nest, resting.

"She's leaving with me," I tell him.

Shit! Shit! Shit! What the fuck is she doing? Danielle just cracked the door open. Edwards is too focused on me to notice and I don't have time to signal Ricci.

I slightly shift my position so Acosta will have to shift his; hopefully he can see why and warn Ricci.

"I'm leaving by myself!"

Paul, I hope you've got her covered.

"No, bitch. You're leaving in a body bag," Edwards barks.

Bang!

Her shoulder. Dani cries out.

Crackle. The sound of a sniper's bullet penetrating the glass window at the same time a second shot is fired from Edwards's gun. I reach back and punch him in the face as three aimed bullets whiz past me.

The stairwell door slams shut after Danielle flies through it. Edwards falls to the floor still squeezing the trigger. I kick the gun out of his hand and run for the door.

CHAPTER TWO

"YO. BRO. THAT SHOT'S WORN off?" Tony shouts.

"I'm all right." Elbow bent like a flexed bird's wing, I use it to push the faucet knobs to stop the water flow. I snatch up a sterile towel. For the past six hours, I've relived every detail of last night from the moment the lights went out on the fifth floor of the hospital to early this morning, hearing my son's heartbeat. Could I have done anything different to stop Dani from falling down those stairs?

Before I join the guys in the restricted area of the operating room, I slide my hands into purple surgical gloves. They've already started on Edwards. I had to make sure my wife is well protected before I left her alone in the room.

Ig looks up from the man on the table. "Stop beating yourself up over it, Bry. Nothing ever goes exactly the way we planned. You know that. She and the baby are fine and we've got Edwards."

It still doesn't sit right with me. Dani and I were left susceptible in that courtyard. Which means one thing. We have a mole in Phantom and that person's loyalty isn't to the United States.

"I want to know why his Shadow didn't notify you when he lost him."

Vin's shoulders roll, and with a slight twist of his head, he cracks his neck. "I've already told him to meet me in two hours." The determination is clear in his response. He *will* get to the answers I seek.

"I'll help you," Tony vows. "The way things went down, there's no way it falls on one man. We're questioning everyone on that assignment. A clear message needs to be sent throughout the branch. Play with our lives and there'll be consequences."

I don't micromanage how Tony, Vin, and Ig lead their divisions. They recognize the finger pointing starts with how well they know their people.

Ig stares at the 3D image of Edwards's torso on the virtual screen. He holds out his hand. "RAGS will stop coming after Dani."

Ever since Edwards came back to life, the anti-government organization, Rebels Against Government Suppression, RAGS, orchestrated ways to get to my wife. Danielle was unknowingly the key to information that can bring down the American government and start World War III.

I place the handle side of the scalpel in his gloved hand. "They'll be more interested in the equipment left in his room."

We have reason to believe RAGS's leadership is being challenged and they've lost control over half the minions. Allowing Dani to leave with Edwards will make them think Edwards recovered the information she's been holding on to for him.

"Is Porter staying on Dani's security detail?" Tony asks.

"Hawkeye Personal Protection Officers are taking over security now with him as point person. I want to use him for something else."

Except for the men in this room, Chen, and Porter, everyone in Phantom are guilty until they can prove otherwise. Once the contract is signed to be a ghost, all constitutional rights are forsaken. We follow an alternative set of laws. Until the mole or moles are dug up from their holes, my company personnel will guard my family.

Vin holds up a metal surgical pan. *Clink,* the bloody slug Ig just pulled out of Edwards drops inside. He uses tweezers to retrieve it from the pan and secures the slug in an evidence bag. He'll do a ballistics test for the report that goes to POTUS.

Ig gestures to the tray holding surgical instruments. I pick up the hemostat and hand it to him. He holds out his hand for the pre-threaded suture needle. We watch him sew up Edwards.

"He was moving around like he wasn't shot," Vin comments.

"The morphine dulled the pain and those ice packs slowed down the bleeding," Ig says without looking up. "Done. You guys can take him to recovery." He steps away from the table while we disconnect Edwards from the machines.

Tony and Vin push the gurney out of the operating room. Ig

steps out of the area. I put another tray of sterile instruments on the stand and grab a chair. I popped a couple stitches when I cold-cocked Edwards.

Sitting under the lights, I pull the surgical top over my head. The gauze covering the wound is soaked. Slowly, I remove the bandage and clean the area with a preoperative skin antiseptic. This one doesn't have that hospital smell that churns my stomach.

Ig walks back into the room covering his hands with a fresh pair of gloves. "You good or do I need to give you a booster?"

"I'm good." The minute we tracked Edwards heading toward the hospital, Ig injected me with one of his engineered pain blockers. It's how I was able to get out of that hospital bed and go after Edwards. My shoulder is numb.

As Phantom ghosts, we're taught to desensitize in order to withstand many levels of pain. It's part of our anti-interrogation training. Even if I felt the needle piercing my skin, I would still sit here and take it.

"Did you see the focus of Dani's attack? Man, she's quick. Now I get why Vin's pride took a blow when she knocked him down."

I'm so proud of my girl's skills, it makes me smile. "Yeah, she's a boxing artist. I was going to let her drop Tony, but she's mad at me, not him."

"That would have been fun to watch in person. The video from the mall when she brought down the tank didn't do it justice. Have you seen Tony's sides? The bruises are visible already."

"She's relentless in survival mode. I should know." I exercised control over her and she fought back with everything she had until I tied her to the bed and shackled her feet. That December morning, the monster I'd hidden from her was released. It scared me because it took *everything* in me to rein him back in. Something about the way Dani kept fighting back made me lose control. Now that I know about Tucker attacking her, I understand why she fought so hard. My monster is there to get me through the ugliness of the job, not make my wife submit to my will.

Ig snips the thread and covers it with a gauze bandage.

Mindful of the new stiches, I put on a clean shirt, then we gather all surgical instruments and used supplies, dropping them in the biohazardous container filled with a chemical that destroys any traces of DNA. This floor is secured, but we can't take chances. We need RAGS to think Edwards is dead—again.

Riley posted a cryptic message, on a black-market site. Rumors of Edwards being alive have been proven to be false.

Ig seals the container, hands me a sling, and waits until I put it on. He grabs his weapon and we leave the OR.

"I know you're faced with an uphill battle with Dani. You're being pulled in different directions. If any one of us can find the balance between the job and the people we love, it's you."

"Thanks, Ig." I'm sure he emailed me a playlist of songs he believes will help. My friend and brother is into music therapy.

When we first met, Ig was a scrawny, nonathletic nerd and a full-fledged medical surgeon at age eighteen. I was in Mexico on assignment. The sailor I was investigating got injured. Ig was the doctor on duty in the emergency room. His unconventional methods saved the sailor's ability to walk.

We kept in touch after I left Mexico. I convinced Langford to give him a shot. A few months later, Ig and his family had dual citizenship. He enrolled at University Colorado Boulder as a music major while Phantom pushed through the necessary paperwork to get him certified to legally practice medicine in the U.S. Ig has this thing about the power of music influencing the mind and body, so he trained to be a Phantom ghost and had the opportunity to test his theories on the government's dime.

Ig holds the door open to the room reserved for top-level government dignitaries. Per the president's orders, it's been set up for two patients and the entire floor cordoned off. If you don't have the security clearance, you're not getting on this floor.

Dani's asleep. Willis and Marie stand off to the side having a quiet argument, if I'm reading their body language correctly. His right hand fisted, the other brushing through his hair, nostrils flared. She's leaning forward, both hands on her hips, lips moving, eyes squinted.

Marie looks up when I walk in. She rushes to me. "Is everything okay?"

I force my lips to turn up in a smile that I don't feel. No, everything isn't okay, but she's mothered me since the day they moved in to help with Emm. I don't want to worry her so I one-arm hug her and lie. "Everything's fine."

She motions for me to sit in the chair next to my wife's bed. A knot forms in my stomach as I stare. Dani's messy hair half covers her face. Her nose is red and her lips are chapped. My girl is strong, but everyone has their limit and we're pushing Dani to hers.

First I use my hand to brush her hair off her face, then lean in to kiss her lips. I ease into the chair and rest my hand on the gown covering her stomach. This pregnancy is supposed to be different. Happy. Shit keeps piling on and happiness is creeping out the back door.

"Bryan?" Marie stands next to me, staring at Dani. "Is your job more important than being the man she deserves?"

How can I answer without betraying my wife or my country?

Willis grumbles. "I told you to stay out of this. If you can't mind your business…"

"Danielle is my business, Willis Percival Langford. She's your business too."

I take Marie's hand in mine. "I promise, when this is over, we'll sit down and tell her."

"You keep saying that, but I see no end. We should tell her now."

Willis exhales. "Danielle is his wife. He decides when…"

Marie's lips tighten and she snatches her hand from mine to point an angry finger at her husband. "She is not his wife. That ceremony was fake."

Her verbal punch was really directed at me. I was expecting Marie to chase me around the hospital room with a scalpel last night. Instead, she verbally let me know just how much I've disappointed her.

They don't get it; most people don't. Dani and I have history. We didn't just meet seven months ago. Our relationship is— untraditional. We have our own secrets. Our own lies.

Before I say something ungentlemanly, I motion for Willis to get Marie out of here. Dani knows all she needs to know for now.

Our marriage isn't legal, but Dani's a Hawk where it matters most. I stare at the beautiful sleeping woman who inspires me to find the balance between the two worlds. Not even my predecessors were able to do it. Their family life suffered because of the job.

There's nothing text book about my wife. She's one of many who beat the stereotype of a foster-kid. She's ambitious. Focused. Driven. Next to my grandmother, Dani is the most *non-swearing* woman I know.

Dani claims she didn't have a connection with anyone other than Edwards when she was growing up. I know for a fact she's still in touch with a few of the students she tutored when she was in college in California. One works for a major Public Relations firm that represents big-time sports celebrities. She called him over the holidays and a couple days later, Willis had autographed boxing gloves for Christmas. Up until her foster father needed full-time care, George and Katherine visited her in Arizona once a year.

Two Secret Service agents come through the door. Immediately, I stand as they check the room. I keep my eyes on the door.

At first sight, my right hand rises. Tip of my forefinger touches the temple point of the frame of my glasses. Palm down. Upper arm parallel to the floor. I salute my Commander in Chief.

"Why aren't you recovering in a bed, Colonel?" He acknowledges the salute, then hands me a big basket filled with colorful flowers and balloons attached. I'm sure the First Lady ordered them.

I set it on the shelf near Dani's bed. "I'm fine, sir."

He motions with his hand. "Your wife?"

The corners of my mouth turn up. "She and my son are doing well."

POTUS shakes my hand and slaps me on the shoulder. He congratulates me and proceeds to tell me how he felt the first time he learned he was having a son, sixteen years ago.

"How's Edwards?" he asks, getting back to business.

"Made it through the surgery. Hawkeye personnel have eyes on him with Porter pulling offsite Watcher duty until I vet Phantom personnel."

He nods. "You have my full support. I want those responsible to pay for their actions against the United States. Just keep me informed."

This is why I work so well with President Hart; he understands that the attack wasn't just on me and my wife, it was on the country as well. As Second Command, I protect the country.

Dani yawns and cracks her eyes open. She blinks a few times. Wipes her eyes with the back of her hands. Her jaw slacks, leaving her mouth open.

"Sir, my wife, Danielle. Dani, President Emerson Hart." I don't miss the quick scowl she tosses my way.

President Hart covers her hand with both of his. "It's nice to finally meet you, Mrs. Hawk."

"Mr. President," she whispers and coughs.

On the mobile tray is a plastic water pitcher and cup and paper-covered straw. I pour her a cup of water. Dani presses a button on the bed's control to sit up, taking the cup.

"I had to see for myself you and your wife are okay. I thought Acosta was downplaying the injuries."

"Of the five of us, he's the most honest."

"I'll remember that." He laughs. "I have to go, but you let me know if either of you needs anything." He walks toward the door, then stops and turns around. "Every year my wife hosts a luncheon for the spouses of our armed forces men and women. Of course, we can't say you're there because your husband is a colonel, but if you're able to travel, we'd like for you to come, Mrs. Hawk."

"We'll let you know, sir." The smile on Dani's face is as fake as it is sarcastic. I'm surprised she didn't come back with a flipped reply for being addressed as Mrs. Hawk.

We watch the two agents follow President Hart out.

I slowly exhale before I turn around to face Dani. What steals my breath is the level of anger I see in her brown eyes. To avoid the argument stirring in her brain, I retreat to my bed.

The pain blocker is starting to wear off and my body's telling me to rest. I focus on a shadow on the ceiling and use a breathing technique to relax me. *Pain is the weakness leaving the body.*

———◆———

In slow motion, Edwards steps out from behind a pillar. Gun drawn. Dani's feet falter. A shot hits my vest on the right. Edwards's eyes buck. He grabs Dani. I reach for my firearm. A shot gets through my vest that just misses Dani's head. I grab her from Edwards and pull her down with me. Edwards looks over his shoulder in the direction the shots came from.

I stop the video there. Edwards's looking over his right shoulder. The tip of my index finger draws a square from the top of the laptop screen down to him. "Riley, mark this square."

I start the video.

A third shot hits my vest before Dani and I reach the ground. Again, missing her head. *Get down!* I'm yelling at him. He's just standing there. I roll Dani off my shoulder to fire at Edwards to make him drop to the ground too. Dani's hands roam my torso. I look for our security. Edwards turns and runs in the gunman's direction.

I stop the video and draw another square from the top of the screen to the point above my head. "Riley, mark this square."

I adjust the headset covering my ears and unfreeze the video.

It doesn't show on the screen, but by this time, Porter's out of the Suburban, firearm drawn. Dani's knee bumps my arm causing me to drop on top of her. The gun falls from my hand. I'm trying not to let the pain show on my face. Before I roll off her, I look to see how close Porter is. I motion for him to go after Edwards.

Mills comes into the frame. Hands empty.

I stop the video and draw a square around Mills.

I unfreeze the video and finish watching to the end and type out the instruction for Riley to list all businesses within the marked squares.

Fingers laced, my forehead presses into the palm of my hands. I exhale long and slow. I've watched the video of the shooting a dozen times. Regular motion. Slow motion. Frame by frame. Each time, I see something else. The one thing that stays constant—Edwards never fired his weapon.

CHAPTER THREE

TONY'S WIPING DROOL FROM HIS mouth as he walks through the door. "Have you seen Nurse Abby?"

"What's up with you and Tiffany?"

"You know the rule: until I introduce her to the group as my girlfriend, she's just a friend."

"Ig's medical staff is on a look-but-don't-date order. Especially after what happened with the last one."

He raises his hands like this is a holdup. "Don't put that on me. *You* know how hard it is to turn down a honey with body and brains. Listen. Women work up the courage to come at a fine, young, dark-skinned brotha such as myself. If the full lips don't get em, then the blue eyes do. Turning them down is an insult to womankind."

Some say he's cocky. We say confident.

I pick up my sweats off the end of the bed and head to the bathroom. "Womankind, huh?" I open the door. "Don't wake up that woman." I point to Dani. "She didn't sleep much last night and I doubt she'll fall for your blue eyes."

He frowns in her direction, unclips his phone from the belt holster, and sits in the chair next to my bed. "We're cool as long as she keeps her hands to herself."

"Thanks again for keeping your head, Tony. I know you wanted to hit her back."

"I couldn't, no matter how much I'm trained to. It would've been like hitting my little sister and risking an ass kicking from my grandma for raising my hand to a female."

We laugh. His grandmother is a sweet and quiet woman, but make her mad and she'll rip you a new one.

I close the bathroom door and get ready for our meeting. The wound slows me down a bit and wearing a sling isn't helping either. I skip shaving. Growing a beard has never been my thing, but three days of not shaving doesn't look bad. I'll shape it when we get home.

Jessi and Nurse Abby are standing by Dani's bed when I go back into the room. Tony is rummaging through the bag Marie sent breakfast in. She called early this morning to check on us. I told her Dani isn't eating much. Marie insisted on sending something with Jessi.

Whatever's in the bag smells good. Marie loves whipping up a batch of Southern comfort food.

I get my sister's attention and ask a silent question by cocking an eyebrow. *How are they?*

Jessi nods. *So far so good.*

Nurse Abby helps Dani get out of the bed.

"Morning, little sis." Tony talks with his mouth full.

Dani winces with each step she takes toward the bathroom. They walk right past him like he's not in the room. The door closes behind them.

"Oh, we're holding grudges?" Tony puffs out his chest. "Maybe I should unbutton my shirt and show you why I'm entitled to hold the biggest grudge."

I herd him closer to the door before Dani bursts out of the stall and finishes that ass kicking from the other night. It's not a good idea to provoke Mama Hawk.

"You didn't push Vin out of the kitchen when he joked about y'all's sex life."

"I didn't love her then." I push him out of the room.

"Bullshit! We took a bet to see how long it'd take you to admit your feelings. We owe Ig ten-racks." He jumps out of the way of a punch aimed at him. He uses that sci-fi character's voice to annoy me. "Right wing's slow it is, young Hawk."

We walk the corridor to the elevator. I nod to the ex-armed forces men and women employed by Hawkeye Personal Protection. They have no ties to Phantom and were Honorably Discharged from the military and therefore can be trusted.

Tony and I reach the elevators. He presses the down button. "All jokes aside, how you doing, man?"

"Them being here was never supposed to be this complicated."

"You could have sent them anywhere, but it was time for you guys to be together. We will do what we have to, to keep them here. Even if that means I take a leave of absence from the sheriff's department and come on as Hawkeye's Executive Operations Officer."

"You serious?" I know wearing the uniform is important to Tony and would never ask him to give it up.

He nods. "I want to help you keep them here. Permanently."

Ding. The down symbol flashes. Tony unsnaps the strap on his holstered firearm and steps in front of the doors. Until Ig clears me, I can't carry a weapon, which means one of them has to babysit when I'm out in the open; POTUS orders.

Thankfully the cab is empty. I'd hate for Tony to order civilians to get out.

We step inside and I push the button for the basement. Tony stays focused on the doors as the elevator passes each floor. He takes his job as my wingman seriously. I know if I'd died in that courtyard, he would have gotten my family out of the country and taken care of them. Hell, so would Ig and Vin. But me and Tony go way back. He comes from a household of women. To him, we're brothers.

The elevator doors open, Ig and Vin are there to meet us. We walk to the SCIF in silence. Due to the nature of our meeting, it is necessary for us to use the Sensitive Compartmented Information Facility here at the military hospital. We usually meet in the underground one in my office building.

Porter stands at attention when we enter the room. I'm not much on formalities when it's just the Elite Team, but I return his salute before sitting at the head of the conference table. It's cluttered with equipment and laptops.

After going through the security scan, my laptop boots up.

"Good morning, sir," Riley says.

I type in the command for the room to be secured.

The airlock door closes us in and the green light comes on. We start with discussing national security and the breach in our department. Each man has his own take on the situation. We agree to hold an impromptu Phantom staff meeting as soon as I'm released from the hospital. Riley will record it, and monitor body functions like heart rates and subconscious movements. Chen will analyze voice tones and eye focus. As farfetched as it may sound, a person doesn't have to be in the same room for their body language to be observed. As long as there's a digital camera that is connected to some form of network communication, it can be tapped into. There's also satellite thermal imaging.

Ricci reads the statements given by the men assigned to Edwards. A copy is in my inbox. Ricci also reports there's an influx of Washington-based military personnel requesting leave. The concern is that their leave dates are the same across the board. So far, none of the men and women are on our watch list, but as a precaution, we will continue to monitor their activity.

Paul keeps us laughing as he gives his report on a worldwide competition taking place here in Colorado next year. It's a Drag Competition. Phantom is keeping an eye on social media sites to assess the threat level since several foreign dignitaries have already announced their intent to attend the *extravaganza*, including the vice president. Opposing opinions are trending right now. The hype behind the competition makes popular sporting events look like the finals of a pee-wee league. All this attention is the perfect arena for a terrorist attack.

Acosta's knees flap like wings as he talks about what he's working on. He does that when he's excited. The man is a genius and has good instincts. He and Ricci are working on a robotics project. I'm helping by designing an interactive software and voice box that makes the verbal responses sound more human and less mechanical.

Porter tells me he's having a hard time hacking Edwards's cell phone. I upgrade his government security level then walk him through the process. First, we put up firewalls so the host provider can't detect us hacking their system. From there, I tell him how to locate the phone's inner brain, then reset the password. Porter is a fast learner. I tell him to let me know when he finds something significant.

My report is brief. I'm not ready to tell them about the second shooter until I have more information. They will hover since I'm not one hundred percent capable of fending off an attacker by myself. We move on to the real reason the meeting is being held in the SCIF— the Edwards situation.

Acosta swipes the screen of his laptop. "Physically Edwards was in good shape. No broken bones that didn't heal correctly. No wounds that scarred his body. No signs of malnutrition or dehydration associated with a prisoner of war under hostile conditions. His lab results showed his levels are above ideal for a man his age. Edwards is in excellent health. There's no way he was a POW in Syria."

Several snapshots of the electrical panel on the fifth floor come up on our monitors. Porter gives a full description of the device. He says the team was able to procure the small box and he stored it in my office for me to take apart and analyze when I get back to work.

The photos change. "Sir, I supervised the team that swept the hotel rooms Edwards's been staying at. No traces of ingredients used to make smoke bombs were found." The black containers were embedded in the large potted plants used to decorate the lobby here at the hospital.

"He wasn't versed in explosives. Do you think he picked it up in Syria?" I ask.

From the corner of my eye, I watch Paul study the photos like he's committing them to memory. One photo captures his attention the longest.

"Pull up number one-nine-seven on the big screen," Paul requests.

The images we were viewing on our laptops now show on the television mounted to the wall.

"Look. The fuse isn't manual and the casings didn't burn. And there's no burn marks on the stems or the lower leaves of the plants. Those weren't made by an amateur."

"How can you tell just by looking at a photo?" Porter asks.

"The smoke and dye were released through multiple, small drilled holes in the casings that created more than one outlet for the particles to be dispersed slowly, making for a long-lasting effect. Plus, the mixture had to have had the right balance of sodium bicarbonate to moderate the reaction of the oxidizer and fuel to keep the casings intact. The fuses were digital. A newbie could never do that."

"Anyone can look up how to make a smoke bomb on the internet," Ricci says.

"True, but those usually tell you to use ping-pong balls with one hole. Light the fuse with fire. And the smoke doesn't spread like a screen and hover like a cloud." He points to the screen. "Those did."

"Were the contents toxic?" I ask.

"The hospital hasn't reported any cases of illnesses or deaths from the people who were in the area at the time of release," Acosta answers.

I direct my next question to Porter. "What about the duffle bags in Edwards's room and the room above?"

"Between the two rooms, there are ten bags. Each bag had nine devices. One bag had ten devices. There are ninety-one devices in total."

We view photos of the black duffle bags from Edwards's room and listen to Porter describe how many bombs each one contained. How they were packed and the distance between each bag.

Paul pushes his chair back, stands, and walk to the monitor. "Go back." The image on the screen changes. "Did all the explosives have this?" His finger circles the photo of a matchbook-sized box connected to the casing with a capped wire sticking out.

Porter starts flipping through the photos. "I believe they do."

"I have to test a few to be sure, but these are made to go off simultaneously no matter where the device is located."

I stare at the screen. "Are they hot?"

He shakes his head. "No. The final wire needs to be connected. It makes them more stable to move. Today's technology is Wi-Fi based. A hacker could accidenty duplicate the signal and trigger them to go off before the intended time."

"Could it be the person who tried to access our feed?" Ricci asks.

"Major Chen tracked the signal to the building across from the hotel. By the time the team got there, the perp was gone. There was just the janitor, an older gentleman. The team swept every office with lint rollers for DNA fingerprints," Porter answers.

Acosta starts flapping his wings again. "Are the evidence bags secured?"

Porter nods. "I personally delivered them to your lab at CU and locked them away."

"I'll get my staff started on them today."

"Send me the building's security footage. Once Ig's finished, I'll do a background check on the tenants and cross reference them with the identities of the people coming and going from the hospital last night."

A corner of Porter's mouth turns down. "It's an old building. No cameras."

"Try the surrounding buildings. Home security systems. Traffic cameras. Anything that will tell us who was in that building or in the area around that time."

Porter acknowledges the order with a nod.

"Did you get the firearms tagged?" Ricci asks.

"Anderson and Ricks did that and moved them to your campus facility."

I like Porter. We left him in charge and he handled himself well under the circumstances. I was his age when I held the title of Delta Team Leader. Paul did the right thing by promoting him last year. Porter is ready to start working with Chen. "How long has it been since you've slept? You kept your eye on everything while we were occupied. Thanks for having our back, Porter."

"I was only doing what the DTL should do."

Paul pats him on the shoulder. "We appreciate it, Porter. Look, after you get a few hours of sleep, see whose name pops up under military explosive experts. Whoever made those bombs has access to materials an ordinary civilian doesn't."

The young Delta writes down the instructions as Paul gives him more insight into what specifically to look for when doing the search. These are things Riley can't handle because they require a more hands-on approach.

I check my watch. We've been meeting for three hours. "This is ESO team communication only, Porter. I will assign two Ghosts to back you up out in the field."

"I understand, sir. Thank you for the opportunity to work closely with you guys."

"That's it for now, gentlemen." I enter the command for Riley to unlock the door. I pack up to leave.

Ig follows me out.

"When can I talk to Edwards?" I ask.

"Give it a couple days. Vin's moving him tonight."

I push the up button. "What about his medical staff?"

"My physician assistant for now. I'll start vetting the other staff once I get back to my lab. By the way, two Shadows and one Watcher are on medical leave." The elevator dings. Ig places himself between me and the doors, his hand on the holstered firearm at his hip.

"Was Chen there?"

"He helped."

Now that surprises me. At least with Vin, the men probably had a chance to talk before he took a swing. Tony, well, let's just say he probably gave them a chance to talk—if they were still conscious after the beating. Chen on the other hand is a killer. Once he decides talking isn't necessary he'll just go in for the kill.

We step off the elevator onto the floor and walk to the room. I open the door and immediately want to tuck tail and run. Jessi's sitting on my bed eyeballing Dani.

"What happened?" I ask, looking between the two women.

Dani's mad-dogging my sister.

Jessi stands with a smart-tablet in her hands. "Your wife refuses to answer my questions."

"Don't refer to me as his wife," Dani threatens.

I set the laptops on the tray and move it closer to my bed. "Ig is discharging me—"

"I'm keeping her here a couple more days," Jessi interjects before I finish my sentence. "If she cooperates, she'll be out by Saturday."

Sorry, big sis, I'm springing us sooner than that.

Ig opens the door to let Jessi walk out first. "I know you, Hawk. This is *my* house. I'll sedate you before I let you tear it down or run off the nurses just to get your sister to change her mind."

The door closes behind them.

"Did you eat?" I ask, reaching for the insulated bag Marie sent.

When Dani doesn't answer, I look up. She's lying back, with the remote pointed at the TV. She finds a talk show. Today's topic. Who's My Baby Daddy?

The irony isn't lost on me.

"Da…" I begin

"Don't," she snaps.

"We need to talk."

"I'm not ready to talk to you, Colonel Hawk."

"When?" Okay, stupid question.

Her response is to cut her eyes in my direction. Eyebrow cocked. Head tilted to one side. Lips puckered. *When I'm damn well ready, that's when.*

A lesser man would back off at this point. Not me. I love pushing her buttons.

"That long, huh? Well, I'll be over there"—I point to my bed—"when you…"

She doesn't take the bait or take her eyes off me. The volume on the television goes up to sixty. Neither the heart monitor nor the fetal monitor beep faster so I know she's not about to jump out of bed to kick my ass.

I laugh and take the bag over to my bed.

———◆———

The glow from the screen of the overhead television is the only light in the room. It's close to midnight. Across the room, Bryan snores— loud. He's been signaling some elusive beast since he closed his eyes. He slept through a bland lunch and eye-revolting dinner.

I can't sleep. I don't want to relive falling down the stairs in my dreams. Or hear bullets whizzing past my ears and Bryan's grunt from the impact. I don't want to feel the coldness in James's stare as he shoots me.

Again, Bryan came to my rescue.

My job is to recognize behavioral patterns, which I did. Bryan calls me baby when he isn't being forthcoming with information. He distracts me with intimate touches when he doesn't want to continue a conversation. His tactics are subtle. In the back of my mind, I recognized what he was doing. What I failed to do was follow through. For the life of me, I can't fathom why.

Mrs. Franklin was good at putting these things in perspective. I can hear her say, *"Females are blinded by one of three things: real love, the need to be loved, or good-sex-love.*

Which category do I fall into?

Why didn't I press him for answers about his reaction to the fireworks on New Year's Eve? Make him believe me when I told him about the trucks following me? Contradict his explanation for the person in my apartment? I don't let my patients get away with it, why him?

You're not in a doctor-patient relationship with your husband.

When I'm with family and friends, I do step out of the primary role of therapist. I don't want them to be guarded around me, or think that I'm internally analyzing their words and actions. Plus, I loved him. I love him. I'm in love with Bryan. He used that knowledge to his advantage, and for that I won't forgive him.

I push back the sheet and lift the gown to watch my stomach flutter.

Which one of us will he resemble more? Will he have long eyelashes like his dad? I hope so. Will his eyes be brown like mine or hazel like his dad and big sister? Will he be tall or average height? Muscular or chubby? One thing I know for sure: I want him to grow up happy and surrounded with love. Bryan and I will not be together, but we will let our children know they are loved.

Distress and fury are a dangerous concoction. When I look at him I want to hurt him. I don't trust that I won't act on my feelings.

Across the room, Bryan stirs, yells out Kourtney's name, then jumps out of bed, knocking over the tray table. Two expensive-looking laptops crash onto the tile floor. He's reaching under the bed for something that isn't there.

Eyes wide and panting. Bryan is panicked. His gaze searches the semi-dark room.

It takes him a minute to regroup. Bryan takes several deep breaths and stands, running his fingers through his hair. He picks up the laptops, put them on the tray, then pours himself a cup of water. He gulps it down and pours another.

He's different. Bryan is restless. Spooked. His gaze turns to me. For a second I think he's going to come over to me. The tears in his eyes are magnified by the glow from the television.

———◆———

Between studying footage of the shooting, and keeping POTUS updated, I pore through branch personnel files. No one is immune to this investigation. With me confined to the hospital, Tony goes to the office. The men and women need to see things are business as usual. If there are any more moles in the department, I want them to think they're in the clear.

Tony informed me his request for an immediate leave of absence from the sheriff's department was approved this morning. I have Riley order business stationary for the new Executive Operations Officer of Hawkeye Personal Protection.

Across the room, Dani is reading the book a nurse brought her. When I woke up from the dream I had last night, I wanted to hold her until the fear of losing her and my daughter evaporated.

Of all the times Dani's been pissed with me, this isn't the best. We need to come to an understanding. She can't leave, and in public, we have to be a happy couple. Behind closed doors, I'll take whatever punishment she wants to dish out.

Not even lunch brought in from Celestina's warms her chilly disposition today. She doesn't know Vin owns the restaurant and the house wine is from his family's vineyards in Italy.

Without access to either one of my offices, I cannot coordinate things from the hospital room. I have to be careful of what I say, and hard copies of the emails in my inbox are a definite no-no here. I feel out of touch in this place. Like the world is moving and I'm standing still.

Dani can be on bed rest at home. Marie will gladly play nurse. Ig viewed Dani's file and confirmed she hasn't had contractions and there's been no bleeding. He advised I wait for my sister because that's her field of expertise, not his. Jessi being *Dr. Hawk* won't budge. She's keeping Dani here until Saturday. I did get her to admit her decision weighs more on the side of caution and not a necessitation.

I consider the many ways I can get us out of here. The quickest is to become the very definition of an uncooperative patient. I hate to undermine my sister, but the big bad world needs me. Unfortunately, Nurse Abby walks through the door right when a plan of action comes to mind. The monster rattles his cage. I smile and undo the latch.

Thursday morning, Ig and Jessi get into a loud discussion outside our hospital room door.

"My nurses are threatening to go AWOL, Dr. Hawk."

"They work in one of the top military hospitals in the world, Dr. Acosta. They should know how to handle a highhanded asshole, like my brother."

"Dr. Hawk, you of all people know my staff is unaware of his status."

"Dr. Acosta, if the visit from POTUS didn't clue them in on his importance, then I'd be worried about their mental capabilities if I were you."

Fingers locked behind my head, feet crossed at the ankles, I lie back and listen to the two doctors talk it out.

Dani shakes her head and mumbles something. The cold stares she's throwing are an indication of her displeasure of my efforts at getting us out of here. *Oh well.*

"Fine, Dr. Acosta. I'll discharge Mrs. Hawk right away."

The room door opens. I was expecting my big sister to storm in.

Ig strolls through the door. He stops once he gets to the end of my bed. Hands on his hips in that doctor stance. "Two hundred per nurse, per hour for each hour each nurse that had to put up with your shit for the past twenty-four hours. Non-taxable and by the end of their shifts today. I already created the payroll run. It's in your inbox waiting for approval."

I open my laptop. Log into the payroll system. Check a few boxes. Type in my pin number. Click submit. "I'll have the checks messengered over in an hour."

He leaves the room without saying anything else.

Ig isn't mad; he knew it was coming. He warned me yesterday about tearing down his house. I just knocked a little hole in a wall.

I ease off the bed and start my victory strut toward the bathroom.

Oh yeah. Uh-huh. I did it. I'm the man. I'm— tripping over the strap of my overnight bag on the floor at the foot of the bed.

Dani laughs.

I untangle the strap, pick up the bag, and keep strutting. *Who's the man? I'm the man.*

CHAPTER FOUR

NURSE ABBY HELPS DANI INTO the back seat of a Hawk-eye-owned Cadillac Escalade. "Take care, Mrs. Hawk."

I'm not a total jerk. The twelve dozen gourmet cookies I ordered along with a thank you note will be delivered to the staff assigned to the fifth floor.

Isaac, our driver, pulls away from the curb. Goodbye, hospital, white walls, and disinfectant smell. I can't wait to get to the office.

It's an overcast afternoon and the atmosphere in the truck is colder than a polar bear's pussy. I'm tempted to ask the driver to turn on the heater. We have a thirty-five-minute ride back to Boulder.

We're followed by an additional Escalade. Hawkeye's two best Personal Protection Officers are assigned to us— courtesy of Hawkeye's Executive Operations Officer. Prince Jawad sent an email to convey his discontent about Isaac being pulled off his detail.

Even if it's just cussing at me, I want to hear Dani's voice. I can handle her verbal anger. Her angry silence makes me edgy. Women are capable of anything when they're so angry they remain silent. Men don't know what to make of them. We find ourselves tiptoe-ing around them. They have the upper hand.

Accidental touches and sad looks aren't going to work this time.

The back seat controls the radio. I turn it on so there's noise in the truck. The keyboard and guitar intro to Justin Timberlake's song comes through the speakers. I take a look at the audio system's screen. An anaconda icon alternates with the song title and artist flashing.

Ignacio.

Dani looks out the passenger window. Every now and then, she wipes her eyes. I ball my fingers in a fist to keep from reaching out to her. If I touch her, Mama Hawk will capture me in one talon and rip out my feathers with the other.

I hum and sing along, hoping to extinguish some of that angry heat burning off her. The play list my boy put together is all male artists pleading their case.

The closer we get to home, the more her fingernail taps her knee. When the truck turns onto Canyon Road she unbuckles the seat belt. Marie stands in the doorway smiling. The driver turns into the semi-circular driveway and stops in front of the steps. Dani twists and grips the door handle. She bumps the door with her shoulder—the safety lock is on.

Isaac comes around and opens her door. Dani bolts. Waddle-walking up the steps. She brushes past Marie, almost knocking the older woman against the open door, and disappears in the foyer. If her body wasn't sore, Dani would be running.

My head falls back on the headrest. I close my eyes and sit for a minute. *This isn't going to be an easy fix.*

I sit up and get out the truck.

Isaac hands me our bags and closes the door. "I'll be back at sixteen-hundred-hours to pick you up for your meeting."

"Thank you, I'll be ready." I walk up the steps and follow Marie inside.

"She went to Kourtney's room."

Why am I not surprised? "Dani didn't eat much this morning."

Marie turns and heads down the hall toward the kitchen. I drop the bags on the bench by the door and follow.

Every time I step into the kitchen, I remember a humid night, lying in bed after *hello-sex* and watching my daughter kick and move in her mother's stomach. This time, we were talking about the design of the kitchen. She said unobstructed view of a big backyard and lots of counter space. I said high tech appliances and a walk-in pantry.

"Those RAGS people aren't going anywhere. Making peace with Danielle is more important." Marie interrupts my thoughts.

I sit at the table. "Willis says…"

"That boy managed to steal information on his watch. He's hard on you because of his failures."

"Just when I think I've got a handle on RAGS, they do something to throw me off."

"Maybe they're doing it on purpose to distract you from the obvious. Have you ever considered that?"

My fingers rub my tired, dry eyes. "Yeah, I have. And if I give one hundred percent of my focus to them, I lose my wife, daughter, and son." It takes a few seconds for me to realize the room got real quiet. Then I figure out why. *Smack!* The palm of my hand hits the table. "We found out Tuesday morning. You can't tell anybody."

Marie stands frozen in front of the open refrigerator door. Jaw slack. Eyes bucked. "A boy. Are you sure?"

"His legs were open."

The glass containers stored on the door shelves rattle from Marie slamming the door. She rushes across the floor and wraps her arms around my shoulder.

"A boy!" she cries. "Danielle wouldn't take your son away from you. She loves you."

"I don't doubt she loves me. The problem is, she also hates me."

Marie steps back. "Hate isn't in her nature. You know that."

"It's possible to love and hate someone at the same time. For as long as you and Willis have been married, I'm sure there were times you've hated him, but it didn't stop you from loving him too."

Marie goes back to the refrigerator and resumes unloading what she needs to make sandwiches. "I'll give you that one. But listen to me, Danielle will come to understand who you are and know the decisions you made were because you love her. Give her space. Let her mull it over in her mind. In the meantime, I may have to pull out our winter clothing. It's going to be awful chilly around here until she forgives us. That girl knows how to hold a grudge."

I wish it were that easy. The necessary lies started nine years ago.

"How's your shoulder?"

Her question pulls me back from the pity-path I was about to travel down. "It's a little sore. I'll be okay once I exercise it."

Marie stands at the counter with a knife, slicing two sandwiches into triangles. *Dani has a big appetite, but two is pushing it.* She adds the pieces to plates with pickle slices, carrot sticks, and a handful of chips. She carries one plate to the table. Marie sets it in front of me, then wraps her arm around my uninjured shoulder. Her lips peck my cheek. "If I can forgive Willis for his transgressions, Danielle can forgive you for yours. Don't accept defeat."

I squeeze her hand. In all the years I've known her, I can count on one hand the number of times Marie's given me a motherly kiss.

"I'm not hungry." I push the plate away.

She pushes it back to me and throws that stern look mothers give their stubborn child. "Ignacio had the pharmacy deliver your medicine this morning. His nurse called and said you need to take it on a full stomach. Your pill is over there on the counter next to that glass of apple juice. Don't make me force you to take it, Bryan."

Damn, Ig got to her before I could. Marie puts the other plate on a tray, along with a glass of milk and sliced oranges. "I'm taking this up to Danielle."

As I eat, I come up with an opening speech for today's staff meeting.

Every member of the Elite Special Operations Team has a regular job for a cover, but we're paid very well to protect the American government and we take that job seriously.

Once the last Phantom Ghost walks into the conference room, I stare at the three hundred and fifty men and women under my command who are physically here or on the video monitors.

"How does that saying go?" I begin. "No matter how good you are, there's always someone better. *We are* the *better!* What other military squad, *worldwide*, is like Phantom? Right now, we're bent over a table getting fucked. So, I have four questions for each of you. Do you like being on the bottom? Or do you prefer the top? Lubed? Or raw?" I pause to see if anyone's bold enough to answer a rhetorical question. "Stand up. Pull your goddamn pants up. Get your shit together or resign right now." I sit in my chair.

That was an all-time best for me. A sixty-second meeting intro.

"Edwards came back for the laptop." Mills is the first to speak; he put his name in the hat for temporary Delta Team Leader since Porter is on special assignment. Others have turned in their interest cards too. *I'm still on the cuff about him.*

The Ghosts of Phantom toss thoughts and theories back and

forth. I watch my monitor. Before apprehending anyone for trea-
son, I need hardcore evidence because the process for Phantom
men and women is much more severe than federal prison. A dead
Ghost can't tell a secret.

One man's words pull my attention away from the screen.

"Maybe Edwards didn't get the information back from Mrs.
Hawk. What if she still has it?" Ross speculates.

He's partially right, Dani *had* something, but I got it before
Edwards could. On New Year's Eve, I realized the key I'd been
searching for was the wedding ring— thanks to Kourt.

When she dangled it on a chain in front of me, I saw the tiny
square hole on the underside of the ring. While giving Dani eleven
orgasms, I searched her body. I had a detector on my tongue. I was
looking for a microchip. The honey-flavored oil made her skin
extra sensitive.

Speaking in Arabic, I told Ig, via a two-way earpiece in my ear,
the chip was implanted in Dani's ring finger. He put a mild sleep
aid in a glass of champagne and left it by the bedroom door. We
waited for her to fall asleep.

I laid her under the covers and went to Kourtney's room to get
the ring while Ig removed the chip from Dani's finger. I turned
on Edwards's laptop and touched the microchip to the ring. The
driver door opened. The chip and the ring gave off a signal similar to a remote control. I inserted the microchip in the hole of
the ring, then placed it in the driver, and I was taken to the last
security measure. I'm presented with a new challenge, a one shot
password. If I get it wrong, the hard drive and external hard drive
will fry.

I end the staff meeting and don't hang around to chum-it-up
with the subordinates. I go to my office and shut the door.

At the start of my senior year of high school I had just passed the
E2 Dan Krav Maga test. Master Simpson was one of few masters in
the world. I was five years old when I started training at his studio.
By age nine, I was training one-on-one with him. I loved working
directly with him.

My friends were talking about joining the military or going to
college out of state. Master Simpson got me an early acceptance
into University Colorado Boulder. At my high school graduation, he handed me a letter signed by the President of the United

States congratulating me on receiving a full scholarship from the government. It paid for my college education, including my PhD in Computer Engineering. Once I became Second Command, I reviewed my file. Master Simpson's recommendation letter was written after my first private lesson. He was preparing me to one day take his place as Phantom's advance technique hand-to-hand combat trainer.

Since armed forces men and women are the only ones who can train for Phantom, I asked to observe each level on the premise that I needed to get a feel for their duties so I know the best approach to teaching combat techniques. Langford reviewed my request and interviewed me. He gave his approval immediately.

Imagine my surprise when I learned my big sister was an instructor. One of the courses she teaches is the art of giving orgasms.

The enlistees gave me a hard time at first because I didn't come through the proper channels. It didn't bother me; I got to see what Phantom was about and found a new love and pride for my country. I wanted to be in on protecting it.

I was anxious to start with Level One. The Watchers. Numbers and computers are like inhaling and exhaling to me. That is my forte. I was helping a Watcher monitor the country's military data base and came across irregularities. I brought it to the attention of Colonel Langford. He did his own investigation, then approached me about doing an accelerated training for the top level, Elite Special Operations.

Being invited to be Phantom is an honor; getting through Maxim Chen's Spook-Camp isn't easy. Chen came out of retirement to work with me and boy did he put me through the paces.

I can admit it now. I was cocky. Hell, at age sixteen I was screwing the most popular girls in school. By eighteen, an Expert Dan. Not to mention, college recruits for soccer were scouting me. Yeah, I thought my shit didn't stink and my misdirected confidence got me put in a six by six cement hole buried deep underground for three months. Being isolated that long makes a man learn a lot about himself. That theory about my shit changed.

CHAPTER FIVE

I T'S LATE WHEN I LEAVE the office. I hadn't planned on staying that long, but I lost track of time. There's a light rain falling
tonight. I ask Isaac to take the long way home. Dani could care less
if I'm there or not.

We have to talk in the morning.

When I walk through the door, the first thing I notice is the
quiet. Even though the girls would be in bed by now, the place
feels deserted without them here.

Before Dani and Kourt moved in, the house was missing something. With them here it feels like home.

"She's leaving," Willis says, as he marches down the hallway.
"She's been packing since you left."

I expected the aftermath to be hard, but I wasn't expecting to
feel— empty.

"Go upstairs and do what you're trained to do. Get that girl on
her back, legs open, and screw your way back into her good graces
again."

His disrespect of Dani is alarming, but I recognize his tactics. I
don't take the bait. Guess he doesn't know I love and respect my
wife too much to treat her like that. Besides, Dani values her body.
She stayed a virgin until she was ready. No amount of pressure
from Edwards could get her to give it up so easily.

"If she wants to leave, I'm not stopping her." That's a lie.

Langford huffs as he charges to breach my personal space. "You
know what you sound like? You sound like a little *bitch* thinking
of his heart instead of his job. Man the fuck up. That girl's walking
and taking your only chance to bring down RAGS with her."

Knocking him on his ass is too easy. Instead, I walk around him.

"Watch yourself," I warn.

I don't look back, yet I take my time walking up the stairs to prove his words didn't rattle me. The side door slams, shaking the glass window. I reach the landing with a smile on my face.

Head-game point goes to me.

I swear he's turned into a nag since Dani and Kourt moved here. You'd think he would be thanking me for having them so close.

A shadow of light from the bedroom spills into the hall.

I walk to the middle of the room and stop. My grip on the brief-case loosens and it drops from my hand.

An open suitcase is on Dani's side of the bed. The photo album from our wedding on my nightstand. On top of it are her rings. Pictures of the ceremony on the floor.

Why is the room spinning?

Stop turning in a circle.

Who's that laughing and talking?

It's the video from our reception playing on the television.

Why is it so cold in here?

The patio doors are open.

Where's Dani?

An uneasy feeling settles in the pit of my stomach. *She wouldn't!* I rush through the patio doors, to the railing. "Dani!" I look down toward the wet ground below. *Please don't let me see her lifeless body.*

It's too dark. I turn with the intention to go downstairs, and stop.

She's here. Sitting on a lounge chair. Knees drawn up to her chest. Feet bare. T-shirt transparent. Jeans darkened by the rainwater.

Dani stares off into the night. Holding something in her hands.

My body catches up with my mind and the chill in the air hits me.

She shouldn't be out here.

Careful not to startle her, I approach the chair. "Come back inside before you get sick."

She doesn't move.

My knees bend so we're eye level. "Please come inside, my love."

She won't acknowledge me.

Slowly I reach out.

"Don't touch me." Her voice is as chilly as the air, but not colder than the ice in her eyes.

"You'll get sick." Dani's being stubborn and stupid. I ease my arm out of the sling and make a move to pick her up.

Her body jerks and she sits up. Her posture dares me to do it. The monster in me is willing to face the consequences of challenging her if it prevents her from getting sick. He's already proven he will control her if need be. But his approach is not the best way to handle this.

I back off and she sits back. Her gaze returns to the darkness. I ease down onto the chair and wait for the storm to pass with her. Whatever brought her out here will make her go back inside, eventually.

The clouds open. Rain comes down harder, and yet we don't move.

"Did you ever want to be with me?" she asks.

"Yes, I did. I still do."

"Why?"

"Because I love you."

"That's not enough."

"Why not?" I ask.

Her gaze turns to me and I see the pain I've caused. It knocks the wind out of me.

"How strong is a relationship that is built on lies?" she asks.

Under the circumstances, is there really an answer I can give her that makes this all go away?

Her gaze turns back to the darkness. She holds up the object in her hands. "A photo like this one is missing from my safe. Did you take it?"

"No," I whisper.

Dani untangles her legs to stand. Looking down on me. The picture falls to the wet seat she just vacated. I keep my eyes on her.

She reaches back. In my peripheral, I see her hand is fisted. I brace myself. I will not block her from slugging me. If it makes her feel better I'll be her punching bag. I deserve it.

At the last second her fingers open and she swings. The sound of the slap echoes, intensified by the rivets of rainwater running down my face. Flashes of light dance past my eye. I sit and wait for the next one.

Blam! The bedroom door slams.

I reach down and pick up the picture. It's Kourt, one-day-old.

The day she came home from the hospital. I remember that day.

I got the call Dani was on her way to the hospital a week before her due date. I was nervous. I planned to be there. The guys and I were in Italy with Vin. He'd buried his grandfather the day before.

I coordinated security for Dani while I flew back to the States. I touched down in Arizona the day after she had the baby and went straight to the hospital from the airport. They were being discharged. Dani was reserved as she secured Kourt's car seat in the back of the taxi. She's the type who needs to figure things out on her own.

I carry the picture to the bathroom and dry it with a towel. I wish she'd let me in instead of shutting me out.

———————

I was okay until Bryan didn't answer my question. I want him to hurt like I'm hurting. To know physical and emotional pain like I know it. My intent was to break his jaw. I was about to do it. Then the look of surrender in those hazel eyes tugged at my heart. In that moment, as my hand was on a collision course with his jaw, I saw something. He didn't flinch, or blink. If I had hit him again, he would have sat there and taken it. Be my personal punching bag.

Frightened by the level of power he'd just given me and the amount of animosity that fueled my actions to begin with, I ran before I did something more and something I'd regret or get arrested for.

Swirls of steam float from the hot water in the tub. The calming scent of mandarin surrounds me. I soak away the chill in my body. My mind was made up. While he was gone, I started gathering my things. Then our wedding album caught my eye. It was a mistake to open it. To reminisce about that day. Forever etched in my memory will be the prayer I said to myself and the vows we took.

Tom managed to capture magical moments and digitally transpose those pictures. Me when I'd taken a deep breath, then stepped toward my happily ever after, and Bryan when the doors opened and he saw me. I mean really saw me.

The conviction of his love for me could not be denied. It showed in his eyes. I've seen that look more times than I can count.

Another side by side photo is of me wrapping my arms around Emma, and of Bryan gazing down at our daughter and uttering the word *finally* as she gazes up at him, happy.

I needed to think about my decision to take my girls and run. Too many memories kept clouding my judgment so I sat out on the deck outside his room. Having a picture of my daughter helped to keep me focused.

I considered going to Max's, but thoughts of the shooting popped into my head. I don't know if he can fight off an attacker wielding a gun. Plus, I don't want to bring that kind of drama to his household. Bryan stormed through the patio just when I had made up my mind the safest place for me to be is here, in this house. The girls and I will live with him, but live separate lives.

In the morning, I'll finish packing my things and move to a bedroom downstairs.

———•———

Dani was up most of the night. Once she finished in the bathroom, she spent the rest of the night sitting on the window seat. I watched her on the camera in the room. She finally went to bed two hours ago.

A group text is sent to the guys letting them know I'm going for a run. In the closet, I pull out jogging gear and get dressed. I secure my phone in an armband and strap it in place.

I go to Kourtney's room. Dani is lying on her back on top of the covers in nothing but an unbelted green robe. One arm covers part of her face. The other on her rounding stomach. Because of her skin color, the red scratches on her neck look worse than they are. The dark purple bruises on her body look painful, but she's still hot in my eyes.

A single breast is uncovered, its coffee brown nipple hardened and begging me to suck it.

In one of the books I read at this stage in the pregnancy, her hair and nails grow fast. Dani's nails are much longer than she normally keeps them and there's a light dusting of pubic hair on her lady bits.

As a self-rule, I've never gone down on a woman I'm assigned to fuck for the sake of obtaining information.

Dani stopped being the assignment the minute I discovered what she'd given up to me. On my first taste of her, I became addicted. Rehab can't teach me to control my appetite for Dani.

The tattoo on her side winks at me. A lady hawk. You would have to know where to look to see the hidden initials. I didn't think she'd do it. I arranged for my guy to go to her apartment. When the picture of the finished product was texted to me I damn near dropped my phone.

Dani is my queen. My wife. Until I moved them to Boulder, my days consisted of work, Emm, and missing a piece of me.

If she didn't consider me the enemy, I'd forgo jogging and get my exercise by waking her with my tongue swiping the hood of her clit. Making her wet and begging me to enter the heat of her Sunshine. I named her lady bits Sunshine because being inside her is like an intoxicatingly explicit day in the sun.

Phantom dedicates time to training its level-seven ghosts in the art of administering orgasms. What better way to interrogate someone than to ask questions during mind-blowing sex?

There are more female spies than there are males. Men get more attention because they work out in the open. Females work behind the scenes—they're sneaky.

I learned three key points. Focus on the woman's pleasure. Master her body language. Know the anatomy of a vagina.

Sex with Dani is so much better than the other women I had. She knows how to turn the tables and focus on me. I didn't have to coach her on the things I like. She studied me and figured it out. I'm not a vocal person in bed, but no walls are up when I'm with her.

Dani stretches and moans. Her toes curl. Back arches. I witness the shiver roll through her like my thoughts made her orgasm. She closes the robe, blocking my view of her body. I know every inch of her. I watch the steady rise and fall of her chest. How arrogant of me to think she'd take her own life because of me. My girl is stronger than that.

I pick up the bear blanket off the foot of the bed and cover her. In case Marie comes in to check on her. Dani keeps the tattoo hidden for a reason.

Knowing this one incident is bringing on the end of my relationship adds more pressure that I don't know how to deal with.

I go downstairs and walk out the door. My lungs expand as I take a deep breath to get my feelings in check. I'm out in the open and need to be aware of my surroundings. Edwards would not have surprised us if I hadn't been distracted by rubbing my wife's stomach. I would not have sent Porter and Mills ahead had I known Edwards's shadow lost him.

I like running the day after it rains. It's like the planet is starting over again. Giving us another chance to take care of it. I stand in the walkway and do warm up stretches while I wait for Porter.

Dawn's light is starting to push away the night's darkness. Whenever I need clarity, I run at this time of the morning.

I spot the black SUV at the corner and jog toward it.

My pace is easy. I block out the sound of the Suburban's tires on the pavement as it tails me and concentrate on the path. The tension in my neck and shoulders isn't because I sat in the recliner all night. I'm stumbling in the dark. Suffocated by feelings.

Seeing Dani lying, unmoving, at the bottom of the stairs I realized how much I'm in love with her. Yes, I've said the words out loud, even changed the pitch of my voice so the words sounded sincere. But I didn't accept the meaning those words stood for and that's why I told the judge to go through the motions, just don't make our marriage legal.

A thoughtless and stupid mistake.

I can't allow myself to focus on that right now. The ultimate goal is to protect Phantom's secret and keep my wife safe, and do it without sacrificing one for the other.

It doesn't take long for me to reach the road that leads to the trail up the mountainside. Porter can't follow me in the SUV from here. He steps out of the vehicle, sniper rifle in hand, and stands on the passenger side of the truck where he can watch me.

I run in place for a second and take a deep breath, then start the climb.

I open my stride as I sprint up the incline. The footfalls of the person behind me aren't a surprise. The minute I sent the text I knew one, if not all, would come looking for me.

He keeps his distance and lets me do my thing.

I'm honored to serve my country and get off on the rush of the job. U.S. Phantom military created the monster in me. I am strong and invincible. I do whatever it takes to get the job done without hesitation. Zero regrets. My family life, on the other hand, is different.

I like being a husband and father. It's a role I will honor beyond my last breath. Our family is— complicated.

So, I run to let the monster and the family man come up with a compromise that Langford swears is impossible to achieve.

Thighs burning. Lungs working overtime. I go past my usual point. I head for higher ground to see the bigger picture. The man running behind me now runs beside me, forcing me to push myself.

Before my first Krav Maga tournament, Master Simpson told me, *if your opponent fails to score points against you, their strategy will be to take you out.* Amelia said RAGS sent her to get close to me then convince me to join their organization. I will *never* be one of them. What better way to bring me down than to go after the one woman who means the most? It's clear those bullets were meant for Dani.

The end is near. I feel it.

One of us will destroy the other.

Phantom will come out on top.

My pace starts to slow.

I walk the rest of the way to the top and stare out at my city. One morning I'll bring Dani up here so she can understand why I built our home here. The prerequisite was visual season changes. A town at the base of the Rocky Mountains is what I found.

My friend's feet crunch the gravel. He's deep breathing.

I unstrap the phone from the holster and use my thumbprint to unlock it. The picture of my family fills the home screen. I go through the videos and send him the file. "Get your phone, you need to see something."

Tony stands next to me. Our breaths make small clouds in the cool air. I wait for him to finish watching the modified video footage.

"That slug Ig took out of you didn't come from Edwards's gun?" The high pitch tone echoes in the valley of the mountain.

I face him. The arch of my eyebrow answers the question better than words.

"Whose?" he asks.

"I don't know."

Tony taps the screen and turns it to face me. "Dude! That was personal."

"It's time we include Dani in on a threat assessment meeting."

"You sure you don't want to ease her into a meeting like that?"

"We don't have time to be gentle."

"How soon we doing this? I need to pad my ribcage in case she makes a move for the door again."

A whistle rides the airwaves to get our attention. Below, my other brothers stand in front of the Suburban idled at the base of the trail. They must have rock-paper-scissors to see which one would tackle the jog.

I whistle back and we start the trek down the trial.

I met Tony second semester freshmen year at University Colorado Boulder. He's originally from south-central Los Angeles and came to CU as a double major.

No one in the dorms knew much about him. He didn't hang with anyone, but liked to party. Why he put up with a semester of hazing from his dorm mate is beyond me. Especially knowing what I know about him now.

On the eve of finals, Tony's dorm mate's car blew up. Not the simple boom. The four-door compact car lifted twenty feet in the air like it was over the hole of a geyser. It started smoking first. An image of a hand emerged from the mist. It lit the fuse and the car exploded into pieces in the courtyard of the dorms. It was like an outdoor light show at an amusement park.

The bothersome dorm mate stood on the steps of the dorm. Shocked.

Campus security couldn't prove Tony did it. They brought in bomb experts, but nothing could be pinned on him. Plus, he had an ironclad alibi— me. We'd just ordered our third beer at the bar near campus at the time of the explosion. He was on his phone most of the time and took a call from his grandmother when the show began.

The day before the start of second semester, we found an apartment off campus and have been brothers ever since. Eventually he showed me how he pulled it off. I was so impressed, I recommended him for Phantom testing. His pyro-tech skills and knowledge of explosives are far more creative than the average expert.

Vin tosses us water bottles when we reach the beginning of the trail. I twist the cap and take a drink.

"I go either way, and prefer warming lubes."

What the hell is Max talking about?

He lifts his chin, looking down his nose at me. "You asked top or bottom. Lubed or raw. I'm answering your questions from yesterday's meeting."

I wipe the sweat from my eyes and laugh with the others. We can always count on him to make us see the humor of things in the most precarious of times.

"You look like hell, Bry. Do you want to talk about it?"

Why do psychologists, even world renowned ones, always want to talk about your *feelings*? Hell no, I don't want to talk about it.

Ig comes to my rescue. "So, what are we doing this morning?"

I gesture to the truck so we can talk on our way back to my house.

Always the playful one, Tony shoves Max and makes a run for the front seat. Max spins, sweeping Tony's feet.

Arms and legs swim in the air, Tony hits the ground, stomach first. Fifteen years and he still thinks he can get one over on Maxim Chen and there'll be no retaliation. Max takes it easy on him.

Tony pushes up off the ground and hops to his feet, dusting the dirt off his clothes. Vin and Ig claim the third-row seats. Me and Max take the middle. Tony crawls into the front seat. Porter makes a U-turn.

In conjunction with Tony's entertaining commentary, I describe the type of meeting I want us to have with Dani included. Max agrees it's time to introduce Dani to our world. He and I debate on how deep to take her. He wants to train her like he trained us. I just want to give her the basics.

"Danielle is an independent person, by nature. Right now, she's piecing her life back together and may lean on you more than she should to feel secure. You know how important inner strength is to her. She views it as self-worth. Her world has been rocked. We need to give her the tools to take back her independence."

"I disagree. Dani's handled much worse."

Max rolls his eyes. "Danikins is far from weak minded. The tale you spin better be good. She doesn't trust you."

"She doesn't trust any of us," Vin corrects.

"We're not going to spin a tale. We are having a Phantom threat assessment meeting over breakfast in my kitchen with Dani as our special guest."

"Hey, Maxie," Tony sings. "As soon as Dani finds out your part of the team, you'll know what it feels like to have your ass kicked by a girl."

Max does that lip pout hair toss thing. "Hey, To'nisha. First of all, Danikins and I are besties. And second of all, I'm not stupid enough to block an angry woman's path."

There's one person who's yet to weigh in on the conversation. His knee bobs as his foot sews the mat to the floorboard. Ig gestures, *I'll do whatever you want,* with his hands. "I don't have these issues. My girl knows all about Phantom and what I do. It's the age difference she sees as a problem."

"Start with a real apology. Like you did on Christmas Eve," Vin suggests.

CHAPTER SIX

"GOOD MORNING, BRYAN." MARIE COUGHS as she closes the side door. "Where is your sling? Aren't you supposed to be resting?"

"My shoulder doesn't bother me much. I needed to get in some exercise. Two days of confinement made me edgy."

Marie coughs again.

"Sounds like you're coming down with something. Want Ig to take a look at you?"

She frowns and bats away the offer with her hand. "It's just a little cold. I'll be fine once I start to move around. Anything special for breakfast?" She starts to unbutton her coat and turns toward the kitchen.

I step in front of her. "Uh— about that. I was planning to make breakfast for Dani. Plus, I gave you the week off because the girls aren't here. Go home. Get some rest so you're one hundred percent when they get home."

Marie stares at me through squinted eyes. Fists anchor on her hips. "I know you, Bryan Hawk. What are you up to?"

Subtle cock of an eyebrow. Slow lick of my lip. Pointed stare in her eyes. Crooked half smile. Even at age seventy-three, Marie blushes and bites her lip and glances away.

I chuckle and turn it down a notch. "My wife and I need to work things out like you said. I prefer to do it without an audience. I don't want you to witness me being dragged down the hallway on my stomach with my hands clamped around her ankle, begging for forgiveness, and trying to stop her from walking out the door."

Marie's lips tighten and shoulders grow stiff.

I realize where the playfulness took the wrong turn. "It doesn't take a piece of paper for me to acknowledge Dani as my wife. Every promise I made was real."

Her eyes water and her eyelashes flap. "You sure you don't want me to stay and give you pointers on groveling?"

I step in and plant a quick kiss on her cheek. "Thank you, but I got this."

She gives my arm a supportive squeeze. I open the door for her. Marie reties the scarf around her head before she walks out. I stand in the doorway and watch her walk the path to their house.

Ig meets me in the hallway. He hands me the laptop and gives me some final words of encouragement.

Each step I take up the stairs is weighted by questions. Will she hear me out? Can I convince her I did this for her? Will she accept my apology? Do I deserve her blind trust?

I knock first, then open the door to Kourt's room. Dani's back is to me. She's still in the robe. I know she's awake.

"If you have questions I'll answer them— honestly."

She rolls over. The swelling around her eyes hits me in the sac. Shame steals the confidence in my approach. The urge to drop to my knees and cry for her is strong. My grip on the laptop tightens.

Dani doesn't budge. Her gaze cuts to the door then back to me. I step to the side so she doesn't feel trapped.

"Are you ready to talk?"

She clears her throat. "Yes."

"What do you want to know?"

"How long have you known James was alive?" There's an accusatory undertone to that question. I understand why.

"Since the end of June. Last year."

"Every question you've ever asked about my relationship with him, you already knew the answer?"

"Most of them, yes."

"You were testing me," she huffs. "Did I pass?"

There's a little of the fire I was prepared for. "It wasn't a test."

"Then what was it?"

"Small details. You would have become suspicious if I didn't ask questions about your past relationships. That's what people do when they first get together."

"How do you know I was telling the truth?"

"For starters, you're a horrible liar. And second, Edwards was sent to Colorado for specialized training before his Iraq deployment. He thought I was a trainee too. He talked about you a lot."

"Why was James chosen? He didn't have a good track record with his Commanding Officer."

"When he showed up in Colorado with the letter we asked the same question."

"How is Amelia a part of all this?"

"She was sent by RAGS to get close to me and have me join because of the clientele my company attracts. I didn't fall for it, not even when she got pregnant on purpose."

"She knew about Phantom?"

"No."

"Where is she?"

"Dead."

"How did she die?"

"She killed herself." Yes, I just told a lie.

"Why would she do that? Was it postpartum depression?"

"Edwards found out about us hooking up. They were— friends. He dumped her. Since she was carrying my child I took care of her. She thought I wanted to be with her and couldn't accept it when I said I didn't." Truthfully, she didn't want Emm to begin with. I convinced her to not terminate the pregnancy in exchange for lifelong protection from RAGS. Months before she gave birth, Amelia signed over her parental rights. She didn't want her name on the birth certificate and refused to look at, let alone hold Emm in the delivery room.

"What laptop was James looking for?"

"The one he used to store stolen information."

"How did you get it?"

"When we learned Edwards was meeting the buyer in an abandoned mosque in Iraq, we flew there to stop the sell. During the raid Edwards shot Langford. I did what I was trained to do and returned fire. Edwards went down. With the team's focus on Langford's injuries, I stashed the laptop and destroyed the one the buyer brought to the meeting. No one knew I had it. I've been working on the laptop to see what's on it. There are four security measures. I was able to hack two of them. The third requires some type of key and I've been searching for it or a way around it." Partial lie.

Dani jerks to a sitting position like she's on a yoga mat. Arms fold across her chest. "So, that's why you knocked on my door and kept coming around? You were looking for a key?"

"Yes and no."

"Don't give me half answers, Bryan."

I exhale long and slow. "Our initial meeting in Arizona nine years ago was because I was looking for the stolen information. Then after I had the laptop, I was looking for the key. No, I didn't sleep with you *because* I was looking for a key."

"And I'm just supposed to believe that?" Her neck rolled.

"It's the truth."

"Four and a half years. No hello. How are you guys? No returned phone calls or emails. Why bring us here if you just wanted a key?"

"Bringing you guys here wasn't just about that laptop."

Lines form around her mouth. Her eyes glare with disbelief. "If you had just been honest…"

Something in me snaps. "If I could pack up and move us to a private island so far off the grid that it would be impossible for anyone to find us, I'd do it right now. For you. For us. But I need you to understand the consequences of our departure. I turn my back on my job. World War Three starts right here, on American soil. We are called Phantom for a reason, Dani. Sometimes we instigate shit. Sometimes we let shit happen. Most of the time we sneak in, kill the enemy, and pretend to be just as shocked as the rest of the world. Once that information gets out, it's the United States against the world. The people you and I love will be dead. Sure, we can bring them with us, but what about the people they love? We can't take everyone with us. So who goes and who stays here to die, Dani? If what you want me to do is turn in my letter of resignation and we leave, there is no turning back. If that is the only way I can convince you I love you and Kourt and did this for you and Kourt and you can live with that decision, then let's go get our girls and disappear right now!"

My tone is more forceful than I intended, but that was no act. That was me in all my dilemmas summed up in a few sentences. I surrender. There is no compromise between the monster and the husband without her cooperation.

Slowly, her shoulders start to relax and her hands fall to her lap.

With caution, I move toward the bed, set the laptop in front of her, then sit next to her. "I don't expect your forgiveness overnight. Our relationship has been complicated and painful and I'm owning up to my part." I try to smile as I trace her vacant ring finger. "I was supposed to propose at the restaurant, in front of our girls. Just the four of us." My hand hovers over hers. Palm down. "I promised to take care of your heart. You know I don't break promises. You *know* me. I'd never intentionally hurt you."

After a minute, Dani's hand flips over. Our fingers interlock. I use my thumb to trace circles on her knuckle.

We sit and let the physical connection sink in.

"Do you remember that day you came to the office to sign papers?" I wait for her to recall the memory before I continue. "You are legally Emm's mother. If I had died in the courtyard, you would have sole custody of her. The adoption papers were filed and granted long before the ceremony."

"But in the hospital…"

"You asked two questions. Is Emm legally my daughter? Are we married? Technically, I only answered one."

"I don't understand."

"I told you I wanted to make sure you guys are taken care of in case something happened to me before we got married. You signed four documents. The final adoption papers for Emm along with her new birth certificate. The others have to do with the house, my estate, and our children's trust funds. We can go over that another time." I unlock the laptop with my free hand and open the file. "This is the classified file on the case. For your safety, we blacked out parts that you absolutely cannot know. It's impossible to get through it in one day. We're having a breakfast meeting in the kitchen in an hour. I really want you to sit in on it so you can learn more about Phantom. Dani, no matter what you decide, I will accept."

I release her hand, kiss her cheek, and stand. I pile pillows against the headboard and wait for her to lean against them. I put two more pillows under her knees and set the computer on her lap. "Comfortable?"

"Yes."

"What do you want for breakfast?"

"One of your loaded omelets." As I turn to go, she says, "Bryan, if I really want us to leave, you would do it?"

"Yes." I leave her to read the file.

The guys look up when I walk into the kitchen. We've been friends for a long time. Words are not necessary. Now it's up to Dani. They give me the mental space I need and go back to preparing breakfast.

Vin is nervous. Family is important to him. The outcome of what happens next affects him too. It affects all of them. When he's like this he sculpts fruit. It's a skill my grandmother taught him to redirect restless energy.

Grandmother would have loved Dani. She died six months before my daughter was born. My daughter's middle name is my grandmother's first name.

I tell them what Dani wants for breakfast.

The hour flies by. I feel like I'm on trial, waiting for a verdict. The person handing down judgment is both judge and jury.

I set the last omelet on a plate and turn off the fire. A barefoot Dani stands in the doorway wearing jeans and a black Hawkeye company sweatshirt that is too big for her. I can't read her body language and that puts me at a disadvantage.

She observes the men in the room.

Ig is the first to break the silence. "Good morning. Grab a seat. Bry will get your plate."

Her stare zeros in on Max.

He scoops up a plate and smirks at her. "That's right, Danikins. Maxie plays with the big boys." He does a dip and a snap of his fingers. He saunters over to her. "I'm still your *fabulous* friend, who just happens to be a closet badass super ghost."

"Does your husband know you're not a badass stay-at-home dad?" She crosses the threshold into the kitchen.

For a moment, Max's face becomes serious. He gestures to the seat across from him. "I love Thomas too much to put him in a situation where knowing the truth can get him killed."

That is true.

Vin pats her shoulder for a greeting, pulls out the chair for her, then places in front of her two skewers of strawberry, kiwi, watermelon, pineapple flowers with green grapes stems.

"You did these?" Dani asks. "They are beautiful. I don't know if I should eat them or put them in a vase."

If any of us say it out loud, Vin will throw a punch, but his cheeks turn the slightest tint of red at the compliment.

Tony greets her with a pat on the crown of her head to show that there are no hard feelings for the ass kicking. He walks around the table and claims the seat next to Max.

"Since we're having a tell-all before the official meeting," Max says, "I'm the one who texted Bry to tell him you were eye-raping him at Back to School Night."

"I was not!"

He bounces in his chair swinging an imaginary lasso above his head. "Ohhh, Danikins. The way you were twirling your hair around your finger and tugging on your earlobe you were picturing him on his back, riding him hard like a seasoned cowgirl."

Dani laughs.

Ig joins the table. "Vin hung the mistletoe and paid the girls to tell you guys to kiss."

Vin growls. "Ignacio paid the DJ at the club to let him take over the turntables and purposely played those songs so you would dry hump Bry on the dance floor."

Dani gasps. "How much do you guys know about our relationship?"

"Everything," Tony says.

"We don't keep secrets," Max adds.

Her eyes grow big. She looks at me. "Everyone?"

"No, just them."

"Why didn't you recognize me in the mall?" she asks Vin.

"My sights were set on the guy behind you."

"What do you mean? Who was behind me?"

"Dani, before he answers, I have to remind you not to discuss this with anyone."

Her spine straightens and she squares up her shoulders. "Confidentiality is a part of my job as a therapist, Bryan."

I acquiesce with a nod and set her plate in front of her, then take the vacant seat on the other side of her. I log on my phone and dial Riley's number so the meeting can be recorded. I start by stating the day, date and time.

Vin answers her question. He tells her about the guy in the store, the kid and the candy, and how he tried to stop her from breaking her ankle.

We dissect the details of the case. Everyone is careful not to mention Edwards's present state of existence. Dani is inducted into the world of real life ghosts.

In these meetings, we have no filter. To someone on the outside, it is unsettling. For that reason, Max keeps a watchful eye on Dani. He lets me know when the dialogue is making her uncomfortable and I change the tone yet keep the discussion on track.

She hasn't run from the table screaming— yet.

Dani is oblivious to our silent way of communicating in the presence of outsiders. We're fluent in American Sign Language. We talk with our hands while the words coming out of our mouths say something different.

The meeting moves from the kitchen to my office. Dani sticks with us. I know the terminology and ideas being tossed around are overwhelming her. I want Dani to get a good look at the monster so she can make an informed decision. And also so she'll recognize the difference between Bryan, the husband and father, and Bryan, the force of nature who protects and serves his country.

———◆———

The meeting ended late in the afternoon. I've been staring at Edwards's laptop monitor. The flashing cursor under the first dash to the eight-letter password has not moved. One chance is all I get to solve the final piece of the puzzle.

Jessi comes in and hands me a beer, then sits in a chair in front of my desk. She got in twenty minutes ago. "Dani in bed?"

I shrug without looking up.

"I didn't see anything in the fridge. What did Marie cook?"

"They have the week off."

She's silent for so long I finally look up. I take a deep breath and wait for it.

Her eyebrows shake hands in the center of her forehead. "That could have ended badly."

I toss my glasses on the desk and sit back.

"Why did you let her leave with him?"

"You know I can't discuss…"

"Screw the job, little brother! At some point, you have to put her safety first."

"And that's what I did by letting her go with Edwards. I was there. I witnessed it. I relive it every time I close my eyes."

"It's just—when I think… I get sick to my stomach. Dani isn't just my sister-in-law. She's my friend too, Bryan. I'm happy she thought to put on that vest."

I pick up the bottle in front of me and gesture, *I agree*. My sister stretches her hand and we touch bottlenecks. *Clink*. Here's to small favors.

"Is Dani talking to you?"

I tip back the bottle and take a long drink then gesture *somewhat*. "She sat in on an Elite Team meeting."

Her eyebrow disappears behind her bangs. "How did that go?"

"She didn't warn us to stay the hell away from her and the kids. So I'm guessing it went well."

"You're lucky you have someone like Dani. I want that kind of love. Someone who looks at me the way she looks at you."

"You'll find somebody who makes you want to do better. A do right girl. But don't be stupid like me and let the lies you tell be the foundation of your relationship. I didn't believe Grandma when she said, 'the dirt always comes out in the wash.'"

"She used to tell you that because you were always hiding things. I was the good one."

"You were the good one all right. You took Dad's car in the middle of the night to go pick up a drunk friend from a bar in Denver and had to ride all the way back with the windows rolled down because she puked in the backseat."

She laughs. "Did I thank you for riding shotgun? Man, was dad pissed."

I finish my beer and laugh with her. "No, your friend was pissed. Dad's underwear was dry."

We laugh more as we remember the highlights of that night. Jessi cussed at her best friend the entire ride back to Colorado Springs. When we pulled into the driveway, Dad was standing there, waiting. Stephanie stumbled out of the back seat. Knees wobbling. Clothes twisted. Pee running down her legs.

The next morning Mom and Dad gave us a one-hour lecture about teenage drinking that included visual aids, then drove her friend home—in Mom's car. Jessi and I cleaned Dad's.

Our friends always thought of Mom and Dad as *the cool parents* because of their realistic views about the times we lived in. After Dad gave me his version of *the sex talk,* Mom put a goldfish bowl

filled with condoms in my room and kept it filled. It wasn't permission to have sex. It was a reminder to practice safe sex. Some
disagreed with their parenting style. Mom and Dad respected their
opinion, and asked others to respect theirs.

When I moved to Boulder for college, Mom continued to sup-
ply me with condoms. And when Tony, Vin, Ig, and I rented a
four-bedroom house near the school, she sent a case of condoms.

Jessi wipes the coughing-choking-laughing-tears from her eyes
and stands. "Well, I'm going up to check on Dani, then going to
get something to eat. Oh, I forgot, I'll be back and forth between
here and Denver for a little while." She drinks down the rest of her
beer. "Check you later, BK4."

"See ya when I see ya, JP1."

CHAPTER SEVEN

I NEEDED A QUIET PLACE TO sit after that meeting with Bryan and his friends. I made myself a cup of tea and came upstairs. Next to the window seat, the deck outside the bedroom is my favorite place to sit and think.

Movies can't come close to capturing the inner workings of a secret military unit. Sitting in on the meeting further convinced me the best place for the girls and me is with Bryan. But do we hide or stay and fight?

Now that the sun has set, a chill in the air is settling in. My feet are getting cold.

I go back inside and start to clean the mess I made yesterday. Bryan's side of the bed is still made. Mine resembles the fall-out after an explosion.

I roll up the sleeves of the sweatshirt and start the restoration of the bedroom. If the girls were home, they'd rip me for the condition of the room. I don't allow them to leave their rooms in chaos before they go to bed.

Two quick knocks, then the door opens. Jessica walks in. "How are you feeling?"

"I'm fine."

"Baby moving. No spotting or contractions?"

"Yes, he's moving. No on the spotting and contractions."

Her shoulders slump. Gone is the confidence that walked through the door a moment ago. "Okay, I'll get out of your hair." She turns to leave.

Why am I being salty toward Jessi? She did nothing wrong to me. Jessi was my biggest supporter when I learned I was pregnant. Put her head together with Max and threw me a raunchy bachelorette party and a demure bridal shower. My attitude is uncalled for.

"Jessi, wait." The clothes in my hands fall to the bed as I fast walk to my sister-in-law.

We embrace.

Shed tears.

Laugh.

Renew our friendship and sisterhood.

"Want some help?" She wipes my tears and I wipe hers.

I exhale and look over my shoulder. "Yes, please."

"When we're done, let's go get something to eat."

"Well, my strict doctor has me on bed rest, so how about we order in?"

"Deal."

———◆———

Dani's in her pajamas, lounging in a recliner with the laptop on. She and Jessi had movie night in the family room. They invited me to join in, but I decided to take a step back and let them do their thing. It felt good to hear her laughter float down the hallway to my office while I worked on Hawkeye business.

I take it as a good sign that the suitcase Dani left on the bed last night is put away. The photo album back in its place. I am disappointed that her wedding and engagement rings are still on my nightstand and not on her finger where they belong.

I jump in and out of the shower, and change the bandage on my wound. Ig said he'd clear me tomorrow if I can make it through one of Max's physical fitness tests. In other words, *shut-up, sit yo' ass down, and let your body heal.*

Dani is still in the recliner when I come out of the bathroom. *Do I sleep on the couch or in our bed?* I look to her for the answer. She's not paying attention to me.

I imagine a coin flipping in the air. It lands in my hand. Tails. I'd called heads.

I get a couple pillows and a blanket off the shelf in the closet and make up the couch. Once I lie down, the tension in my body eases, some.

It's not long before Dani starts to move around and the lights turn off. The silence in the room is— awkward. The elephant in the room grows bigger.

Gone is her angry silence, but there is an invisible line dividing us.

"I don't want you to whisk us away to a private island. I want you to do your job. Maybe I can help. James was fascinated by audio-hypnosis. Maybe what you're looking for isn't a key, but a word or phrase. Check the CDs he made me."

"Where are they?"

"In one of the boxes in the storage cabinets. I'll look for them in the morning."

"He tried that audio-hypnosis stuff on you? Is that why you repeat phrases when you're in fighter's mode?"

"Keep fighting. Protect yourself." Her laugh is short. "My foster father told me to chant so I had something to focus on other than being hit." The bed covers rustle. "Do you know anything about my parents? If you did a background check on James, you did one on me too."

"Your mother didn't have ID on her when she arrived at the hospital with a gunshot wound to the chest. She was in active labor. All the nurses had time to do was get her name, Antoinette Dominique Beaudry-Tatum, and before she died, she named you. No relatives were located." God forgive me for the blatant lie I just told.

"Kourtney's family roots start with you, Bryan. I've had the genetic tests done and can pass that on to her and our son, but names of people and their importance to the family will have to come from your side."

"They can never find out..."

"You don't carry that burden alone," she whispers.

Silence descends upon us. I wonder if she's thinking about that conversation we had a while ago about Kourtney's birth certificate.

The faint howl of a coyote rings out. Its pack answers. Tony and I need to go out and mark the boundaries so the coyotes don't come within a mile of the property. Especially now that we have a family dog, Trevor.

"How long has Phantom been around? How did it start?"

I tuck my right hand under my head and stare up at the ceiling. My left hand rests on my abs. I get comfortable. I have a feeling this is going to take a minute. "It was created by President Wood-row Wilson in nineteen seventeen to detect and extinguish acts of espionage right after the United States entered World War I. The first man to hold the position of Second Command was Herman Johnson, a Marine."

"Has it always operated out of that office building?"

"No, headquarters is wherever Second Command wants it to be. The only restriction is that it's here in Boulder, Colorado. Lang-ford's headquarters was a series of warehouses near the college. I chose the office building because of my company. Some customers like to visit the home office before they sign the contract."

"How do you separate the two?"

"Hawkeye Personal Protection occupies the entire fourth floor. Phantom occupies the first, third, fifth, and sixth floors of the building. The first floor is underground. The second floor is equally shared, but manned by a Phantom Watcher because it's the lobby and garage level. Riley uses facial Recognition Software to identify anyone entering the building and alerts the Watcher. He knew who you were and the purpose of your visit before you told him your name. He was reprimanded for staring at your ass."

"By you?"

"No, Max. I was going to blind him." I hope she knows I'm not joking.

"How many men and women are there in Phantom?"

"Including my team, three hundred and fifty."

"What about Hawkeye?"

"Roughly fifteen hundred."

"Why so many?"

"My Personal Protection Officers are global. I don't just have U.S. customers."

"Were any at your holiday party? Did I meet them?"

"Yes, there were a few there because they were working, guard-ing their charges. The woman you sat down for dinner with, she is the PPO for Prince Jawad. She accompanies him to all of his social engagements. Isaac, the PPO who drove us home, is Prince Jawad's main protection officer."

"Why is he here? Is Isaac his first name or last name?"

"Tony pulled him off the prince and put him on your detail to replace Porter. We call everyone by their last names."

"Are there anymore assigned to the girls and me?"

"Since the shooting, yes. I should also tell you, there's a team of ten who've been guarding the house since the New Year."

"So, it wasn't fireworks going off. That's why you guys reacted the way you did."

"Yes. I didn't want to scare you. That's why I didn't tell the truth."

"What are Shadows and Watchers?"

"Watchers provide support to everyone in the field using satellites. Shadows follow people."

"Are there others?"

"Phantom is broken up into divisions. Watchers. Shadows. Sweepers. Field Operatives. Security. Delta. And Elite Special Operations."

"What do they do? I'm sorry, am I asking too many questions?"

"No, Dani. It's okay. I want you to ask questions. Sweepers search for evidence or clues for information. They also clean up evidence. Field Operatives do reconnaissance and gather information. Security secures people, places or things. Most are Secret Service Agents assigned specifically to the President. Deltas are our first line of defense for hostage situations and counterterrorism. Elite Special Operations is us."

"Do you know who was in my apartment?"

"No." *I know who trashed your apartment.*

"So, Max is a badass Super Soldier?"

I fake a long yawn. "Yes, and you need your rest. The girls come home tomorrow."

His story isn't mine to tell.

————◆————

Now that Dani is asleep, I leave the room and go down to the garage. She brought a bunch of boxes from the apartment. I search through the storage cabinets until I find the box.

I pause for a second to give myself a mental pep talk. Technically I'm not invading her privacy. She said she'd look for the CDs in the morning. I'm just expediting the process by saving her the hassle.

The tape along the center seam tears off with one pull. I peel open the flaps. The first thing I see is her senior yearbook. I lift it out of the box, thumb through the senior pictures and find the one of her in a blue cap and gown. Wow. Look at her. Fifteen years old. High school graduate. Valedictorian. Dani still looks the same.

I flip through more pages. There's a picture of her on Edwards's back. His arms hooked behind her knees like he's giving her a piggyback ride. Her arms around his neck. Hands on his chest. Chin on her arm. Her long hair swept to one side. They're smiling for the camera. Dani's smile doesn't reach her eyes. The caption underneath reads, *Cutest Couple.*

I curb the instinct to rip the page out of the book. It was taken four years before I came along. I scan another section of the yearbook and come across a page that makes me do a double take. The smiling, brown eyed, toothless baby in the full-page ad is the reason I take a second look. I thought it was Kourt's baby picture. It's Dani's. The message from her foster parents reads *Congratulations Danielle. Continue to be exceptional. Love, George and Katherine.*

I close the book and rummage through the contents of the box until I find three bundles of CDs. There are—I count—fifteen in total. Some are labeled *songs*. Some are labeled *pictures*.

I stack the boxes back in the cabinet and take the bundles to my office. The scanner on my desk reads my handprint. Everything unlocks in my office and I'm logged onto the desktop computer. One day I'll show Dani where she went wrong that time she tried to search my office during the holidays. If she'd kept her hand on the scanner four seconds longer she would have had access to the drawers and closet.

I number each disk using an ultraviolet marker then one by one, slide them in the external drive connected to the desktop via USB. Riley copies the audio and visual files. After I remove the last disk, I type in the request for the audio files to be transcribed, verbatim.

An incoming virtual call box pops up on the screen. Vin's Rottweiler icon flashing inside. I tap the dog and the box opens. He looks amped.

"What's up?"

"One of the guns Edwards had may match the one that killed Dani's parents."

I feel the shock being broadcast through my face. "How soon will you know?"

"I'm leaving for Los Angeles in a couple hours. I've been in contact with a detective who agreed to let me view the case file. She's even willing to search the storage to see if they still have the evidence. The case is twenty-eight years old, but it's unsolved so there's a good chance it's still there."

How did Edwards come to possess the alleged weapon that gunned down Dani's parents in front of their apartment building twenty-eight-years ago? The list of questions I have for him keeps growing.

I exhale. "Do you have someone to keep an eye on Edwards while you're gone?"

"Yes, his name isn't on the list that Riley compiled and Chen already interviewed him. His name is Torres; he's been in Phantom for five months."

"Make sure he knows his assignment is Elite communication only."

"He's fully aware of the consequences should he fail to follow my instructions."

"All right, let me know what you find in LA."

Vin nods and ends the chat. My fingers skim through my hair and cup the back of my neck, squeezing. What he uncovers could plug in the holes of the sketchy information we have on what happened to her parents. I started this quest the day I introduced myself to her. Dani's wrong about one thing. Our daughter's family roots do not begin with me. I know where to find both sets of Dani's grandparents. When I do finally tell my wife, I want to be able to tell her everything. She deserves to know *her* family history. I believe knowing will give her a sense of belonging so she can have a true bond with me.

I don't want Dani to give up being the strong woman that she is. Her inner strength is a turn on. But she needs to realize that even the strongest woman needs a shoulder to lean on. Deep in her soul, where her strength comes from, I want Dani to know I have two perfectly good shoulders that will hold her up. Two capable hands that will catch her if she falls. Two working feet that will walk and run for her. And a beating heart that will always love her beyond its final thump.

I put the CDs back in their cases, bundled the way I found them, put them back in the box in the garage, and go back upstairs.

Thoughts, questions, and information plague my mind. I lie awake. I can visualize what I'm trying to accomplish. It's the multitude of indiscernible details that's blocking my path. Somehow these elements are connected, that much I know for sure. But the order in which they fit together eludes me.

The clock on my phone tells me it's four thirty in the morning. I give up trying to sleep, fold the covers and put them away. I change into workout clothes to go put in a couple hours in the gym in the garage. Before the girls get home, there are business calls I need to return and emails that require a reply. Phantom and Hawkeye Personal Protection operate twenty-four hours, seven days a week.

———◆———

The constant vibration from my cell phone on the bathroom countertop interrupts my shower. Half in, half out, I reach for the device to see who's texting me. One from Kourt. One from Donovan, the lead PPO assigned to the girls. One from Romano, the Watcher assigned to my parents' home.

I open Donovan's first. He's letting me know my parents are leaving the house but taking the girls to the stables before they head here. Next I open Romano's. She's sending me a copy of how she's positioning the other PPOs at the stable to ensure the safety of the girls and my parents. I smile when I open Kourt's, happy I saved hers for last. She sent me a selfie from my old room. Mom said she begged for that room. I tap out a quick reply and set the phone back on the countertop and rinse the shampoo out of my hair.

With a towel wrapped around my waist, I stand at the sink, in front of the mirror, to slowly peel off the waterproof bandage covering the wound. The anti-scarring gel is cool as I smooth it over the stiches. Eventually I'll have to tell Dani about the shooter.

Shifting my head left and right, I check out how well the facial hair is filling in. I pull out the clippers from a drawer and shape it a little. My grooming routine didn't become this meticulous until I met Dani. I want to always look good for my woman. I wonder if she likes the beard.

Dani is deep under the covers when I come back into the room. The only thing sticking out are the natural curls of her hair.

I get dressed, then go down to the kitchen. Breakfast is a bowl of cereal that I eat at my desk. I log on to my computer and start from the bottom and read emails. Porter sent me an update on his progress with Edwards's cell phone. Vin sent a copy of the ballistics report along with his travel itinerary. Ig's email says he'll be in his lab most of the day running DNA tests for that office building across from the hotel Edwards took Dani to. Tony is in the field doing the assessments of the explosives in the duffle bags. Then he's going to the kennel to start working with the four dogs he's acquired.

Trevor is one of Tony's trainees. His previous owner encouraged him to be aggressive. Tony rescued him, along with five others, from a raid on the coordinator of a canine fight club. It's crazy to watch how gentle Tony is with these dogs knowing the beast he becomes when it comes to protecting his country and the people he loves.

"I see things worked out with Danielle." Willis steps in my office, uninvited.

My hand freezes with the spoon almost in my mouth.

"How are you going to proceed now that Edwards is dead? You can't get information from a corpse."

"We found a few leads among his belongings."

"Why are you sitting on your ass? Why aren't you following those leads? Have you spoken with the Shadow who was tailing him?"

Why aren't you home taking care of your sick wife? "Vin interviewed him."

"You should have been the one to question that man. When I was Second Command I had my hands in every aspect of operations."

I stare him square in the eye. "I read Ricci's report and I'm moving forward. Protecting Dani is my priority."

"That's why Phantom's going to *hell* under your leadership. Protecting the American people takes precedence over where you stick your penis every night."

"Get. Out." My tone is so calm, Langford hesitates before following orders.

He keeps his eyes on me as he quietly leaves my office. It was wise of him not to turn his back. The monster is pounding the door and foaming at the mouth. One more crack aimed at my relationship with my wife and I'm going to forget who he is and beat the shit out of him.

I reply to the emails and open the visual voicemail messages and read through those. Some clients got wind of the shooting. I'm contacting them to calm their fears and reassure them Hawkeye Personal Protection takes their safety seriously. I paint on the fake smile and make the first video conference call. "Prime Minister. As you can see, the rumors are false..." Necessary lies come easily.

CHAPTER EIGHT

THE FRONT DOOR FLIES OPEN, knob hitting the wall. Hurricane Cuddles followed by Hurricane Sweat Pea sweep through the foyer with Trevor following close behind, his bark echoing throughout the house.

I bend and scoop up my girls in my arms, ignoring the discomfort in my shoulder. "Hi."

"Where's Mommy?" Emm looks around.

"Upstairs I think."

She squirms out of my arms. "Mommy," Emm sings. She runs up the stairs.

I shift Kourt to my right side and wrap both arms around her. She throws her arms around my neck and we squeeze. I inhale the sweet scent of my baby girl.

Trevor stands on his hind legs. His wet nose brushes my arm, followed by his tongue. He whines. I reach down and scratch his head. "I missed you too, boy."

He barks.

Kourt leans back to hold my cheeks in her hands. "What's with the hair on your face?" She turns my head to get a better view.

"I'm growing a beard. What do you think?"

She gives me the thumbs up, then leaves a wet kiss on my cheek. "I'm gonna go say hi to Mom." She jumps out of my arms and runs for the stairs. Trevor goes with her.

My mother's coming up the steps with the girls' jackets and backpacks in her arms.

I meet her in the doorway. "How was the drive?"

"It was good. Not much traffic. We stopped at the stable before we got on the road." She sighs when I relieve her of the girls' things. "Emma wasn't feeling well and didn't want to get out of the car so your dad took Kourtney horseback riding while I stayed with her."

Emm seems fine now. I lean in and kiss Mom's cheek.

Dad grunts. He struggles to close the trunk and balance the girls' suitcases with more bags in his hands. I drop my load on the bench by the door to go help him.

Mom stops me with a hand on my chest. "Let him do it. Dani told him not to buy them anymore toys, he didn't listen, so *he* has to face her wrath."

I wink at Dad and tell Mom, "Let's go sit in the family room."

As I lead her in that direction, I gesture for Dad to take the extra bags to my office. Dani isn't the only one who knows how to sneak things in the house undetected. I bet if she knew there are surveillance cameras throughout the house she wouldn't have been so smug about helping Mom hide stuff in Jessi's room.

"We loved having the girls for a week. Do you think Dani will let them come for a couple weeks in the summer? I promised to take them back to the seniors' center."

"I'm sure she wouldn't mind."

Trevor barks. He sounds like he's at the landing. His nails tap dance on the hardwood floors. I hear the animation in Kourt's voice, but can't make out what she's saying. Trevor is helping her tell the story.

"Are you sure it's safe for you to walk down the stairs? Your stomach's blocking your view," Dad jokes.

"Very funny, Dad," Dani laughs.

Mom meets them in the doorway. Dad has his arm around his daughter-in-law. They have become best friends since that morning she was ready to pulverize him.

Dani pulled her hair back into a ponytail of curls and she's wearing long pants. The collar of the yellow shirt hides the scratches on her neck. Her rounding stomach is prominent behind the tight fit. A lightweight sweater covers the bruises on her arms. For once, she's not barefoot.

Mom hugs her. "How are you feeling?"

She gives Mom a one-arm hug. Emm's holding onto her other hand. "I'm fine. How were my girls? They didn't give you a hard time, did they?"

Mom laughs. "We had a great time."

They move to the sofa and Emm sits next to Dani, practically in her lap.

"How was Colorado Springs?" Dani asks the girls.

"It was *great,* Mom," Kourt proclaims. "I loved it there and Grandpa got us our own ponies." He elbows Kourt and they whisper back and forth. "Don't worry, Grandpa. I bet you can outrun her. She's got that baby in her stomach," Kourt says out loud.

My cough covers the laughter.

She turns to her mother. "Grandpa said he couldn't send us home with bunnies for Easter because you'd make him take them back."

Mom comes to their rescue. "The son of the man I'm partnered with at the seniors' home owns the stable. He saw how much the girls loved being around the ponies and gave Bry a good deal. You know how Emm feels about animals, so it was either the ponies or two rabbits. And the rabbits were *not* staying in Colorado Springs."

Dogs, cats, and possibly birds Mom can handle. She draws a line at any pets that don't make noise.

Usually Emm's the one who goes on and on when it comes to horses. Right now, she's quiet, tense, and focused solely on Dani. I stop paying attention to the back and forth banter about the ponies versus the bunnies, and watch my daughter.

She climbs onto Dani's lap. Touches Dani's face, shoulders, arms and hands like she's checking for injuries. She then settles on her mother's lap. Resting her head on Dani's chest. Over Dani's heart.

No one else notices Emm's protective behavior. And Dani keeps her arms wrapped around her daughter.

"I don't know about you guys, but I'm hungry," I say. Something's up. I need to question Dad.

"Come on, girls, help me make lunch and finish telling me about your spring break." Dani slides Emm off her lap. "Any special requests?" she asks me.

I shake my head.

"I'll help too," Mom says and follows them out of the family room.

While they're in the kitchen, Dad and I sneak the extra bags up to the girls' rooms and hide the new stuffed animals and toys.

I wait until we're in Emm's room to question him.

"Son."

"Dad."

We speak at the same time. I gesture for him to go first.

"Is everything okay with you and Dani?" he asks.

I frown. "Why do you ask?"

"Dani called the girls Thursday evening. She didn't sound like her normal jovial self. She sounded really upset." He watches me. "You and Dani are still newlyweds and that's a big adjustment even for couples who have been together for years before marriage. Add a pregnancy and more pressure is put on you. A marriage license is more than a piece of paper; it's a binding partnership that cannot be easily walked away from. You guys will have good days and not so good days. It's how you two approach the not so good days that will strengthen your marriage. I know I've instilled this in you since you were a young boy and I know I don't have to remind you, but a man never lays his hands on a woman in anger. He walks away and calms down."

Words escape me. Who the fuck does he think I am? For god's sake, I have two daughters and I'd murder any man who put his hands on them. Why would he think I'd hit my wife?

"From the moment your mom found out she was pregnant with you, there was no pleasing her. The mood swings. The cravings. I didn't think we'd survive for nine months. We argued so much Jessi would cry. Even though I knew I'd never do it, I daydreamed of dropping Nancy off somewhere in the Rockies, then going back for her after she had you. Instead, I found gardening. It helped me stay out of her way. What I'm getting at, son, is sometimes Dani may be unreasonable, especially while *infanticipating*. Instead of trying to please her, find a hobby that relaxes you and keeps you out of her way for a little while."

"Okay, Dad. Let me stop you there. Know this. If I ever have the balls to raise a hand to Dani, you'd know I was in a fight. She'd get in some good hits and I'd probably have to move back home because she'd kill me in my sleep. You haven't seen her in action like I have. I was there the day she dropped Vin and trust me, I never want to be on the receiving end of that kind of ass kicking."

He laughs. "Tell me how she did it."

"Man, Dani showed no fear. She threw the first punch." While we rearrange the stuffed animals in Emm's room, I tell him, punch for punch, how my five-foot-nine-inch wife took down Vincenzio the Tank Ricci.

"You're favoring your right arm. Did you hurt yourself?"

"No," I frown. Why would he pick today to notice I'm not lifting with my dominant hand? "Did anything happen with Emm while she was with you guys?" I ask to take the focus off me.

"She was a little homesick and kept using her iPad to try and contact Dani. A young family moved into the Malone's old house. Friendly couple, Theo and Ellen Akers. The girls played with their triplets. Why do you ask?"

"Emm's all over Dani."

"Emma's excited about finally having a mom. Son, you're a great dad, but look at how much she's blossomed. You never told us much about her birth mother."

And I'm not telling you now. "Guess I'm not used to Emm being clingy, and you're right, she isn't the same little girl she was this time last year. She's finding her voice."

He slaps me on the shoulder, "Just wait until boys start calling the house. That's when you need to pay attention to their behavior." He laughs, leading the way downstairs. "You won't have to worry about Kourt. She can handle herself. She knocked the wind out of that boy when he tried to kiss her."

My eyebrows meet my hairline. "Excuse me? What boy?"

Dad laughs harder. "Let her tell you about it."

We sit in the family room. He turns on a gardening show. I check my phone for updates from Vin.

"Dad. Grandpa. Lunch is ready," Kourt shouts from the kitchen.

"I could have done that," I hear Dani tell her.

"Well, why didn't you?" Kourt snaps.

That sarcastic mouth is going to get her in trouble. Lately, her sweet disposition is replaced by sarcasm. We've been giving them a little freedom of speech because we're all adjusting to our new family life, but Kourt's testing the waters a bit too much. I hurry to the kitchen to be the buffer between mother and daughter. I have a feeling Mama Hawk is almost to her breaking point with our daughter's mouth.

We eat lunch out on the patio. Trevor runs around the yard chasing birds. Even in April, there are patches of snow here and there further back in the woods. The leaves on the trees are a healthy green. I'll wait until May to uncover the pool and get it ready for the summer.

"So when do we find out if I'm getting another granddaughter or finally a grandson?" Dad looks at us.

Dani and I haven't talked about when we'd tell everyone. Is she waiting for me to spill the beans?

"Why are you asking?" She spears a fork full of salad then puts it in her mouth. Chewing slowly, she cocks an eyebrow.

His shoulders rise and fall like a little kid not wanting to verbalize the truth.

She swallows and takes a sip of sour strawberry lemonade. "You want to get a good deal on a pony for him too?"

The legs of his chair grate on the stoned patio. Dad jumps to his feet. A goofy smile on his face.

Mom's hand slaps the table. "I knew it."

Kourt pouts. "Who wants a stinky boy?"

"I know the perfect name to give him." Dad pulls Dani out of the chair to wrap his arms around her.

"I bet you do." She laughs. "Emm told me about the stuffed animals you bought them at the zoo."

Dad's face turns red. He looks like he wished a hole suddenly opened under his feet to suck him in.

───◆───

Dani took the girls upstairs to unpack after Mom and Dad left. I've been in my home office working. Vin's icon flashes in the center of the video chat box. I exhale and steady myself for what he's about to divulge. This is the update I've been waiting for.

I make sure the door is closed and tap the answer button.

"It's the gun," he says. No greeting. No leading up to it. Vin would not say it if he wasn't one hundred percent sure. He knows how important this story is to me. To Dani. To our family.

My nails rake through the hair on my chin. I briefly look away from the monitor to soak in this piece of the puzzle. Where it fits at this moment is unknown. Does it bring me closer or further from the truth?

"Detective Campbell found everything I requested. It took a while, but I scanned the case files. Made models of the evidence. She's one of the top detectives in the precinct and is willing to reopen the case. Make it a bi-state investigation."

"What did you tell her?"

His lips turn up in a cocky smile. "I said I want to close the missing person's reports on the teens so their parents will have some closure. Campbell said she'll keep digging to see if the gun is tied to any other unsolved cases."

"When's your flight?"

"Six hours. I rebooked for a later one. I'll have time to read through the information, then send you a summary."

I smile. This detective must be attractive if he's spending more time in LA than he has to.

Wait for it.

"I'm going to hit some spots before I head to the airport. Want me to bring Dani some cupcakes?" Translation: he's made plans with Detective Campbell that have nothing to do with his reason for being in Los Angeles.

I nod and laugh as my finger rubs my temple.

"Will two dozen hold her until my next trip to LA?"

"Yeah, man."

And then I see it. He let the façade slip for a millisecond. Vin and I have been friends for a long time. He's holding back.

"What aren't you saying?"

Vin's eyes close and he takes a deep breath. When they open, he stares into the camera. "Gut feeling—it was a hit."

The other shoe is dangling from the tip of the toe. Ready to drop.

Vin wants to go through the information before he says anymore. I agree, then sign off after I tell him to have a good time with the detective.

I sit at my desk. Stunned. Paralyzed.

Someone put out a hit on Elizabeth and Daniel—Dani's parents? Why?

Sitting here is not productive and I can't follow up until Vin sends me the info, so I lock up the office and go search for my wife and kids.

Emm's door is the first one on the left. I knock, then open it when no one answers. Dani and Emm are cuddled on the bed. Asleep. Emm's hand resting over her mother's heart.

I pull out my phone, snap a few pictures, and cover them with a blanket.

Across the hall, I knock on Kourt's door.

"Come in," she calls out.

I crack the door open and poke my head in. She's sitting at the table with Trevor and two stuffed bears.

"Whatcha doing, Cuddles?"

Trevor throws a look that says 'I'm wearing a pink hat and boa, what do you think we're doing?'

The hostess is sporting an orange hat with matching gloves, boa, and shiny jewelry. "I'm having tea with Mrs. Fuzzy, Mrs. Daisy, and Mrs. Trevorah. Would you like to join us?" She mimics an English accent.

I curtsey. "I'd love to, milady." I stride into the parlor.

"I don't have a man's hat and tie for you."

I'm secure enough in my manhood to play dress up and have a tea party with my daughter. "Give me what you've got, baby girl. And call me Mrs. Bryanna."

She laughs, goes to the chest and brings back a purple hat set, earrings, and necklace. "Your hands are too big to fit in the gloves."

I clear my throat and channel an English woman and use the best feminine voice I can pull off. "I prefer to drink my tea without them, love. They just get in the way."

Her lips twitch. She sets a purple teacup and saucer in front of me and pours make-believe tea while I get dressed.

"How do you like your tea, madam?"

"Three sugars and a spot of cream please." That time I sound just like a proper English lady with a baritone voice.

She can't hold it in any longer. Kourt laughs. We go back and forth perfecting our accent. Topping one another. Kourt's competitive. She gets it honestly. Look who her parents are.

Kourt, the bears, Trevor, and I drink make-believe tea and talk. She tells me how happy she is to have a grandma and a grandpa like other kids. And she can't wait to turn in her family tree report on Monday.

I ask what she liked most about visiting Colorado Springs. She says sleeping in my old room and helping grandpa in the garden. Kourt gets animated, using her hand and arms as she talks about their visit to the zoo. She enlightens me about all the plants that attracted butterflies.

For next year's science experiment, she wants to create a controlled environment for plants and insects and show how well they thrive without human interference. My baby girl's intelligence continues to astound me. I tell her she should talk to Uncle Tony about building a habitat. Environmental Design was one of his majors.

I ask how she liked riding a horse. The smile on her face tells it all. I don't think she takes a breath and the words are a run-on sentence. She tells me about her pony, Cuddles. The lady who took a long time helping Emmy. Mr. Banks, the stable owner, taught them how to brush their ponies.

The conversation evolves into the long test my dad gave her after looking over her spring break homework. Going to the *old-people's home* with Grandma.

Kourt talks about the family with triplets who live across from Grandma and Grandpa. "I liked climbing trees and playing football with Stuart. Savannah and Sarah wanted to play with Emmy, but Emmy mostly stayed in the house crying for Mommy. I punched Stuart in the stomach."

"Why?"

"Because he tried to kiss me. Grandpa said I did the right thing and if any boy tries to do something to me, I should defend myself. Please don't tell Mommy. She won't let me go back in the summer."

I do my best not to laugh while I cross my heart and let her know her secret is safe with me. I also tell her to try telling boys how she feels before throwing the first a punch. Deep down it does my heart good to know she's not into boys yet.

"Mommy slept in my bed while I was gone, huh?" She pours more tea for us.

"A couple of nights. How do you know?"

"My sheets are different and Mr. Cuddles wasn't where I left him. Did she cry when I was gone?"

"She missed you. We both did, but Mom's happy you weren't afraid to be away from home."

"Dad, can we plant a butterfly garden in the yard? Just me and you."

"Why don't you want your sister to help?"

"Emmy hates digging in the dirt. I learned about butterfly gardens at the zoo."

"Okay, let's research it after dinner. We really should find a way to include your sister."

Her eyes roll and lips smack.

"Kourt. Can I ask you a question?"

She nods.

"Why aren't you happy about the baby?"

Her gaze drops to her hands.

"You can always be honest with me."

"You'll forget about me," she whispers.

Her words resonate like a punch to the gut. I'm winded. My baby girl believes I'll abandon her. I reach across the table and use my fingers to gently lift her chin. "I think about you and Emm all the time."

She moves her chin away and uses the back of her hands to wipe her eyes. She looks at me. The message in her eyes, *I don't believe you.* Kourt's gaze drops back to the cup and saucer on the table in front of her.

"Is that why you don't want your sister to be in on the garden?"

Her lips tremble and her breathing becomes uneven. She nods. Trevor whines and starts to bark. The hat on his head falls to the floor. He's reacting to the change in Kourt's demeanor.

I cup her chin and wait for her to look up at me. "Trevor's been cooped up in the house too long. I think the three of us can use some fresh air."

The shutter of a camera captures us sitting at the table. Kourt and I look toward the door.

Dani's lips twitch. "Am I interrupting?"

"We're cleaning up and taking Trevor for a walk." I hand Kourt my hat and boa.

"You coming with us, Mommy?"

"Let me go wake up Emma."

Our daughter shoves away from the table. Upset. Trevor barks and nudges her hand with his nose.

I stand and help her put away the toys. I'll wait until it's just the two of us to see what triggered her reaction.

Dani and Emm wait for us at the bottom of the stairs. I open the side door. Trevor takes off running for the pond. Kourt races him. Emm holds her mother's hand and walks slowly down the path between us.

This is real.

We pass the guesthouse. It looks like no one is home.

Willis sees my relationship with Dani as part of the business. He knows what it takes to succeed on an assignment, even if the subject of the case is someone you know. In his eyes, national security trumps family. I disagree and that's why we bump heads on this RAGS case.

He got permission for full disclosure nine years ago, yet Willis never told Marie everything. He believes if his wife knew them being in the same bar on the same day, at the same time was no coincidence, she'd be crushed. Now with that, I do agree. Look what happened when I told Dani.

Pierre, Marie's fiancé, was a RAGS runner. He was at the bar to pass on top-secret information obtained from a military mole. Marie showed up unexpectedly. Her outburst drew too much attention and the buyer walked out with the cash.

Marie stood up to leave; Pierre hit her over the head with a beer bottle knocking her unconscious. He would have killed her if Willis hadn't stepped in. Once Pierre and his buyer were apprehended and the information destroyed, Willis's next assignment was to find Marie's affiliation with the anti-American government group. He was engaged to a woman named Carolyn at the time, but up and married Marie three months after accepting the extended assignment.

The first several years of their marriage, he volunteered for assignments that took him out of the country. The day Carolyn married another man; Willis accepted the Second Command position and came home to his wife.

For a while, Willis would take off for a week to meet up with old military buddies for a fishing trip once a year. But since they've come to work for me, the fishing trips increased to three or four times a year. Some longer than a week. I've never questioned him. I doubt he'll admit to his true activities. I do know Willis never comes back smelling like someone who's been camping for a week, and Carolyn has been divorced for fifteen years.

A team of ten ex-Navy SEALs, now Hawkeye PPOs, are watching us while I'm unarmed and spending quality time outside with my family. I spot one high up in the treetop lookout point. A person would have to be trained in the art of covert observation to notice him. I acknowledge him with a nod. He signals with a quick flash of the setting sun's ray bouncing off a mirror aimed at the pond.

———————◆———————

"So—Grandpa got you a telescope. How did you manage that?" I whisper to Kourt. We're sitting on the sofa in the family room. Emm's in the kitchen with Dani.

"Me and Stuart were lying on the grass in the backyard looking up at the sky."

"Is that when he tried to kiss you?"

"No, Dad," she sings. "We were looking for the smiling face in the moon."

"Did you see it?"

"Nope. Grandpa said we needed a telescope and the next day he came home with one."

"The box isn't opened."

"That's when that stinky boy tried to kiss me and I let him have it."

"Want to go set it up? See if we can find the face in the moon?"

Her eyes light up. She nods so hard, her braids dance.

We hold hands and run upstairs to her room. I hid the telescope on the top shelf of her closet out of Dani's line of sight. It's not an expensive one, but it'll do for casual stargazing. If Kourt is really interested in astronomy, I will get her a more expensive one. The CEO of an aerospace engineering company requested a consultation for Hawkeye's services. They just won the bid for a government contract. One of the products the company makes is a compact, high-powered telescope that would be perfect for her.

On our way out the back door I grab a picnic blanket from the laundry room.

"Emm, Kourt and I are going to look at the stars. Do you want to come too?"

If we allowed our girls to use profanity, I know Kourt would have called me every profane name known to man. The look in her eyes tells me so.

"That sounds like fun, Emm. Go with them," Dani encourages.

"Are you coming?" Emm asks her mom.

"No, sweetie, I'm going to put my feet up."

"I'll stay inside with you. You might need me."

"I'll be all right, Emma. Go look at the stars with Dad and Kourt-ney." Dani looks at me. She looks tired and needs some quiet time.

I end this by tucking the telescope under my arm, throwing the blanket over my shoulder, and taking the girls' hands, leading them out the door.

After the chill burns off Kourt's attitude, she bombards me with questions about the constellations. I have to look up some of the answers on my phone. She tells me dads are supposed to know everything. I counter with, sisters are supposed to share.

CHAPTER NINE

MONDAY MORNING ROLLS AROUND AND I have another Elite Team meeting. Dani's still under doctor's orders so she won't be going in. That takes one worry off my plate for the day. Marie's nothing cough turned into a full-blown cold over the weekend so it's up to me to make breakfast, and since Dani doesn't have to get up, I'm getting the girls ready for school too.

I've never needed an alarm clock. Dani, on the other hand, uses one and hits the snooze button a few times before she gets out of bed. I sit up, swing my legs around and set my feet on the floor. I stretch and stand, rolling my left shoulder. It's not too tender this morning.

I look toward the bed. Dani's half lying on a pillow underneath her stomach and half on her side, hugging the pillow under her head. She's kicked the covers off her naked body. Her pajamas are on the floor. She must have gotten hot in the middle of the night. If she'd let me, I'd kiss every bump and bruise on her body to make them feel better. Instead I go pee.

I think about the full schedule I have today while I empty my bladder. Morning meeting with the guys. Video conference with POTUS in the SCIF. Review list of nominees. The list goes on.

As the toilet flushes and I turn to walk away, I pause mid step. The last time I left the seat up and Dani came in after me, her exact words were, *I'll shove a large catheter up your dick hole and crazy glue the bag to your thigh if you don't remember to put the seat down.* She got in my face, *you're living with a woman now, so put the seat down after you use it.* I turn around and do just that.

The heat of the water is a few degrees more than I normally have it and I set the showerheads to pulsate. Sleeping on the couch is making my neck stiff. My wife hasn't invited me back into our bed yet so that's where I rest my head at night. It's not too bad. It stops me from rolling onto my shoulder in the middle of the night.

It's been seven days, twenty-three hours, fifty-nine minutes, and twelve seconds since we last had sex. I could use some stroking. Dani's appointment with Jessi is on Friday and even if we can resume our *sexcapades,* there's no guarantee she's ready. She seems perfectly okay with having the bed to herself.

Shower gel and my hand is no match for the tight, warm pleasure her body gives, but it's a temporary solution for the itch. The one consolation, I don't have to cuddle with my dick when I'm done.

The bathroom door opens. I wipe the steam from the glass and watch my naked wife zombie walk in. Dani's never been embarrassed about using the bathroom or being nude in front of me. She picks up the trail of pajamas I left at the door, drops them in the laundry basket, and sits on the toilet. This is our normal weekday morning routine. I wonder why she's awake.

The toilet flushes and she joins me in the shower room. Without the usual shower cap. Her body jerks as soon as the sting of the hot water hits her. She jumps out. I quickly turn down temperature.

"Good morning," she says, testing the water with her hand before stepping back under the streams.

I ogle her body and return the greeting. My day just got a bit better.

Pretty brown eyes wide open and staring up at me. She flashes a toothy grin. "Rock, paper, scissors. Loser gets the girls up."

My left fist pounds my right palm. Her right fist pounds her left palm. We count: one, two, three. I choose scissors. She chooses paper. Kourt isn't a morning person, add a week of sleeping in and she's a poked grizzly bear. No one is ready for the stubbornness on a Monday morning after a break from school.

I take a chance and kiss her shoulder. "Thank you."

Her wet body brushes my right side. She's reaching for her body wash. If I didn't know better, I'd say she's purposely trying to turn me on.

It's difficult, but I control my body, get out, and leave the bathroom before I force her up against the glass, drop to my knees and say a proper hello to Sunshine with my tongue.

I usually take my time with the grooming routine. I rush through it while she's still in the shower. This morning, Dani's playing a dangerous game of sexual-indulgence versus abstinence. I get out of there before she sees how close I am to playing along. *And I won't play fair.*

Selecting the right look is crucial. Everyone in Phantom knows I was shot. I don't want the moles to think I've been weakened. In the closet, I take my time laying out a power suit and matching it with proper accessories. Power tie and pocket hankie. Expensive cufflinks, belt, and shoes. My timeless titanium watch compliments the look.

On my way to the stairs, I hear my sister and Dani talking in Emm's room. I head in that direction.

"Do you think I should call their pediatrician?"

Jessi yawns. "Nah, it's just a little stomach bug. Keep her home with you today."

I walk into the room. Emm's in her underwear, cradled in her mother's arms. Dani's in her robe with a towel wrapped around her hair.

"What's wrong?" I ask.

Dani touches our daughter's forehead with the back of her hand. "She said her stomach hurt, then threw up." Dani points to the pile of covers on the floor at the foot of the bed. Emm's pajamas on top.

"She'll be fine. No fever and no abdominal pain. It's probably just a twenty-four-hour stomach virus," Jessi says. She's still in her scrubs. The bags under her eyes mean she didn't sleep much last night.

"Bryan, can you take those out of here? The smell is starting to get to me." Dani covers her mouth and nose with her hand.

Careful not to get puke on my clothes, I pick up the bundle and step out into the hall. Kourt comes out of her room still in her pajamas. She fans her nose.

"Gross! What stinks?"

"Your sister's sick."

"She gets to stay home?" Her tone is chock full of indignation.

I lift the bundle higher, letting the smell answer the question. Kourt backs away.

"Finish getting dressed and be downstairs in thirty minutes.

What do you want for breakfast?"

"Nothing," she shouts.

I laugh all the way down to the laundry room. I double bag the foul-smelling covers in trash bags. I'll drop it off at the cleaners on my way to the office.

Apparently Kourt didn't take me seriously when I told her to be down in thirty minutes. She's ranting about having to go to school. Under duress, I help my daughter get into her uniform. Pull her hair into a lumpy ponytail, couldn't find her comb and brush. I pack our grilled cheese sandwiches and apple slices to go, and pour her milk into one of my travel mugs.

We rush out of the house.

Kourt proceeds to tell me Emm is faking. "She just wants to stay home with Mom."

Through the earpiece in my ear, I hear a beep, then Riley's voice. "Good morning, sir. POTUS is calling from a secured line."

"Put it through."

"Put what through, Dad?"

I take a quick look at her in the rear-view mirror. "I'm on the phone."

"No, you're not."

I point to my ear.

It must be important if he couldn't wait for our scheduled video conference call. The beep was Riley securing the line before alerting me to the call.

"Good morning, sir?"

"You're talking to Grandpa? Hi, Grandpa," Kourt yells.

"Kourt. I'm on the phone." My tone is harsher than intended.

"The man CIA picked up is one of Amir Mahdavi's."

Mahdavi is the leader of Islam Liberation Army, an infamous terrorist group in the Middle East. They have close ties to Al-Qaeda, ISIS, and two others who are at the top of our watch list. We've been looking for Mahdavi for nine years. He never stays in the same place for more than twelve hours. ILA was the buyer Edwards was selling Phantom information to.

I read the report last night, but it didn't indicate the man in custody was ILA. Unfortunately, I can't talk with Kourt ear-hustling from the back seat. We're three miles from the school. I can listen for that long.

"Give me details."

"Details about what? Are you talking to me, Daddy?"

"Kourtney. Allison. Hawk. Be quiet!" I have to get her out of this truck. I push the button and the hazard lights start flashing. President Hart is talking in my ear, giving me the specifics of the CIA's operation in Yemen. It's a good thing Porter's been on my security detail before and knows the importance of the hazards. He pulls ahead of me. We use defensive driving maneuvers to get my daughter to school. The chaser Suburban stays on my tail. Kourt's pouting in the back seat.

The president is still talking when I pull up to the drop-off curb. I keep the motor running. My shoulder works in tandem with my hand to get the door open. I hop out and open my daughter's door.

Kourt resists as I unhook the seatbelt. She struggles as I lift her off the seat and grab her backpack. She glares as I help her out of the truck.

"Mom walks us to class."

I kiss her cheek and gently push her toward the gate. "Have a good day."

"You forgot my lunch."

I hop back into the driver's seat and pull away from the curb. Now I can actively participate in this conversation. We have a small window of time to execute a mission. If Mahdavi's men are in Yemen, then it means the man himself is on his way.

The Elite Special Operations Team is always ready for covert operations. ILA have many enemies. The United States one of them. If we succeed in eliminating their leader we will be doing the world a favor.

By the time the CIA go through their protocols to find Amir Mahdavi, he'll have moved on to his next overnight hideout. That's why POTUS is giving Phantom this assignment. We're exempt from the protocols of the United States law. He doesn't have to submit a Presidential Finding. He won't have to obtain congressional approval for us to execute a covert operation because legally, Phantom doesn't exist. He won't know when or how we go about this mission. It's not to keep him out of the loop. POTUS needs plausible deniability if we're caught.

"Are you up for this, Colonel?"

"Yes, I am, sir."

"I'll forward you the recordings from the clandestine operation CIA used to apprehend the man in custody. Godspeed, Hawk."

"Thank you, sir. We won't let you down."

I end the call and maneuver through traffic to get to my downtown office. On the way, I dictate a text message for Riley to send to Chen, Tony, Ig, and Vin. A quick glance in the back and I remember the trash bag. The guys won't be at the office for another hour. I stop at the cleaners, drop off the covers and ask if they can deliver them to the house when it's ready.

I pull into the parking garage of my building. Normally I go through the main entrance; this morning, I take the elevator straight to my floor. President Hart's transmittal was uploaded to a secured file in our network that only he and I have access to.

———————◆———————

I look up at the clock: it's eight fifteen in the evening. We've been at it since the guys got here this morning. Max gave me a fitness test. Ig cleared me to return to active duty and POTUS signed off on it.

Max also vetted five of the twelve members of Delta. From the list, I selected two to back us up in the field.

Since we're leaving at daybreak, we head home to pack.

I know what awaits me when I walk through the door. An angry wife and an even angrier daughter. I forgot to make Kourt a lunch. I kind of heard her say something this morning about it, but I was listening to the president and not my daughter. She had to eat the school's lunch, which she doesn't like. I forgot to pick her up after school too, and to top it off, I hear she had a bad day. I'm sure they have unkind words for me.

I close the inner garage door and walk down the hallway. Dani's moving around in the kitchen. I stop in my office to leave my briefcase on the desk, then head that way.

"Hey." I lean on the doorframe and watch her. She gives me a quick over-the-shoulder look, but doesn't stop cleaning the kitchen. "Is Kourt in bed?"

The dish towel in Mama Hawk's hand is tossed aside. She turns to face me head-on. My instinct is to take a step back and prepare for the strike.

"I told you that woman has something against me and now she's taking it out on my daughter." She folds her arms. "As a teacher, if she had concerns about our child's family history report, she should have discussed it with us. Not our daughter. And certainly not in front of the whole class." Dani's got that neck rolling thing going on. She is pissed. "I'm asking you, Bryan, is she one of your no-strings-attached chicks?"

I look my wife straight in the eye. Keep my tone even. My shoulders square. Body relaxed. "No, she's not."

Dani stares me down like she's weighing the truth behind my words. I maintain the composure. The first sign of weakness and she'll attack. This is the price I have to pay for my transgressions. If she's this mad, why didn't she go up to the school?

I count the seconds till she unfolds her arms. Dani turns her back to me and picks up the dish towel. From where I stand, that counter top is clean, but from the set of her shoulders, I'm guessing Dani's trying to smother the fire inside with mundane chores. If this were a television commercial, the kitchen would sparkle.

"Are you hungry? I can warm up something for you."

"I'm good. I ate at the office."

"Kourtney didn't come down for dinner."

That's my cue. I head upstairs to our daughter's room.

At her door, I knock and wait for her to answer.

"Come in, Mommy."

I open the door. Kourt is in bed. "It's Dad. May I still come in?"

She frowns and nods. Trevor raises his head and watches me from his post at the foot of Kourt's bed. I close the door behind me, walk over to the desk, and grab the chair. When I turn around, I notice Mr. Cuddles on the floor. I rescue him, then set him next to her and sit in the chair.

"I hear you had a bad day."

She nods again.

"Do you want to talk about it?"

Her fingers play with the covers as her head shakes side to side.

"I can't make it better if we don't talk about it."

"Dad, can I ask you a question?"

"Ask me anything."

She holds up her pinkie finger. "You promise to answer?"

I hook mine to hers. "I promise to give my best answer."

"If you had to choose between me and Emmy, who would you choose?"

Whoa. Talk about blindsided. "I'd choose both of you."

"But what if you could only choose one? Like say there's a fire and I'm in my room and Emmy in hers. Who would you save?"

"Where's this coming from, Kourt? What was said to make you think you're not important to me?"

Her lips start to tremble. "You yelled at me. I've never heard you yell at Emmy. You didn't walk me to class. You used to always walk Emmy to class." Her voice cracks. "You forgot my lunch. And you forgot to pick me up." She turns on her side, away from me. "Never mind. Forget it." She sniffs.

Trevor whines and crawls up the bed until he's lying beside her. She throws an arm over him.

"Baby girl, I'm sorry. I was on an important phone call. That's no excuse…"

"It's okay, Dad."

"No, it's not okay if I made you feel like you don't matter to me. Kourt, please look at me."

"I'm sleepy. Can you turn off the light?"

My eight-year-old daughter just dismissed me. *Damn.* I don't know how I should feel about that, but it's important I answer her question.

"Baby girl, I would fight the fire. Stop it from getting to you and your sister. I wouldn't stop fighting it until I put out *every* flame that tries to harm my girls. I would never choose one over the other. I choose both of you." I kiss her cheek and reach for the lamp's switch.

"I remember you, Dad," she says.

I wait for her to say more or tell me what that means. She keeps her back to me. I flip the switch and leave her room.

Across the hall, I check on Emm. Her light is out and she's already asleep. I go in and kiss her cheek.

As I walk to my room, I try to curb my anger as a parent. I know she went after Kourt to get my attention because I've been ignoring her attempts to get in contact with me. But a line was crossed today and it's up to me to force that woman back on her side.

I change into jeans and a T-shirt, and go back downstairs to my office. Dani's in the family room running the carpet sweeper. The house will be sparkling from top to bottom before she goes to sleep. Maybe I should lift the ban on her working out. She needs an outlet for that angry energy she's carrying around.

I place my hand on the mouse pad. "Riley. Locate Mike. Whiskey. Two. Zero. Zero. Five." The desk drawers unlock. I grab my firearm and bike key, and lock it back.

"Target's location is place of residence, sir."

This won't take long. I secure my gun in the hip holster and put on a jacket to cover it. On my way down the hall, I meet up with Dani. She looks me up and down with a cocked eyebrow.

I answer her silent question. "I have to make a quick run. It should take less than an hour."

She doesn't respond.

I feel her watching me as I walk out the door into the garage.

I lift the tarp off the EBR 1190SX motorcycle. The garage door rolls up. I push the bike down the driveway, secure the helmet on my head, and start the powerful engine.

As I speed through the streets of Boulder, I see flashes of Kourt in my mind's eye. Her as an infant. A toddler. The smile on her face the day she and Dani moved into that house in Arizona. I've stood in the background and watched her grow. My daughter means everything to me. The thought of losing her love tightens an invisible band around my heart.

I don't bother knocking. I use my key to let myself in and storm into her bedroom.

Burning red candles are on the dresser, nightstands, and in glass holders on the floor around the bed. Wicked-shaped shadows flicker on the walls. *What the fuck!*

I cough. The smell of her perfume is suffocating. *She's out of her damn mind.*

"You're late, baby," she croons from her position in the middle of the bed. Lying flat on her back on a black comforter. A scoop of chocolate ice cream covers each breast, a cupcake on her hairless mound.

"First you start with my wife and now you're dragging my daughter into this? Get back on your side of the line before I throw you back."

She snarls, then levitates to her knees like a demon. Holding the cupcake between her legs. "There's no record of that *bitch* being your goddamn wife. And her little brat is *not your daughter, Bryan!"* She throws the cupcake. I smell the chocolate frosting as it passes by. It misses me by less than an inch.

I wouldn't give her the satisfaction of moving out of the line of fire. "If that had hit me you'd be nursing a broken hand." Yes, I've been taught not to hit women, but this one doesn't know when to stop. She's lost it. Look at her. Naked and on her knees. Streams of chocolate ice cream running down her body. A hundred candles burning in this room making it so hot in here it feels like hell.

"Why her, Bryan?" she whines, changing tactics. She crawls to the edge of the bed and throws her arms around my neck, rubbing her ice cream-covered titties on my clothes. Her tongue traces my ear. "I would have given you more children if that's what you really wanted."

Her body jerks when I shove her off. I take a step back. She's trying to leave traces of her stench on me for Dani to catch. Oldest bitch trick in the book. She lifts her enhanced breasts in the palm of her hands and her tongue takes a swipe at the smeared ice cream.

This dizzy woman thinks I'm going to screw her. I respect my relationship with Dani too much to even entertain the thought. No other woman can achieve what my wife gives me in and out of bed. Especially the one kneeling in front of me.

"How could you get her pregnant!" Her attempt at seduction failed and she realizes it.

I turn to leave. We're not having this conversation again.

"Before you make it home, she'll know *everything* about us. About me. *I* bet if your precious Dani knew you spent those days before the New Year with me…"

The monster strikes before she finishes the sentence. My hand captures her by the throat. I throw the demon back on the bed. Draw my weapon and shove it in her smug mouth.

"If you so much as say hello to my wife, I'll slit your throat, fly to Texas and slit your parents' throats too. If you tell my daughter she's not mine again, I'll cut your fucking tongue out and hand deliver it to your parents before I put a bullet in their heads. Understood?" The monster speaks with deathly calm while staring into her eyes. I'm beyond my limits with her.

My hold on her neck tightens. I push the gun in deeper. She

gags. Real fear covers her eyes. Tears seep down her temples from the gag-reflex. Her body trembles. She knows I'm serious.

"My daughter worked hard on that report, *Malinda*," I say her name like that because it leaves a bad taste in my mouth. "Don't you ever belittle her place in my family again."

She nods. Her face is turning red. Her eyes start to roll back.

I rope in the monster and force him back into his cage.

I retract the gun, but keep it in my hand as I walk out of her house, slamming the door behind me.

My gaze searches the neighborhood for anyone who might be watching. I holster the weapon and throw my leg over the bike. I take one last look over my shoulder at the house. Malinda's standing in the window. The candlelight gives the illusion of her burning in hell. Too bad it's not really happening.

I pull away from the curb before I go back in and knock over the candles then block all her exits.

Yes, I spent three days with her, but it was business. We flew to Texas to investigate the person asking questions about Malinda Williamson, the second-grade teacher who took a job at a private school in Boulder, Colorado. He was a RAGS hitman. Now that I'm certain we have moles in Phantom, I know that hitman's search for Malinda is connected to her trashing Dani's apartment.

Who trashed my apartment? Dani asked during the meeting the other day. The lie rolled off my tongue without a second thought and the guys backed me up. *I don't know.* We couldn't tell Dani Malinda said she went to the apartment to protect them from Corporal Dial. We most certainly couldn't tell Dani we installed surveillance cameras in her apartment here in Boulder, and I own the building.

I watched the recording. The look on that woman's was face stone cold. She tore pictures and trashed the living room and Dani's room. Malinda's been watching us since October. Her phone calls, text messages, and unexpected visits to my office increased the more she saw me with Dani. At least she's smart enough to not bring that mess to my house.

Traffic is light. I head home to get ready for this mission to the Middle East. At a stoplight, I catch a whiff of Malinda's perfume and I look around to see if she's following me.

Shit! It's on my clothes.

I can't walk in the house smelling like this.

The light turns green. I speed down the street. At the next intersection, I make a right and keep straight. Tony lives a half mile from me. I can shower at his house.

I park the bike in his walkway and ring the doorbell just in case he has company.

"You alone?" I ask as soon as the door opens.

"Yeah. Everything okay?" He steps back.

I push past him.

"Yo! Dude. You didn't!" The door slams.

"What? No! Of course not." I drag a hand through my hair. "She must have bathed in that stuff." Even I hear the disgust in my tone.

He points to the stairs. I take them three at a time and walk down the hall to one of the guest rooms. I open the closet and get my duffle bag. I drop it on the bathroom floor and get out my clothes. We all have *emergency gear* at each other's houses.

I wash that woman's scent off me.

My relationship with Malinda Williamson is not something I want to explain tonight. Dani would definitely leave if she knew the truth behind that lie. Well, partial lie. I haven't been with Malinda in years. Yes, she was one of the past no-strings-attached-chicks.

I step back into the room and get dressed. The perfumed clothes go in a plastic bag. Another bag to drop off at the cleaners.

Tony is in his den playing a video game. That's how he prepares for a mission.

I go to the kitchen and get a couple beers out of the refrigerator.

He still hasn't completely furnished this house. A stove, refrigerator, and microwave in the kitchen. A bed and flat screen television in his room and one guest room. The other two are used for storage. Nothing is in the dining room or living room. In the den, a sofa, coffee table, flat screen television, and every gaming console on the market. No pictures on the walls. Not even ones of his family. I've walked in his shoes so I don't question why.

Controller in hand, Tony's fingers move like synchronized swimmers. The virtual car zips through the imitation streets of Brazil. I set a bottle on the table in front of him and sit on the other end of the sofa.

"What did she do now?" he asks.

"She threatened to tell Dani and I lost it."

"Huh?"

"She said she was going call Dani before I made it home. I made her choke on the barrel of my gun."

He looks at me, yet the car on the screen doesn't veer off path. He's waiting for an explanation.

I drink down half the bottle. "Kourt read her family history report in front of the class and afterwards Malinda told her she needed to write about her real family history. The Edwards family. Kourt argued that she is a Hawk. Malinda told her she's not related to me and Emm. The other kids laughed."

"Dawg. What's the real reason you went over there tonight?"

My index finger and thumb rub my brows. "Kourt asked who I would choose if I could only save her or Emm."

The virtual image on the screen pauses. "Damn. What did you say?"

I grunt. "How was I supposed to answer? Daddy loves you, but about five years ago..." My voice trails off. "A phone call just wouldn't have gotten the message across. She needed to see that was the wrong button to push."

"Stop beating yourself up over a past you can't change, Bry. If you hadn't done what you did, they would be dead and you know it." He turns his attention back to the television. "Process and move forward."

I wonder if he's taking his own advice. By the state of his house, I doubt it. He's right though, I can't change what happened, but I can prevent my daughter from crossing paths with Malinda Williamson again. I pull out my phone and call Barrett.

———◆———

I make it back home at a decent hour. After securing my firearm, I make sure the house is locked up and check on the girls. Mr. Cuddles is back on the floor when I open Kourt's door. Trevor's still lying next to her.

Emm's not in her bed. The light isn't on in her bathroom. Her slippers aren't on the side of the bed. The next place I check is my room. She's lying in bed with her mother.

Dani's not asleep, but her eyes are closed.

In the closet I change into my pajamas, then grab pillows and a blanket off the shelf.

I lie on the couch staring up at the ceiling. Across the room, the bedcovers rustle. Dani's waiting for me to say something.

"I don't want the girls going back to school and I don't want you going back to work."

"Why?"

"I'm doing this to keep you and the girls safe, baby."

"Humph," she grunts. "Safe from RAGS or safe from your booty call chick?"

CHAPTER TEN

WE LOVE IT WHEN WE have a solid lead on the leader of a terrorist group. Amir Mahdavi's reign with Islam Liberation Army is about to end. We'll make such a good example of him that others will think twice about stepping up to fill his shoes within ILA.

Acosta plays his favorite underground rap songs the whole time we're heading to the outskirts of Yemen in a stealth bomber specially made for Phantom. Our heads bob to the heavy beat of the bass, soaking in the lyrics as we check and double-check our gear and weapons.

Blacked-out HALO jumps are the perks to the job. So is soaring through the abyss of the night sky, a weightless ghost about to strike down the enemy. The rush is like the pleasure of ejaculating without feeling sleepy afterwards.

For this type of mission, we wear customized uniforms meant to prevent all DNA fingerprints from escaping from head to toe. Sweat, hair, tears, snot, eyelashes, even the dead skin cells a person sheds daily are DNA fingerprints. The uniforms also conceal our body heat so we cannot be detected by satellite imaging. Basically, we are ghosts.

This is Porter's first covert operation with the Elite Special Operations Team. Hell, ever! He's shadowing me. Although he's trying to hide it, the wide-eyed look is a sign of nerves. Going in for the sole purpose of killing many is totally different from going in to extract someone. We all had to start somewhere. And we were all nervous our first time.

Thirty minutes out, Acosta turns off the music. Individually, we go through our pre-strike ritual.

I kiss the picture I carry of me holding my baby girl for the first time, then tuck it next to my heart and secure my armor vest. A picture of my wife and kids is in my helmet.

We form a circle. Paul leads us in prayer. Which isn't easy considering our oxygen masks.

Ricci starts the strike chant.

I do a final communications check with Chen, who is back at headquarters acting as Watcher. Ready to alert POTUS if things don't go our way.

We have a small window of time once the doors open to avoid detection. Mahdavi's been able to escape capture because he possesses a sensor that detects a radar cross section. With the ramp door open we're vulnerable and so is the aircraft.

Calmness settles over me. We look to Acosta. If he doesn't fall in line, we know to abort mission. It seems like forever before he gives the thumbs up and gets into place. We mirror his actions.

The cargo ramp opens. All sounds are drowned out by the fury of the night air. Acosta jumps first, disappearing into the blackness. Ricci's next. Paul follows. Porter looks back at me. I nod and he executes a textbook exit. All newbies do. I'm the last to jump.

Free falling. One after the other. We slice through the night heading for the drop zone.

Acosta is spread eagle to reach a slower terminal velocity. Paul brings in his limbs, increasing his speed. He has to get underneath Acosta. If we're spotted, he'll set off a charge that momentarily hides us so we can veer in another direction.

I reach low altitude and pull the cord to release the chute. A slight jerk, then my speed starts to slow. As the ground draws closer, I pull the toggles toward my chest, the chute inflates. I glide-walk into a landing and immediately disconnect. I look to my right. Porter has a second of trouble with disconnecting but recovers quickly. Technique comes with experience. He'll get it.

Everyone drops to their stomachs. We store our chutes and oxygen masks. We're two miles from the compound, which is far enough that the dogs can't hear us. The area is blacked-out so they will bark at the slightest sounds.

Porter is on lookout. Ricci detaches the kennel pieces and starts to assemble it.

Paul unpacks six remote-controlled toy dump trucks from his

pack and hands them to me.

I unpack tiny cameras and secure them inside the cabs of four. Then get the other cameras and attach them in the open-box beds of the last two. I pull out the controller and a tablet. I log onto the tablet—the screen's set to night vision mode—and make sure Paul has a visual from the cameras.

Acosta takes two toy dump trucks and fills the open-box beds with doggie treats saturated with a liquid tranquilizer.

Paul attaches explosives to the other trucks. Once that's done he tests the long-range control box and uses the controller to punch in the code. The infrared signal is locked.

We're good to go. I hold the tablet in front of Paul so he can watch the progress of the dump trucks as they roll across the sand toward the compound.

We move within a mile of Mahdavi's camp.

At the entrance, Paul stops the toy trucks. Two guards are at the gate. He maneuvers one dump truck to the left and another to the right. They're the ones carrying explosives. The other four stay put.

Ricci and Acosta ready their sniper rifles.

I give Porter the signal. He rolls onto his back and starts spinning the rope attached to a six-inch bullroarer. The two German shepherds in the compound immediately pick up on the sound and start barking.

The two guards open the gate.

The dogs race across the sand toward the sound of the bullroarer. The armed guards split up, one going to the right, the other to the left. Ricci and Acosta track them in the telescopic sights attached to the rifles.

The dogs stop at the dump trucks with the treats.

Ricci and Acosta squeeze the triggers, the sounds muffled by the silencers.

Both guards drop.

Porter stops spinning the rope. We listen to the dogs devour the treats.

Paul drives the last two toy dump trucks through the compound's entrance. He presses the button and the hydraulics on the modified toys lift the open-box beds high enough to allow us to see if anyone comes to investigate why the dogs are out the gate and the guards have left their post.

We wait.

In three minutes, the dogs are down and no one else comes out.

I signal, with my fingers, the countdown to set our watches.

We conducted our own clandestine operation prior to leaving the airfield. We know which structures to target and how many inhabitants are present. Staying low, we venture into enemy camp and slip through the entrance, unnoticed.

Vin goes to the right heading for the building where the radar and weapons are stored. It's his job to make sure our evac helicopter can't be tracked or fired upon.

Acosta's on sniper duty and heads to the structure in the center of the compound. It's his job to cover us as we move about the grounds.

Paul's position is outside the gates. His job is to keep Mahdavi and his men in, and their backup out. He's also loading the German shepherds in the portable kennel.

Porter and I are going for Mahdavi in the building straight ahead.

Blackout curtains hang over the windows. Body heat from the four men inside the quarters shows us their positioning. I use sign language to tell Porter what he is to do once we enter. He nods. We creep inside. Porter fires counterclockwise taking out the three men at a table. I take out our main target.

I stand over his body to give visual confirmation that Amir Mahdavi is down, then fire three shots in his head and three in his chest.

Porter pulls out his case and starts working on the computers. I pack up documents and photos laid out on the table. I take a second to look at a particular set of pictures of a woman and a young boy. *Who are they? It's not Mahdavi's wife and kid.*

Porter motions that he's done. A hacking virus will spread through Islam Liberation Army's network. It's one I designed specifically for this mission.

We exit the building.

Two dancing flashes. Pause. One motionless flash. Pause. One long dancing flash. Ricci uses Phantom's optical communication to signal he's completed his task. The men in his target building have been executed and the radar dismantled.

I nod to Porter. He gives the same signal.

We look up. Acosta signals, all clear.

Sticking to the shadows, we run along the buildings of the compound where others are sleeping. We leave small packages of explosives then meet up at the gate. I stop my watch. Like the ghosts we are, we're in and out in eight minutes.

The extraction spot is a five-mile jog away. At each mile, we switch off lead and lookout. Towing the portable kennel with us. Even though Mahdavi's no longer a threat to us in this desert, who's to say someone else isn't.

A stealth helicopter hovers within ground effect. Vanessa Larson, from Delta Team, releases six ropes and covers us with the rifle in her hands as we climb up. Ig and Vin tether the kennel to their lines and start the climb. Paul keeps an eye on me. When I reach the top, he takes hold of my pack and pulls me in. I don't need babysitting, but because of my recent injury, the struggle was real.

To commemorate Porter's first mission as an honorary Elite Team member, Paul hands him the detonator. The kid smiles like it's Christmas morning. He presses the button and in the distance, we watch the compounds crumble in a ball of fire and smoke.

We head home.

————◆————

The three most important people in my life are out near the pond taking advantage of the warm weather we're having in Boulder today. I trade my business suit for a pair of shorts and a T-shirt, then go down to join them. This is what I want to come home to every day, family time with my wife and kids.

Kourt's running across the grass guiding a soccer ball with her foot. Trevor's trying to get it from her. A month ago I started teaching her soccer drills. She picked up on them like she'd been playing the sport for years.

Emm's standing at an easel. Paintbrush in hand. She tilts her head to the side while the brush moves up and down the paper.

Dani's sitting on a blanket looking through a magazine. The sun highlights the burgundy streaks in her brown hair. Her eyes are hidden behind dark shades. The bruises are hidden under her clothes.

I sit down behind my wife, wrap my arms around her. For a hot second her body stiffens. I startled her. Then Dani relaxes into my embrace and gives me a nudge in the ribs. Emm's body language draws my attention. The paintbrush in her hand hovers over the paper. Her eyes show a flash of fear. She looks at her mother, then smiles, and her body visibly relaxes.

"What are you painting, Emm?" That's not the question I really wanted to ask.

"A picture for Mommy."

"Treevorrr," Kourt sings. I crane my neck to see what's going on. She's chasing him. He dashes to the right with the soccer ball between his teeth. "Drop it." She laughs.

Dani turns the page of the magazine. "Marie's still under the weather. I have steaks marinating in the refrigerator. Can you put them on the outdoor grill?"

I press my lips against her ear. "Anything for you."

Her body twitches. I'm tempted to lick that spot behind her ear and capture her earlobe between my teeth just to make her wet. I exercise restraint. She has a doctor's appointment tomorrow morning. Hopefully we'll get the thumbs up from Jessi.

Kourt drops onto the blanket, out of breath. "What do you think about putting the butterfly garden near the big window?" She points toward the house.

"Sounds good to me. Did you do the research?"

She nods. "That spot gets lots of sunlight. It's close to the house so the butterflies will be protected from the winds. And a pipe for the sprinklers is close by."

Emm abandons the easel and joins us on the blanket.

"I guess we better make a list of things we need to buy so we can get started," I say.

Dani takes hold of my hand guiding it down to her stomach. We wait. I feel the tiniest thump against my palm. I didn't think anything could top being outside with my family, but this moment is pretty damn close.

"Girls, give me your hand," she says. She places their hands on her stomach so they can experience this too.

———◆———

I groan and stretch, and wipe the sleep out of my eyes. I don't usually sleep this late, any day of the week. Earlier this morning, at exactly four thirty-six, my daughter knocked on the door, then came in singing happy birthday. When she finished, she wanted to know why I'm sleeping on the couch. I came up with some excuse, then walked Kourt back to her room. Neither Dani nor I could go back to sleep after that. We lay awake listening to nature's nocturnal sounds. Kourt's question became the elephant in the room. Even I asked myself: why aren't you sharing a bed with your wife? The husband replied, *you're too much of a coward to ask her if it's okay.*

Sunday, April twenty-seventh, my thirty-fifth birthday. I look up at the ceiling. The nature of the job means we never get down time, but I'm making it a point to not let it interfere today because my wife asked.

The bathroom door opens and I don't move. Dani comes out naked, fresh from the shower, her body shining from the moisturizer spread over her flawless skin. Most of the bruises faded. The others are starting to fade.

She straightened her hair and pulled it into a ponytail on the top of her head. It still touches her back.

My gaze skims every inch of her, the evidence of our son causing a pouch in her stomach that makes her even sexier.

When she was pregnant with Kourt, it showed in her face and her curves disappeared; she was round. This time it's showing in her breasts and hips, and her nose is starting to spread. With each step my goddess takes, her breasts bounce. They are to me as my thighs are to her. A turn on.

"Ready for what the girls planned for you?"

"I told them I just want to catch a few games on the sports channel. Is that why you're up this early?"

"You will get to watch the baseball game. Put that stuff away and get in the bed. Your first gift will be up in an hour." She comes to me and kisses my forehead. "Happy birthday."

My fingers close around her wrists. They have a mind of their own this morning. I pull her arm. Dani's lips inch closer until they're a breath away from mine. As always, I let her make the final decision.

She closes the gap with a long peck. We stare at each other. Another peck. Her tongue brushes my lips. I open and at the first taste, everything around us disappears. It's just me and Dani. My eyes close and I wait for the moment when this kiss becomes way more intense.

Dani's hand doesn't touch my cheek. This kiss isn't the intimacy we've shared in the past.

I'm past mechanical sex. I want what we had. I want that connection back that puts us on a different level. Women are under the misconception sex means nothing to men. That's not true. A man who truly respects the woman he loves, adores the bond they have in bed.

What would make this kiss degrading is if she climbed on top of me.

Dani pulls back. She smiles. I wait for the touch of her thumb sweeping across my bottom lip. It doesn't come. She leans in for more. This kiss is different, it's deeper. Fueled by sexual hunger, not our bond.

I can't... I break the kiss before things go further. The kind of sex I want with my wife is not what she's offering this morning.

"Thank you." I don't know what else to say. I release her wrist.

"I need to get dressed so I can help the girls. Your daughter is adamant about sticking to the schedule. Go, get in the bed."

I fold and put away the covers, then crawl into bed and lie on my stomach. *Oh, I've missed my bed.* My eyes close right away.

The next time I wake up it's late in the morning. From my position on my stomach I reach for my phone and open Dani's reply to the snapshots of the wrapped present the girls left and the breakfast I was served in bed earlier.

The two oddly shaped chocolate chip waffles, overcooked scrambled eggs, extra crispy bacon, and uneven melon cubes. My message asked if Trevor helped. Her response was sent five minutes ago. Two snapshots. One of Trevor with his paw on the box while Kourt and Emm pulled tape. The other of him wearing an apron and a whisk between his teeth.

Three knocks at the door. "Come in," I say.

Kourt pokes her head in, and Trevor rushes in. He stands on his hind legs, with his front paws on the bed. He licks my face. "He's telling you happy birthday," Kourt translates.

I sit up and scratch him behind the ears. "Thank you, boy."

"It's eleven o'clock. Time for you to get up, open your present, and be downstairs in one hour, Dad." She picks up the breakfast tray.

"Copy that, ma'am." I salute her. "Where's your sister?"

"Getting in the way." Her head tilts and her lips turn down. "Come on, Trev, we need to finish the family room." He follows her command and she closes the door behind them without any explanation.

I pull the paper off the gift box and lift the top. Inside are Colorado sports teams' jerseys. "So this is why Kourt kept asking about my favorite team." A handmade card falls onto the bed when I lift a jersey out of the box. "Happy Birthday, Dad. Love, Cuddles, Sweet Pea, and Trevor." At the bottom of the card, written in Dani's handwriting: *and The Baby.*

After a quick shower, I stand in the closet trying to decide what to wear. Since I don't know what my girls planned, I go for a pair of cargo shorts and my new Rockies' jersey. They are the only Colorado team playing today.

Twenty minutes early, I go downstairs. The doors to the family room are open. "Put that down, Trevor!" Kourt scolds him. "Emmy, don't put that there."

"Why not?"

"Ugh. Because. Just leave it."

"Mommy said to let me help decorate, Kourty."

"I didn't help you make that stupid breakfast so don't help me decorate the family room?"

"You said you didn't wanna help."

"Because it was a stupid idea. You're a copycat. We gave Mom breakfast in bed for her birthday."

"My idea wasn't stupid."

"Yes, it was. Now go away."

"No, I'm helping like Mommy said I could."

"Get. Out. Emmy!"

Trevor barks. I stand in the doorway to the family room. Shocked. Kourt is in her sister's face. Her head snaps, she looks my way, then around the room. My daughter's eyes water. "See what you did!" she yells at her sister, fingers balled tight. "Ugh. You messed up *my* surprise for Dad."

"Kourtney." Dani brushes past me. "I told you to stop shouting at Emma. And let her help you. It's a lot to do and you didn't give yourself much time to do it alone."

"I had time, Mom. But because of her, he's seen the room before it was ready."

Colorado sports teams' memorabilia is in unopened packages. One side of the room looks like it's going to be a concession area equipped with popcorn machine, hotdog machine with a bun warmer, a variety of chips, and bagged peanuts. Water bottles and soda cans are on ice in a bucket on top of a bar. In another bucket are bottles of beer on ice. The best part is the eighty-five-inch LED ultra HD television with a red bow attached to it.

I hide my eyes behind my hands. "I didn't see anything, Cuddles. I can go to my office and wait for you to come get me."

"Never mind," Kourt growls. I hear footsteps stomp past me. "Come get me when they're ready!"

"Bryan, go to the kitchen," Mama Hawk commands. "They'll come get you when we finish in here."

My hands drop to my side and I turn to leave. Kourt is sitting on the bottom step. Arms folded. Trevor sits in front of her, panting.

I follow orders and go to the kitchen.

Tony's stirring something in a pot on the stove. His friend Tiffany stands next to him. Things are getting serious between them if he brought her here today. I hope it's not because the woman he is still in love with just got engaged.

"Bry, Tiffany Grant. Tiff, Bryan Hawk."

She shakes my hand. "I don't know if you remember me. I came with Tony to your holiday party. We didn't get a chance to talk then, but I'm happy to meet you. I've heard so much about you guys."

Tiffany looks like one of those models you see on the cover of magazines. She is a jewelry designer. Celebrities and the very wealthy commission her work. Her jewelry store looks more like an art gallery. It's located in Denver. She's been hired to design and make the diamond crown for that drag competition.

I didn't peg her for the type Tony would date. Booty call, yes. Girlfriend, no. But then again, I haven't spent time around her. They've been hanging out since that night at the club when he, Summers, and Ramirez had to interrupt my date with Dani because Malinda showed up.

Vin walks through the door. "What's going on in the family room? Kourt and Dani are in a standoff."

I rub the back of my neck. "Man, I don't know. I think the girls have been at it all morning." Should I go back in there and referee?

Nope, stay out of it.

Ig walks in next. "Tony, Dani said put the chili in the crockpot and bring it in." He walks to the refrigerator and takes out a vegetable platter, courtesy of my wife no doubt, and containers of condiments.

"I'll take the things to her," Tiffany offers.

We wait until she leaves the room, pushing the cart down the hallway, to pounce.

Vin starts with the jokes. Even Ig gets in on it. I pay him back for all the digs I had to endure the day I met my wife.

Emm skips through the door. "Are you ready for your surprise, Daddy? Close your eyes and we'll take you to it." She's wearing an Avalanche jersey and a black half apron with the number thirty-five painted on it.

Kourt smacks her lips and rolls her eyes at her sister as she walks through the door. She's wearing a Broncos' jersey and a black half apron with the number thirty-five painted on too, except it looks like Trevor helped. "Close your eyes and *I'll* take you to your birthday surprise. It *was* my idea."

Emm pouts. "It was my idea too."

"It was both your idea." Dani's mommy-warning tone carries down the hallway. I'm guessing her patience is wearing thin with them today.

I think I need my hearing checked. If I'm not mistaken, Kourt just mumbled, *"the hell it was"* under her breath. Judging by Vin's face, he's is standing closest to her, he needs his hearing checked too.

"It would make me happy if *both* my girls led the way." It's my attempt to relieve the pressure that is sure to explode on my birthday. I close my eyes and hold out my hands. The girls take me back down the hallway to the family room.

"On three, open your eyes," Kourt grumbles. "One, two, three." Trevor barks. She says it so fast I don't know to open my eyes until she tells me to.

I hug my wife and daughters. "Thank you, this is awesome."

My girls lead me to my seat and my wife brings me a beer and a bag of peanuts. What Dani is wearing distracts me for a moment and I pause before taking the bottle and the bag from her hands. With my finger, I signal for her to give me the three-sixty view of her sports outfit. She's geared-up in a Nuggets jersey, too short retro basketball shorts that show off her legs, and basketball kicks to match. She must have used makeup to cover the bruises. "You look like you're ready to play ball."

Her gaze drops to my thighs, then stops in the area of my body where the hawk rests in his nest. Her thoughts show on her face. They mirror my own.

She bends at the waist and presses her lips against my ear. "Meet me in your office for the seventh inning stretch and I'll play with your balls."

The hawk twitches. Screw being a gentleman. We're sneaking off to my office for a quickie.

"Happy Birthday, little brother." Jessi rushes in, her purse and keys in her hand. She breaks the spell Dani cast on me. "Sorry I can't stay. I have to get to the hospital." She gives me a hug and runs out the door.

"Ooooh, Dani, you keep this up and my husband will want a taco instead of sausage," Max croons from the doorway. I stand to shake hands with Tom and Max. Penny hugs my waist. She's wearing a jersey and a black half apron too.

Porter comes in behind them.

After introductions are made Dani saunters over. "Here's the remote. The girls and I are your waitresses."

God, I love this woman.

Midway through the Rockies, Dodgers game, my cell phone knocks against my thigh. Incoming alert. I exercise discretion, ease it out my pocket, check to make sure Dani and Kourt are distracted enough, then read the content.

Riley's deciphered some chatter on the black-market website. It's been busy since the news of Amir Mahdavi's death spread. Many have speculated as to who's behind it. ILA is threating revenge on its enemies until the guilty party comes forward. The usual stuff when a terrorist leader is executed.

I wouldn't be worried about the alert except an anonymous post was flagged by Riley because of a specific list of words are being used.

The post reads. *I have proof the United States is behind this attack on Islam Liberation Army. They used a covert team of men to sneak into Mahdavi's quarters. Assassinated him and stole information.* The post prompted monetary offers for the evidence.

When I look around, my friends are watching me. I sign for them to meet me at the downtown office once the game is over.

I order my second fully loaded chili cheese dog from my waitress, Cuddles. My wife steps in front of me with a plate of carrot sticks and ranch dip. My eyelids lower, teeth clamp down on my bottom lip. Mesmerizing her with *the look* as I pull a twenty out of my pocket with my right hand, I use the left one to pull her onto my lap. I wave the bill behind her back. Small fingers take it. I distract Dani by picking up a carrot and slowly sliding it between her lips, relieve her hands of the plate, leaning in to whisper in her ear while holding the plate behind her. I wait until Kourt takes the plate and moves away from us before I speak softly in my wife's ear. "I'm imagining those lips wrapped around something else."

Over Dani's shoulder, I watch Kourt feed Trevor the rest of the carrot sticks. *That's my girl!*

Other than the guys, no one else knows we're faking our way through the rest of my birthday party. Counting the seconds to the end of the game.

CHAPTER ELEVEN

TEN STRAIGHT HOURS OF NONSTOP monitoring the worldwide web. Hacking IP addresses. Following the chatter on the black-market website. Rumors are starting to spread amongst world leaders. Allied ones are calling President Hart. A small online gossip rag picked up the story and is reporting the White House denies any involvement. Quoting an anonymous source as saying, *"No armed forces units were in the area of Mahdavi's camp."*

We don't believe anyone captured our movements in Yemen; however, technology changes hourly, and we have to accept there is a small possibility someone did.

With Riley's help, Chen views satellite recordings for the window of time we were in the Middle East. We came in under the cover of darkness and left the same way. Only used vetted Phantom personnel. The rest were not aware of our activities.

Every aspect of our mission is under the microscope. Each one viewed from the angle that it is the evidence the nameless person has to expose us.

Riley's analyzing data. We put it up against facts. Riley assesses images. We map it on a chart. Riley translates and transcribes audio files. We reevaluate, reenact, and recollect the key points.

Nothing.

We can't find how or where we were exposed. I make a phone call to the head of a major motion pictures studio and let him know to get ready to send out a media blast about their latest movie release. That will buy us more time to investigate.

Coming up on the twelfth hour, we catch a break. The miscreant posts another comment and we track it to a college dorm room in Massachusetts.

Nineteen-year-old Braxton Hollis. Blogger slash hacker slash gamer slash mathematician who posts government conspiracy theories. According to his web history, he stumbled upon the black market site while attempting to hack an offshore account the same day he made the post about the United States' involvement in Mahdavi's death. He lied about having proof.

That kid doesn't realize the magnitude of his words caused a rift in world peace. It's up to us to teach him that his balls haven't dropped yet. He's not ready to run with the big boys.

To my knowledge, Phantom has never fucked with someone just for laughs. And because we've been working nonstop on this, I figured a good laugh is overdue. We put in a video call to the studio owner, tell him to put the film back in the vault and explain how he could help us.

We go all out to give The Kid the twenty-four-hour, proverbial Hollywood hacker movie experience.

Late-night distress call from the girl he has a crush on. Dorm room door kicked open. Bad guy snatches his laptop. A cloak and dagger meeting in the student parking structure. The high-speed car chase, under gunfire, in a sleek, 2014 supped-up Hennessey Venom GT that uses verbal commands to drive. There's a private jet waiting on the tarmac and a sexy flight attendant in a revealing uniform. She keeps The Kid's champagne glass full. He wakes up in bed, in the luxury suite of a hotel room in Paris. Hands covered in blood. A dead flight attendant next to him. The French police are pounding on the door. He's handcuffed and taken into custody. Interrogated by the French General Directorate for Internal Security. An intense station shootout with a mysterious man. Escape through a bathroom window. Needle in the neck. The Kid wakes up in dorm room, convinced it just was a dream. Late for class he rushes across campus. Sees his dream girl and smiles. Takes his usual seat in the middle row, middle seat. Turns on laptop ready to take notes. Screen goes in and out. A forty-five-second recap of his dream plays on the screen. All of a sudden, he feels a searing pain on the inside of his left arm. The kid yanks off his jacket and stares at the handle he used to make the post written in an ink that leaves a permanent burn in his skin. His laptop catches fire. He runs from lecture hall. One by one, in different areas on campus, the people he encountered in his dream show up in his reality. Federal agents take The Kid into custody. POTUS holds a press conference exposing the hoax, but not The Kid. In conclusion, the president sings the praises of the armed forces men and women who fight to keep our nation safe.

I've given Edwards ample time to recover from his injuries. His accommodations are stellar despite my wanting him dead or placed in a six-by-six cement hole in the ground. He's sitting in a chair, leaning forward, elbows on his knees. I stand with Ig watching him.

Edwards jumps out of the chair and starts to pace. He pounds his forehead with the palms of his hand. "Stupid. Stupid. Stupid." He stops pacing and charges the glass wall. "Get Hawk in here! Now!" His fist slams into the shatterproof wall.

He can't see us.

"How long has he been like this?" I ask.

"Charisse said it started this morning."

He stomps back to the chair and sits. Head in hands. Elbows on thighs. One knee bobbing like a jackhammer.

The door panel opens, and I enter. Edwards doesn't look up. Instinctively, my left hand slides into the pocket of my pants to shield the view of my wedding band. I stroll across the room and sit in the chair across from him. "You bellowed?"

"Let me out of here." His voice is low. Pleading. His words are spoken to the floor.

"Nine years in a Syrian prison and not a scratch on you. How did you manage that?"

Slowly his hands lower. He mad-dogs me with a smirk. "I learned early in life to adapt to my surroundings. Keep my head down. Blend with the background. Too bad Danielle didn't heed the lesson. Center of attention. Wanted by both sides." He huffs. "She kept it under lock and key until you turned up. Then she unlocked the deadbolt on that chastity belt. Parted those golden thighs and now she's the main attraction of the event. Just because you're tappin' that don't mean she's fighting your battle. I made the mistake of trusting her too."

He wants a reaction out of me. I know my wife in a way he'll never know her. I could stoop to his level and toss the innuendos, but what would that accomplish?

I shift in my seat, getting comfortable, right ankle resting on left knee.

His whole body subtly stiffens, like he was expecting me to attack.

"Why'd you come back, Edwards?"

"I thought you'd start with something simple, for instance— what does Danielle have that they want?"

I smile at him, keeping my chin up and eyes leveled. "I like starting with the difficult questions then working my way down to the things I already know."

"Eight years and you don't know shit." He tsks and mimics my posture. "Who you seek is closer than you realize."

I square my shoulders with confidence even though I know my reply is a lie. "Again. Already know."

"Bullshit, Hawk. I get it. She gave you the ring." Self-assurance now showing on his face. "When did she give it to you? Before or after you broke her in?" He huffs. "Amelia was certainly dick-whipped after you fucked her. Why am I here?" He gestures with his hands to reference the room.

I sit up straight. Both feet on the floor. "You had no idea how much power that ring holds; otherwise you'd be asking—no— correction, *begging* for protection. You didn't come back to the States for the ring or the laptop. Someone spooked you out of hiding. You want to know why I am going through the trouble of keeping you alive? I neutralized your sudden existence on this earth because the minute you rose from the dead you pulled my wife deeper into the shit hole you've dug with RAGS. You gambled with your brother's life and you see what happened. If it comes down to your life for Dani's, I'll hand you over and not give it a second thought."

A bit of that cocky self-confidence he displayed a minute ago slips from his body language. His gaze cast down to his feet, and he laughs to himself. "Who calls themselves Rebels Against Government Suppression and expects to be taken seriously?"

"How did you end up with the gun that killed Dani's parents?"

"Old family heirloom."

"Your parents are serving a life sentence for a bank robbery that resulted in the deaths of the guard and two tellers. The guns they used were confiscated."

He lifts his head. "I didn't say it's *my* family's heirloom."

"You're wasting my time, Edwards." I stand and button my suit jacket. Adjust the sleeves. "Option one. You help us bury everyone affiliated with RAGS. I'm not just talking about the leader. I want every single member. Do that and Sergeant James Andrew Edwards of the United States Army died in action on Wednesday, May eighteenth, two thousand five just like the official death certificate reads but is living happily ever after on a private island under the protection of the United States Phantom military. Option two. I torture the information out of you, then hand you over to RAGS, and the official death certificate will still read Sergeant James Andrew Edwards of the United States Army died in action on Wednesday, May eighteenth, two thousand five because there will be no need to have a second one issued. They'll kill you." I turn my back on him and walk toward the door.

"Toussaint lived by that old saying. 'Keep your friends close and your enemies closer.'" He tsks.

"Don't request my presence again if all you want is to talk in riddles and clichés." The door closes behind me.

————◆————

Malinda's at the front desk demanding to see me. She's been texting and calling since my birthday. I want to finish my report for POTUS and go home, but I take a break and allow her to come up so she can say whatever she needs to say, then go away.

I stand and wait for her to walk through the door.

"Why do you hate me so much?" she begins.

"I don't hate you."

"Then what is it about Danielle that…"

"Don't make this about her. You're acting like a jealous ex and we were never together. What do you want, Malinda?"

She frowns. "I came to apologize, Bryan." Tears pool in her eyes. "The change still isn't easy for me. I've decided to move back to Texas once the school year ends—"

"Why wait?"

She continues as if I didn't interrupt. "—and I wanted to make sure we're okay."

"We're good as long as you remember your place. I've always been honest with you. And I take all threats seriously. I'll do whatever I have to, to keep my family happy."

"I have no intention of coming near your *family*, Bryan." She walks around my desk. I track her movements. Malinda stretches on her toes to kiss my cheek. "Goodbye."

She leaves my office.

I sit in my chair and instruct Riley to do a full trace on Malinda's whereabouts for the last ten months. That wasn't a sincere goodbye.

Max walks through the door. A smirk on his face. "Did she really think you bought that *emotional* voice and those *crocodile* tears?"

"She wasn't trained by the best."

He snaps his fingers two times, then drops to the sofa. He crosses one leg over the other. "Malinda's a wild card."

"I thought it would be easier to keep an eye on her here than if she was in Texas."

Fingers intertwined and hooked around his knee, Max rocks back. "Sooo, what did she do this time?" His lips twitch from suppressed laughter.

It was just a matter of time before one of them asked what I walked into when I went to her house. I go to the refrigerator and grab a bottled water, offering it to Max. He nods. I toss it to him, then grab one for myself and sit at the other end of the couch.

"Man, Max. I thought I was in an insane asylum for sex-addicted looneys."

Right away he starts to laugh. I get comfortable and tell him how Malinda offered herself to me, *again*. How the shadows on the wall freaked me out. Her lack of proper planning, she didn't anticipate the level of anger she stirred up. And how her threatening to expose me to my wife pushed me over the edge.

To my chagrin, Max brings up the last time I was in Pecos, Texas. Whenever I was in the area on business, I'd stop by Malinda's to see how she was doing. Most times I stayed at a hotel. There were times I slept in her guest room. On my last visit Malinda and I stayed up late talking. Against my better judgment, I decided to spend the night there instead of going to the hotel. She waited until I'd fallen asleep to sneak into the bed and wrap herself around me. I fought her off and held her until she gave up and we fell asleep. Some people don't believe a man can resist a naked woman throwing herself at him, but it's possible. Especially when said woman has burned him before.

My cell phone beeps. It's a text from Dani asking if I can stop by the store on my way home. The next text from her is a long grocery list.

———•———

Dani is adjusting to being a stay-at-home mom. Her taking over the run of the house gives our home a different vibe. It looks brighter. There are family photos decorating the walls now.

Marie can't seem to shake her cold. She refuses to go see a doctor. She claims the home remedies are working. I don't contradict her to her face, but from the sound of her voice and her inability to get out of bed, that *back-home* stuff isn't working.

Dani takes her food and tea whenever Marie is up for a visit. She's trying to convince the stubborn old woman to seek professional help.

Willis doesn't seem worried about his wife's health. His nonchalance is a bit cold, bordering on uncaring. We have an unspoken agreement to keep our end-of-the-day-recap short and on topic. Don't ask me about the progress I'm making with RAGS, and I won't point out you're being an asshole to your sick wife. It's in our best interest if he'd just email me his report every evening.

I snag the handle of three reusable bags in each hand and carry them into the house. Just as I round the corner, Kourt comes stomping down the hall with Trevor on her heels.

"Kourtney Allison Hawk, don't walk away when I'm talking to you," her mother yells.

She ignores the summons and heads for the stairs. Dani flies out of the kitchen, frustration written on her face.

I have a moment of hesitation. *Should I?* The hard thumping on the wood of the steps and the irritated tone of my wife repeating the command decides for me. I step in Dani's pathway. "Take a breath."

She glares at me. "I've taken a breath. Your daughter needs to come back and explain herself."

I go for humor to defuse the situation. "Why are they my kids when they do something you don't like? And your kids when they're little angels?"

"Mother's law," she barks.

I can't resist a battle of the quips with my wife. Her quick come-backs are a turn on. "Hmm, can't say I'm familiar with Mother's law."

Her lips twitch. Her eyes smile. "The male brain is too inept to master Mother's law." She faces me head-on, her eyes checking me out from toes to head. Lingering on my thighs.

"Is that so?" I don't think she's aware that she pulls her earlobe and twirls her hair around her finger when she's—thirsty.

"Scientific fact. Would you like for me to show you?"

I'm about to win this one. I slowly close the gap between us by forcing her to step backward until her back is against the wall. My hands can't touch her, I'm still holding grocery bags, but other parts of me can. I lean in, my lips against her ear. Instinctively she leans her head to the side giving me more of that sexy neck.

Oh yeah, I'm the victor of this round. "No need. My male brain holds the knowledge of a hundred ways to make you come. Pick a number between one and one hundred." The tip of my tongue leaves a wet trail up her neck making her moan long and slow.

Her nails dig into my biceps. A shiver rolls through her body. Inwardly I pat myself on the back. *Yep, my ego is stroked by the knowledge that I possess the ability to make my wife orgasm simply by drawing the outline and her naughty imagination coloring it in.*

I give her a minute to come down off the high, then step back. Her eyes stay on me. I kiss her cheek, then take the bags to kitchen.

"Hi, Daddy." Emm smiles. She's standing on a stool in front of the counter with an apron on.

I set the bags on the table and go to my daughter, kissing the top of her head. "How's my big girl?"

"I'm fine. I'm helping Mommy make dinner." She points to the cookbook Marie gave Dani for Christmas.

Dani drifts into the kitchen and starts unloading the bags. "Did you get everything on the list?"

"Yep, there are more bags in the truck. How come we're out of everything?"

"I haven't had a chance to get to the grocery store."

While pushing a full grocery cart down an aisle at the store, it occurred to me that Dani hasn't been away from the house since the shooting. The furthest she's gone is Willis and Marie's or down by the pond, but that doesn't count. Both places are on our property.

I watch her move about the kitchen. "You guys have been cooped up for a week and a half. How about I take my three girls out to dinner tonight?"

"I already have my mind set on cooking. Plus, Emma's helping me."

"Hey, Emm. I need to talk to Mom about something real important. Can you go up to your room until we're done?"

"Sure, Dad." She jumps down off the stool and walks out of the kitchen.

I go to my wife and pull her into my arms, my chin on top of her head. We never talked about how *she* felt about what happened. She's asked questions. Participated in a meeting. Agreed to homeschooling the girls and taking a leave of absence from work without putting up a fight. I'm so used to seeing Dani strong and confident—a survivor—I didn't recognize her anxiety.

I kiss the top of her head. Her body stiffens. I whisper the words I'd written on the card I attached to the eighteen long-stemmed yellow roses I gave her on her birthday. They are the words I use to describe her.

Dani's arms wrap around my waist, her hands grip my shirt like she's afraid to let go. I hold her close until she conveys her fear through tears.

That night in the courtyard of the movie theater was scary for both of us. Getting shot at comes with the job for me. I've been doing it for seventeen years. I know how to pick myself up, dust myself off, and keep it pushing. For someone who's never experienced something like that in real life, it makes you see the world through a different pair of eyes.

I don't want her to be afraid to be out in the open. I was so focused on my reasons for getting her to stay that I didn't grasp what Max was trying to get me to see. Dani experienced a traumatic event. As one who vowed to pick her up if she fell—her husband—it is up to me to help her get through this.

We move over to the chairs at the table. I sit her down and go over her security detail and what she needs to do when she wants or needs to go somewhere. I leave it up to her to decide if she wants to drive or be driven by a Personal Protection Officer when she leaves the house.

The girls don't know about the guards, but we agreed to teach them a safe word like my dad taught me when I was little. If there's ever an emergency and someone other than those in our inner circle needs to take charge of them, the girls will know it's okay to go with that person.

I wipe her eyes with my fingers. "You and I are going somewhere. Be ready in thirty minutes."

She stares.

"Trust me."

"What about the girls?"

"I got this." I could kiss my big sister right now for having perfect timing. She blows through the kitchen door heading straight for the refrigerator. "Jessi. I'm taking Dani out. Can you watch the girls?"

With her head hidden behind the door she says, "Sure. We'll go to a movie."

"No," Dani shrieks. "I don't want them leaving the house."

Jessi leans back, a twisted look on her face. Her gaze bounces between Dani and me. I answer with a quick shake of my head and a cocked eyebrow. *Just agree and we'll avoid a panic attack.*

My sister nods, understanding. "Good, I really didn't feel like getting out of the house. We'll make nachos and have movie night here."

Dani visibly relaxes.

"Go get dressed. I'll bring in the rest of the groceries. Jessi and the girls can put them away."

I wait for Dani to leave the kitchen to explain to my sister what's going on. She pats me on the back and tells me how proud she is to have a little brother who knows how to take care of a woman.

I send out a group-text to the Hawkeye PPOs who guard my wife and daughters. It includes the address to where I want to meet. The next text I send is to the guys.

I get the rest of the grocery bags out of the truck, then go upstairs to have a conversation with, as my wife claims, *my* daughter. I knock on the door and wait for permission to come in.

Granted access, I open the door and step inside. Kourt is sitting on the floor, back up against the bed. Knees drawn to her chest.

Trevor lying at her feet.

Stacked on the bed are her iPad, cell phone, telescope, laptop, and a few other things.

I sit on the floor next to her. "Want to tell me what happened?"

"Emmy's acting like a big baby all the time. She just wants to be with *Mommy*," she mocks her sister. "Emmy won't go outside unless Mom goes too. She won't play video games. Or watch TV. Or do anything if Mom isn't there!"

She's pleading her case and not telling me what happened. I wait until she's looking at me to raise an eyebrow.

Kourt exhales. "I said I wish I didn't have a sister."

I raise the other eyebrow.

"And I wish it was just me, you, and Mommy." She looks away.

"Do you really mean that?"

She nods.

"Why?"

Her shoulders rise and fall.

"Kourt."

"I just do, Dad. Can't I just feel something and not know why?"

"You have the right to your own opinions, Kourt, but if you are going to express them in a way that hurts someone you should also be able to explain why you feel that way."

"I didn't hurt anybody."

"Yes you did, Kourt. Your words hurt Mom. Emm. And your words hurt me too. I love you and your sister and your brother. We are a family of five. Not three."

"I know."

"I'm taking Mom out tonight. You and Emm are having movie night with Aunt Jessi. Be nice to your sister."

She frowns. "Okay."

I give her a quick kiss and climb to my feet. "Now go help Aunt Jessi in the kitchen."

"Can I keep my stuff?" She gestures toward the bed as she stands.

"You'll have to ask Mom." I wink and leave her room.

Across the hall I knock on Emm's door.

She and I talk about clinging to Mom so much. I remind her that Dani is pregnant and sometimes needs to rest, by herself. She says she just wants to make sure Mom is okay. I assure her it's my job to take care of Mom. I encourage her to spend more time with her sister and less with her mom, then send her down to help put away groceries.

I open the door to my room. Dani steps out of the closet dressed in jeans that hug her hips and ass. No top, she's holding two in her hands. Her full, round breasts fill every inch of their bra cups. Barely.

I take a minute to appreciate the view. She doesn't notice me ogling her body. When she bends at the waist with her ass taunting me, an imaginary lasso circles my torso and vise clamps burrow out of the hardwood floor to keep my feet in place. I salivate.

Dani straightens and turns around, startled. I didn't hear myself make a sound, but hell, I may have. Her lips move, but I don't hear her speak. The tops in her hands are presented one at a time.

She frowns and stares at me. I focus on her full sexy lips.

"Bry, which one? Jeans and this long sleeve top okay? Or jeans and this sweater? You didn't say where we're going."

You butt-naked in my favorite position would be better. I swallow. "The light blue top is fine. Wear tennis shoes." My voice sounds a little hoarse to my ears.

She goes back into the closet.

I run to the bathroom, close the door, and wash my face with cold water. *Dani did that on purpose.*

When I come out, she's not in the room. I change and go down to the kitchen.

Emm pouts and whines about not going with us. Kourt smirks and mumbles under her breath, *I told you.*

I take my wife by the hand and take her away before she gives in to our daughter.

Dani is quiet as we head toward University Colorado Boulder in the early evening traffic. It takes me longer than usual to get to the campus. Which is fine; it gives the guys time to set up.

I park in the designated stall outside of Vin's building on the north end. It's the only one with the most square footage. He is after all the Phantom Weapons and Security expert. Those aren't his only talents. Beneath his rough exterior, Vin is a nice guy with a big heart. It truly bothered him when Dani and Kourt didn't trust him when they first met him in December.

I met Vin on the last night of my training in Italy. He and two friends were hanging out, targeting tourists to rob. Their first mistake was picking me. Thinking I'd go down without a fight was the second.

From his size and threatening body language, naturally I assumed Vin was the leader. So when I spoke, my words were for him. It was the other two who rushed me. Vin pulled a handgun. That made me fight even harder. Once I knocked the gun out of his hand, the two friends ran off. Vin stood his ground and in that moment, he had my respect. Right or wrong, Vin was committed to finishing what he'd started. He'd gotten in some good punches. Eventually we realized neither was willing to surrender. As if we had one mind, we stood up straight and shook hands.

I went to pick up the weapon and found it to be hollow. It looked like a real Glock, not a plastic toy. I looked closely at it and laughed. It had no trigger. No open barrel. And no magazine that disengaged.

He told me it was made of wood and he'd painted it to look real.

We laughed all the way to my hotel and sat in the lobby talking. Before I left, I made a phone call. A day later, Vincenzo Luca Ricci had dual citizenship and a full scholarship to the University Colorado Boulder.

I open the passenger door and help my wife climb out. "What are we going to do here?"

"You will see."

With my hand low on her back, a hair above her ass—yes, I'm copping a feel—I lead her to the entrance. I swipe my access card and open the door, allowing her to enter first. The area is quiet. Dani looks around at the bare walls and cocks an eyebrow. I point to the other door.

We walk into another room. Her eyes widen. We're standing behind a clear shatterproof wall. On the other side, Max, Vin, Ig, and Tony fire weapons at targets that are a football field's end zone away. The sound is muffled. This is the waiting area.

"There are some things you need to practice."

"Okay."

"Treat all firearms as if they are loaded. Never point your weapon at anyone or anything unless you are absolutely sure you're going to fire it. Know who or what you intend to shoot—and what's beyond it or them."

Dani smiles. Understanding the reason we're here. I'm taking a page out of her foster father's book. He taught her to box as a means to build her confidence when she was bullied. I'm going to teach her to kill anyone who dares come after us again.

At first she's shaky and awkward with handling the guns, but once she finds one that feels right in her hands and she becomes more at ease with it, the gawkiness is gone.

Three hours into the training the eight men and women of Hawkeye Personal Protection arrive and Porter walks in with the food I asked him to bring. We sit in the waiting area and Dani gets acquainted with her security team. Each PPO tells her a little about their background and their approach to personal protection. Porter goes over the areas he feels Dani can enhance her own safety, having been assigned to her after the break-in at her apartment. He points out that she was only aware of him in times when he stepped out of the shadows because of a possible threat.

The purpose of this meeting is to allow her to be an active participant in her and the girls' safety. Dani accepts that she has to drive one of my trucks because they are armored. Her Range Rover is to stay parked in the garage or I'll drive it. Vin is retrofitting and armoring the Tahoe I bought her.

By the end of the evening, Dani is feeling more confident about being out in public. Porter will act as lead and will assign the teams according to where and when Dani or the girls go somewhere.

I'm still not ready to tell her about the second shooter. That bit of information will push her back inside.

When we get home, I take the time to show her the security room under the stairs and how to use the surveillance system. She laughs when she realizes operation sneak-in-shopping-bags was a bust. And apologizes for snooping through my office in December.

I take Dani's right hand, kiss the palm, and place it over my heart. "This hand unlocks my world." I guide it to the scanner on my desk that looks like a mouse pad. The rolling light moves up and down then in and out. Her palm print loads on the computer's monitor. When it stops, clicking sounds can be heard around the office.

"Open the desk drawer," I tell her.

She pulls the drawer open then closes it.

I gesture for her to sleuth through my office and stand back while she does. Dani opens and closes doors and drawers. She freezes when she opens the cabinet where some of my rifles are stored.

"They're the ones Ig and I used the night someone was lighting fireworks."

Once she's done I hand her a business card-size paper and tell her to read it aloud and enunciate.

"Delta. Lima. Hotel. Five. One. Nine. Zero. Six."

Clicking sounds can be heard around the office. "The office is locked up. That code is yours—do not give it to anyone. Do not say it in front of anyone, even though voice recognition is what unlocks and locks things, someone could record you. Your right handprint gives you access to every floor in my building except the first floor. It also opens and closes the security room under the stairs. If you had waved your right hand over the sensor on the adjacent wall that December morning, the door would have opened for you."

I lead her out of my office. Room by room, I show my wife how secure our home is.

CHAPTER TWELVE

THE WEATHER IS GETTING WARMER and Dani wants to take the girls shopping for summer clothes. Tony volunteers to go with us, even though Porter assigned a team of two females and three males to shadow us. It's early enough in the afternoon that I trust the mall not to be crowded, yet the open floor plan still makes us easy targets. Dani doesn't want to carry a gun when the girls are with us.

We go in and out of stores all afternoon. She wants them to have options and stick to their individual styles. I arrange for the packages to be delivered to the house. I want to keep my hands free.

Shopping doesn't bother me. Kourt, on the other hand, is bored so she picks on her sister to entertain herself. Her antics are upsetting Dani. I take matters into my own hands and start a game of hide-and-seek to get Kourt's focus off Emm. We duck under clothes racks, behind counters, blend in with window mannequins.

Dani's annoyed, but keeps her cool. Tony refuses to play. He says he's not going to be caught in the path when Mama Hawk strikes. *Coward.*

Emm is tense and stays by Dani's side. She's not letting her mother out of her sight.

The game of speed-walking-tag becomes intense and super competitive. Kourt knocks T-shirts off a shelf and I accidently knock over a mannequin. Dani finally loses her cool. She grabs me under the arm and tries to pinch the skin. She can't get a good grip. I'm all muscle.

Teeth clenched, my wife leads me toward the door. "Let's take the children to the play area, *Tony.*"

I try not to laugh. She thinks she's hurting me. Kourt, on the other hand, can't hold it in. Her laughter makes Tony laugh and Dani's fingers pinch harder. I make a face and Kourt bends over holding her stomach.

Out of nowhere a man bumps Dani. I grab her waist, switch our positions and reach for my gun. Concurrently, Tony grabs the man's cane. Without the stability, the old man is off balance and drops to one knee. The two female PPOs position themselves to grab the girls. The other three draw their weapons, but stay in the shadows watching the people in the mall.

"I'm sorry, Dr. Hawk. I didn't mean to startle anyone," the old man says.

"That's Mr. Brumfield. He is one of my patients." She tries to step out from behind me, but I'm in defensive mode and block her.

Mall security is coming our way. Before they can intervene, Tony identifies himself, but doesn't relinquish the cane. The mall cops shoo away the looky-loos and keep the walkway clear.

Dani grips my arm, a cue to let me know it's okay and allow her to come from behind my shield.

"Mommy, are you hurt?" Something in Emm's voice makes me look her way.

Eyes wide. Cheeks flushed. Panting. Beads of sweat breaking out on her forehead and upper lip. Our daughter is shaking. *Is Emm having a panic attack?*

"I'm fine, sweetie." She motions for Tony to return the old man's walking aid, then hugs her daughter to her breast. Dani rubs Emm's back until she starts to calm down.

What the hell was that?

"Dad, may I go play?" Kourt asks, uninterested in what's unfolding in front of her.

"Stay where I can see you." I signal for someone to follow her.

"Are you hurt, Mr. Brumfield?" Dani asks. "Bryan, help him up."

The old man waves his hand in protest of my assistance. I do it anyway, because my wife told me to. Once he's steady, I release him. I'm still in defensive mode.

"I'm sorry. My husband and his friend are a little over protective," Dani says.

He rubs his knee. "I just wanted to say hello and see how you're doing. I understand you're taking a leave of absence."

"Have you been assigned another therapist yet?"

He shakes his head. "I'm not comfortable with any of the others."

"Let's sit and talk for a minute," she tells him. My attempt to protest is cut off with a raised eyebrow from my wife. "Bryan, please get Mr. Brumfield an ice pack for his knee and a bottle of water, then take Emma to the play area so we can have some privacy?"

"I'll go," Tony offers.

The old man extends his hand to me. "Terrance Brumfield."

I clasp his hand with a little more force than necessary and shake. "Bryan Hawk."

With my assistance, Brumfield hobbles over to the closest bench. Dani is still holding on to Emm. My wife asks if he needs a doctor to look at his knee. He assures her he's fine.

Tony comes back with a bag of ice and water bottles for Dani and the old man. He coaxes Emm to go with him to the crafts table near the play area. Since Dani and Brumfield are having a therapy session, I step away. Far enough to give them privacy, yet close enough where my wife is in eyesight and I can get to her in a few steps if someone else approaches them.

At the end of their session, I arrange a ride home for Mr. Brumfield.

Dani doesn't scold me and Kourt for our behavior in the stores. She goes straight to the kitchen to start dinner, as soon as we get home. The girls go to the family room.

Willis storms into my office. "My security clearance is limited."

"We're going through evaluations and promotions. Anyone not active in the branch has limited access."

"Since when?"

"Since I became the head." That was a dig at his leadership abilities since lately he's challenged mine.

He huffs. "You spent the day shopping? Don't you own Hawkeye Personal Protection? Your best men couldn't handle a little shopping spree?"

"Is that all?"

"I'm meeting up with my Army buddies in a couple of weeks. I hear that new guy Ross is an excellent Watcher. Maybe you should have him fill in."

"I'll take care of it."

My desktop computer rings. Porter's name flashes on the screen. I raise an eyebrow at the man standing in front of my desk. He leaves, unhappy.

I connect the video group chat. "Good evening, sir. I was successful in hacking one of the numbers Edwards called frequently. The phone's battery was low so I only got a minute eighteen seconds of the person's conversation. There was a lot of background noise, but it sounds like a male talking."

I grab my headset and put it on. "Play the recording."

A small rectangle box pops up on the screen phone. The play, pause, fast-forward and rewind controls are grayed out. The slider is blue and starts to move across the bottom. There's crackling sounds of static along with dogs barking to muffle out the man's voice. I tell Porter how to filter out the dogs and he replays the recording. The man's voice is more audible.

"Did you catch the language he was speaking?" I ask.

"It sounds like Louisiana Creole."

"You understand what he's saying?"

"No. He was talking too fast. I know some words, but not enough to tell you what was said."

I have Porter play the recording again. "See if Ig can translate."

He shakes his head. "I tried. Major Acosta is fluent in contemporary French."

"The man sounds like Marie when she's mad." I usually tuck tail and run when Marie is pissed off. The Southern upbringing comes out in more than just her words. She took it easy on my dad that morning she chased him around the table with a wooden rolling pin. Although she's a part of our inner circle, Willis's last act as Second Command was limiting Marie's clearance level. Therefore, I can't ask her if she can translate.

"Major Chen hasn't cleared any of our other Linguistics Specialists yet. Do you think Valentine can do it?"

I shake my head. "She's at a training camp with her daughter."

"I might know somebody." Porter's mouth twists and both eyebrows arch. "She's not Phantom, but I know she can translate for us."

"How do you know her?"

"We were stationed in Kentucky at the same time. She's from Louisiana and she's Creole."

"Give Vin her info. If he clears her let's bring her in and see what she can do. What else you got, Porter?"

"I researched military explosive experts. None came close to doing what Paul and Stavros can do so I looked for civilians on the government's list and came up with someone, but his file is locked. Here's something interesting though, Elijah Hopper's name came up too."

"The guy who owned the apartment building where Dani lived when she first moved to Arizona?"

"One and the same. He scored high on the military's aptitude test."

"Tony didn't come across any military information on Hopper when he did a background check in December."

"It's not in the database. I'm looking at files on microfiche. Hopper's name is on an old military watch list from nineteen forty-seven. I requested a hard copy of the file. Of course I was transferred three times before I received an email saying there is no military file on Elijah Andre Hopper."

I hear the rapid clicking of the keys on his keyboard, then a copy of the email shows up on the screen. Porter is doing a hell of a job with his research. I don't want to say it out loud, and from the gleam in his eye, Porter's thinking it. Someone didn't want Hopper's military file found.

We end the video chat when Emm knocks on my office door to let me know dinner is ready.

At the table, Kourt and I fidget as we sit on the edge of our seats, waiting for the bomb to drop on us for being rambunctious in the stores today.

Dani is in a good mood. Calm and relaxed. She keeps the conversation going. Kourt and I sit back and relax and enjoy the meal.

After dinner, I tell Dani to get off her feet, the girls and I will clean the kitchen. She kisses my cheek and goes upstairs. Every five minutes, Emm goes to check on Dani. Kourt rolls her eyes and shakes her head.

When we're done, I go back to my office.

A little after midnight, I shut down my computer, lock up the office, and stand. My arms reach for the ceiling, stretching my back.

My nightly routine is to check all windows and doors in the

house, then go upstairs and check on my girls before I go to bed. Jessi isn't home tonight.

Dani's laid out on the couch with her nose in a book when I walk in our bedroom. I pause for a second. The pillows and blanket I left on the couch this morning are gone. Does that mean she wants me in our bed? "Why are you still up?"

She holds up the book without taking her eyes off the page. "Couldn't put it down. I'm just about finished."

I strip out of my clothes, grab my robe, and go into the bathroom.

Hands on the glass, staring out at the Rockies, I let the hot water pouring from the showerheads hit the back of my neck.

The lights dim. I stay still and wait. I listen to her soft movements around the bathroom.

The spray from the showerheads behind me disappears. A smile spreads across my lips. I don't want to wake from this dream. *Pop.* A bottle's cap opens. The smell of my shower gel mixes with the steam circulating the space of the shower room. A shiver runs down my spine as Dani's hands inch across my shoulders. Crawl around my back. I close my eyes.

Her touch moves down my sides, stopping on my hips. The lightest peck from her lips kiss the center of my back and my body reacts to the anticipation of pleasure I can only find with my wife. Her fingers trace the shape of my ass, twice, brush the crevice of my crack.

Smack.

Cheeks clench. I should feel the sting, instead I welcome the rush. A first for me. Her hands circle my butt again. This time my sac embraces the rush of pleasure.

Her touch is gone, but her soft lips rain kisses on my spine. I groan.

The bottle top pops open again. Air bubbles seep out with the gel, then the plastic bottle drops to the shower room floor.

Smack.

The front of my thighs stings and I jump. Surprised. Completely turned on.

Dani takes her time washing my thighs. Inner. Outer. Front. Back. My abs tighten. Ready for her hands to grope my dick. She brushes over him and cleans my stomach. My chest. Dani's lips continue to shower the middle of my back with soft kisses as her nails rake down my slick abs. Over the speed bumps along the way.

The skin of my hawk tightens. He reaches for her touch.

I suck in a breath of steam. My wife's fingers finally wrap around my dick. The hawk. She holds him. Slowly strokes him. Down to the base. Up to the tip. Pleasurably circles his head. *Aahh!*

My legs open with coaxing from her knee and her sultry command to *spread'em* and I obey.

One hand creeps lower. Cupping my balls. Coddling them until they're squeaky clean.

"You and Kourt were acting out today, Mr. Hawk." She releases me.

Oh shit! I'm in trouble.

My dick jumps at the faint buzz of the waterproof finger vibrator.

"Kourt… was bored… I … I was just… trying to keep her… entertained." She's got me stuttering. The vibration of her finger toy moves between my legs. Just under the sac.

"You were excessive in your entertainment, Mr. Hawk." Another shaking finger circles the head of the hawk. *Oh damn, she's torturing me with two.* "I'm not going to ground your daughter, she was following your lead."

My gulp is audible.

"But you, on the other hand, will be punished." That sexy, domineering tone makes the hawk itch to fly in the heat of Sunshine.

She starts jacking me off with one hand while keeping a constant vibration against that sensitive spot between my balls and asshole.

"How do you want me to punish you, Mr. Hawk?"

Fuck! If she keeps talking to me with that tone, I'm going to come.

My balls scream for relief. Precum drips from the tip. The visual of her hand getting me off is too much. I close my eyes so I can make this last as long as I can.

"I asked you a question, *Mr. Hawk?*" More pressure is added to the constant vibration while the stroking hand slows down to a turtle crawl.

Dani is the only woman I've given up complete sexual control to. I'm okay with her being in charge. My wife makes me weak in the knees in and out of bed.

I'm at the brink of orgasm. The need to release is so powerful it hurts.

"I'm sorry," I find my voice.

"You *will* set a better example for your daughter. Won't you?"

I nod.

"I need to hear you say it, *Mr. Hawk*."

That's it! I turn around and face her. This is not a game anymore. Dani stares me in the eyes. Daring me to touch her without permission. To prove she means business, both vibrating fingers concentrate on that spot just under the hawk's head.

My balls are weighted. Teeth sink into my bottom lip. Eyes close. Water pounds my face. Knees lock. A tremor travels…

What the hell?! My eyes snap open.

Dani's hands are gone. Her eyes are fixated on the cusp of my neck. She snatches off the finger toys. They fall to the shower floor. Vibrating against the tile.

Cautiously, she reaches out. The tips of her fingers brush the healing flesh of my gunshot wound. Her lips tremble. Chill bumps break out over her body.

Before I can stop her, Dani flees the shower room, snagging a towel from the rack. The bathroom door closes behind her.

I press the button on the control panel to stop the water flow, grab a towel, and rush after her.

Our bedroom is vacant.

"Dani?"

I didn't hear the bedroom doors close.

I stand in the bathroom's doorway desperately searching the room with my eyes.

She wouldn't go out on the deck.

She's not on the bed.

"Dani?" I call out to her again.

Stop for a second, Hawk.

Think.

I look down at the hardwood floor. Her wet footprints stop at the closet door. I follow them and knock. "Are you okay?"

I hear her crying. She sounds like she's right by the door. I turn the handle and push, but something's blocking it. "Please answer me."

"I'm okay," she whispers. It sounds like she's sitting on the floor in front of the door.

I take a breath and sit on the floor too. "I'm right here, Dani. I'm not going anywhere. When you're ready to talk, I'll be right here."

The minutes fly by and she's still crying.

I try singing to her.

She cries harder.

I've lost all feeling in my butt and still my wife cries.

Finally I realize I'm not helping. "Dani, what do you need?"

"Max," she whispers. "I need to talk to Max."

There was a time when I was her anchor. The one she needed in a crisis. My chest tightens. I know the change is because of the lies. I thought I was forgiven and we were moving past that.

"I'll call him." I tried to keep the disappointment from my tone.

My body feels heavy as I stand. Instead of the cell phone, I make the call from the house phone. Max says he'll be here in fifteen minutes. After I relay the message, I go down to the laundry room and get dressed, then go to the security room under the stairs. I type in the code to the security system and turn off the cameras in the house so Dani and Max have complete privacy.

I notify the men guarding the house that I intentionally turned off the system and to increase patrols until I turn it back on.

In my office, I grab my bike keys and go out the inner door to the garage. I put on the helmet and push the bike to the center of the driveway.

Exactly fifteen minutes after he hung up, Max pulls up in front of the house. He stares at me as he walks up the steps. I wait until he rings the doorbell and Dani opens the door to start the engine and pull out of the driveway.

I blow through the stop sign at the corner.

Numb. I feel numb and reckless. Instead of slowing down to take the curve, I shift gears, pick up speed and lean with the bike, keeping it steady. I take the curve going eighty. The sign says thirty. I don't slow down or look for oncoming traffic. I merge onto the main road and head to my office building.

———◆———

Bryan takes off on his motorcycle. Tears blur my vision and I stand in the doorway crying. Max wraps his arm around my shoulder and guides me back inside. He locks the door and we walk down the hall to the kitchen.

"Do you want coffee or tea?" I wipe my eyes and move around the kitchen, guilt propelling me to keep moving instead of sitting and facing my friend.

"Whatever you're having."

I fill the tea kettle with water and put it on the stove. I feel Max's eyes following me around the kitchen. His silence is his question. *Why am I here, Danikins?*

"Kourtney looked so happy today when she played around in the stores with her dad. She's been in such a bad mood lately. He's never been privy to a rebellious Kourtney so he's unsure of how to deal with her."

"I can't wait to see how he handles menstrual mood swings and boys picking her up." Max chuckles.

I keep my back to him. "You know, I usually don't find beards attractive, but the one he's growing looks good on him. Don't you think?"

He doesn't reply. I exhale and turn around. He's giving me the duck lips, reiterating the unspoken question.

"I'm afraid, Max."

"Of what?"

I turn my back and get cups out of the cabinet. "I don't know."

"Honey, it's my job to teach them how to lie believably. With a straight face. Right body movements and facial expressions to authenticate the lie. How and when to change the pitch of their voice to make the lie believable. You are not one of my students, Danikins."

The tears start to flow from my eyes again.

"Sweetie, I threw all kinds of men at you. But you didn't respond to them like you do to Bry. I guess it didn't help that he threatened those men before they took you out."

I gasp and turn around.

Max comes to me. He guides me to a seat at the table and turns his chair to face me. He holds my hands in his. "I didn't teach him to lie about being in love. That's an emotion no one can fake. You looked past the physical attraction and saw the man. Bryan accomplished something not even Edwards could. The distance only strengthened it. You're not afraid of him. So what's frightening you?"

"Since the shooting, we haven't slept in the same bed. The last time we kissed was on his birthday and before that it was before we left the movie theater on the night of the shooting. I know I haven't been the perfect wife." I pause for a second. "Is that the correct description for my status?" Max doesn't answer. It was a rhetorical question anyway. I exhale and continue. "He's apologized. Gone beyond explanation to get me to understand the reasons behind the deception. But something in me just can't let it go. Today was— different. I see how important his relationship with Kourt is to him and I found it to be incredibly sexy. Bryan always let me control our sex life, so tonight, I joined him in the shower, ready to reclaim our physical intimacy. From his reaction, he felt the change in my mood. When he turned to face me the scar jumped out at me. I felt—guilty."

"Guilty of what? You didn't shoot him."

"Bryan puts his life on the line to protect me and this country. I'm afraid I may be one of those who are trying to tear it down."

His eyes grow wide. "Excuse me?"

"Max, I think I'm a trained RAGS agent and it's my job to kill Bryan."

"Huh?"

I wipe my nose with a paper napkin. I'm not getting through to him. "I fit the profile."

"Lots of people fit the profile, Danikins, but you didn't join the military and you don't have political aspirations."

"Come on, Max, I know you guys are thinking it. Maybe they went for something different."

"Yes, we considered it a long time ago. And after investigating you it was ruled out. Why do you think you're the enemy?"

"Back during the holidays, I dreamt of being chased by dogs I couldn't see, and in the end Bryan saved us. Now I keep having this dream of Bryan and me as an older couple. We're sitting on the bench wrapped in a plaid fleece blanket while our children and grandchildren ice skate on the uneven surface of the frozen pond. Their laughter and playful taunts make it a joyful winter afternoon. My Bryan whispers in my ear. He's the one I fell in love with the first time he took care of me. The one who I leaned on when I felt the world drifting away. My Bryan took care of me in my lowest of times, and celebrated my happiest of moments. My Bryan made love to me for the first time and didn't walk away three years later. He was there to watch our child grow up. He had no secrets. No lies. Then I hear a woman whose words are spoken like a song. 'Yé un shyin, piti'. The chilling breath of evil winds rips through the bare trees. I'm surrounded in darkness. My family is gone. The angry growl of dogs slithering through the darkness mixes with a rhythmic click clicking.

"A three-year-old Kourtney tugs on my pant-leg. She's clutching Mr. Cuddles and reaches for me. *Where's Daddy?* she cries. I pick up my daughter, hold her to me, and utter the words that are both truthful and reassuring. *Daddy had to go away, but we will see him again. Where's Ma?* she asks. I press my hand over her precious heart, *Emma will always be right here.* The clicking grows louder. Constant. The dogs howl and whine like the sound hurts their ears. Every lie Bryan's ever told is knitted into a massive pulsating black yarn replica of a heart. Anger creeps into my body. From out of the darkness, four sets of eyes stalk toward us. I reach behind me. My fingers wrap around the cold steel of the weapon tucked in the waistband of my jeans. *Close your eyes and cover your ears, baby girl,* I tell my daughter. She struggles to follow orders while holding Mr. Cuddles. I squeeze the trigger. *Bang! Bang! Bang! Bang!* Kourtney flinches in my arms with each shot. One by one, the dogs fall. I wait. They don't move, but one whines. His emotional pain is a sinister joy to hear.

"Slowly, I lower Kourtney to her feet, then I step forward, checking over my shoulder to make sure she doesn't follow. The dog whines again, begging me to come closer. My heart tells me not to enjoy his torment, but my head overrules, saying he deserves it for being a liar. With my foot, I nudge one dog. Its lifeless body slightly moves. I step over it. A warm mystic wind circles my ankles. I don't look back because I know who it is. I nudge the other two dogs, while the one close to death watches me. Tears stain the fur around his hazel eyes. Each breath is taken with much effort. I take the final step, hovering over him. His eye searches mine, like he's trying to tell me something. My heart feels unconditional love for the dying canine. 'Yé un shyin', that evil voice whispers in my ear. I point the gun at him. The warmth of the mystic wind momentarily blinds me. *Only you,* he says. And without thought or regret. *Bang!* I squeeze the trigger."

Max scoots his chair closer. I lay my head on his shoulder. Tears

and sorrow steal my ability to finish the story. We ignore the whistle of the tea kettle. I stumble over the words of my plea. "I need
you… to help me… figure out if I'm conditioned to kill him…
Max. And if I am… help me find a way… not to."

CHAPTER THIRTEEN

I GO HOME LONG ENOUGH TO check on my family, grab a clean suit, shirt and underwear, then come back to the downtown office. Being away from them isn't easy, but it's necessary.

Max told me about the dream. To help Dani, I have to stay focused on the goal. Obliterate RAGS.

I refuse to accept that she was sent to kill me. It is not in her nature to deceive people. That dream is manifested by remnants of resentment toward the lies. If she were sent to kill me, then she's had plenty of opportunities to do it— and didn't.

In the back of my mind, the monster shouts, *you're forgetting the shooter was aiming for her head!*

Screw him. So what? I hid Amelia when the order came down from RAGS's leader to eliminate her for failing her assignment. I *know* my wife. Dani is not a follower. She's an alpha. It's what attracts me to her.

Dani helps others, even those who have been salty toward her. Prime example: Melissa Valentine. Dani talked her down from committing suicide in the parking lot at the school.

It helps to have the full support of my boys. They agree, Dani isn't a murderer. Max is helping her analyze the dream. She said it started *after* the shooting, but became more detailed after we taught her how to fire a gun.

Once Edwards was *supposedly* dead, Willis assigned me to find out Dani's connection to RAGS. It took a year of close observation to clear her. I was thorough with my investigation. Danielle Lauren Hawk is not a minion for Rebels Against Government Suppression.

Yes, the name of the homeland radicals may sound ridiculous, but their influence is strong. Worldwide. And they did not train Dani.

Their founder, Dominique Elian Toussaint, globalized his fight to take down the American government by force and rebuild it as a single political party dictatorship with him as the dictator. He stood behind his right to free speech as an American citizen to spread *his* views amongst those who were looked upon as inferior because of their sex, race, religion, sexual orientation, or income. He promised that under his reign, everyone would be treated equally.

Toussaint skirted the lines of legal financial support to keep from going to federal prison. Encouragement poured in from foreign radicals who wanted the American government to fall.

Dominique Elian Toussaint was executed four and a half decades ago.

His followers claimed POTUS ordered the hit because Toussaint posed a serious threat to the sanctity of our government's structure.

Toussaint left behind a wife, two rumored mistresses, four sons by his wife, a rumored son by one mistress, and a rumored daughter with the other.

His successor to RAGS is unknown. The new ruler hides in darkness since ascending to the throne yet continues to exploit those whom society continues to label inferior. RAGS is responsible for many violent attacks that have taken place on American soil. Willis couldn't shine a light on the successor's whereabouts, but I intend to.

The guys and I divvy up the transcribed files of the CDs Edwards made for Dani and comb through them. We come to the conclusion: yes, Edwards tried to condition her.

Porter is running a background check on people Dani has spent time with. Her foster parents. Study group associates. Neighbors.

Ig has Larson probing into the lives of Dani's patients.

Max and I debate about him modifying a version of his form of training as a means of reconditioning, should it be necessary. I hesitate, not because I don't think it's a good idea; Max is considered the best in the business for a reason.

The root of my hesitation is, ninety percent of his training is inhuman. Anyone who comes out of it with their sanity intact is exceptional. We made it, but who's to say my pregnant wife will, even if his methods are altered for her.

If I can just concentrate on the puzzle pieces, I can start putting them together. We roll up our sleeves and start transferring the pieces from my head to three vision boards labeled RAGS, Dani, and Other Shit. Everything is posted on these boards, including things that may or may not be relevant to the case. Even the photos of the woman and child I found in Mahdavi's hideout are on the OS board.

Tony posts on the Dani board his findings on the explosives in Edwards's hotel. He explains why. "Those small boxes attached to the devices aren't our only problem."

"How's that?" Vin asks.

"The bombs are designed for chemical warfare. It's invisible and odorless. Ig is testing the effects, but I do know out in the open the chemical loses most of its potency. But in a controlled environment, like underground subways, it becomes an entity hunting us like animals." A map of the United States shows up on the television. The cities with underground means of public transportation are highlighted. "Five million people ride the New York subways daily. These odorless smoke bombs strategically planted in the tunnels could affect everyone who rides the trains."

Vin rushes to his laptop on the conference table. "The target is Washington, DC," he says as his fingers punch the keyboard. The list of military personnel and their leave request dates come up on the screen in typewriter speed. "Only a handful were granted leave, I bet the others go AWOL. They'll want to be as far away from the toxic air as possible. Everyone on the list will be out of the DC area on the same days: May ninth, tenth, and eleventh."

"Today is the third," Ig says.

What the hell is Edwards up to?

I make a secured call to President Hart. Within the hour, all military branches are on high alert and leaves have been revoked. The rats will go down with the ship.

I've expanded Riley's monitoring to include other black-market sites and all international intelligence agencies.

Ig helps Porter complete the deciphering of the contents of Mahdavi's computer. Islam Liberation Army declared war on the United States. A large financial transaction was made between him and an unknown with an offshore account, the wire transfer generated from an IP address here in Colorado on June 26, 2013.

We haven't made the connection between the woman and child in the photo and ILA. Facial Recognition identifies her as Selam Bahta, a thirty-three-year-old Ethiopian woman. She works as a registered nurse in a health care center in Addis Ababa. We're guessing the child in the pictures is her son. The background check did not turn up a husband.

Ig calls for a dinner break.

I think of Dani as I put carrot sticks on my plate next to the foot-long Philly cheesesteak sandwich and fries. I lift a bottled soda from the cooler and go sit on the sofa.

My plate balances on one thigh and a tablet on the other. I place a video call.

Her smiling, sleepy face fills the screen after the third ring. "Hi." Dani's lying on her side, hugging a pillow, eyes at half-mast.

I look at the time. It's two in the morning. Behind her, I see the top of Emm's head. "Sorry, didn't mean to wake you."

"It's okay. I'm in that zone between sleep and awake."

"Why?"

"Well, first, it's too quiet. I'm used to you calling hogs all night."

"Hey, I don't snore." I laugh.

She chuckles. "I'm too much of a lady to record you then play it back in the morning."

The camera on her end moves, the mic picking up the sound. I hear a click and her background becomes a little brighter. More rustling and the camera goes out of focus for a second, then I see what's going on. Dani turned on the light, lifted her pajama top, and is holding the tablet over her stomach. I watch it jump and flutter. The baby is moving.

Her face comes back on the screen. "Your son is keeping me awake."

My son. "How are things on the home front?"

"Everything's good. Willis is staying in one of the rooms off the laundry room. Marie sounds horrible. The girls miss you."

Just them?

She covers her yawn behind her hand.

"How's Kourt? Is she behaving?"

Dani shrugs. "She's trying." Another yawn stops her from saying more.

"Try singing to him. I remember it used to work when Kourt was restless at night."

A flash of sadness fills her eyes.

"I have to go. I'll try and call the girls in the morning."

"Okay, Bry. Goodnight."

"Night, Dani." I disconnect and stare at the board labeled RAGS.

"You know you can't keep avoiding her," Tony says as he claims the other end of the sofa.

"I'm not. In case you haven't noticed, we've got a lot going on here."

"Long gone are the days you can put in sixteen hours. I could see if we had to go out on a mission, but we're home. Trying to figure out how all those"—he gestures to the boards—"fit together. We've got this, Bry. If anything comes up, you know I'll call. Go home."

———◆———

"Where we going?" Kourt asks. We've been on the highway for forty minutes.

"Thought you guys might like to visit your ponies."

"Really, Dad? The whole day?"

"Yep, and we can stop by Grandma and Grandpa's too."

"Mommy, I don't feel too good," Emm moans.

"What's wrong, sweetie?"

"My stomach feels funny."

Dani looks over her shoulder. "Do you think water will help?"

Kourt blurts, "Eww, Emmy. Don't throw up!"

"Pull over, Bryan," Dani urges.

Signaling, I check the mirrors, then cross four lanes of traffic while unhooking my seat belt. I get to the shoulder and stop. The truck rocks from the abrupt way I pushed the gearshift into park.

Dani tugs on her seat belt.

My shoulder bumps the door as I pull back on the handle. I sprint around the back of the truck to the passenger side back door. I get it open in time. Emm leans out, the seat belt making it difficult for her to go far. She hurls.

I jump out of the way as the contents of her stomach barely miss my brand new kicks.

Dani is out of her seat, coming to our daughter's aid. She

unbuckles the belt and helps Emma climb out. Trevor barks and jumps into the front seat.

The Escalade tailing us pulls up behind. A Hawkeye PPO hops out. "Do you need medical assistance, sir?" he asks, phone up to his ear, ready to make the call.

"I think we're okay." Dani pulls a package of wet towelettes out of her bag. She wipes Emm's mouth. "Bry, can you hand me a bottle of water from the cooler?"

I step around the regurgitated breakfast and walk to the back of the truck and pop the hatch, get the bottle, twist the cap and take it back to Dani.

"Here, sweetie. Rinse your mouth. Don't swallow the water." Dani pours a little into Emm's open mouth. "Let's go back home. She doesn't look too good."

"Nooo," Kourt sings. "That's not fair!"

"Cuddles, your sister is sick."

"Daddy, I want to go home." Emm clings to her mom.

"We're turning back, Kourtney," Dani decrees.

My daughter kicks the back of the driver's seat, folds her arms across her chest, and huffs.

I help Emm back into the truck. Dani climbs in next to her. Trevor happily remains in the front seat.

The PPO opens the hatch on his truck and comes back with an absorbent that he covers the vomit with. Once it solidifies, he puts on gloves, uses a beach shovel-size scooper to lift the clump off the pavement, and dumps it in a biodegradable bag. He signals the second Escalade that we're heading back.

I drive along the shoulder until the third car blocks the lane and I can pull into traffic. We take the next exit, make a left, and get into the lane that puts us back on the highway, heading home.

"We ate the same thing for breakfast, Emmy. I don't feel sick." Kourt is unhappy about the change and it shows in her tone.

"Sweetie, you know Emma's been having an upset stomach for a while." Dani's trying to reason with our daughter.

"Dr. Spencer didn't find anything wrong with her."

Thankfully there isn't much traffic in this direction. It shouldn't take long to get home. I can't drive and physically referee Dani and Kourt at the same time. I offer Kourt a consolation prize. "Cuddles, soccer drills or flag football when we get back to the house?"

"Football," she shouts.

I remind her that I don't believe in taking it easy just because she's a kid. If she steps on my field, we are going to play and play hard. My baby girl loves a challenge and claims I won't be able to keep up with her.

She loves sports where she gets to run, kick, hit, throw. Kourt is the outdoorsy type like me. The first time I took her jogging, she asked about the old scars on my knees and legs. I told her they're battle wounds from the sports field.

Occasionally, I check on Dani and Emm through the rear-view mirror. Emm is falling asleep and Dani alternates between kissing our daughter's forehead and staring out the window. She looks worried.

I pull up in front of the steps instead of parking in the garage. Dani climbs out, trying to lift Emm.

"I've got her." Emm climbs into my arms and I carry my big girl into the house and up to her room. Dani's on my heels.

"I'll get two flag belts," Kourt says, following us up the stairs.

Dani rushes ahead and opens Emm's door.

I lay our daughter in bed. Adjust the pillow. Kiss her forehead. My phone vibrates. I unclip it and step out into the hallway to answer.

It's Tony. "Hey, man. Sorry. Did you guys get far?"

"No, we had to come back. Emm got sick. What's up?"

"Edwards is demanding to see you. Ig tried to get him to wait till you came in, but the guy is out of control."

"Did he say what he wants?"

"He asked the PA what day it was, and when she told him, he lunged for her and tried to choke her. She fought him off and pushed the panic button. Ig and Vin got him strapped to a chair right now."

"How's Charisse?"

"For a thickie-thick, she can move and kick ass."

"I'll be there in thirty." I end the call.

Dani's standing in the doorway. Disappointment in her eyes, but an understanding smile on lips.

"I have to go in."

"Go in where?" Kourt demands.

I turn around. *Shit, I forgot about her.* Understanding is not in her eyes or her posture.

"I have something important to take care of at work, Cuddles."

"Go, Bryan. I'll explain it to her," Dani says.

I kiss my wife's cheek and go to kiss my daughter. She ducks out of the way and throws the belts down at my feet.

Dani says, "Kourtney, we talked about how sometimes Dad has to take care of important things and we may not like it, but we have to let him do his job. He doesn't like it either. Dad really wanted to spend the day with us."

I can't stand the hurt look in my baby girl's eyes. I start to walk away.

"You work too much!" Kourt's accusation hits my back and it sticks with me all the way to the bedroom where I change clothes.

The heaviness of her words settles on my shoulders as I walk by my baby girl sitting on the top step crying. "When are we going to start the garden?!" Her pain makes me stumble as a band squeezes my heart.

"We will do the garden, baby girl."

She doesn't look up at me.

I leave the house.

———————◆———————

I park in the structure of my building and take the elevator to the first floor, which is underground. The scanner reads my fingerprints and the exit door opens.

Motion sensitive lights automatically come on to light the path of the tunnel I walk to get to the facility. The sound of my footsteps echoing in the empty concrete underpass mirrors how I feel inside for disappointing my daughter. I can't blame her for being upset. I have been working a lot and I can't tell her why. The shooting took the RAGS case to a new level. Trying to snatch Dani is one thing. Trying to kill her is another. I have to put an end to them before they come after my baby girl. *I will* declare war if anything happens to her.

At an unmarked door, visual confirmation grants me access.

Tony and Ig look up when I walk into the section of the first floor where detained suspects are held. My eyes focus on the man behind the soundproof glass wall, tethered to a chair.

"He stopped yelling about five minutes ago," Ig says.

I hand Tony my weapon, phone, and keys and wait for Vin to remotely open the panel so I can enter Edward's cell.

I don't hide my ring this time as I walk across the tile floor toward an empty chair.

Edwards tracks me with his eyes.

First impression—he's in pain. Not physical pain. It's the kind of pain a man feels when he believes he's lost everything. His soul. His reason for wanting to live.

I recognize that level of pain. I faced it in the mirror for five long years. If it weren't for Emm and my friends I wouldn't be here.

A split-second decision is made. Mentally I hear Tony and Vin calling me every *dumb-fuck* they can come up with while Ig's knee drills a hole in the floor with his foot because of the bad vibe he's getting. I keep my eye on Edwards and squat to undo the straps around his ankles first, then watch his feet as I rise to remove the restraints around his wrists.

I hover before moving away. My fingers press the button through the buttonhole of my suit jacket. It opens as I sit in the chair across from him.

His jawline tightens from his teeth pressing tightly together. The charge in the room takes on a static energy of anger. Edwards's torso is leveled. Knees bent. Knuckles strangle the arms of the chair. Feet rooted to the floor.

Out of habit, my elbow brushes my side, seeking the surety of the butt of my gun. It's not there. I slightly shift in the seat, my right shoulder leading to protect my dominant side.

I mind his posture.

With the curl of the upper lip, the beast lunges. His crazed battle cry sounds off. His attack propels the chair I'm in to tip back. I use the momentum of the pummeling furniture to keep our velocity moving and shoulder roll, flipping Edwards onto his back. I land on my knees over him. The first strike I sink to the side of his head. *For putting them in the middle of his shit.* The second punch, my wedding band slices the skin of his cheekbone. *For shooting my wife and making her fall down the stairs.* His scrawny fists of desperation and suffering bury into my sides. His batter is wild and unfocused. Mine fast and calculated. The third, *for pulling me away from my daughter for this shit.* We scrap for different reasons.

Edwards land a solid kidney punch. I maneuver us in a wrestling pose he can't escape or counterattack. A choke hold. Like a magnetic pull his hands grip my forearm. He kicks and thrashes, trying to find leverage to break out of the hold. I seize his legs with mine. Edwards coughs and struggles for air. My mouth turns up and I squeeze more.

The person kneeling beside me is familiar. He's applying pressure to the points in my wrists while someone else pulls Edwards out of the hold. My name is said along with the command to *let go.*

My body slackens. The weight of Edwards is yanked off me. I lie on my back staring up at the ceiling. My lungs inflate and deflate at their normal pace. My heart beats at its resting rate. The brawl wasn't long enough for me to work up a sweat.

"Kill… me," he hacks, leaning away from Vin's support.

I lift my head to stare at the fool. Blood streams down his cheek. One eye swelling. *I'm down for granting wishes.* This time I won't pull back on the punches. He's upset about something and is lashing out. But I'll be damned if he takes his shit out on me. Another stunt like that and I'll break his fucking neck.

"You good?" Tony asks.

"Yeah."

He offers his hand. I take it and he pulls me to my feet. I straighten my clothes while I survey the opponent. My fingers trail through my hair and smooth out my beard.

Tony stays close. There's no need. I'm in control of myself— as long as Edwards stays on his side.

Ig uprights the chairs and restores the sitting area.

Vin leads a vehement Edwards to a chair. I ease into one across the room. Vin sits next to him. Tony beside me. Ig is at the sink.

I cock an eyebrow and tilt my head when Edwards stops flexing his fist long enough to look up at me.

"One mistake. I've been in hiding for nine years and I make one stupid mistake." Edwards takes the wet towel Ig hands him. "I was living under the radar everybody thought I was dead. Then in May last year, I clicked on an online article about a couple, serving consecutive life sentences in separate federal prisons in California, beaten on the same day, at the same time, May twenty-second, two thousand-thirteen, seven-forty-five in the evening. The husband was expected to recover from his injuries, but the wife was touch and go." He bundles the towel and holds it to the laceration on his cheek.

I don't see the connection to today's date and some felons getting a beat-down a year ago.

We give him a minute to compose himself.

His gaze includes the guys. "I can't fathom why I cared about what happened to that man and woman. They'd been in prison since I was three years old so it's not like I knew them. But I couldn't sleep or function because their story weighed heavy on my mind. It took me a few weeks to plan it out so that I didn't compromise the life I'd been living for almost a decade. I drove five hundred miles from my hiding spot. Bought a burner phone and called the prisons. Something in me had to know Leroy and Bertha Mae Edwards were okay."

His parents.

"Two days after I made the calls, men barged into my home. Knocked me out. When I came to, my family was gone. The burner phone I'd ditched was on my wife's pillow and ringing. I was told I had twenty-four hours to be at the Israeli Syrian border. I didn't know what to do so I called someone here in the States. He told me to put back on my old Army fatigues and use my old military ID to get me there in time. But I was late because I got detained by Syrian soldiers. The burner phone rang and I listened to them beat my wife. That was at the end of June. It's almost been a year since I've seen them."

"Who is, *they*?" I interrupt.

"I don't know who, *they* are! We thought it was you."

"Why me?"

"Because the prison guards were paid by one of your people to look the other way while my parents were beaten."

"Which one of my people?"

"Eugene Mills..."

"*That son of a bitch.*" Tony shoves to his feet. The chair's legs scrape the tile floor as it travels a foot back. "Mills left you and Dani open on purpose." He pulls his phone from the inner pocket of his jacket.

I motion for Edwards to continue talking. "What convinced you I wasn't the one who took your family?"

"Deidra was lurking around the hospital after you were shot."

"Deidra?"

"Amelia never told you about her?"

I shake my head.

"Did you know she was bisexual?"

"Yes, I knew."

"Deidra Billups is Amelia's high school girl friend."

"And she was at the hospital?"

He nods. "There's only one reason Deidra would've been there." He pauses. "To kill Danielle."

"Because Dani failed her assignment like Amelia?" It was meant as a bluff to see how much he knows about Dani's connection to RAGS.

"Amelia and Deidra think she's the third person who accepted the assignment to flip you."

Vin huffs. "Is she?"

"No. There was no third person. That was part of the lie Jamal and I told to get RAGS's top female closers to turn against each other. You know how ruthless females are especially if the object is a dick. Amelia and Deidra were competitive. But to make sure they went hard for the victory, we tossed in a third person."

"Why Dani?" Ig asks.

"Listen. I didn't make it a secret that Danielle held on to her virginity like a precious gift. People assumed we were screwing because we lived together. Her hooking up with Hawk a week after I was gone wasn't a good look since I'd known her longer than two seconds."

I lean forward. "Why did you show up in the courtyard?"

"To warn Danielle. If those people took my wife and son from our home in Ethiopia a year ago to force me to be their mule. They were…"

"Wait." I hold up my hand. "You were hiding out in Ethiopia?"

Head tilted to the left, he nods.

"Is your wife Selam Bahta?"

"How do you know her name?!"

"The boy in the pictures is your son?"

"What pictures?"

Ig hands me my phone. I access the file and turn the screen toward Edwards. His shaking hands reach for the phone. I release it. Slowly, he brushes the screen with the tip of his finger. From where I am, I can see the images change. At the last photo, a small drip falls on the screen.

He looks at me with a solemn expression. "Those had to have been taken the day the men kicked down our door. Do you know if they're still alive?"

"Are you still mixed up with the Islam Liberation Army?"

"Who?"

I repeat the name of the organization.

Lips primed, Edwards shifts in his seat. "I don't know those people."

"These photos were found by a CIA agent amongst the belongings of a terrorist from ILA. They were the buyer of the information you were selling. They probably want their billion dollars back or the product they purchased nine years ago." Of course I couldn't tell him how I really came across the pictures.

"That money went to an offshore account. Hopper paid for my new identity and my new life in Ethiopia."

I lean forward, eyebrows knocking into each other. "Elijah Hopper?"

"Yeah."

"Hopper's dead."

"Elijah Hopper is alive and living right here in Boulder, Colorado."

No fucking way!

Vin taps his phone and holds it so that the camera is facing Edwards. "Start from the beginning."

The four of us sit and listen to the man we once thought of as a traitor spin a tale that contradicts the information we gathered on him when I first started working the case.

Jamal, the intellectually superior twin, and James, the physically superior twin, were groomed by RAGS trainers, using a military-style form of discipline since the age of three. As teenagers, they were a powerhouse that catapulted the threat of RAGS to the security of the government's classified information.

The twins loved the rush from hacking into forbidden databases to steal information. The higher the level of classification, the bigger the monetary reward.

The thrill had become an addiction for one twin and, instead of playing by the rules, he made up his own and pocketed the money. The other twin viewed the climb as a futile attempt to tear down the government when RAGS had nothing better to offer the American people.

In 2003, the intellectual twin stumbled upon the highest level of classified information in U.S. history. The payout was going to be beyond anything RAGS's leader could ever give them— freedom for one twin's best friend, the ultimate perpetual high for the other.

It took two years for them to gather and store information on RAGS and Phantom. The twins thought outside the box. Everything fell into place until I found the anomaly that made both sides realize they had been hacked.

Phantom and RAGS were in a dead-heat to cover their tracks while the twins shopped for buyers. In May 2005, Elijah Hopper approached the twins and introduced himself as the man in charge of Rebels Against Government Suppression. They were shocked. The identity of RAGS's leader was as big a secret as the existence of a phantom military organization. The twins figured the only reason Hopper introduced himself was because he wanted to be the one to kill them. Hopper gave them a choice. Turn over the information *or* die right then and there. The intellectual twin convinced Hopper that it would take a couple days to gather all their files. They knew the real story behind Hopper's threat.

Jamal came up with a third option. He engineered the microchip and gold ring external drive and transferred the information to them. James married his best friend Danielle. The twins implanted the chip in her finger while she was in a drug induced sleep. The next morning, Jamal deployed to Iraq in James's place. James flew commercial to Europe.

Jamal met the buyer in the mosque in Iraq and things didn't go as planned. Langford's Elite Special Operations Team showed up. Jamal was killed and James couldn't reclaim his identity. The United States Army declared James Andrew Edwards dead.

He called Hopper.

"Why did you attack my PA?" Ig asked.

"In order to keep my wife and son alive, I have to call a phone number by three o'clock this afternoon to get the final instructions on where and when I'm supposed to deliver the duffle bags."

I check my watch. I have four hours, fifty-nine minutes to investigate his story and decide if I believe him.

I fix Edwards with a pointed stare. "Are you the twin that got off on selling out his country or the one who wanted a way out for his best friend?"

"The one who wanted a way out for his best friend," he vows without blinking or looking away.

CHAPTER FOURTEEN

PHANTOM HAS NEVER BEEN THIS close to closing the books on the RAGS case. We have the name of its leader, and soon, we'll know the date they're going to pull off their next strike on the United States.

In the SCIF, here in my building, my team and I start the tedious process of verifying Edwards story. Max weighs in on it too. In his professional opinion, Max believes Edwards is telling the truth. He freezes the part where Edwards leapt from the chair. Max points out the look in Edwards's eyes.

If my wife and children were being held by unknowns who are going to kill them if I don't call in on a certain date at a specific time, I'd have the same crazed look in my eyes.

I give Tony and Porter the green light to take the cell phone to Edwards so he can make the call and get the final instructions. Riley will attempt to trace the call.

While I wait, Chen forwards Phantom personnel files for me to pore through so I can put together a special Search and Rescue team to extract Selam and Solomon once Riley locks in on the location of the call.

I choose a Watcher, a Sweeper, a Field Operative, and a Delta.

No one questions my choice to lead the Search and Rescue team. Vanessa Larson. Yes, we give Vin a hard time about his abrasiveness, yet the females he trains are equally as qualified in the field as the males before they move on to Tony.

Larson moved up the levels of Phantom under Vin's discipline. He didn't allow her to settle for just being a Watcher. He recognized potential and challenged her to be the first woman to hold the title of Delta Team Lead. Today she's taking the first steps. Her performance will determine her promotion.

The SCIF phone rings. "Edwards is supposed to have the bombs in Maryland by the eighth. The automated voice rattled off the address to where he is to park the car," Tony reports.

"Was he able to talk to his wife?"

"No, they put his son on the phone for like two seconds. Really tore him up. I almost feel sorry for his ass."

"Tell Edwards, if we get coordinates from the call, I'm sending in a team for his family."

"Roger that."

I end the call.

Visitors from all over the world ride the DC metro lines because they provide access to tourist attractions including the White House. I alert President Hart and give him a playbook to follow.

We disperse.

I go to my office and plant credible cyber information about the bomb threat, and the capital's threat level has been raised.

Edwards said the two times he's met up with Hopper was in an office across the street from the Pine Village Hotel in Boulder. The B-list place he took Dani after they escaped from the hospital the night I was shot. Vin coordinates a meeting with the building's owner to make them a generous offer.

Mills just signed in for his shift. Tony is on his way to have a *chat* with him. I warn Tony not to go too far; we may need Mills for something bigger. I know the command flies over his head. There are certain people he has mercy for. Betrayers are not one of them.

Ig goes to his laboratory on the campus of CU to test the lint rollers for Hopper's DNA fingerprints.

My time is divided. Thankfully I'm a gifted multitasker. I'm listening in on the president's closed session meeting with his Joint Chiefs of Staff, and commenting, via a one-way earpiece, when he's questioned about the direction he wants to go as it relates to the threat. I'm also reading the growing file on Deidra Billups. For the last task, I enlist Vin's help, then call my baby-momma. Amelia's existence is one lie I hope I never have to confess to my wife.

The growl from the depths of my stomach reminds me I haven't eaten since breakfast.

Amelia answers on the first ring; her location isn't registering. I order her to meet me at *the spot* in two hours. At first, she protests saying I have no right to demand she meet me at the park around the corner from her house. My silence prompts a dubious plea of innocence of any shady activities on her part. I say nothing. She exhales and agrees. I disconnect the call.

I don't get why she had to hem and haw before doing what she was told to do.

Riley's virtual image comes up on my screen. The location of the person on the receiving end of the call Edwards made this afternoon loads onto the screen. Jaw slacken, eyes bugged out, I pull up the satellite view. *It can't be. We destroyed that one.*

The call was answered from the rubble of an abandoned mosque in Fallujah, Iraq. The same building Langford's Phantom Elite Special Operations Team raided nine years ago to stop Jamal from selling the highly classified information. The situation just became much more serious. I'm about to send a covert team into an area of Anabar under heavy fighting from both sides. *Shit!*

"Take your contacts out and put on your specs." Tony strolls into my office.

My gaze drops to his knuckles. They aren't bandaged so I take it he shot Mills instead of doling out the customary ass kicking. "Which hospital and is he expected to live?"

The belly laugh emanating from my friends is contagious.

Porter knocks, then stands back. An ethnically ambiguous young woman wearing a Class A Junior Enlisted Army Service Uniform enters and stands a foot over the threshold at attention.

I step from behind the desk and approach them.

She displays proper military courtesy and waits until I am six paces away to render a salute. "Specialist Fontenot, NCO from the Way Station reporting for duty, sir."

No, I didn't come through the customary channels of the United States Armed Forces to get to where I am in Phantom, but I respect the traditions and protocols as if I did. I return the salute and say, "At ease, Soldier."

Sophie Fontenot snags the seat next to Porter at the conference table. "Thank you for the opportunity to work with you all." Her laid back Southern purr reminds me of Marie.

"Welcome to Phantom. Have you had the chance to listen to the recording that's in Creole and translate it for us?"

"Yes, sir, I have. The gentleman was telling someone: 'let her know the doctor cleared him to travel with a private nurse and the arrangements have already been made. George will be leaving on Friday, May ninth. Make sure you tell her to give him his medication prior to leaving the facility.' There was a short pause and then he told the person, 'the check should go to her.' Another pause then he said, 'assure them that we are not displeased with the facility. Look, just tell them it has become difficult for us to travel back and forth to California. We are his appointed caretakers. We have power of attorney. And we don't owe them an explanation. Trust me, moving George is what's best for all of us.' Another pause. 'I know she's finally happy now. That's what we've always wanted for his daughter.' And that's where the phone went dead." She recited the conversation without referring to the folder in front of her.

I lay my pen on the note pad. "How many times did you listen to the recording?"

"Twice, sir. The first time I just wanted to listen. The second time I wrote it down word for word."

I'm impressed. "How certain are you of the translation?"

"One hundred percent, sir. Nowadays, most people speak the English-based form of the language, but my granddaddy insists we speak traditional French Creole. And that's the form the gentleman was speaking. I swear he and granddaddy would get along. Only old folks talk like that."

Porter nudges her. Sophie's cheeks tint.

"What does, yé un shyin, piti mean?"

"Was that all that was said?"

"I believe so."

"It means, 'they're a pack of dogs, child.'"

"Thanks. Your hotel and meals are covered by Phantom while you're here."

Her eyes cut to Porter then back to me. Her cheeks turn a deeper red.

"Thank you, sir. And if there's anything else I can help you all with while I'm here, please let me know."

"There is something else."

Her eyes light up.

"Have Larson catch you up on the background checks she was doing. I understand you are majoring in criminal investigation."

Her shoulders bounce with excitement. "Yes I am, sir."

"I'll see to it that this assignment be credited to your internship. We need that information and Larson's been reassigned." I address Porter. "Get Fontenot settled at a Watcher's station in The Nest. Have Riley give her a temporary access code, cell phone, and assigned a vehicle."

"Yes, sir," Porter replies.

"Vin, take her to the range. Put her through the paces until she passes, then issue a service weapon."

Vin rises to his feet twisting his neck. *Crack! Crack!* His shoulders roll. A gleam in his eyes. That's the look he gets when he gets to work with someone he sees as having potential. He motions for the young woman to follow him.

A quick furrowed glance at Porter, she rises out her seat. Shoulders back, Sophie Fontenot strides out the room with Vin.

Before I dismiss Porter, I give him the updates on the traced call and tell him to review Larson's plan of action and clear it with Tony before her team deploys.

The minute the door closes behind Porter, Tony pounces. "So she's Porter's girl. She's cute, huh? That Creole blood is strong in her genes. Her coloring is a shade lighter than Dani's."

"How old is she?"

"Twenty-one, today. I bet I know what Porter's giving her for her birthday…" He starts singing and dancing and doing that ab roll dance that male strippers do.

While he's living out his fantasy of dancing at a strip club I check my firearms. I secure one in my ankle strap. One in the belt holster on my left and another one in a holster at the small of my back.

"What, no knife?" Tony watches me.

"Do you think I should? I mean it's Amelia."

"In that case I'm shadowing you."

"I need you to follow up on something." I gesture to the mounted flat screen, then type on my keyboard to bring up the footage of the shooting. "I isolated the areas around the courtyard and had Riley enhance them. There are still some blind spots…"

"The stores in those squares don't have real time security systems so you want me to see what kind they have and if it still has the footage from the day of the shooting," he finishes my sentence.

I shut down and fly out the room before he protests. The last meeting with Amelia didn't go well. This one may not either depending on how fast Vin can work his magic.

———◆———

Fresh baked breads, homemade cured meats slow smoked in a specialty rub, kosher pickles, and beer mustard. The smells taunt my taste buds. The people ahead of me in line snicker at the temper tantrum my empty stomach is throwing.

I discovered this deli when I was scouting office buildings in the area. It's on the other side of downtown Boulder and across the street from the park I'm meeting Amelia at. Ownership has been in the same family for three generations.

The staff is preparing for the early dinner rush. In about ten minutes, this place will be packed and the wait for a table can take up to an hour on a good day.

The young man behind the counter gives the customary friendly greeting without making eye contact, but when he looks up to take my order, his posture changes.

"Pastrami on rye. Toasted. Light mustard and an extra pickle." I start to walk away, then turn back. "Add a small side salad with ranch instead of the chips."

His eyebrows almost meet his hairline and he'll have to push his eyeballs back in their sockets. I never ask for a side salad with anything. The change in diet can be accredited to my wife.

I sit at a table near the window, take out my phone, and survey the deli.

A familiar mahogany cane and the labored gait of the man at the door catch my attention. The cabbie cap, cardigan, starched collar white shirt, dark necktie, creased slacks, and loafers must be his everyday attire. Mr. Brumfield is an old school gentleman. He removes the cap from his head, holds the door open to allow the three women behind him to enter first.

I smile and stifle a laugh when the elderly man behind Mr. Brumfield nudges him with an elbow and vaudevillian flashing eyebrows and a grand gesture with a rolled up magazine in his hand. Brumfield bats at the man with his cane and steps inside the deli.

My food is set in front of me. I put the phone away and thank the teen. My stomach flips as I pick up one half of the piled-high sandwich, open my mouth wide, and chomp down.

Mhmm. The tender meat strokes my taste buds. *Oh yeah. Oh yeah.* The hungry man in my head does the cabbage-patch.

I have to bring Dani here. She'd love this place. There are a lot of little places in and around Boulder I want to take her.

I take another bite.

"Mr. Hawk?"

I look up before the meat makes my taste buds come for a fourth time. Brumfield and his companion stand a few feet from the table. I place the sandwich back in the basket, pick up a napkin to wipe my hands and mouth as I rise out my seat. Mr. Brumfield waves me off and gestures me to sit back down.

"Didn't mean to disturb you, son. Just wanted to say hello. See how the family's doing."

I nod. "Hello, sir. Everyone is well, thank you for asking. And please call me Bryan. How is your knee?"

His hand comes down on my shoulder. "I've had a bum knee all my life. Kept me from joining the military so I went to school to become a chemistry teacher."

His friend clears his throat.

Brumfield's eyes roll skyward and the corner of his mouth jumps. "This young man is the husband of my therapist." The cane flicks in the direction of his friend. "That dirty old fart is my best friend since high school."

"Good to meet you, Bryan. May we join you?"

My eyes do a quick sweep of the room. All the prime tables are already occupied.

"Don't feel obliged to acquiesce, son." Brumfield's fingers squeeze my shoulder before his hand drops to his side.

"No, it's okay. Please have a seat."

The two men get settled at the table.

"What branch you serve in?" the friend asks.

"I beg your pardon?"

"Army? Navy? Air Force? Marines?"

"Neither."

"Come on, son. The way you positioned yourself, pretending to be occupied by the phone, but scoping the joint. Your command-ing aura. Calling us sir. I recognize a military man when I see him."

I take that as a compliment. "I own a company where I only hire ex-armed forces men and women because of the specific needs of my clientele."

"Well, fuck me sideways. I thought that was you." The surprised man unfolds the magazine, turns it so that the smiling face on the cover stares up at me.

The twitch in Brumfield's downturned mouth pulsates. "Language!"

The friend ignores him. His wrinkled index finger taps the title across the top of the world's most recognized financial monthly periodical publication. "This is you? Bryan K. Hawk the fourth?"

"The one and only. I didn't serve, but I honor my country in other ways."

Their food arrives at the table. We eat and talk about my business. The conversation shifts when the friend asks how I balance a billion-dollar company and marriage. It gets a little touchy when I tell him we already have two daughters and a son on the way. I tiptoe around the fact that our girls are two months apart, but not twins. Brumfield's mouth twitches when his friend cusses or asks straightforward questions about my relationship with Dani. Yet his eyes brighten every time I describe how having her in my life has made me stronger.

I motion for both checks and apologize for leaving so soon. I'm meeting Amelia in fifteen minutes and want to get to the spot before her. The men thank me for letting them join me. I shake their hands before I leave.

"What kind of *man* fucks up a culinary masterpiece with a salad?" Eli scowls as he watches Bryan walk out the door.

"The kind who wants to be around for a long time with his wife and family, that's who."

"I'm just saying, Terry." He throws his hands up to let them fall to the table. "The homemade chips compliment the sandwich."

"Oh stop it. You're just trying to find a reason not to trust him. But you have none. Bryan isn't working for one of them. Everything he's done proves it. That boy genuinely loves Danielle. Wants to do right by her. Unlike James."

"Well, one of them is in bed with Islam Liberation Army and I can't figure out who."

"Elijah Hopper, you are too old for this stuff and George certainly can't help you. I beg you, properly introduce yourself and tell Bryan what's going on before it's too late."

A long breath of air expels from my friend's mouth. "Let's see how he handles the bombs in DC. Then I'll know for sure he's on our side."

"How many tests does Bryan have to pass to earn your trust? The minute he took Command he cleaned house. Changed procedures. Keeps an ear to the ground and stays on top of threats. Every person you've tried to sneak into Phantom, he's blocked. If Mills wasn't flipped from the inside, Hawk would know about him too. But after that attempt on Danielle's life, I bet they know about him now. Hawk is a far better leader than any of his predecessors. Don't condemn him because he wasn't military before joining Phantom. Elizabeth and Daniel turned over in their graves when you orchestrated that little plot to make him think his job was threatening Danielle's security. In spite of your efforts, that boy still found a way to take care of her, but in the background. You didn't know until *I* told you what he was doing. He brought her here when James returned from the dead. The only reason they are not legally married is because he asked the judge not to sign and file the paperwork and I'm sure that was more for Danielle's protection than him wanting to hold onto his bachelorhood. Just as strongly as you feel he's working for RAGS— I *know* he's not. I cleared him long before the ink dried on his contract. You of all people witnessed how well I did my job when I was a Phantom recruiter."

"Somehow one of them got a hold of your formula and made those deadly smoke bombs. It's become difficult to keep up with who're the good guys and who're the bad guys. I've been inside well past my years. Maybe it is time to tell Bryan."

———•———

I watch Amelia saunter toward me. Both hands in the pocket of the white jacket she's wearing. My elbow brushes the butt of my gun as I rise from my seat on the park bench. My grandmother told me to always stand for the woman I'm meeting, even if she's my enemy. The gesture will put them at ease long enough for me to gauge their intentions.

Amelia smiles and takes her hands out of the pockets. They swing freely at her sides. She picks up the pace. "Hi."

I nod and wait for her to sit first. The space between us is friendly enough that passersby don't mistake us for a couple.

"What's up?" she asks.

There's no need to dance around the subject. I keep my gaze on the people in the park. It's another nice early evening in Boulder, Colorado. With the time change, families stay later.

"This is the only chance you get to tell the truth. Who is Deidra Billups? And why did you sic her on Danielle?"

I don't have to be looking at her to know she's shaking. The small vibrations of the bench give her away.

"She's a friend from high school. We haven't talked since before I had the kid. I don't know why she'd go after your wife."

"Don't play this game, Amelia. I helped you get out because you said that wasn't the life you wanted to live anymore."

"Oh, so I'm Amelia now because someone's trying to off your precious Danielle?"

"Never forget, I have the power to make you Amelia Faye Goodman again. I'm sure RAGS would just *love* to see you alive and well. That kind of change in appearance must have cost millions."

"I swear, Bryan. I haven't been in touch with anyone from RAGS since you faked my death and paid for me to go to Switzerland for cosmetic surgery."

My cold gaze shifts to the woman seated next to me on the bench. She flinches. "When I track your phone what am I going to find?"

"Nothing." Her head shakes adamantly. Eyes wide. "I go to work. To the gym. And back home."

I push to my feet and adjust the sleeves of my jacket. "You can let your girlfriend know I'm going to put a bullet in her head when I catch up with her." I start to walk away.

"How's my little girl doing?" Amelia shouts.

I freeze and turn around. She's standing. Hands clutching the lapels of her jacket.

"You never wanted children, remember." This time I keep walking even though she asks again.

Vin gives the thumbs up as I climb into my truck. I knew Amelia was going to lie about Deidra. The whole reason for meeting her here was so that Vin could locate and reprogram the frequency blocker she installed in her car. Riley couldn't track Amelia's movements in the car because of it. And she's not smart enough to leave her cell phone at home when she's out doing dirt.

My personal cell phone rings when I get off the elevator on the fourth floor of my building. No need to check the caller ID. Tony's in my office. Ig is at his lab. And Vin's on his way back to his building to pack the weapons and gadgets we'll need for our trip. Dani has a special ringtone.

It's Willis calling. I send the call to voicemail. If something's going on at the house, I'll get a call from the men who are patrolling it. I close my office door, take off my jacket and roll up my sleeves. Tony and I need to concentrate on installing microchips on nine-ty-one bombs.

Somewhere around ten, my eyes start burning. I take out my contacts and put on my glasses. That's when I notice the red light on the phone's headset is flashing. "Riley, play voicemail messages."

"First voice message from—" There's a short pause then the call-er's voice says, "Retired Colonel Willis Percival Langford." Riley says the time stamp, then the recorded message plays. "Call me back."

Bastard. I laugh. Formal greeting and a command for a message. If he could, he'd still be Phantom's Second Command at the ripe old age of seventy-eight. I humor him because of who he is in our lives. Still, he needs to remember his place. He's not above an ass kicking.

"Second voice message from— Kourtney Allison Hawk… Sorry for yelling at you. We can do the garden when you're not so busy. I remember you."

I blink to clear my vision.

"Riley, call Willis Langford." Yeah, I know it's late and he's prob-ably asleep. He said to call, so I'm calling.

Langford answers on the second ring. We go through our usual *end of day report*. He wants to know if I've found someone for onsite Watcher duty. He's leaving for his trip on Monday. I don't reply. Instead, I ask if Marie is feeling better. He doesn't answer. As I'm about to end the call, Willis speaks up.

"I have extra time on my hands before I leave. Kourtney and I can start the garden since you're busy."

A kamikaze mix of emotions boils in me.

Should I or shouldn't I?

Fuck-it.

"Thanks for the offer. My daughter and I got this. Maybe if you'd spent time planting a garden with your own daughter twenty-nine years ago, she wouldn't have run away pregnant at age sixteen." I disconnect the call.

Yes, that was a low blow, but if he wants to drag my children into this he better be prepared to have his thrown in too.

The screensaver on the monitor lights up. The hawk stares at me. I reach out and tap its left eye. The hawk evaporates and is replaced by one of my favorite pictures. It's the picture of me holding my daughter for the first time. She was so little. Five pounds, fifteen ounces. The love I felt for her then is stronger today. "Bear with me just a little longer."

I access the cameras in my house and check on my girls. Kourt and Trevor are asleep. I wonder how Dani feels about being a two-dog family. Trevor is Kourt's through and through. He's replaced Mr. Cuddles, her original nighttime bed buddy. I'm not sure how I feel about that.

Of course, Emm's not in her bed. I switch to the camera in my room. She is snuggled up against her mom. Dani needs to set boundaries. I'm not sharing a bed with my wife *and* our daughter. I understand Kourt's frustration with Emm being clingy. I'm getting there and I'm not around much these days.

Tony's hand clamps down on my shoulder. "We're almost at the end. I feel it. Then you guys will be in the clear."

"I hope so."

CHAPTER FIFTEEN

I T'S MIDNIGHT WHEN I WALK through the inner garage door. I go through my nightly routine making sure the house is locked up, then head upstairs to check on the girls.

Kourt's room is my first stop. I kiss her cheek, pat Trevor's head, and close the door behind me.

A light from the room at the end of the hall shines through the gap between the base of the door and the hardwood floor. It casts my shadow on the wall. I knock.

The heavy footfalls of my sister come toward the door. It opens. Jessi stands to the side of the doorway wearing holey sweats and a worn, outstretched, faded shirt, a toothbrush in her mouth.

"That thing in Denver. Are you finished with it?"

"Yesss," she sings.

"Good. I'm going to need you to stick around the house more."

"Not a problem."

"Call Vin and schedule some time for the range."

"That serious?" she asks.

My lips tighten as I nod.

"I'll hold it down on the home front while you save the world, little brother."

It's been too long since I've told my big sister how much I love and appreciate her for always having my back, even when I'm wrong. I hug her. Tomorrow isn't promised, so I'm embracing mines today. I leave my sister standing in the doorway, the unexpected words and gesture surprising her.

Emm's curled around her mom in our bed. Both asleep.

I take a shower and put on pajamas.

As gently as I can without fully waking her, I untangle Emm

from around my wife, lift her into my arms, and carry her to *her* room and put her in *her* bed. I kiss my daughter's cheek, then jog back to my room and crawl in bed with my woman.

"Is everything okay?" Dani whispers.

"Just wanted to come home for a couple hours and hold you if that's okay."

She scoots closer. My shoulder becomes her pillow, my hand the blanket rubbing her stomach.

"Have you talked to Emm about why she's clinging to you?"

"Yes, we've talked about it."

"Does the conversation fall under doctor–patient confidentiality?"

The quick laugh from Dani shakes our bodies. "No, it was a mommy–daughter talk and I wasn't sworn to secrecy so I can disclose the information. She had a dream that I got hurt and went away and I wasn't her mom anymore. She looks out for me because she doesn't want to lose me. I asked her to tell me what I was doing in the dream that made me get hurt. She couldn't remember."

"I wonder what prompted the dream."

"She had a dream when they were with Mom and Dad for spring break. I asked her to tell me what made her the happiest about spring break with Grandma and Grandpa. She named: sitting outside with the nice older ladies at the special home that smelled like a doctor's office, going to the zoo, and painting pictures on the rocks around Grandpa's garden."

"What about the stable and Sweet Pea, and Kourt said they played with triplets?"

"The stables fell in the category of the saddest parts of spring break. She said being there wasn't as fun as she thought it would be."

"She didn't go into details?"

"No, and I didn't push. I know you and Kourtney think I'm being too accommodating with Emma, but something about that dream really frightened her. I'm helping her get through it and she is getting better. She's not on my hip every time I move around the house." Dani covers my hand on her stomach and adds a little pressure. A flutter brushes my palm. "What have you told Emma about her mother?"

The answer rolls off my tongue without a second thought. "You are her mother."

A breath of exaggerated air blows past her lips onto my shoulder.

"Oh, you mean the woman who gave birth to our precious daughter. I haven't told her anything about Amelia."

"Why not?"

Now would be the time I'd distract Dani with sex, but that valley of distance is too far to leap over and I don't want to miss the ledge and pummel to my death. I'm faced with two options. Tell her the truth or feed her a fact that has nothing to do with Amelia.

I opt for the fact. "It's almost over, Dani. We're close to bringing in RAGS's leader. We know his name and a location he frequents. We're going to DC to stop an attack. Don't go anywhere without your PPOs and carry that gun Vin gave you."

———◆———

I'm up and out before Dani and the girls wake up. I make sure the men guarding the house stepped up patrols. Now that Dani knows, they don't have to hide in treetops or inside Trojan trees when she and the girls are outside.

As onsite Watcher, Willis should have spotted them at the beginning of the year. None of his end of day reports noted movement around the property. Maybe it's time the Langfords retire. His mind hasn't been on his job for a while now. And it's taking Marie too long to shake that cold. I just hope taking care of four people instead of two isn't why her immune system has deteriorated so quickly.

The Watcher at the reception desk stands at attention when I enter through the lobby door. "Good morning, sir."

"You're Ross, right?"

"Yes, sir."

"Come see me at the end of your shift."

"Yes, sir."

The elevator door opens; I take it to the first floor. All video communications with POTUS are to be held in the SCIF until the moles are found and handled.

Everyone is already here except for Porter. I look at my watch. Zero, five, fifteen hours. The door will lock in exactly fifteen minutes. We eyeball each other. Smirks on our faces.

Vin's fingers fly across the keyboard of his laptop and the tracking chip on Porter's car shows us exactly where he is.

His car is doing eighty down a public main street a mile and a half away.

Vin accesses the dash camera.

We laugh as we watch Fontenot drive and Porter get dressed while wearing a seatbelt. He waits to the last minute to tell her to turn right.

I must say, Sophie Fontenot can drive. She makes the wide turn without braking, back tires surfing the pavement and kicking up smoke. The camera picks up the white clouds in the rear window. She remains in control of the vehicle. The look of pride on Porter's face is priceless.

They pull up in front of the building at zero five twenty-two. The couple kiss. *Yeah, we know that morning after kiss.* Porter jumps out of the car. Fontenot's head drops back to the headrest and she laughs nervously. Vin switches to the building's cameras.

Porter's running past the guard's station with the handle of his briefcase clamped between his teeth as he buttons his shirt, suit jacket in the crook of his arm. In the elevator he slips his arms in the jacket, reaches inside one pocket and pulls out a travel-sized bottle of mouthwash.

The elevator doors open and Porter looks around wide-eyed, then holds the bottle to his lips, the used mouthwash refills the small container.

By now, we're busting up laughing.

His rapid footsteps pound the concrete. We turn our chairs to face the door and wait. Ready to haze him when the door locks us in.

Porter runs in the room and the door closes behind him. Panting, he skids to a stop. The briefcase falls to the tile floor.

I don't have to look at the others to know we're all wearing the same blank gaze. Like the Elite team we are, we rise from our seats as one.

Porter stands at a seasoned soldier's attention, waiting for the reprimand.

We stalk toward him. Porter keeps his eyes front. All parts of him mannequin stiff.

I reach out and untuck the collar of his suit jacket. Smoothing it out for him.

Tony unbuttons his shirt then re-buttons it, the right way. Straightens the tie and pocket handkerchief.

Vin fixes his hair.

Ig re-loops his belt.

Porter stands there, clearly at a loss as to why we're adjusting his clothes instead of reprimanding him for being professionally late not timely late.

We stand back to survey the young man we've just dubbed our little brother.

Vin howls. "You're stomping like a big dog! Woof! Woof!"

"Man, I would'a pissed my pants if my girl took a turn like that going eighty." Tony shakes his hand.

"You got a little mouthwash—" Ig points to the corner of Porter's mouth.

I also shake his hand. "You're ready for Instructor Hawk. She'll teach you a hundred ways to make a woman come."

Porter's neck turns the color of a tomato. His fingers trail through his hair. He tucks his shirt into his pants and fastens his belt. "Did I mention Sophie street drag races?"

He waits for the shock to leave our faces. That five-foot-nothing young lady likes to drift? Porter apologizes again. We sit around the conference table assuring him we know all about that morning quickie, so he's forgiven.

We're so proud of him. Our crest already has a bird, cat, dog, and a reptile. We can add a fish. A piranha.

The video conference starts. President Hart sits in the office he really works out of. The Oval Office is for formal presentations.

President Hart is the first to speak. "The Department of Homeland Security along with the FBI and cross-trained law enforcement officers are gearing up and ready to deploy as soon as they have the names of the people to bring into custody. The search team has been advised not to engage the suspects or attempt to handle the bombs if they come across any that are left unattended. Why can't we just duplicate ninety-one smoke bombs? Why bring the real ones?"

"We don't have enough time to make exact replicas of ninety-one smoke bombs," I answer. "Distribution is going down today, during evening rush hour. Paul and Acosta already used three as testers. The casings were preserved, but they are filled with ordinary ingredients for an ordinary smoke bomb."

Paul leans forward. "Even if one of the carriers spots us and wants to connect the detonating wire it will take them a minute because it's not as simple as pushing it through a hole or pushing it down. The bomb will have to be steady when the wire box is opened and closed. They couldn't do it on the fly and not expose themselves to the contents. Once it is connected, the device is too hot to be moved even using a robot. RAGS do not use suicide bombers to further their cause."

"Our people will carry containment boxes that Paul designed based on the devices we're up against. They can be assembled to fit in any space at any angle. The containment seal is a quick hardening agent that will prevent ninety-seven percent of the smoke from seeping through," I tell him.

Acosta takes over from there. "The timeframe for life expectancy should anyone be exposed to the chemicals contained in the smoke bombs, even if it's as small as three percent, is six hours. Ricci re-engineered portable odorless gas meters to look like cell phones and Hawk designed the software for our people to use to detect gas seeping from the devices. If any are, we will have a two-man team posted at each station's entrance wearing Level A hazmat suits to handle the situation."

Vin and I go over our evacuation plans for POTUS should the situation call for it. We can't be certain that Edwards was the only mule. President Hart still refuses to leave DC but has sent the Vice President and those in the line of succession to opposite corners of the United States under heightened security. He is First Command of Phantom and we respect his decision to stay visible. I, however, press to have more of my people there to assist with the protection of him and his family. President Hart agrees. Chen has cleared all but five people in the investigation of the mole.

Larson checks in with Paul. The team touched down in Iraq. They are assembling a command center and surveying the area around the abandoned mosque. I hope they locate Selam and Solomon before the raids begin. If one person sounds the alarm, Edwards's wife and son will be killed. I won't give him an update until we have something solid to tell him.

Acosta's wings start flapping. He's reading a message on the laptop in front of him. "The results from the lint rollers are in. It's Elijah Hopper."

My thumb and index finger squeeze and release my eyebrows in a mechanical pattern. "What did you have to match it to?"

"I sent him the DNA report from the military file I found," Porter says.

"Of course, nothing's one hundred percent." His wings haven't slowed down.

"What about a probable match to a sibling or offspring?"

Paul's fingers tap the keyboard of his laptop. "He's never been married. Name doesn't appear on anyone's birth certificate. I found someone who could be his half-sister, Katherine Patton. Same father, different mothers. She married George Franklin."

My hand drops. "Back up. Did you say Katherine Patton married George Franklin?"

He nods.

"Dani's foster parents are George and Katherine Franklin."

Ricci reads from his laptop. "Katherine and George Franklin granted temporary guardianship of Danielle Lauren Tatum on February fifteenth, nineteen eighty-six. Given full legal guardianship on April third, nineteen eighty-six. Danielle Lauren Tatum was granted emancipation as a minor at age seventeen on February fourteenth, two thousand three."

"Where are her foster parents now?" Porter asks.

I know this answer without looking in Dani's file. "He's in a high-end nursing home for patients with Alzheimer's. Whatever George's pension and social security don't cover, Dani pays it. Katherine still lives in the house in Los Angeles."

They raise questioning eyebrows; *how do you know?*

"I monitor Dani's bank accounts and investment funds. Plus, she talks to Mrs. Franklin twice a month and sends her pictures of the girls to share with her husband."

Porter holds up a copy of the transcribed conversation. "Could that be the George that Hopper's talking about?"

I nod. It is possible.

"We know George will be arriving at the Denver airport on Friday. I'll search the airlines' manifests."

And that is exactly why I want Porter to work this with us. He's quick on his feet.

The deal on the quick sale purchase of the office building complex closes. It helps to have governmental backing to push these kinds of things through overnight. Hawkeye Personal Protection now owns the building where Hopper leases office space. As the new owner, I am contracting V.L. Ricci Security, Inc. to assess the building's current security system and upgrade it as soon as possible. I have Riley draft a letter to the tenants to let them know I will honor their current leases and have no intention of raising the rent. That should make them more open to embracing the new safeguards.

The puzzle pieces are beginning to fit together.

At seven hundred hours, I head up to my office to meet with Ross. Porter rides the elevator with me.

"What do you know about Ross?" I ask.

"We hung out a couple times, like in a group of us. I remember the last time we went to a club he was checking out the older women. If you need to know something specific, I can ask around."

The doors open on my floor. "No, that's okay." I head to my office and go straight to my desk. Ross's military file is on my screen. His CO is a Navy Phantom recruiter. The recommendation letter says the sailor's extensive knowledge of the complex's computerized guidance system coupled with a keen sense of observation and commitment to duty qualifies him for consideration.

Ross scored in the ninety-nine percentile for a Watcher. Ninety-eight percentile for both Sweeper and Field Operative. Ninety-seven for both Security and Delta Team. Had he scored a ninety-six or lower in any category, he wouldn't have made it to the next level.

Three thousand armed forces personnel test each year; only ten percent pass. Out of that ten percent, an average of five clear the background screening.

For Phantom, it's an invasive look into a person's past, which includes their entire family tree, friends, significant others. Anyone a recruit has come in contact with from birth to present is put under a microscope. Affiliation with known enemies of the state, no matter how small, will disqualify a candidate. Since becoming Second Command, that is one of the recruiting tools I enforced due to the number of RAGS moles I uncovered in our ranks after Langford resigned.

He thought micro managing every aspect of the operations kept the enemy out, but it had the opposite results.

I, on the other hand, built a team I trust to do their job. Paul, Acosta, Ricci, Chen, and I share our vision for Phantom.

Ross knocks on the door. I tell him to come in and have a seat.

When someone is told to meet me after their shift, it's usually for a next-level reprimand and they look scared. That isn't the case with Ross. He cruises across the room and sits in a chair in front of my desk.

I didn't see any disciplinary notes in his file; therefore he has no reason to be anxious about this meeting.

We exchange the obligatory greetings.

"How do you know the retired Colonel?"

"Colonel Langford came up to the nest a few times. We talked."

Willis said he *heard* Ross was a good Watcher. "What did you guys talk about?"

"The job mostly. And what I like to do on my downtime."

"Fishing, right?" It was in his file. He'd go fishing with his father and uncles in South Carolina.

"Yes, sir."

"Langford is the onsite Watcher at my residence. When he goes on vacation a Phantom Watcher is assigned to cover until he gets back. Is that something you'd be up to doing?"

Nodding vigorously, Ross says he's up for it. He pulls a mini pad from the inner pocket of his work jacket and unclips a writing pen from the breast pocket. Ross takes notes as I describe his duties. I let him know that Dani and the girls are home full time, but I do not tell him about the team guarding my home. Let's see if he's a better onsite Watcher than Langford.

I have Riley send a message to Willis informing him that Ross will shadow him starting today, then take over on Monday when he leaves for his *fishing* trip.

Dani doesn't sound too pleased when I call her and let her know about Ross. She said she doesn't like telling Kourt half-truths about why all these people are around all of a sudden and why they now have a safe word. Emm just goes with whatever Dani tells her; Kourt is a bear of a different color.

A lot goes into our travel arrangements, especially when we're taking equipment. The upside to this trip is we're going to DC, and not out of the country. Barrett did the final inspections on the plane before we arrived.

A late morning rain shower sweeps through Boulder. He helps us load the cargo.

The last piece of equipment is stored and the door closed and locked. I tell them to give me a second and I step to the side with my phone in my hand.

"Hello?" She answers on the second ring.

"Just wanted to let you know we're taking off. If you need to get in touch with me, go through Riley and the call will be forwarded right away." *What I really want to say is I love you and I miss you already.*

"Be safe." Her words are dry and I know why.

"I didn't tell Emm about that woman because Amelia never wanted to be a mother to begin with. I never want my daughter to feel unwanted, so I don't talk about that woman with her."

"Thank you, Bryan."

A clap of thunder rumbles overhead. Tony's motioning for me to hurry up.

"I have to go. I'll call you when I can." I disconnect the call and board the plane.

Barrett turns on the seat belt sign and reviews the safety guidelines over the intercom. It's regulations and he's a by-the-books person so we sit and listen.

The plane moves in line and waits for clearance. I stare out the window at nothing in particular. My mind replays that last conversation with Dani. I should have told her last night why Emm knows nothing about Amelia. I should have told her last night that Amelia is alive and here in Boulder. Maybe we could have resolved this suffocating distance and gotten back on the same page last night.

After take-off and the seat belt sign is turned off, I count to three and mentally flip the switch to monster mode. We pull out laptops and maps and review what we're going to DC to accomplish.

Three hours and twenty minutes later, we're landing at the airport in Virginia. Two black Escalades are parked in the hanger where the plane will be secured while we're here.

We load equipment into the trucks and head to 1600 Pennsylvania Avenue.

It's a short drive and we enter the grounds via an alternate entrance. President Hart meets us in the Phantom office. Porter is a little star stricken.

I immediately log into our network and enter my itinerary and the number to the secured phone I'm carrying while we're here in our nation's capital.

POTUS hands us all-access passes so we can move about the grounds without question, then leaves for a meeting. He'll be in and out of this office as time permits.

Porter and I upload the website that we're using for the purpose of identifying the ninety-one people carrying the bombs, and Hopper.

Acosta's wings flap so fast I'm surprised he's hasn't levitated off the seat. He's super excited to be here and can't wait to get started.

Ricci is mapping out an alternate plan to secure POTUS in the event there are other bombs or there are moles here in the White House. This one will differ from the one in place should there be a missile attack, invasion, imminent terrorist attack. The goal is to get POTUS in the air, not underground.

Paul and Acosta go to the command center set up for the team who will neutralize the bomb carriers. In the controlled environment, Paul and Acosta will teach the men and women how to handle the bombs.

Porter will stay in the Phantom office and act as Watcher. He'll also monitor the activities in Boulder.

My first destination is the situation room.

I like walking the halls of the White House. It's another perk of the job. I want to bring Kourt here. She'd probably try and take it all in in one day.

"Bryan?"

I cringe at the screech of the woman calling my name and sauntering toward me with a smile on her face.

"Bryan Hawk, is that you?" Gloria Perry approaches with the intention to hug me.

I gently redirect the gesture to a friendly handshake with an extra squeeze to ease the sting of rejection. "Yes, it's me. How are you?"

"I'm doing well. Hey, I read that article the magazine did on you. Wow, so Hawkeye is doing that good? I'm happy for you." She moves to rest her hand on the breast pocket of my jacket. It's an intimate gesture of familiarity.

Again, I redirect her and put a little more distance between us.

"What are you doing here in Washington?" She shifts the folders in the crook of her arm.

"Time to renew government contracts. I was just on my way to a meeting."

"We should get together for a— drink." Lip caught between her teeth, Gloria's eyes remove my clothing, settling on the area of my package.

It's a turn on when my wife eye rapes me. I'm put off when other women do it. "My schedule is packed while I'm here."

Gloria's gaze shifts around the busy hallway before she steps into my personal space. I fix a pointed glare in my eyes. She ignores it and brushes her breast against my arm as she leans in to whisper in my ear.

"My office is still in the same place it was two years ago. I would love for you to come in for a...quickie."

"I have a better proposition. The next time you're in Boulder, my wife and I will take you out to dinner."

Gloria jerks back. Eyes wide. Her gaze drops to the band on my left hand. "You're joking, right?"

"It was good seeing you." I step around the stunned woman and don't look back. It's times like this I'm happy all my no-strings-attached flings were in other states. Don't shit in your own yard, you will step in it one day.

Dani gets a kick out of watching women react to me, and how I, the gentleman that I am, politely turn them down. I doubt she'd be as amused if she saw how a woman I've actually slept with reacts to seeing me again.

I'm not as generous when it comes to men checking out my wife and I'd definitely be on the warpath if I came upon one who's actually slept with her. Lucky for me, she's only been with one person.

The President's Emergency Operations Center is the final destination on my circuit of the White House. It's my favorite place. Although it's existence is known to the world, Hollywood hasn't come close to capturing its full functionality or its size. I go through a series of identification protocol before I'm allowed inside.

Power.

The energy produced by this bunker is— power.

I breathe it in and get to work.

With Riley's help, I test the communications systems between the presidential bunker and my bunker back home, hidden underneath the pond. In case of an emergency and POTUS is relocated to the bunker, my team and I go underground too.

The vibration in conjunction with a staccato alert comes from the phone attached to the belt holster. It's time for me to head back to the Phantom office to get ready for our real purpose for being in our nation's capital.

I take the long way back to avoid running in to Gloria again. People in a hurry zigzag around me as I stroll the West Colonnade. I turn down another corridor and make it to the wall-sized portrait of President Woodrow Wilson. Behind it is the entrance to Phantom's office. I key in the code and the door opens.

"Hold the door," Acosta shouts. He and Paul are jogging this way.

Ricci is already seated at one of the stations working with Porter. "According to the real-time data, there have been seven attempts to hack military satellite communications in the past hour that have not registered with the Department of Defense."

"Have you been able to trace it?"

Porter nods. "Yes. It's coming from the residence of a Presidential cabinet member."

Her picture comes up on the wall monitor. Secretary of Health and Human Services, Nora Owens.

It's time.

CHAPTER SIXTEEN

I LOVE MY JOB. CUSTOM-MADE WEAPONS hidden on my person. Advanced technological gadgets. This time, I don't mind the closely tailored suit. I look good and I'm ready to take on RAGS. End their reign of terror on the United States.

After today, Dani is free. Our secret is safe.

We're coming up on the traffic circle on Massachusetts Avenue NW, Barrett at the wheel of the mini-van. Ig's got the underground music going. We're thirty minutes ahead of rush hour. And five minutes behind a Ford the same make and model of the one Edwards had in Boulder; we brought the license plates with us—it's all in the small details.

The Ford is being driven by a Sweeper who fits Edwards's description. All ten duffle bags in the car. Edwards was told to leave it unlocked and parked at the Metropolitan Garage. It's the closest to the Bethesda station.

I can't help but to be excited. This is the shit I get off on being a ghost. I'm confident once we have the ninety-one carriers in custody, we can *persuade* them to plea deal and give up the others.

Barrett turns onto Wisconsin Avenue. The station is in the heart of the business district in Bethesda, Maryland.

We go through our rituals.

I carefully unfold the picture of me holding my baby girl and kiss it. The photo is starting to show signs of wear and tear. I could print another one, but I can't duplicate the handwriting that describes what happened to make this particular photo so special. I tuck it next to my heart.

The van stops two blocks away. Ig is the first to step out. As always, I'm the last man out. We look like Fortune 500 executives just getting off work. Optical sunglasses covering our eyes, we pull out our phones and follow the other business folks to the station's entrance.

On the platform, we spread out.

The microchips Tony and I added to the devices are numbered. Once a bomb is removed from the bag, the chip gives off a signal that flashes on our phones. If the trigger wire is connected, the number is red and we'll cause a commotion that will prompt law enforcement to block the entrance to prevent the carrier from entering the station. If the number is green, the carrier will enter the station and we'll digitally identify them. The number will flash on our screen when the device is five feet from one of us.

We each have a one-way earpiece tucked in our ears. Chen can't hear us, but we can hear him. Two-way frequencies are much easier to pick up. He'll direct the other Phantom ghosts who are riding the rails, which train the carrier is on and what the device is being carried in.

Porter is the first to get a hit. He accidently on purpose bumps into the carrier and apologizes, by patting the man on the shoulders while his phone zeroes in on the device. It's in the backpack. Porter touches the frame of his optical glasses, snapping a picture of the guy. It automatically uploads to the website. I look at the image. Male. Caucasian. Bald head. Gray eyes. Mid-twenties. Five ten. Hundred sixty pounds.

Not the guy I'm waiting for.

A seventy-eight-year-old Black male, five ten, thinning salt-and-pepper hairline, beer belly and military posture is who I'm on the lookout for. I don't expect him to be a carrier. Edwards claims Hopper isn't the one behind the attack, but if I were him, I'd be here to see who shows up. Take note of which ones are stabbing me in the back. Sit by them on the train and hold a conversation.

Hopper's a different type of leader. He hides from his people, whereas I like for them to see me. That could be the reason the entity is starting to crumble and his position is being challenged. No one believes he's real anymore.

At the seventeen-hundred hour mark the platform starts to fill up with people getting off work. I constantly scan the crowd. At one point, I zero in on a woman who looks like Marie from the back except this salt-and-pepper-haired grandmother is groping a younger man and wearing tight-fitting clothes. Marie is more conservative with the way she dresses, and certainly wouldn't be all over a man a few years older than her granddaughter.

Ricci is the next to get a hit. He moves around the platform until he comes across the person. Ricci drops his briefcase. It pops open, the carrier helps him retrieve the papers and pens. He scans her and touches the frame of his glasses as he says thank you. The device is in her purse. Her image loads. It's newly elected Congresswoman Chandra Mann.

A presidential cabinet member and now a congresswoman. It'll be interesting to see how many more step into the sunlight.

Number eight flashes on my screen as the carrier walks toward me. I stop him and ask for directions.

At eighteen hundred hours, we've identified sixty-eight carriers. Armed forces personnel, commissioned and noncommissioned. Elected officials. Heads of international corporations. Law enforcement officers. Regular people. Males and females are evenly matched. Various ages and ethnicities. Still no Hopper. I'm not giving up. I can't go home until we have him.

I can't face Dani if I fail.

The second team of Sweepers and Field Operatives take over. There are only so many times a person can slightly change their appearance before someone starts to take notice. The platform is still busy.

A distinctive whistle sounds out over the noise of people talking. I look up from my phone. Acosta points to the escalator. Stepping off is a gentleman fitting Hopper's description. I can't see his face because of the snapback cap with the army insignia he's wearing. Everything down to his gaited walk tells my gut it's him. His head turns left to right like he's searching for someone.

Paul and I approach from opposite ends.

All at once the last twenty-three devices show up on our screens and a train is approaching.

Do I give up Hopper and help the guys identify the carriers? Or, do I let carriers get away and go after Hopper? The team watches me, waiting for a decision.

Shit!

I signal to go after the carriers.

———————

"Hey, little sis," he says when I answer the phone.

I reach over and turn on the lamp on the nightstand and look at the pony clock. It's nine thirty. "Is Bryan okay? What happened, Tony? Oh god, please don't tell me he's hurt."

"Calm down, Dani. No, he's not hurt, but he's hurting."

"What do you mean?"

"He made a tough call. It was the right one, but he feels like he's let you down."

"I don't understand. Let me down how?"

Tony exhales then tells me about their trip to Washington DC. The leader of the organization that threatens my life was there and Bryan had to decide to take down one man or the last twenty-three who posed a threat to thousands. I made the choice for us to stay and fight and that's exactly what he did.

"Did he say he let me down?"

"We don't have to say how we feel. As brothers, we just know it."

"Where is he?"

"The office. We've been back since yesterday evening. When we touched down he told us to go home and he went back to the office to work. This morning he didn't sit in on the debriefing. Told me to write up a summary and he'll read it later. He needs you, Dani."

"Thanks for calling me, Tony."

I end the call and lie there for a minute.

I promised to love Bryan unconditionally and walk beside him. Travel this journey with him. Step for step. Fall for fall. Run for run. Fight for fight. I haven't been living by that promise. The engagement and wedding rings are collecting dust on his nightstand. I took them off because I thought they didn't mean anything to him. I watched our wedding video and cursed myself for standing there being all in love.

But in his own way, he told me the truth then: *I am your protector even when it seems that I'm not. This is real. We are real… what we have will be tested, but my love for you will not falter.*

No amount of training can teach a person to speak with that much emotion, because it comes from the soul.

I laugh to myself. He avoids people. I give people the silent treatment. Kourtney is moody. Emma is turning out to be the normal one in the family.

Careful not to wake her, I ease out of Emma's bed and rush out of her room.

I fast walk down the hall to Jessi's room. Her light is still on. I knock on her door.

"Can you listen out for the girls? I'm going over to Bryan's office."

Her smirk and knowing eyes start at my feet, then work their way up.

"Sure, not a problem, little sister. But come on, let big sis help you get fixed up." She grabs my hand and we fast walk to the other side of the house. "Go shower. I'll find you something to wear."

While I'm in the shower, she brings in four dresses for me to choose from. I pick the one that buttons down the front.

Jessi approves of the selection.

I moisturize my body and wrap a towel around me and walk back into the bedroom.

Jessi laid out the dress on the bed. She's rummaging through the closet.

I stand in the doorway watching her, horrified by the mess on the floor. Dresser drawers dangling from their slots. "What are you looking for?"

"The lingerie you bought back in December. Where is it?"

"My booty is too big and breasts too large to fit into that lingerie."

She opens another drawer. "You won't be wearing it for long. It's been too quiet in this bedroom. I know you guys are going to rip each other's clothes off. Oh, I packed you an outfit to come back home in." She gestures to the satchel hanging on the door handle.

"You are going to clean up the mess your making in my closet, aren't you?"

"Sure you are," she chuckles and finally comes across the drawer I stashed the lingerie in. "Here, put these on while I get your blow dryer. Bryan can't take his eyes off you when your hair is sporting the natural curls look." She hands me sheer green bikini panties and the matching bra, then leaves the closet.

The body moisturizing cream makes it easy for me to wiggle into the panties. The material screams for relief from being tortured and stretched. The cups of the bra look more like see through pasties than an actual bra, but hey, this is for Bryan, not me. Well, me too because it's been *too* long since we've had sex.

I pick up my robe off the floor and put it around me and go sit at my vanity by the glass doors.

Jessi walks out of the bathroom with the dryer in her hands.

"Take off the comb attachment," I tell her.

"You're not going to scream like Kourtney, are you?"

"I'm not tender headed like her and her father."

We laugh.

Over the noise of the blow dryer, Jessi and I review my strategy. Bryan uses sex as a means for interrogation; I'm using sex as therapy for my husband.

When she's done, I drop the robe and put on the dress and go stand in front of the full-length mirror.

My breasts look like they're about to burst out of the top of the dress. I turn to the side. My chest poke our more than my stomach. I turn to the back and look over my shoulder. Wow, I'm boobs, hips, and booty for this pregnancy.

Jessi unbuttons the first two buttons.

"I can't walk through the lobby of his building looking like this."

"Take the elevator from the garage."

"There are cameras everywhere in that building."

Jessi runs back into the closet and comes back with a lightweight cream-colored shawl with fringe and wraps it around me. "Take it off before the elevator door opens."

I sit on the edge of the bed and slide my feet into the wedge sandals she pulled out for me to wear.

I grab my keys, phone, and wristlet purse and start for the door, then stop.

I go back.

"Thank you, Jessi. I love you." I throw my arms around my sister-in-law.

"I love you too, Dani. You guys are good for each another."

I go to his nightstand, dust off the wedding ring and engagement ring and slip them on my finger. Bryan is my husband, maybe not in the legal definition of the title, but where it counts— in my soul. I rush out the bedroom door.

"Hey, no running in those wedges," Jessi warns.

———◆———

An alert from the front desk pops up the screen. I pick up the phone and press the button. "What is it, Zimmerman?"

"Sir, Mrs. Hawk was just dropped off. She's taking the elevator from the garage."

I release the button, push back from the conference table, and stretch, then walk out of my office and go stand by the elevator.

The doors open.

Dani jumps like I startled her. She finishes the motion of unwrapping the sweater with frilly stuff. A smiles spreads across her lips.

My gaze drops to where the tops of her breasts are pushing out of the green dress she's wearing. I guess they're too big for her to get the buttons closed.

Her hair is down. My fingers itch to get tangled in the curls. I'm always reminded of the first time I met Dani, when her hair was curly like this. I know it sounds cliché, but my outlook on relationships changed that day.

I check out the woman who makes me want to be her husband. Be the man who slays the bad guys so this world is safe for her.

The dress stops midthigh to show off her long legs and toned thighs and sexy curves. She hasn't gained much weight, but no one could mistake that she's carrying my son.

"Hi," Dani says.

"Hi." I step aside and gesture with my hand for her to lead the way to my office.

Oh yeah, that dress is hugging her like skin.

Dani stops at the conference table. "If you're busy, I'll leave."

I relieve her of her sweater and bag. "No. I need to take a break. My eyes were starting to cross." I lead her to the sofa. "Is everything okay?" I hang up her things on my way to the refrigerator. I pour her a glass of water and add a cucumber slice.

"Yeah," she sighs. "Everything's fine." She accepts the glass. I sit on the other end of the sofa and sip my water. "No, everything isn't okay. Bryan, are you sleeping with somebody else?"

What the... "No!... What are you... Why would you think that?"

She sets the glass on the table and takes a deep breath. "Why didn't you come home when you got back from DC? Why aren't you sleeping in our bed?" She looks around the office. "It sure doesn't look like you sleep here." Her eyes settle on me. "Yes, I was angry and hurt and distant. I apologize for my actions. But now you're being distant. Either you're seeing someone else or you're hiding from me again. So, which is it?"

"Hey." I reach out and take her hand, pulling her closer to me.

"Be honest. Is there someone else?"

My desk phone beeps. "Sir, Prince Jawad is on line two."

Dani jumps up from the sofa. "It's ten thirty at night, Bryan. Why is your secretary still here? Alone with you in the office?" Fire is shooting from her eyes now.

"Sir?" Riley asks.

"He's busy!" Dani yells, her gaze sweeping the office.

I try not to laugh. "Take a message, Riley."

"Roger that, sir."

It occurs to me that I've never told Dani about Riley. I go to my wife and attempt to wrap my arms around her. She shoves away from me, which makes me laugh out loud.

"I can give you something to laugh about, Bryan." She kicks off her shoes. Mama Hawk's threatening to wreak havoc in my office.

I walk over to the conference table and turn on the television mounted to the wall. "Riley, introduce yourself to Mrs. Hawk."

The virtual image instantly appears. "Good evening, Mrs. Hawk, also known as Delta. Lima. Hotel. Nine. Zero. Five. Eight. I am Riley. Riley stands for real-time, interactive-intelligence, localhost, encryption, yottabyte. Colonel Hawk created me to operate as a single device with many technological capabilities."

Dani gasps. "Why do you look like me?"

"I'm sorry, I do not understand the command."

"Bryan, your computer secretary looks like me!"

"I am a virtual ghost."

"Bryan?"

I laugh. "Riley, alpha list calls only. You're dismissed."

"Roger that, sir." The monitor goes blank.

"To break it down in simple terms, Riley is a real-time super-computer I built. It operates on an interactive intelligence software I designed and update frequently since technology constantly changes. The U.S. armed forces' networks are on a loop-back through Riley which Phantom monitors for the purpose of detecting breaches. Due to the nature of what we do, Riley encrypts outgoing communications and deciphers encrypted messages floating in cyberspace. The hard drive for a computer this vast requires a data center the size of a small state. Mine is very well hidden underground. No one really pays attention to the fact that I give simple verbal commands and Riley responds with precise words. The more complex commands are given manually along with guidance for completing the tasks. Riley is not a she. Riley is not one of those Hollywood supercomputers that talks and thinks or threatens to take over the world. Riley is a machine. Its virtual image is inspired by you because you inspire me. *You* are my everything."

Dani smiles. "Nice save, Hawk."

I point to the sofa. "That has a pull-out sleeper. When I'm here overnight I sleep on it. You've seen the bathroom so you know I can shit, shower, and shave here if I need to. Don't forget I know you, Danielle Lauren Hawk. Asking me if I'm having an affair isn't the reason you came here tonight." If she really thought I was screwing around she would have confronted me wearing kickboxing gear and her face covered in petroleum jelly. "Which one called you?"

Dani's hand cups my cheek. "Anytime *you* shut yourself off and they can't pull you out, your best friends worry. I worry. I want them to call me when you're hurting because you can lean on me." She smiles. "Bryan, I've made a couple decisions. First, you and I are no longer giving RAGS power over us. You did the right thing and I'm so very proud of you. I'm a healer, that is my job and it gives me joy to help people work through their issues and be a better person. But if those smoke bombs had killed anyone because you chose me over them, I couldn't be a healer anymore. How do I live with myself knowing I heal people mentally yet my man allows people to be harmed because of me? You will get another shot at him."

I pull my wife into my arms and hold her.

Really hold her.

"What's the other decision you've made?"

"We're going to tell Kourt…"

I don't let her finish. My head is shaking so fast I'm getting dizzy.

"Hear me out, Bryan."

I let her go and make it to the bar in four determined strides. Ice cubes clink against the glass. I smother them with a healthy pour of scotch. Hard liquor isn't my thing, but I need something to stave off the panic that is trying to overthrow me.

In the mirrors on the bar, I watch Dani approach me. She takes the glass from my hand before it touches my lips and sets it on the bar. I didn't realize I'd stopped breathing until she loosens my tie and unbuttons the top buttons. Her hands slide up and down my chest, our gazes lock. I follow her breathing until I start to calm.

"Usually when something's bothering her, she crawls into my lap or she asks me to cuddle and we talk. She hasn't done that in a long time. Lately, Kourtney's been quick tempered and rebellious. She doesn't sleep with Mr. Cuddles anymore. And ever since that thing with Ms. Williamson and the family history report, she's been really impatient with Emma. Before it escalates from verbal impatience to physical aggressiveness, you and I need to sit down and find out what's bothering her."

My scalp is burning. "I don't see how telling her will make her be nicer to her sister. Kourt asked me who would I save if there was a fire and I could only save one of them. We tell her what I did and she'll think I don't love her."

Dani reaches with both hands to loosen my fingers in my hair. "Bryan, I understand your fears and will help you explain it in a way that she'll accept."

"Trust me, Dani. She won't." I push past her and go to the window. Downtown Boulder at night sums up how I feel inside. Dark and empty.

Dani's reflection in the glass grows larger as she walks up behind me. Her hand slides down my back. She steps in front of me.

My vision blurs. The lump in my throat is blocking my airway. "Please let this be one we take to the grave."

Dani holds my cheek in her hand. It's a touch of understanding, but it's not the one that I associate with us. The touch that is just ours.

The unshed tears make her eyes as light as mine. I start to pull away, then her thumb brushes my bottom lip.

The shift in the air between us is noticeable.

The floodgates of locked up emotions are about to be breached. Dani places the other hand over my heart. The tip of her thumb traces my bottom lip again. It's what I'd been waiting for. The touch that made me feel something I'd never felt with a woman. Loved.

Need takes over. I reclaim what is mine. My hands capture her head as I back her up against the glass and attack her mouth.

Greedy for a taste.

My queen lets me in right away, matching my hunger.

In the recesses of my mind, I tell myself to be gentle. Her hard stomach presses into me.

One of us, or maybe both of us moan. It's hard to tell.

Dani fumbles with the buttons on my shirt. My fingers tighten around the material and pull. The sound of the tear ricochets off the walls and buttons hit the glass wall and the tile floor.

I lift Dani off her feet without breaking the kiss. Her legs rope around my waist.

Somehow, I get us over to the sofa without falling and sit her on the cushion.

She watches me like I'm the main attraction at her private strip show. I make quick work of my belt and pants. I stand in front of her in navy blue socks.

The hawk dancing in her face.

If she does not want this I will back off. I've always given her the final say so.

The turn up of a corner of her mouth mixed with a cocked eyebrow and a nod is the green light. Her fingers push a button through its hole on her dress.

The light from the lamp reflects off the metals on her finger.

I drop to my knees and capture her hand.

"This time, they are glued to my finger," she whispers.

I bring her hand up to my lips, then lean in to kiss her. My fingers work the rest of the dress's buttons.

Every button I push through a hole is followed by a kiss to show how much I've missed her. Dani's reactions show me how much she's missed me too.

A soft peck on the temple. Her eyes close and nipples harden.

Quick peck on each eyelid. Her lips part and a sexy breath of air escapes.

A lingering peck on the cheek. Her thighs open wider and the spot in the cusp of her neck pulsates at twice its normal speed.

There are ten buttons on her dress; by the time I reach the last one, my wife is on her back panting.

I peel the dress open and stare at my woman wearing a see-through bra that can't contain her breasts yet restrains her brown nipples. And the see-through panties that enclose her hairless pussy and shine with her wetness.

Hmm, where do I start?

My fingers brush down the center of her body. The breath catches in her lungs and her pelvis rolls. She is more sensitive to the touch.

I have no desire to play the number game.

The motions of her breasts hypnotize me. I palm them and squeeze. Her thighs press together. I don't bother with the front clasp of the bra. My teeth capture a chocolate brown nipple inside its wrapper.

Dani's hand cups the back of my head as her back arches up, pushing deeper in my mouth. Her moans are a stroke to my inner ego. I like knowing I have sole ownership of every single sexual experience she's had. Dani is my queen.

I twist and pull the other chocolate treat. She cries out. I keep an eye on her to gage pleasure versus pain. Her breasts are really tender with this pregnancy.

My mouth switches to the other nipple.

She bucks.

Dani takes my hand, leading it down her body until it's between her legs.

Together we rip the material of the panties. She tosses it and recaptures my fingers.

We fondle the hood of her clit.

Our fingers trace the lips of her pussy. Spreading the wetness. Testing to see if she's ready.

We penetrate and stroke her walls.

Dani's meeting the action of our fingers with every thrust and roll of her hips. She's never been afraid to show me what she wants in bed. I don't mind being the follower. That type of sexy confidence is an ultimate turn on, and the view isn't bad either.

The hawk bounces and twitches, eagerly waiting his turn to be snug in the warmth of Sunshine.

We stroke faster.

"Please— Bryan." My name is song like a note being held.

I watch her. Waiting for that second before she holds her breath, unable to stop the orgasm.

She sucks in air and I lift her up and then sit down with Dani squatting over me. I grip my dick while the other hand on her waist guides her down on me.

Welcome home.

Sunshine is hot and wet and tight. She molds around me. Contracting and drawing me in deeper. Her heat hugs me.

Dani holds onto the back of the sofa. She bounces. Riding that good feeling.

It's been too long and I can't hold back. My feet press into the rug, my hips push upward. Over and over.

The applause goading us on.

Dani's close to a second orgasm, her juices are thick and heavily coating me.

I feel my lips moving, but I don't know if words are spoken. My brain shuts off as the moment of transparency spreads through me. My guard is down. I'm exposed. I share my soul with Dani. The gratification lifts me up. Her walls clench. My thigh muscles strain to hold the position as I release inside her.

I relax and push her naturally curly hair off her face and attack her mouth. Dani shifts to put her weight on her knees. The movement makes the hawk slip out of her. A wave of electricity shoots through my sac, but I don't break the kiss. I make out with my wife until she's out of breath.

She holds me and I hold her. We don't move or talk. My wife and I reclaim what was snatched from us in that courtyard. Our closeness. Our intimacy. Our untraditional relationship that works for us.

"I love you."

"I love you more."

We hold each other for a moment longer.

I gaze over her shoulder and laugh.

"What's so funny?" Her lips press into my neck.

"I've never had sex in my office. We left the door open."

Dani jerks back. Eyes wide open. She looks over her shoulder. "Is anybody besides us on this floor?"

"I don't think so."

"What?!"

My eyebrows stretch toward my hairline and I scratch the back of my head. "I mean I'm pretty sure we're the only ones here."

She dismounts and reaches for the remains of my shirt. "Bryan! That isn't funny. What if someone saw us? Or heard us?" Only the top two buttons are still attached. Another one is dangling by a breath.

"If they did it's too late to do anything about it." I stand and strut over to the door. Closing it and locking it. When I turn around, she's staring at my thighs. The theme music plays through my mind. "Now stand back, so I can pull out the bed, and take my time with you." I slow strut back.

Dani picks up her glass of water and moves away. She walks over to the bar and pours herself another.

I shove the coffee table to the side, toss the cushions over the back of the sofa, and pull out the bed. I'm happy I changed the sheets this morning.

Something occurs to me as I watch Dani over at the bar. Whenever she got too close to the truth or the topic of conversation is uncomfortable for me, I resort to sex to get her off topic instead of talking it through with her. If I'm going to have a real relationship with Dani, I need to change my ways.

"Dani, can we talk about this thing with Kourt?"

CHAPTER SEVENTEEN

"WAKE UP, SLEEPYHEAD. WHERE'RE THE plans for the garden?" I bounce on my knees on Kourt's bed. Trevor barks and jumps with me.

She cracks one eye open, looks at the clock, then groans, covering her head with a pillow. "It's five ten in the morning, Dad." She yawns from behind the pillow. "It's too early to get up."

"I'm going to go wake up Emm. Get up. Put on some old clothes and be downstairs in twenty minutes." I take the pillow off her head, tossing it on the floor.

Across the hall, I open Emm's door and bounce on her bed too. She pulls the covers over her head. "Are you crazy, Dad?"

"Nope. Get up. You're going with me and Cuddles."

"Is Mommy going?"

"Nope. We're having a daddy-daughter day."

"No, thank you. You and Kourty can go."

I pull back the cover and lift her out of bed. "Go wash your face, brush your teeth, put on some old clothes, and be downstairs in twenty minutes." I push her toward the bathroom and run out.

I poke my head back in Kourt's room. "Nineteen minutes," I yell. Kourt sits up in the bed, frowning, her dog licking her. "Thanks to Trev, you don't have to wash your face. Now get dressed."

I jog to the other side of the house and join Dani in the shower. She greets me with a smile and soapy towel. We spent the night at my office, talking and reconnecting and sexing.

Today, I'm giving her an early Mother's Day gift. A day without the girls. Max is coming to pick her up and they will spend the day shopping and doing whatever else they do when they're together. Which I'm sure will be something they have no business doing.

"I've got fifteen minutes to shower, get dressed, and meet the girls downstairs. So keep your hands to yourself."

Her gaze drops to my feet. Snakes up my legs. Wrapping around the hawk.

"Hey." I lift her chin. "Eyes up here." My hand mimes wiping my face.

"I know, but I like your thighs better."

"No-no. Up here." I point to my face.

"Are you sure we can't..." Her voice trails off as her fingernail outlines of the symbols tattooed on my ribcage.

Be strong!

"Fine." She pouts. "But can you wash my back?"

I catch the towel she tosses as she pivots and bends at the waist. Hands on the bench. Dani hikes up her butt and looks back at me. I lose the grip on the towel. The hawk stirs.

I forgot how much fun sex in the shower with a horny pregnant Dani can be.

Of course that shower quickie makes me late. Her laughter taunts me as I run out of the bedroom wearing a tracksuit and go make sure the girls are ready for our daddy-daughter day.

Kourt is sitting on the edge of her bed, tying the laces of her sneakers. I knock and open Emm's door. She is lying under the cover.

I go to her dresser and find a pair of old jeans and a T-shirt and toss them on her bed. I know she's awake. "Get up, Emm."

In the closet, I pull out a pair of sneakers and grab a sweatshirt off the shelf. When I come out, she's sitting in the middle of the bed.

"Why isn't Mommy going?" Emm whines.

I pick up her brush from that vanity thing Dani bought her and walk back over to the bed. "I've already told you: this is a dad-dy-daughter project." I brush her hair into a ponytail and wrap a holder around it to keep it in place.

"Get dressed, Emm." The extra bass in my voice is a warning that she heeds. I step out of the room and wait for her in the hallway.

Kourt stands in her doorway, her lips turned down. Arms folded. Her dog by her side. "Go let him out to do his business. By the time he's done, Emm should be ready."

"Lets go potty, Trev," she says.

He barks and runs off.

After three knocks and a final warning, Emm's door finally opens. Strands of hair hang loose from the holder. Shoelaces untied. I drop to one knee and tie them.

"Who's going to make sure Mommy doesn't get hurt?"

I'm trying to keep from yelling at her. Dani doesn't have a hard time getting them to their mommy-daughter day outings. I take her by the hand and lead her downstairs. She protests.

"Just leave her here, Dad," Kourt demands and Trevor barks in agreement.

"No, the three of us are going to spend the day together. Mom has other plans."

Emm plants her feet on the floorboards. "Where is she going?"

"Out with Uncle Max. Now come on."

"I'm going with Mom!" Emm stomps her foot.

When did she start doing this foot stomping shit?

"Stop being such a cry baby!" Kourt stomps back. Trevor prances, siding with her.

"I'm not crying, Kourty!"

"Yeah you are, Emmy!"

"That's enough shouting. We're going to the nursery." I start for the door, holding Emm's hand. Trevor's barking and jumping around. "Quiet down, Trevor, before I leave you here." He runs to the door like *no you're not.*

"I'm sitting in the truck till it's time to come home." Emm pulls against me.

"That's fine. Me and Dad don't need your help anyway."

"Blah, blah, blah," Emm mimics. "Digging in the dirt is for boys."

"Making a butterfly garden is for anyone," Kourt defends.

"You're such a tomboy."

Kourt gasps and Trevor barks.

"Enough, you two." I manage to get them in the truck and we head to the nursery.

It's another cool Boulder morning. Few clouds in the sky. This is the perfect day to start the garden.

The nursery is eleven miles from us. Tony knows the owner well.

My first impression of the small nursery is that it will have a limited selection of the plants we're looking for. Once I drive through the gates I'm forced to change my mind. There are rows and rows of flowers and plants and lawn decorations and planters. Beginner to professional, this nursery offers everything a person needs. And the outside effectively hides the amount of land it sits on.

The minute we get out of the truck, Emm uses her phone to check up on Dani. I take it from her, tell my wife to have fun, and end the call.

Emm glares at me— looking just like the woman who gave birth to her.

I leave her standing there while Kourt and I look for the gardening tools on our list.

This is supposed to be a group project. I use Emm's eye for color to make her a part of this garden. "Can you help Kourt pick out colorful plants and flowers for the garden?"

She folds her arms. "I don't want to. I need to make sure my mom is okay."

I know she's become more outspoken since Dani's been in our lives, but giving me attitude is a new behavior that needs correcting. "Unfold your arms and watch your tone, Emma."

She backs down and joins her sister.

Kourt's reading the tags on a selection of scrubs near the entrance. Trevor's sitting at her feet. The nursery's owner and I load tools and equipment in the back of the Silverado, then go inside so I can pay for them.

"Thanks again, Mr. Adams." I shake this hand. He's not open this early on Saturdays, but he made an exception for me.

"Anytime. I will deliver the plants and flowers week after next to give you guys time to ready the soil."

I keep an eye on the girls through the window. Kourt and Trevor move over to the first row of flowers. She stops to read the tags and mark her list.

Emm drags her feet behind her sister.

I turn back to Mr. Adams. He hands me a pamphlet and goes over the best method to prepare the soil.

"Shut up, Emmy!"

"I don't have to, Kourty!"

I look out the window.

Kourt is facing her sister. "You're messing up my day with Dad."

"I can say whatever I want."

Kourt takes a step forward. "I'm warning you, Emmy!"

Emm stands up straight. "Tomboy!"

The list and pencil fall to the pebbled ground. "Don't call me that!"

Arms stiff against her side, fingers tight in a fist, Emm leans forward. "He's *my* dad!"

What the hell?!

Shocked by both my daughters' behaviors. I snap out of it and run out to head off what's coming next. I'm not going to make it in time.

Kourt charges. She shoves her sister hard enough that Emm stumbles back and hits the rocks on the ground— hard.

Emm scrambles to get to her feet.

Kourt is hovering over her, fist drawn back. I grab her by the waist, lifting her off her feet before she takes a swing at her sister.

Emm's on her feet ready to defend herself. She's in a fighting stance similar to Dani's.

I turn Kourt around to face me. "You are never to put your hands on your sister like that again. Do you understand me, Kourtney Allison Hawk?" I yell.

Fear flashes in her eyes. She whimpers. I've never used this tone with her, but she's leaving me no choice. Trevor's showing his discontent by barking at me.

I look at the other one.

"You will stop complaining. And don't you ever call your sister out of her name again. Do you understand me, Emma Rose Hawk?"

She nods.

Kourt contorts and wiggles until she's free from my hold. She runs to the truck. Trevor by her side. She climbs in and slams the door after her dog jumps in.

I check Emm's hands and arms to make sure she wasn't injured. Once she passes inspection, she stomps off to the truck.

Mr. Adams stands in the doorway of his office.

"I probably handled it all wrong."

"I have five girls. That was nothing. Wait until they start borrowing each other's things without asking. That's when the real fights happen."

I'm the head of a multi-billion-dollar company, Second Command of a secret branch of the military that's been around for almost a hundred years, and nothing has shocked me more than this fight between Emm and Kourt.

Dani said Kourt's hostility toward her sister was growing. I didn't realize it was that much.

Why did their relationship change?

I pick up the list off the ground and follow Mr. Adams inside. He creates an account for us in his system. I hand him my credit card and the paper.

He whistles. "I'm impressed. Your daughter did her homework."

"Yeah, she's into saving the planet." I look through the window where I can see her steaming in the truck.

He pats my shoulder. "You did the right thing. I've had to step in the middle of many fights in my house. My advice to you is to not take sides. Stay neutral even when you know one of them had every right to haul-off and hit the other. If you're outnumbered by the women in your house like I am, and want peace, walk the middle line. Even when your wife is at odds with one of them."

"Thank you, sir."

He laughs. "I didn't become the number one nursery in the state because I love gardening." Mr. Adams hands me back my credit card and the receipt to sign.

He tells me he'll email before billing me for the plants. I leave the office.

The atmosphere in the truck is like fire and ice. In an attempt to get us back on track, I take the girls to my favorite diner for breakfast. It's around the corner from my building.

The waitress, Yvette, greets me with a one-arm hug and fawns over the girls as she shows us to a booth by the window so we can keep an eye on Trevor.

He's content in the bed of the truck with a bowl of water and a chew bone.

Kourt scoots in first and moves all the way over. I go second to keep some physical distance between the two. They haven't made up yet. Emm slides in next.

Yvette hands the girls a kid's menu and a pack of crayons. Kourt pushes the pack to the center of the table and opens her menu.

"I'll give you girls a minute. I already know what your dad wants." She goes to wait on another table.

"What do you guys have a taste for?"

Crickets.

"The breakfast pizza is good."

More crickets.

"I apologize for shouting. You guys were best friends. When did that change?"

"Kourty doesn't want to be my sister anymore."

I wait to see if she denies or confirms the accusation. The menu in her hands hasn't moved. The grudge is settling. Kourt is shutting us out.

Daddy-daughter day is circling the drain.

"Nothing can change you two from being sisters. You two owe each other an apology. You don't have to do it now, but before the day ends, you need to do it."

I wave for Yvette to come take the girls' order.

When she leaves, I try an ice breaker. "If you can go anywhere this summer where would you like to go?"

"Somewhere far, far away where nobody can find us," Emm says.

Kourt looks out the window, doing her best to not be a part of this conversation. I'm in over my head with this. Kourt's scared. I have to remember she's not used to being reprimanded by a male.

I pull out my phone.

"No cell phones at the table, Dad," Emm reminds me.

"I know, Sweet Pea, but this is important. Can you forgive me this one time?"

"Okay."

I open the text window and type out an S.O.S. to Dani. Emm's mood swings I know how to handle, but Kourt's personality is so much different. Dani predicted the fallout of Kourt's behavior. We can't turn a blind eye to it any longer; she went after her sister.

Dani's reply pops up right away. Her advice helps and now I know how to bring my daughter out of her funk and hopefully get her to tell me what's bothering her.

"Your last day of school is coming up. Any plans?"

"Mom signed Kourty up for softball at the park and I'm taking art classes."

"Wow, that's great. Are you excited about playing softball, Cuddles?"

She picks at a piece of imaginary lint on her sweatshirt.

"I can take you to get your cleats."

Crickets.

"Mom already got'um," Emm answers for her sister.

I'm determined to get Kourt to talk. "Want to go to the batting cage to practice?"

Her shoulders rise and fall. Okay, that's a start.

"Mommy let Dylan come over. He and Kourty played catch. He's playing on Kourty's team."

Dani conveniently forgot to tell me about that play date. She knows how I feel about that little boy. I wasn't chasing girls at that age. He'll corrupt my child before she's a teenager.

I turn to Emm. "When do you start art classes?"

"The same time Kourty starts softball." She starts rattling off all the things she wants to learn to draw. Emm dominates the conversation when she knows she's in trouble or overly excited.

"I was thinking about planning a camping trip for us this summer."

Kourt sits up showing signs of coming around.

Emm huffs. "Do we have to sleep outside with the bugs?"

"No, you guys can sleep in the tent. I like sleeping under the stars."

"What about Mommy?"

"You guys have mommy-daughter time. Why can't I have daddy-daughter time?"

"I don't like all this digging in the dirt and camping stuff."

"You guys will get a chance to pick what we do."

"What if we want to get manicures and pedicures?"

"Then I'll sit in the chair with my feet in the water and my fingers soaking in bowls right along with you guys."

Kourt laughs then catches herself.

"Can we pick out a color for your toes?" Emm giggles.

"Depends on what color you pick."

It's still early when we finish our breakfast and go home. Dani's already gone.

I drive the truck to the side of the house and unload the equipment. We measure then rope off the area for the garden. Kourt is slowly coming around. She still hasn't said anything, but she laughs when something funny happens or is said.

The morning chill wears off and they shed the sweatshirts. Turning soil is a lot of work. I don't mind. I'm spending time with my daughters.

I ask them what they want to be when they grow up. Emm immediately says she wants to be an artist and have a horse ranch. She would only let nice people work at the ranch. And she'll paint pictures of the horses all day.

Since she's the resident artist, I commission her to paint pictures on the stones we're going to lay down to outline the garden.

Kourt shrugs her shoulders, but I already know she wants to be President of the United States.

"If I could take you to the White House to meet the president, would you go with me?" I ask.

"What do you want to be, Dad?" Emm asks.

"A super ninja who flies and shoots laser beams from my eyes. I'd save the world from evil villains."

Emm laughs. "What would you call yourself?"

The shovel in my hand falls to the ground. Feet apart. Chest out. Shoulders back. Fists anchored on my hips. An imaginary gust of wind making my red cape wave behind me. I use my hero voice. "Super Hawk."

Kourt giggles. "How would you save the world?"

I know my wife is going to kill me for this, but I'm making headway with our daughter. It's warm out and we can be in and out without her ever knowing.

"First I'd fly around in the sky and see if anyone is in trouble." I run a circle around the turned over ground with my hands out like a flying super hero. Trevor joins me like my faithful sidekick. "And when I find someone I'd swoop down from the sky like this." On my second pass, I pick up Kourt in my left arm, then Emm in the right. "And fly them away to safety." I run with them in my arms toward the other side of the house, their laughter and squeaks of fun making the consequences all worthwhile.

We round the corner and I charge up the steps to the patio.

"Daddy, what are you doing?" Emm yells. "Mommy's gonna to be mad."

"Mommy's not here to stop me." I run full force, hold them tight against me, and jump. My feet walking on air. My trusty sidekick flying with me.

Kourt screams.

We hit the water. Our combined weight pulls us down in the

deepest part of the pool. I'm not worried. I know Kourt can swim. I paid for her to take lessons every summer at day camp. I taught Emm how to swim when she was two years old.

My Nike's touch the bottom. I bend my knees, release the girls, grab hold of their feet and push them up toward the surface. I kick my legs to shoot them through the water. They break the surface like graceful aquatic mammals.

We tread water in the center of the pool.

"That was so cool!" Kourt smooths back the hair in her face.

Emm swims for the steps. "You are in so much trouble."

I go after her, pick her up, and toss her back into the water. She shouts, going under, then comes up laughing and splashing water at me. I take off my shirt and toss it on the patio.

"Dad, did you know Mom has a lady hawk tattoo right here?" Kourt points to her side.

"Yeah, she's a copycat."

"What's the funny arrows right here?" Kourt points to my rib-cage.

"They are Sumerian numbers and alphabets."

The back door slams. I grab the girls and we move to the center of the pool. We watch Mama Hawk fly toward us.

Trevor barks.

"Quiet, boy," Kourt tells him.

"What. The. Hell. Bryan?!"

"Baby, you do such a good job of keeping the house clean and we didn't want to track dirt inside so we thought the best way to get it off would be to jump in the pool. That's what we were thinking, huh, girls?"

Kourt nods her head. Emm shakes her head.

Come on, girls. Help me sell this. "Okay, here's what really happened, baby. Trevor was playing on this side of the house and we heard a big splash. We ran to see what it was. He'd accidently jumped into the pool. Kourt jumped in to save him and I wasn't sure if she could swim so I jumped in after her. Emm forgot I knew how to swim so she jumped in to save me. Turns out we all know how to swim, even Trevor. Isn't that what happened, girls?"

If Dani could, she would jump in this pool and strangle me with her bare hands. But I'm safe; she just got her hair done. I learned the hard way, don't mess with a Black woman's hair after she just gets it done.

Lips tight. A slow nod of the head. Dani stares at me. "That's okay. Stay in as long as you'd like." She turns and walks back to the house.

Kourt covers her ears when the door slams. "Maybe we should get out."

"Mom said we can stay in," I assure them.

"No, Dad. Mom was daring you to stay in."

"No, she wasn't. Come on, you and Emm against me and Trevor." I mentally prepare myself for the tongue-lashing I'm sure is waiting for me when I step foot in the house.

After throwing four rounds of a relay race, and who can hold their breath under water the longest, the girls and I finally climb out of the pool.

I walk in the kitchen holding one girl in each arm and Trevor following behind us. Dani and Max are sitting at the table eating a snack. He gives me the *you've done it now* head shake.

"You have to wash, blow dry, and braid their hair." Dani dips an apple slice in peanut butter.

Kourt gasps.

I puff out my chest. "Okay, I will." To drive the cockiness home, I throw the smirk back at her like it's no big deal. I've washed and blow dried Dani's hair before. Doing it for my daughters is no different. We walk out of the kitchen to the tune of Dani and Max laughing. I tell the girls to go take a shower and get dressed and then I'll do their hair.

What I didn't know then, but I know now, Kourt is tender headed and she has a head full of thick, long hair that she absolutely hates getting washed, blow dried and braided. I can sympathize; I'm tender headed too.

Kourt cries and wiggles the whole time I have her on the bathroom counter over the sink washing her hair. "Please don't get water and shampoo on my face and in my ears."

I try my best, but the more she squirms, the more water and shampoo get on her face and in her ears.

To blow dry her hair, I have to sit on the floor in her bedroom with my legs locked around her. "Please stop, Daddy!" she cries. "Just let it dry on its own."

I look to Emm for advice. She shakes her head.

"You can be the better parent and let my hair dry naturally. It's better for the environment!" Kourt looks over her shoulder, ducking and dodging the comb attached to the blow dryer as I try to work it through her tangled hair.

Trevor lies on the bed whining and barking. Upset because his best friend is in distress.

By now I'm sweating like I've been working out in the gym for hours. Once I finally get her hair dry down to the roots, I pull out the comb and hair oil from her bucket. You'd think I was about to torture national secrets out of her. My inner thighs tremble from the workout they get keeping her in one spot.

"Dad, you have to put that orange stuff in your hands and some of that oil stuff and rub them together, then run your fingers through her hair before you use the comb." Emm demonstrates. She's watched Dani and Marie do it.

I relax my thighs for a second to get the bottle of coconut oil, and Kourt breaks free. She speed-crawls for the door. Trevor's barking, cheering her on.

"Baby girl, if you sit still and let me braid your hair, I promise to take you to the teddy bear store and you can pick out two new bears." I'm dad enough to know when I need to bribe my children so I can prove a point to their mom. Unfortunately my daughter hates getting her hair combed more than she loves stuffed bears. I exhale and crawl after her. I get her locked down again by the door. Emm brings me the hair bucket. Kourt kicks, screams, ducks and dodges.

It takes me a total of three and a half hours, from start to finish, to do my daughter's hair. Now I understand why Dani mentally prepares herself to do this every other weekend and why they're both exhausted when she's finished. I give Kourt something for her headache and let her take a nap.

It takes less than an hour to do Emma's hair. I know she's not tender headed. I've done her hair millions of time.

"Where are the girls?" Dani looks up from the book she's reading when I walk into the family room.

I lift her legs and exhale and sit on the sofa next to her. I put her feet in my lap and massage them. "Kourt's taking a nap and Emm's drawing a picture of Super Hawk." I close my eyes, resting my head on the back of the sofa.

LIES YOU TELL 207

"I cut my day short because I thought you were struggling with Kourt."

"Thanks, but you didn't have to do that. Your advice helped and she was starting to come around."

"I don't remember giving permission for you guys to be in the pool."

A wicked thought crosses my mind. I crack my eyes open, grip her feet tighter. "Sometimes you have to modify the rules a bit." I tickle her feet.

She draws her knees toward her chest, trying to free her feet. "I'll remember that, Mr. Hawk." She laughs. "You're not done yet."

My fingers freeze. Dani leans over to pick up a bottle of dog shampoo. "His tub is in the laundry room." Gone is the laughter. It's been replaced by another twist of the lips.

I refuse to admit defeat.

I snatch the bottle from her hand and call for Trevor. I abandon her feet and go wait for him in the hallway. He barks. His nails tap the hardwood floor as he runs down the stairs. He stands on his hind legs. Paws on my chest. I hold up the shampoo bottle— Trevor drops to the floor.

"Did you just… Dani, did he just…" Trevor's lying at my feet on his back. Tongue hanging out on one side. Eyes wide open. "I can't believe the dog just fainted."

Dani snickers.

Deep inhale and extra slow exhale, I bend and push the eighty-pound dog down the hallway, through the kitchen to the laundry room where we store his tub.

He loves bath time just as much as Kourt likes getting her hair combed. Military physical training is a walk in the park compared to the punishment I'm receiving for the pool fiasco.

———◆———

As I do every night after I make sure the house is locked up, I check on the girls. Emm is knocked out.

Kourt's still awake when I open her door.

I sit next to her on the bed. "I didn't mean to scare you today. Sometimes I may yell, but it's to get your attention. Make sure you hear what I'm saying. I've never spanked Emm and I have no intention of ever spanking you. I will ground you guys first."

"Do you think I'm a tomboy?"

"I think you're a kindhearted girl who likes to play sports. Throws the best tea parties. And wants to save our planet. If that makes you a tomboy, then I'm a tomgirl because I like putting on feather boas and hats to have a tea party with you and the bears. I actually liked doing your hair today and if you let me, I will keep doing it. And I'm looking forward to gardening. Look, baby girl, it's unfortunate that people put labels on everything. Don't let that stop you from doing what makes you happy. What matters is how you identify yourself. And I will talk to your sister about calling you names. I don't know where she learned that word."

"From those girls at Grandma and Grandpa's."

"Cuddles, what happened today? Why aren't you best friends with your sister anymore?"

She shrugs her shoulders.

"Being called a tomboy isn't the only reason you were upset, was it?"

"No."

"Do you want to talk about it?"

"No."

"Scoot back." I wait for her to make room for me. I kick off my shoes and lie on my side facing her, my head propped up by my hand and elbow. Trevor joins us on the bed. I make room for him. "My job has been keeping me busy. I haven't been around much. You and I haven't hung out like we used to. Does that make you mad?"

"A little."

"What if I tell you things are going to change. We are going to do more family things together. Will that make you not so mad?"

"I guess so."

"Baby girl. Mom and I know you're angry about something. We don't know how to help you because you won't tell us what's going on. If you can't tell us, you have other adults in your life who love you. You can talk to them."

Her lips start to tremble. A tear rolls down the side of her face, into her ear. "I was tired of her whining for my mom and messing up my day with you."

It doesn't escape my attention that she referred to Dani as *her* mom and Emm was messing up *her* day with me. Emm and I have had years of one on one time. I'm guessing the reason behind her anger is that she wants it too. "You know, you didn't answer my question. If I can take you to the White House to meet the president, will you go with me?"

"Just me and you?"

"Just us."

"Yes, I'll go with you."

"Okay, I have another question."

"Okay."

"What do you remember about me?"

"Huh?"

"When you left a message on my work phone, you said you remember me. What do you remember?"

"I don't remember saying that. Dad, can you sing me a song so I can go to sleep?"

"What do you want me to sing?"

"Anything."

Only one song comes to mind. Baby Mine. I hummed it to her over the phone that night in December when I raced to the apartment because she made the emergency call about an intruder.

CHAPTER EIGHTEEN

BRIGHT CLEAR BLUE SKIES GREET us this early Sunday morning. A day outdoors is calling my name. The girls and I could finish preparing the soil, but I'm— happy and I want to be with my family and friends.

I text the guys and invite them over for a cookout and a flag football game.

Tony sent his mom and grandmother on a seven-day cruise to the Mexican Riviera. I know he's not busy today.

Ig's parents are in Florida with his sister and Holly's out of the country at a gymnastic training camp for Melissa. So, he's free today.

Max and Tom decided to stay in Boulder this year and text back saying yes.

Dash thanks me for the invitation, but he and Fontenot have plans today. He adds the winking emoji. It sounds strange to think of Porter by his first name.

Vin is the last one I text, only because on Mother's Day we give him space. His reply comes back right away. *What do you need me to bring?* I'm a little shocked. He usually wants to be alone. He'll go hiking or rock climbing. We keep an eye on him from a distance. Every year, the guys and I make sure flowers are delivered to the gravesite of his mother and grandmother in Italy. Vin doesn't speak to his older brother, but Salvatore sends us thank you emails with pictures of the flower display.

Arms above my head, I stretch my back. I don't know why I feel so happy. Technically I should be drained. My five months' pregnant wife screwed me 'til I cried uncle an hour ago. How she outlasted me fogs the brain. Granted we went three weeks and four days without sex and both acquired a massive amount of pent-up sexual energy, but Dani was overly enthusiastic. If she weren't pregnant I'd swear she'd taken a performance enhancement supplement in order to ride me nonstop for hours.

Jessi and I need to have a talk about my wife's sex drive. She wasn't like this with Kourt. Is it because she's carrying a boy that makes her so horny? If she keeps this up, she'll wear herself out.

I must check out the books Dani's been reading. There is no way she perfected blow jobs without reading up on it. That's the other reason my hawk is so— flaccid. He was squawking by the time she let him come.

The bathroom door opens and Dani steps out. Robe unbelted. Eye cocked as she poses in the doorway with her hands on the frame.

I clear the sleep from my throat. "Morning, beautiful."

The brightness in her eyes and the smile on her lips warms my body. We've reconnected in every way. The distance between us lessens with each minute we spend together. Dani was right to bring me back home. She helped me see that using work as an excuse to stay away was not just affecting our relationship, it was affecting Kourt's behavior too.

Dani pushes away from the door. Her hips roll as she dances toward the bed, the sexy moves even more appealing with bouncing breasts and a swollen belly. The lady hawk sways too.

"Good morning," she sings.

"How are you feeling?"

Dani purrs as she cat crawls on the bed.

"That good, huh?" Deep breaths. Take slow. Deep. Breaths. She's not ready for another round.

Or is she?

Dani sheds the robe and yanks back the covers. Still on all fours. My eyes slam shut and I make exaggerated snoring sounds.

She giggles as she straddles my hips, the heat between her legs warming the sleeping hawk. Her vanilla and light rose scent hovers over me.

Something hard and sharp dusts circles around my nipple. "What's the plan for today?"

"Throw something on the grill. Have a few people over," I answer in between snores.

"Mmm, what's on the menu?" Her heat slow-strokes my dick.

My abs constrict. If I give in, we'll never make it out of bed. Before she knows what's happening, I urge her up higher as I scoot down until she's straddling my face and holding onto the headboard.

The heady aroma of her arousal and the heat from Sunshine make my mouth water.

Since my woman wants to rule the bed this morning, I put her in a position where she's in complete control, does not have to utter a word, and will zap her of some of this early morning sexual energy she's got going on.

Every place that's licked is because she wants it there.

Slow and easy strokes, fast and hard is because of how she moves.

High up on her knees or knees spread wide so she's flat on my face, Dani controls how much stimulation she can handle. My job is to French-kiss her pussy.

———◆———

The meat in the freezer will take too long to thaw, plus Dani mumbled something about wanting to make her special barbeque sauce before her eyes closed.

I make a list and get the girls up.

This morning, Emm doesn't give me a hard time about leaving Mom at home by herself to go the market with me.

Kourt is excited about the flag football game and asks if she can play too. I'm not surprised. She likes football and is not afraid to take on grown men much bigger and taller than her. She's in a much better mood this morning and the girls' camaraderie is back to normal.

We work as team at the market. I read from the list and push the basket. They pull items off the shelf. I pretend not to notice the two bags of cookies they slip in the basket. They pretend not to notice the family size bag of chips and jar of dip I add.

I jokingly ask for their opinion about us bribing Mom with her three favorite ice creams so we can swim today. Yes, I know since becoming pregnant, ice cream doesn't agree with her digestive system.

Kourt smirks. "It's your nose, Dad. You share a room and bathroom with her."

Emm reminds me of how much we suffered the consequences. We bypass the frozen desserts aisle and opt for fresh fruit.

They help me bag the groceries at checkout and we leave the store.

Willis is toddling around the garage when I pull in. I'm in such a good mood today, I invite the Langfords to join us. It doesn't even bother me when he accepts, then mumbles something incoherent under his breath.

I've come to realize, Willis is an unhappy old man who lives in yesterday and looks for things to bitch about. Phantom is accomplishing what it set out to do: dismantle RAGS. No, we don't have Elijah Hopper in custody, yet. But we have ninety-one people who want a plea deal. We'll have their elusive leader and the rest of their members soon.

Dani's in the kitchen chopping onions on the cutting board. I set the bags on the counter, wrap my arms around her waist, and kiss her cheek. "I thought you were sleeping."

She points to her stomach. "After that last one, he wouldn't stop moving."

My day just got better.

"Mommy, what can me and Emmy help you do?" Kourt asks.

We both do a double take. Kourt's been so snippy lately, we forgot she is a polite little girl.

"Put on your apron, wash your hands, and you two can help me make the barbeque sauce."

"What do you want me to do?" I ask.

"Clean the chicken. Put one layer in each pan and pour the marinade over the pieces. I made it while you guys were gone. It's in that white bowl in the refrigerator.

I kiss her cheek again. "Thank you."

"For what?"

"For not giving up on us."

"You do know you're on your fourth chance."

"Are you seriously keeping count?"

She laughs. "Of course I am. I'm a woman— right?"

———◆———

The guys help me set up yellow and red cones to mark the end zones and yard lines. Since Kourt is playing, we get together and modify the rules a tad and then draw straws for team captains.

Kourt jumps up and down and turns cartwheels. She's a captain. Vin turns backflips to outdo the other captain. She's yellow team and picks Max, Ig and me.

Vin's red team and picks Tony, Willis, and Tom. He jokes that having an old man on his team is like having an eight-year-old as a captain. If she were allowed to, Kourt would flip him off and call him a mitch. The scowl on her face says so.

On the sidelines are the cheerleaders: Dani, Emm, Penny, and Trevor. He looks at me like, a cheerleader— really?

The cheer squad claps and side steps and chants for each team. Trevor barks.

Jessi runs out the back door. She delivered a baby late last night and is just now getting home. "I want to referee!" She runs back inside to change clothes.

Marie is sitting in a lawn chair with a purple blanket over her legs and a straw sunhat on her head. I'm happy she's feeling well enough to sit outside today. She's our scorekeeper.

Penny's Chihuahua, Bella, snags the roll of annoying crowd heckler.

Right now, we're enjoying the show Kourt and Vin are putting on over the coin toss.

"I called heads, we have the ball," Kourt shouts.

"You called tails, we have the ball."

"Get your hearing checked, Uncle Vinny. I said heads." Boy, is she letting him have. It's like watching a miniature Dani go toe to toe with Vincenzio *The Tank* Ricci.

Kourt shocks us all—she reaches out, snatches off Vin's flags, drops them to the ground at his feet, and executes the perfect military about face. "Cheater," she yells over her shoulder. Then marches toward our side of the field.

There is a moment of silence before we bend over laughing, including Vin. Dani stands on the sideline frowning. My teammates and I high five our captain.

It's good to know my daughter isn't going to let a man take advantage of her.

Jessi runs out the back door wearing basketball shorts and a T-shirt. A whistle on a string hangs around her neck.

For an eight-year-old Kourt knows how to strategize and use

what she has. Yep, proud papa's grinning ear to ear as my daughter tells us what position each of us will play and why.

Kourt and Vin's verbal tug of war sets the tone of the game. She's determined to outdo him and he's determined to stop her. The rest of us are pawns in their game of flag football chess.

My daughter is our secret weapon. The other team doesn't see her as a threat. She uses that to her advantage. Max throws her a long pass. She catches it, rushing for the touchdown, scoring the first points of the game.

Proud papa smiling as I watch my daughter spike the ball and do a touchdown dance in front of Vin. The cheerleaders join her in the end zone to celebrate.

"Hey! Cheerleaders have to stay neutral," Vin protests.

Dani laughs. "When your team scores, we'll dance for you."

As promised, they dance a two-step with Tom when he scores.

The end zone shenanigans are just as entertaining as the flag football game.

It's almost half time, we are down by two, and Kourtney comes up with a crazy play.

The ball is snapped, we run back to the huddle. Breaking away, we run around in circles bent over like we're protecting the ball. The other team can't tell who has it. They're so busy chasing us around the field pulling our flags that they don't notice Max sashaying his way into the end zone.

Jessi blows the whistle. "Touchdown."

"No way!" Vin gawks at Max voguing in the end zone with the football in one hand.

Kourt's hairbrained play is not only comical, it's effective.

The sideline cracks up laughing. "That just proves my sister is smarter than you," Emm shouts.

Vin runs over to wrestle Emm to the ground and tickles her.

Kourt shoots across the field. "Don't mess with my sister!" She jumps on his back.

"No fair double teaming my captain," Tony tickles Kourt.

"He started it!" Penny yells and jumps on Tony's back.

"Half-time." Jessi blows the whistle, then joins the ticklefest. Trevor runs around the dog pile of bodies, barking. Penny's heckling dog yaps from her blanket.

While the others watch the melee, I go over to check on Marie.

She smiles as I sit on the grass next to the lawn chair.

"How are you feeling?"

"Today's a good day for me."

"Don't overdo it. We miss you."

She bats away the comment with a flick of the hand and rolling of the eyes. "Oh, hush that. I know Danielle's taking good care of you guys."

"I guess I'm just used to having you around. I was thinking, now that Dani's here, you can cut back on your days. Take more time for yourself."

Marie's brow furrows. Her eyes water. "Are you firing me?"

I reach out and take her hand. "No, of course not. It's just that I've never seen you this sick and I'm guessing it's because the workload doubled with four people in the house now."

"You know I love you guys. This isn't a job. We're family."

"Yes, we are and that's why I want you to take care of yourself. Who else will give me advice when I mess up with Dani again?"

"You'll be happy to know I have a doctor's appointment tomorrow."

Jessie blows the whistle, signaling the start of the second half of the flag football game.

I jump to my feet and press a kiss on the back of Marie's hand. "It makes me very happy."

I jog over and join my team on the field.

The score is up and down.

At one point our team is ahead. My daughter is holding her own. She manages to pull Willis's flags when he had the ball.

She looked so much like Dani chasing after him with that singled-minded focus on her face. Marie stood and cheered the loudest. Me, the proud papa, I did a two-step before I high fived her.

It's the final quarter, we're down by one.

"Hey, Kourt," Vin shouts, "we're hip to your tricks."

"I've got a whole lot more of um, Uncle Vinny. You'll be eating my dust by the end of the game." She sticks her tongue out at him.

I want to laugh, I really do, but the look on Dani's face warns me not to. Kourt's been trash talking since the start of the game.

She brings us back to the huddle for her next hairbrained game play.

On the snap Kourt runs toward the sideline, then cuts off, running past Tom, who is standing with his legs open and watching us keep his team off Max. He doesn't see Kourt cut again and run behind him.

Max fake throws to Ig and lobs the football to Kourt. It sails through Tom's legs, by a pubic hair.

She catches the ball, turns, and runs for the end zone.

"Go, Kourt, go!" Yellow team cheers.

Kourt crosses the line, tripping over her feet, and hits the ground. Hard. But still holding the football.

We all freeze waiting for the tears.

The air stops moving. Birds stop chirping.

You can hear a rat pissing on a cotton ball it's so quiet.

Trevor and Emm are the first to react. They're running across the yard. Dani's on her feet. Trevor's barking like he's commanding Kourt to get up.

Heart pounding, my feet kick up grass to get me to my baby girl. The guys are right with me. Vin and I neck and neck. We're three feet away when Kourt turns over with the biggest smile on her face.

"Look, Daddy, I got my first battle wound!" She points to her bloody scraped knee.

I pick her up off the ground. "Yep, your first. Mommy will clean it up for you."

Emm holds her sister's dangling hand and walks with us. "Are you okay, Kourty? That looks like it hurts."

"I'm okay."

I sit her down in the chair her mom vacated. Ig checks her knee before Dani cleans and bandages it.

Uncle Vinny helps her to her feet. Kourt slowly limps back onto the field. "Baby girl, are you sure you're okay to finish? Jessi can call tie game."

"I'm going to finish this football game. Besides, my knee isn't bothering me. I limped over here to fool the other team."

"What do you have in your bag of tricks?" Uncle Max asks.

She looks over her shoulder, then whispers her idea. Ig and Max fall out laughing.

"I don't know. What if he drops you? I'll have to tie Mommy's hands and feet together so she won't kill him."

"He's not. Uncle Vinny would never let anything happen to me. Come on. Please let's try this."

"I don't know."

"Trust me, Dad. Have any of my plays gone wrong?"

I guess I can't argue with that. "If you get hurt you have to explain this crazy idea to Mom and convince her to let me back in the house."

"Deal."

We shake.

"Hey, Uncle Vinny. I need to talk to you for a second." She slowly limps to the center of the field, wincing for maximum effect.

Vin jogs over to meet her. They hold a brief discussion in center field. Inwardly, I shake my head at how easily he falls for her act. *How early do girls learn the art of manipulation?*

The two team captains shake hands and we get into formation. I send up a silent prayer because I know Dani will castrate me if our daughter gets hurt.

I call the play and she snaps the ball, I hand it off to her, then scoop her up in my arm, rushing down the field in Tom's direction with Ig and Max on my flanks.

It all seems to happen in slow motion.

Willis comes right for us. I hand her off to Max, blocking Willis, snatching both his flags. He's out for this play.

Max and Ig rush down the field and I run to the end zone watching the stunt unfold.

Vin is covering me shouting instructions to his teammates.

Tony comes at Max, who hands off Kourt to Ig then trips Tony with his feet while pulling both his flags, and jumps into Tom's arms. All in a ninja like movement.

Vin stands right in front of the end zone. Ig switches direction, now carrying Kourt, the ball cradled in her arms, her braids flopping.

I haven't breathed since the play started. I block out everything else, because here's where the plan can go seriously wrong.

Ig is within two feet of his target. He launches Kourt to Vin. Out of reflex Vin reaches out to catch her. Ig snatches off Vin's flags while Kourt tosses me the ball, landing safely in her uncle's arms.

"Touchdown!" Kourt screams as Jessi blows the whistle.

"That wasn't a touchdown!" Vin protests.

"No one pulled my dad's flags!" She jumps out of his arms, gloating and pointing and galloping in circles around him. "In. Your. Face. Uncle Vinny."

Eyes bugged-out, Vin tracks her movements. "You were faking?"

"Yep." She dances her way over to me, takes the football out of my hands, kisses it, then throws it to Vin. "That'll teach you to cheat me on a coin toss."

Our team celebrates in the end zone for a vogue- robot-cabbage patch-victory dance.

"That was ridiculously brilliant. Well played, Kourty Bear." Vin gives her a high five.

We go back to the patio and I fire up the grill. Dani brings out the chicken and hands me a beer. After a lot of begging, she takes the girls inside to change into swimsuits. Cover's Kourt's hair with a swim cap and lets them play in the pool.

Dani has on her suit too, with a see-through skirt tied around her waist. She's looking too damn sexy in the orange one piece that ties like a bikini at the bottom. I can understand why some men find a pregnant woman provocative.

She catches me staring at her and puts an extra sway in her hips when she walks over to me. Today she's not hiding the lady hawk tattoo.

Her hand slides down my chest, stopping low on my abs. "Not even my world-famous barbeque sauce can doctor up the taste of burnt chicken, so keep your eyes on the meat and not my booty."

"I'm a born multitasker, my love." I palm her butt and give it a little squeeze.

Marie calls out to Dani. She stretches on her toes to give me a kiss, then joins Marie and Jessica near the pool.

Max dances over. He's changed into eye-blinding yellow board shorts.

"What did you do to her yesterday? I had to beat her off with a stick this morning."

He raises both hands in denial. "All I did was ask her to help me with something I want to surprise my husband with for our anniversary and yo' freaky wife took it to a whole different level." He looks around to make sure no one's listening. "Let's just say I'm a little jealous that Danikins knows more about giving the ultimate blow job than I do."

"What did she tell you?"

"Sweetie, just sit back and enjoy the ride." He saunters away with an extra swing to his hips.

Today, the guys and I don't talk Phantom business. We relax and chill.

We sit at the table for a family meal and a recap the flag football game. Kourt explains, in detail, how she came up with that last play.

"I can't believe you let her take that kind of risk," Dani scolds.

"Every play we executed came from our team captain," Max tells her.

Dani's eyes narrow. "Who were the adults and who was the child?"

I know she's not angry.

"Sorry, little sis, but I blindly followed my captain. She came up with stuff I didn't think of," Ig laughs.

"I'm all for Kourtney playing sports and being competitive, but I want her to learn good sportsmanship."

"My sister, let me tell you what my dad told my mom and grandma. Athletes play to win. Friendship or kinship don't belong in the game. It's the attitude off the field that matters. My niece recognizes that. Kourty's a true athlete. After she humiliated Vin, they walked off the field as uncle and niece." Tony toasts Vin with his beer bottle.

"Hey— I wouldn't call it humiliation."

"Dawg, you got beat by an eight-year-old."

"Who you cheated in a coin toss," Kourt adds.

"My plan worked. You got out there and played hard."

"Danikins, she paid attention to *everything*," Max laughs.

"Her dad used to pay attention to everything too," Willis mumbles.

My foot twitches, but I'm not the one who kicks someone under the table this time.

Willis jumps in his seat.

"Oops, sorry but that, old man. My foot slips." Tony winks.

"Yeah, I bet it did, sonny."

"Did you see the look on Kourtney's face when she was chasing down Willis?" Marie laughs.

I shift the focus off the game to how good the food is.

"Mommy put her foot in it, huh, Uncle Tony."

"She sure did."

After lunch everyone migrates to different areas of the yard.

Kourt takes Tony around the side of the house to show him where we'll plant the flowers for the butterfly garden. She told him she wants to build an ecosystem habitat for the upcoming school year's science fair. Big words and concept for a third-grader, but my little girl is into this stuff and I encourage it like I encourage Emm's interest in animals and art.

Emm and Penny pull out two jump ropes and teach me how to jump double-dutch. The biggest fun is Uncle Vinny knowing how to do tricks while jumping.

As the sun starts to get low in the sky, Willis takes Marie home. She's not feeling well.

Dani and I relax in the hammock built for two. Our eyes hidden behind sunglasses. She's been on her feet most of the day and didn't put up a fight when I *suggested* she join me.

From her lax limbs and slow breathing, I can tell Dani's starting to fall asleep. I hold her close as the hammock gently sways.

In the background, music plays through the speakers on the patio. Jessi, Tom, and Max's friendly card game is turning hostile by the second. Quiet Tom is equally as competitive as my sister.

Emm pulled out her easel and art supplies. She and Penny are drawing.

Trevor's sleeping in the chaise by the pool. He finally found a spot where he can get some peace from the four-legged five-pound guest whose been yapping at his hind legs since she got here. Personally, I think if he growled at her one good time, she'd shut the hell up and leave him alone.

I watch Uncle Iggy and Uncle Vinny teach Kourt how to bicycle spike the soccer ball into the net.

Tony's sitting at the table with a laptop in front of him.

This is my life now and I like the direction it's going. When I signed the contract to become Phantom, I'd resolved myself to being a lifetime bachelor. I preferred it. Carried a platinum membership card to *Bachelorhood* in my wallet. I didn't believe in that romantic stuff people read about in books or went to movies to see. That kind of love wasn't real. It was a politically correct word made up to disguise a couple's intense sexual attraction. When Amelia got pregnant, I revised my status to *single-father bachelor.* The first-time Dani smiled at me challenged my outlook.

I'd seen her from afar when I investigated Edwards— tailed her for a week. Viewed her through a camera lens so I knew what she looked like. Knew her smile. But when it was directed at me. Only for me. Things changed.

In the beginning, I convinced myself it was because I found her sexually attractive. If it were just sexual though, I could identify it, conquer it, add her to the list, and move on. Phantom didn't teach me how to deal with that instant attachment after only a few days of nonsexual interaction. It started to affect my approach to the assignment. But I still didn't identify it with love, not even when my friends joked about me falling for Dani. Not even when I whispered the word in her ear the night she told me she was pregnant. She needed comforting and women find security in hearing the words, *I love you.*

The things that have happened these last four weeks opened my eyes. I discovered what *love* is. I was in love with Dani nine years ago. I'm even more in love with her right now.

Dani yawns and shifts, causing the hammock to swing.

"Are you happy?" I ask.

"Huh?" She squirms until she finds a comfortable position.

"Do I make you happy?"

"You make me very happy."

"Will you marry me? For real this time? Just the two of us tomorrow morning?"

She takes my hand, placing it over her heart. It's beating fast against my palm. "Yes."

———◆———

Dani kisses my cheek when she walks into the family room. She's changed out of the dress she wore to the courthouse earlier this morning. "You're not going to work?"

I'm dressed in jeans and a collared shirt. I pretend to be distracted by the newspaper in my hands. "Later on. I want to go with you guys to the aquarium." I bend a corner of the paper and peek around it to watch her water a plant. "It's been a while since I've been there. I hear the new exhibit opens today."

Yesterday, I overheard the girls giggling about Dylan meeting them at the aquarium. Emm and Penny kept referring to him as Kourty's *boyfriend* so I pushed back my mid-morning meeting and asked Tony handle the small things on my schedule.

I duck back behind the newspaper when she looks my way.

"Max and Penny will be there too, Bry."

I hear the smirk on her lips. She knows why I'm going.

"The more the merrier. I should see if Uncle Vinny wants to go. I'll pay for lunch."

"Don't you dare say anything to Dylan. I invited him and Jennifer."

"Baby, I'm going so I can spend time with my wife and daughters, not to mess with an eight-year-old boy whose corrupting my little girl."

"How do you know he's the one doing the corrupting?"

"Cuddles isn't boy crazy."

"If it lets you sleep at night, keep thinking that way." The newspaper is snatched out of my hands, and she points a finger in my face. "I'm warning you, Bryan Kendall Hawk the fourth. Do not mess with Dylan. He is *their* friend and he likes hanging out with *both* of them."

I'm a hairline away from getting in trouble so I give my wife the best innocent smile I can muster up. "You have my word. I won't say anything to Dylan." There are other ways to intimidate people that do not include verbal threats. By the time I finish with him, he'll run the other way when he sees Kourt. It's bad enough they play on the same team.

She walks away with the paper in her hand and waters another plant. My lips twitch. Have I completely lost my touch? How does she know I'm up to something?

———◆———

The aquarium is crowded. Kourt wants to know why I went through a separate entrance. I can't tell her it's because of the gun holstered to my hip underneath my shirt, so while I check in with security, I step over to the information desk, give a donation, and show her the receipt.

We stand in the atrium to map out our visit. Dylan taps my arm. "Mr. Hawk, can I talk to you for a second?"

Dani tosses me a quick warning glare, then turns her attention back to the map on the podium.

"Sure, what's on your mind?"

He gestures for us to step to the side.

Back straight, shoulders squared, Dylan Hill looks up at me. "My grandpa told me he didn't like my dad at first because Dad didn't have a pot to piss in when he was my mom's boyfriend. I want you to know I'm doing extra chores around the house and I started a yard raking business to earn enough money to buy a pot to piss in so you'll like me enough to say I can ask Kourty to be my girlfriend."

My jaw drops.

"Dad said he's still paying for his. How much did yours cost and are you still paying for it like Dad?"

He's serious. Rearing back, the laughter shoots from my stomach. Dylan's reaction makes me laugh harder. I hold my hand out to him, a sign of respect for the little guy's tenacity. He places his hand in mine and we shake.

"Dylan, my pot costs *a lot* of money. I had it specially made and I paid it off a long time ago. You need a good job to even buy one. But I tell you what, when you do have a pot to piss in, I'll let you ask my daughter to be your girlfriend."

"I want to fly fighter planes like my grandpa did so I'm joining the Navy when I graduate from high school. Is that a good enough job, sir?"

"I'd be honored to have a Navy Fighter Pilot date my baby girl." I pat his shoulder. "And if you're serious about joining the Navy, you should talk to Dr. Barrett. He was a Fighter Pilot too and is certified to fly all types of aircrafts."

Jennifer walks over and ruffles her son's hair. "Is everything okay?"

Dylan ducks away, giving her that look little boys give their moms when she's embarrassing him. He is trying to have a big boy conversation with the father of the girl he wants to date and his mom is treating him like a little kid.

My respect level for him moves up two notches.

"I was telling Mr. Hawk I'm going to wait until I have enough money to buy a pot to piss in before I ask Kourty to be my girlfriend."

"I'm sorry, Bryan, my dad encourages Dylan's crush on Kourt-ney. We've asked him not to."

"Grandpa said nowadays young men don't respect women like they did when he was growing up. And no grandson of his is going to disrespect females. He said he's going to teach me to court a woman the right way and keep my tallywacker where it belongs. I don't know what that is, but it sounds important." He leans away from his mother whispering, "Grandpa said Grandma kept his tal-lywacker under lock and key after they got married."

My laughter draws attention. *I like his grandpa already.* "How much do you charge to rake a yard?"

"Grandpa gives me five dollars to rake his front yard. Dad gives me seven for the front and back."

I pull out my wallet and hand him a hundred-dollar bill. "I have a big yard with lots of trees."

Dylan stares at the bill in his hand then up at me. "Thank you, Mr. Hawk. Grandpa can bring me over tomorrow morning. Don't worry, I have my own rake and bags."

I look up in time to catch the smile on Dani's face.

I love you, she mouths to me.

I love you more, I mouth back.

CHAPTER NINETEEN

TUESDAY MORNING, MARIE RETURNS TO work with a clearance from her doctor. She and Dani sit at the kitchen table dividing the household chores. They look like two superpowers negotiating a peace deal. I pretend to be engrossed in the emails on my phone when asked to take sides.

Before I leave for work, I check the calendar to verify the time of Dani's prenatal appointment and the time the girls have to be at the park. I add it to my schedule and head to the office.

When I step off the elevator Porter is waiting for me. "I've been monitoring a new post on the black-market site. It came up two hours ago with a billion-dollar for sale sign in the yard of a haunted house. Well, an image of a haunted house. Seventy-five people already put in a bid. You need an invitation to bid and to get an invitation you have to crack the Spam Bot security four-digit code that reboots every eight seconds. Riley can't help."

And so my day begins. He follows me to my office. I gage the time using the platinum watch my wife gave me. "Forward a copy of the post to Vin. Tell him to contact his Field Operatives to see if there's any street buzz about this haunted house. Edwards and his brother created a similar post when they sold classified information. Start manually recording the codes. I'll be in meetings most of the morning, but will come find you when I'm done."

I put down my brief case and head to Tony's office. The door is open, but I knock anyway as I enter.

From the looks of things, he's settling in to the role at Hawkeye. There are pictures on the walls. Plants in the corners. Gaming consoles near the flat screen. Mementoes here and there. Tony's office is more decorated than his house.

"Do you miss the uniform?" I ask.

"I miss the out that it gave me from being in the center of chaos twenty-four-seven." His hands sweep to include the room as he walks toward the conference table. "I don't miss the sporadic shifts I had to take to make up for the times Phantom business took precedence."

"Feeling claustrophobic already?"

"A little."

"Man, I appreciate you taking a leave of absence to help me out."

"Bros for life."

Dap-dap. Hand-slap. Finger-snap. Bro hug.

We sit across from one another.

"Nora Owens is demanding immediate release." He begins with Phantom business. "She claims Americans will die if we continue to hold her against her will."

"Nora was a Presidential Cabinet Member; POTUS stands firm on his one-time offer. Leniency in exchange for Hopper. Send Chen to interrogate her."

Tony smiles. "The rest are cooperating. So far, the task force has arrested three hundred people. The U.S. Attorney General is ready to file charges once her office has the evidence that will stick. I have Sweepers working in the background to help the task force dig up what they need."

"Do we have anything we can use to barter against Owens?"

He shakes his head. "And my best Watchers haven't been cleared by Chen yet, so I'll have to do the background checks."

"Let me see how close Fontenot is to finishing with Dani's patients. I'll ask if she wants to take on another assignment."

"That'll work."

"Any names we should be concerned about?"

"Langford's name came up a couple time and I asked him about it on Sunday. He brushed it off with some lame ass excuse. I'm on it though."

A video call is announced on Tony's laptop. "It's Larson."

I move to the other side of the table next to him

"Good morning, Colonel. Lieutenant Colonel. We have a possible location on Selam and Solomon, but it's hot. Any signals will give us away. We need to black out."

Tony's shoulders square. I sense the wheels turning in his head and sit back and let him do his thing. Delta is under his dominion. If she fails, everyone will look at him because it was his responsibility to make sure she was well trained for the task.

He starts drilling her on the evacuation plan. He throws what ifs and she responds. If he doesn't like her answer he throws it at her again and again until she comes up with a response that is more to his liking.

It's not that he doesn't think Larson's capable of succeeding, he's concerned because this is her first solo mission where she's the lead. He's on the other side of the world and if something goes wrong he can't pull her out right away. "You bring everyone back to Boulder no matter what."

"Roger that."

"How long?" Tony asks.

"Seventy-two hours."

"Fine. Seventy-two hours exactly."

She signs off and his whole being changes. A seriousness wraps around my brother. He'll let it go once Larson checks in.

We move on with the meeting. He hands me a stack of service contract requests for Hawkeye Personal Protection. The article is the reason for the interest. I have the luxury of being selective with my clientele like I am with who makes it into Phantom.

I hand him the paperwork for the approval of bonuses for the ex-Navy SEALs who guarded my home. Now that the situation with RAGS is contained, they aren't needed. I tell Tony to give the men some downtime, at full pay, before reassigning them. He wants to add a bihourly mobile patrol of the house to the rotation, just as a precaution.

I have about twenty minutes before my next meeting. I take the elevator up to the sixth floor, better known as *The Nest*.

It's surrounded by photochromic glass walls, has an open floor plan of cubicles, and over twenty billion dollars in technology and equipment. It's also the most active floor in the building. Everyone in here is a Watcher.

"The Hawk is in The Nest," the Watcher Team Lead calls out. Her voice travels around the room. One hundred men and women stand at attention.

"As you were," I announce and nod to the captain. "Which cubicle is Fontenot assigned to?"

She escorts me to one in back.

Strike one.

Fontenot is on the phone when I approach. Terrance Brumfield's file open and in front of her on the desk. I wait for her to finish her call.

"How are you coming along with Dr. Hawk's patients?"

"This is my last one. I had to ask Major Ricci to access Brumfield's military file."

"Brumfield was in the military?"

"No, he has a classified civilian file. It's the last bit of information I need and I can complete my final report."

"That was fast. Have you come across anything we should be concerned about?"

"No, sir, but if I do I will inform Major Ricci."

"How do you feel about another assignment? Major Paul needs help with background checks."

Her eyes brighten, but they dart side to side. She leans in. "I'd really like that, sir."

I look around to see what the problem is. Three Watchers quickly avert their eyes when my gaze sweeps over therm.

Strike Two.

"I'll have Ricci contact your CO. When you're finished, report to Paul."

"Thank you, sir."

Before I leave, I check my phone for Ricci's calendar today and type out a quick note for him to visit the nest.

The WTL rises as I approach her office. The slight blink of worry in her eyes confirms the displeased look I'm projecting is exactly as intense as I intend it to be.

"Have a good day, sir."

The energy I sense from the back row of cubicles is not acceptable. Fontenot doesn't strike me as the type to take shit from an equal. I'm guessing she doesn't want to make waves and therefore hasn't addressed her concerns with the Lead Watcher.

I will not tolerate the dissention. Watchers are our eyes because we can't see everything— in the moment. Petty shit is a distraction that put the lives of the rest of us in jeopardy. It's the Lead Watcher's main duty to maintain a cohesive floor. Fontenot shouldn't be made to feel as if she has to stifle her excitement for being asked to work another assignment just to keep the peace.

My next meeting is a blur. The Nest is heavy on my mind especially knowing Larson and her team are blacked-out and will need guidance once they come back online. I send a message to Ricci to handle it— now.

I take the elevator down to the first floor and go to the SCIF. President Hart asked me to blindly sit in on the video conference meeting with ten heads of state. The General Secretary of the Communist Party of China sent notification that his Naval vessels are scheduled to do maneuvers in the Sea of Japan starting Friday. Today is Tuesday. The leaders are looking to President Hart to initiate a call to action from NATO to send a cease and desist message to China.

The meeting lasts well into the early afternoon. Before I sign off with POTUS, he lets me know how he really wants to handle the crisis with China. A team of Field Operatives are on their way to China.

I go back to the fourth floor, get my laptop, and go check in with Porter.

"Are you still keeping a record of the codes?" I ask.

"Yes, sir," he replies without taking his eyes off the monitor in front of him.

I set up my laptop next to him on the desk and pull a chair around. He scoots over and makes room. The fresh note pad in front of his has at least one hundred codes written down; there are five more next to him. It's been five hours since I had him manually record them.

I create a spreadsheet and start keying in the codes. Riley reorganizes them after I finish with the first note pad. It's evident the system is on a loop and the four-digit alpha numeric codes don't change. Just the order changes. I tell Porter to stop writing and look at the screen. My world is a series of numbers; I see what's going on. I want him to develop the skill of recognizing these patterns.

He leans over and stares at the laptop's monitor. I turn it his way and lean back to let him go through his process. Porter has a photographic memory.

A smile creeps across his face. "It's an anagram."

"Yes, and with Riley's help, you are going to decipher it." Normally I'd sit in front of the computer until I figured it out, but this may take hours and I've other things on my schedule today. So, I'm delegating authority. Porter can handle this one.

I go back to my office and put out the mini fires that require my attention until it's time for me to meet Dani at Jessica's office.

———◆———

"The girls are finally settled in the family room. I promised to make sure you wouldn't exact revenge while they sleep." Dani stands in the doorway of my office smiling.

"Oh, I'm going to get them back when they least expect it," I vow. They started it by painting my toenails blue while I took a nap on the sofa in the family room after we came back from the park.

"Trevor is acting as watch dog and I'm going up to take a long hot bath."

"If that's an invitation I'll join you in a second. This is the last video I need to look at."

"What are you watching?"

"Video of the shooting."

"Can I see it?" She walks in, closing the door behind her.

I don't think twice about the answer. I push back from the desk and stand, offering her the chair.

She's bright eyes and smiles as she sits and pulls up to the desk.

I stand behind the chair. "Riley, play video."

Instead of watching the monitor, I watch her reaction. I know the exact moment Edwards steps in front of us because her back straightens. Her body jerks after each shot is fired. Her hand trembles as she reaches for mine. Silent tears roll down her cheeks. Dani's reliving that night.

"You don't have to watch this."

"Why are you watching it?"

"I'm trying to find something."

"I don't get it. The theater was full of people that night. Why were we the only ones walking in the courtyard after the movie let out?"

How perceptive of her. "Remember you had to pee and wanted to beat the crowd to the restroom, so we left right when the end credits started to roll. A man in his late fifties had a heart attack in the theater. The lobby was packed by the time you came out of the restroom and we went out the side door. When the shots were fired, a few people came running in our direction. Porter had to show his identification because one was an off-duty police officer."

"Did the man die?"

"No, but Ig reviewed the man's medical history and tested his blood. Ig found traces of a drug that can cause a heart attack." I tell her the whole story. It's like what happened at the mall when that kid spilled his candy. The man felt a bite in his arm when he stood to leave the theater. Ig found a small puncture wound in the man's arm.

"Can Riley slow down the video? I want to watch it again."

"Riley, replay the video frame by frame."

The images on the monitor play like a slide show. We walk out of the theater. I move behind her. Edwards walk up. First shot. Second shot. Third...

"Stop!" Dani yells out and shoves back from the desk. The chair slams into me. "That bullet would have killed me if you had not shifted our positions."

I nod my head.

"James was trying to kill me?"

From the angle of the camera, she can't see his face. "Edwards never fired his weapon."

"What?"

"Riley, play video number four frame by frame." I stand by Dani as we watch the scene unfold from a different angle.

"There was another person," she says. "You're trying to see who shot at you."

"Yes, but the person wasn't shooting at me." I leave her to inter- pret the rest herself.

"How can I help?"

I was expecting more tears, even shock— not an offer to help identify the shooter. I pull up another chair beside her.

We view all the videos I have from that night.

———◆———

Hump day is turning out to be just as busy at the previous day. People in and out of my office. The constant ringing of my desk phone and the nonstop buzzing of my cell phone. I do press the pause button to take a call from my daughters and niece. Dani is laughing in the background as they promise to get me back for rubberbanding their braids to one another then setting the house alarm to sound off at six forty-five before I left the house.

I remind them they started it.

A call comes in from the Watcher at the lobby desk. I disconnect from the girls to answer.

"Sir, there are two gentlemen here to see you."

"I don't have anyone scheduled. If it's about Hawkeye, send them to Paul."

I listen to the Watcher convey the message and hear the visitor's reply. "Tell him it's Terrance Brumfield and he'll want to see us."

Ricci and Fontenot tear into my office demanding my immediate attention. I exhale and gesture for them to give me a second and tell the Watcher to escort the gentlemen to the lobby conference room and I'll be down in a minute.

Fontenot slams Brumfield's file on the desk in front of me.

Vin is the first to speak. "She found a connection between Brumfield and Hopper."

"What?!" I snatch up the file and read the highlighted areas of the report.

"Terrance Brumfield, Elijah Hopper, George Franklin, and Willis Langford went through Military Entrance Processing Station at the same time. Back then, Phantom recruited right out of MEPS based on the Armed Services Vocational Aptitude Battery test. Brumfield didn't pass the physical because of a childhood knee injury."

"Brumfield wasn't Phantom."

"That may not necessarily be true. Fontenot couldn't access Brumfield's file so she called me for help. I can't get into it, you can't either. Only POTUS."

"I tried looking into Franklin's and Hopper's files too. Same situation," Fontenot adds.

There is a journal that each president passes down to his successor. I pick up the secured phone and put a call in to President Hart. He's in a closed session meeting. I send him an urgent message.

"Do you at least have a photo of Hopper?"

"Last page of the file. I took his service picture and asked one of the tech guys to age the facial features."

I flip to the last page and gawk at the man we've been searching for. No word, in any language, can describe the emotion that fills me. I ate lunch with Elijah Hopper. Talked about my wife and kids— my company. I was sitting with the enemy.

Something is wrong with the Facial Recognition system. I'm trying to see who was identified in the last five minutes. Then it hits me.

If I could fly I'd flap my wings to take me high in the sky, then dive, at full speed, down to the lobby, and swoop in with my talons ready to snatch up the Watcher on duty.

Instead, my chair flies across the floor and hits the glass as I get to my feet and run out of the room. The elevator can't get here fast enough. I pace in front of the door. On the third pass, it opens. "Lobby," I yell before Riley can ask.

As it travels down two floors, I try to rein it in. The door opens and I run to the Watcher's station. Ricci and I jump the counter at the same time. I manage to shove the Watcher to the side and discover he was trying to delete the last two entries in the latest recording.

Terrance Brumfield's information fills the screen. I go to the next record.

The Watcher scurries around Ricci.

Elijah Hopper's name flashes on the image on the screen.

That fucking Watcher knew exactly who was standing at the desk requesting to see me.

Fontenot takes down the Watcher with one good punch to the boys.

I run to the conference room. The doorknob leaves a dent in the wall. I stand in the doorway glaring at the two men seated at the table.

"How do you take down your enemy?" Brumfield asks.

Wrinkle lines cross my forehead. "What?!"

"How. Do. You. Take. Down. Your. Enemy?"

It's the last question on the written test to become a ghost. "You become the enemy."

Elijah Hopper gestures to the chair across from them. "Have a seat, son. There are some things about Phantom and RAGS and Danielle's parents that we need to school you on before you go after Langford."

The microchip, the wedding ring, and the laptop are stored in the safe in my office. I pull them out and take them to my desk.

Hopper's and Brumfield's tale play over and over in my head.

George Franklin, Terrance Brumfield, Elijah Hopper, and Willis Langford became friends the day they met for MEPS. Since Brumfield's knee took him out of the running for getting into the military, Second Command found a way around it by making him a civilian employee of Phantom. The other three went into the military and the United States government paid for Brumfield to go to college.

Brumfield's locked classified file says he's a retired biochemist who engineered the recipe for the odorless smokeless bomb. To the public, he is a retired high school science teacher. Daniel Tatum, Danielle's father, was one of his best students. Daniel confided in Brumfield that Elizabeth's father, Willis Langford, was working for RAGS. Hopper, Franklin and Brumfield plotted against Langford to stop him from destroying the democracy he'd taken an oath to protect. Hopper's locked military file reads: he's a Phantom Ghost working undercover in the inner circle of RAGS since 1985. How do you take down the enemy? You become the enemy.

George Franklin started showing signs of dementia in 2005. Langford suggested the friends take turns staying with George for a week to give Katherine a rest. When the symptoms worsened, the decision was made to put George in the nursing home and the friends continued to visit him. Two years ago, Langford happened to visit on a day when George was remembering the old days. He inadvertently told Langford James is alive.

Langford came home and instigated a coup to overthrow the leader of RAGS who is also the descendant of the founding father, Dominique Elian Toussaint.

Last year, Brumfield's deadly smoke bomb recipe was stolen right before Edwards's wife and son were taken.

That brings me back to why I'm in my office with the laptop, ring and microchip. Once the program loads I take a deep breath. "Please don't let me be wrong about them."

Hopper gave me what I needed to unlock the last security code. I type in the eight-character password that has been right in front of me all this time. Even I have used its definition when I talked about Dani being an artist when she's boxing. I key in the capital letters. P. U. G. I. L. I. S. M. Pugilism— the art of boxing.

The screen's monitor goes black. A puppeteered piece of white chalk draws a door, then a stick figure that resembles pugil sticks.

The stick figure comes to life, jumping up and down, shadow boxing.

A robotic voice comes through the laptop's speakers. "Hello, Jamal."

The stick figure folds its arms and taps. Animated question marks dance around its head.

My fingers type out the words as I say them out loud. "Hello, Pugil. Please open the door."

"Okay." The stick figure pulls a skeleton key out of an invisible pocket, unlocks the door, and walks into an empty room. It begins to draw ten treasure chests. Each with a skeleton lock.

The figure turns back to me. "Which one do you want to open first?"

I go with the first number that pops up in my mind. "Box number five."

The figure unlocks the box, then draws a bed in the lower right corner of the screen. He climbs in bed. "Wake me when you need me."

The box opens. Labeled files fall out of the box like they're on a conveyer belt.

I click on the first file. Photos, audio recordings, and documents open.

As I go through each file in each box, the puzzle pieces on the board come together.

———◆———

I don't know how long I've been standing in the shower with my eyes closed and my forehead against the glass letting the hot water hit the back of my neck.

"What's wrong, Bryan?" Dani steps in with me.

Why didn't I hear her come into the bathroom? *Your mind is still trying to process decades of information.*

"All this time," I whisper, tilting my head back to let the water hit my face.

"Talk to me. You've been distracted since you got home and you didn't eat dinner."

This is one of those things I can't talk to you about. At least not yet.

She ducks under my arm and stands in front of me. I bring my forehead down to hers and stare into her eyes unsure of what I'm searching for.

You know what you're seeking. In her eyes, you want to find the reason why it never occurred to you that the real leader of RAGS has been by your side all this time. Advising you.

Dani cups my cheek and uses her thumb to trace the line of my lip. She rises on her toes to kiss me, then wraps her arms around my waist. "What do you need, Bry?"

"I need you..." My voice falters. *I need you to be strong because we're at war and the people we thought were our friends are actually our enemies. I need to know you really love me and want a life with me.*

"You have me. You've *always* had me." She kisses me again.

I close my eyes and put my everything behind this kiss. Transferring my soul to her for safekeeping. Only she can pull me back from the darkness.

Of their own accord, my hands run over her baby bump.

The water is turned off. She takes my hands, guiding me out of the shower room. My feet step onto the soft fibers of a floor mat. I look down. *When did she put that here?*

I look around the bathroom as if I'm seeing it for the first time. *When did she do all this?*

Dani reaches for a towel and runs the warm cloth over my body, then uses it to dry my hair. She's putting me first. I reach for a towel and return the favor.

She takes my hand. We walk side by side to our bedroom and into our closet.

I look around at how her clothes and accessories blend nicely with mine. My closet no longer smells of my cologne.

Our closet smells of a perfect balance between her and me.

No one scent overpowers the other.

She reaches for the moisturizer, squeezing some in my hands first, then hers. We spread the cream over each other's body, keeping a connection with our eyes while we touch.

Dani moves over to the chest of drawers. It's new and it looks custom made. *When did she exchange this one for the old one?*

She steps into a pair of panties, then opens another drawer, pulling out the silk pajamas she bought me when she went shopping on Rodeo Drive. I never thought I would be a silk pajamas type of man, but I like the way they feel against my skin.

She squats in front of me, holds the bottoms open so I can step into them, then pulls them up my legs. The waistband rests low on my hips. I help her into the pajama top, only fastening the middle two buttons.

I follow her out of the closet into our bedroom. With my eyes now wide open, I notice the changes she's made to make this a married couple's bedroom. It's the balance between us as a couple with children, and us individually as man and woman.

The throw over the back of the couch and colorful throw pillows. The many photos of us and the girls on the mantel of the fireplace is our family. The ultra-sound picture of our son in the middle.

Gone are the shades that hung over the glass doors, replaced by drapes that frame the view of the mountains. Reminding me of why I love the outdoors and why I opted for glass doors instead of windows.

The leather reclining chairs and mounted television have been moved to another area in our room. Our son's custom-made crib and mattress now sits there along with the matching changing table and rocking chair I conveniently forgot to tell my wife I ordered.

We go around the room and turn off the lights and climb into bed. Dani scoots close to me, encouraging me to rest my head on her chest. She holds me.

The light from the moon shines through the glass doors and the sounds of nocturnal animals helps me stay in the here and now with my wife. I peel back the unbuttoned section of the pajama top and cover her stomach with my hand. "I love you," I tell both of them.

My eyelids get heavy. I finally allow my body to relax. The rhythmic rise and fall of Dani's chest calms me. She's already asleep and I feel myself drifting off too.

A high-pitched scream of terror coming from the other side of the house filters through the closed door of our bedroom.

I forgot to make sure the house is locked up and now my children are in danger!

CHAPTER TWENTY

ROLLING OUT OF BED. GRABBING my gun from the safe under the nightstand. Jumping to my feet. All executed in one military-trained movement, I run out of our room pushing my feet and legs to get me to the other side of the house.

Just as I pass the stairs the sound of Dani's bare feet slapping the hard wood floors echoes behind me.

Emm's bedroom door flies open. She runs from her room crying.

I hide the gun behind me as she sprints past me into her mother's arms.

"What's wrong, sweetie?" Dani wraps her arms around our child.

Willis comes charging up the stairs with his weapon. *When did he get back?*

Jessi stumbles from her room in her usual nightclothes and looking flushed.

Kourt moseys out of her room, wiping the sleep from her eyes.

"I saw someone in my room," Emm cries.

"Get back to our room. Jessi, go with Dani and the girls," I order, pushing Kourt toward my wife.

Dani grabs our girls by the hand.

"Wait," Kourt yells. "Where's Trevor?"

Shit! He would have started barking when Emm screamed.

"I'll find him. Go with Mom. Now!"

Dani tugs our reluctant child as she runs back to our room with my sister trailing behind.

Willis nods twice. I rush into Emm's room.

The fingers of my right hand slide along the wall as my eyes adjust to the darkness. I find the switch and flip it and do a visual assessment. Unmade bed. Bathroom door cracked open. Windows closed. Closet door closed. Nothing sticking out from under the bed.

Willis stands guard on the other side of the door in case the intruder gets past me.

I take my time to searching.

There are no signs of anyone other than my daughter being in here. Her windows are locked. I'll call in Sweepers to go through the room to be certain.

"Why are you back? Where's Ross?" I ask Willis when I open the door.

He lowers his weapon. "Sent him home. Fish weren't biting so we came back early."

"Have you seen Trevor?"

"Last time I saw him, he was in the family room."

"Where's your wife?"

"Asleep in the downstairs living quarters. She wanted to stay close. Said you seemed distracted."

"Go check on her."

Willis nods and rushes down the stairs.

I run back to our room. Dani has Emm cradled in her arms. They are sitting on the couch. Kourt is lying on my side of the bed, hugging my pillow. Jessi paces the floor.

"Did you find him?" Kourt asks.

"I'm going downstairs to look for him."

"By yourself?" Dani asks.

I don't answer. I go to the closet and get the laptop out of my briefcase then activate the Hawk alert. The guys and I came up with codes when we each moved into our own places.

I pull a pair of jeans off the hanger in front of me and a pair of boxers out of the dresser.

In the room, my phone goes off four times.

Dani brings it to me.

While I reply to the messages, Dani hands me a shirt and socks, then pulls my boots off the shoe rack.

"Open the floor safe. Get the Glock and two magazines and give them to Jessi."

She follows the order without question or hesitation.

I try to locate Trevor using the tracking chip code. The black dot flashes on the house address. After I tie the laces of the boots, I grab four magazines from the safe and shove them in each pocket and fast walk out of the room.

My front door opens as I jog down the stairs. Tony and Vin step into the foyer.

"Room-by-room, we stick together," I order once they cross the threshold with their weapons drawn.

Willis creeps out of the security room. "The cameras are offline. We're blind. What do you want me to do?"

"Find your wife and stay with her."

The rodent scurries away. I go into the security room and shut down all the lights in the house and digitally lock certain doors.

Tony, Vin, and I get into formation. Flashlights and guns in our hands, we search the first floor of the house starting with the sitting room.

We take our time. If someone's in here we'll know.

Vin is on point. I've got right flank; Tony has left. We come to the inner garage door. Slowly, Vin eases it open. A whine greets us. We do a visual check. Vin gives the "go-ahead" signal.

"Trevor?" I whisper.

He whines again.

We break formation. Vin goes forward. I go right. Tony— left.

Trevor whines.

I round Dani's Range Rover. He's lying on his side, his shiny black coat highlighted by the flashlight. His back is to me, but I can see the rapid rise and fall of his ribcage. I check under the truck and the interior and do the same for the other vehicles before I come to the front of him. A pool of vomit is near his mouth. "I found him."

"All clear." Vin comes out of the gym.

Tony and I mimic the all clear call.

I drop to my knee at Trevor's side, holstering my weapon.

Tony walks toward us. "Looks like he's been poisoned."

"Get him to the vet," I command.

Tony opens the backdoor to Dani's truck. I lift Trevor off the ground and lay him down.

Vin jumps in the driver seat. "Where's the key?" He flips down the sun visor and opens the center console.

"Under the seat," I tell him.

He gets the key and starts the engine. Tony runs over placing his hand on the sensor. The garage door opens.

Vin throws the truck into reverse, backing out of the driveway. The tires kick up smoke as they spin on the asphalt. He takes off in the direction of the twenty-four-hour veterinarian clinic.

The garage door closes. We walk back inside and go to the security room. Tony logs into the interior cameras. I take the exterior cameras. I dedicate one monitor to the camera in my room so I have eyes on Dani and the girls. I dedicate another to the room the Langfords are in.

I rewind the exterior cameras' footage to the hour before Emm screamed.

It's a lengthy process to view, but Tony and I work fast. Every few minutes, my gaze shifts to see Dani and Emm talking.

"I went all the way back to eighteen hundred hours, the time you came home. Nothing," Tony says without looking up from the monitors.

"How did Trevor end up in the garage?"

"From what I can tell the door cracked open after you walked through."

"You know that's bullshit Tony."

He pulls up the video of me pulling into the garage in the Suburban, climbing out of the truck, walking through the door, closing it behind me and walking out of view.

The door cracks open.

I leave the security room with a flashlight. Inspecting the faceplate and strike plate on the door. The catch is pushed in.

Twisting and turning the knob, I try to dislodge it, but it won't move. I storm back into the security room. "I don't like being fucked with in my own home, Tony. Who fucked with the lock?"

"I'm telling you, Bry, there's nothing on the monitors. I've gone frame by frame on the one in Emm's room too."

"Bry, can I talk to you for a second?" Dani stands in the doorway of the security room. She's using her phone's flashlight to navigate her way around the house. She's changed into sweats and one of my sweatshirts.

I pick up a battery-operated lantern and follow her into the family room.

"Have you ever shown Emm pictures of Amelia?"

I shake my head and set the lantern on the coffee table to give us some light.

"What did she look like?"

"Tall, brunette, brown eyes." I shrug. "Why are you asking these questions?"

"I asked her to tell me what the person in her room looked like. She said the lady had a long blond ponytail, blue eyes, red lipstick and a lot of makeup on her face. She was wearing a black shirt, black vest, and black jeans with a black belt and black high-heeled boots. When I asked about the dream where I got hurt she couldn't remember any of the details, not even what I was wearing, but she was able to tell me every detail of the person in her room even though the room was dark."

The hairs on the nape of my neck stand up. An uneasy feeling setting deep in my gut, but I wait for Dani's conclusion before I let that feeling take over.

"Bryan, Emma loves horses. We read about them all the time. We've read about stables too. She didn't have a dream about me getting hurt. Some woman spoke to her when she was at the stables. That woman told her I was going to die so I wouldn't be *her* mom anymore. If you hadn't shifted positions, I would be dead."

Anger starts to boil in my blood. I pull out my cell phone and type out the command for Riley to locate Malinda Williamson.

Dani silently sits on the sofa watching me.

I think back to my teatime with Kourt. She told me about going to the stables and the man who takes care of their ponies *and the lady who took a long time helping Emm.*

Fuck!

"You figured out when that woman said something to her, didn't you?"

I nod.

"Do you know what day of the week that was?"

I shake my head.

"Monday."

That was the same day someone took a shot at Dani.

"That's why she's been having anxiety attacks and why she got car sick when we were going to Colorado Springs." Dani wraps her arms around herself. "I should have picked up on it then."

Dark thoughts run through my head that involve a hundred ways I'm going to torture then murder that woman.

"Bryan, did you buy this?" Dani points to a plant on the coffee table next to the lantern.

I shake my head.

"Where did it come from?"

I shrug my shoulders, walking over to look at it.

"Bryan, this is a Peace Lily. It's poisonous for dogs and it looks like Trevor was chewing on it."

There's soil and parts of chewed up leaves on the table near the plant holder. "Trevor doesn't chew on any of the other plants inside or outside. Why would he chew on this one?"

Dani grabs the newspaper, spreading it out.

"Don't touch anything," I bark. I run to the kitchen and return with a pair of serving tongs, rubber gloves, and dishtowels.

Dani ties a dishtowel in the back of her head to cover her mouth and nose. She slips her hands into the gloves, and turns over the plant holder emptying its content onto the newspaper.

"What is that?" she points to chunks in the soil.

Covering my nose with a dishtowel, I use the tongs to sift through the soil, picking up one of the chunks. I hold it closer to the light. "Looks like a doggie treat. Where in the fuck did this plant come from?!"

"It was delivered this afternoon, right after Danielle took the girls to the park."

We turn toward the door.

"The card that came with it is on the mantel above the fire-place," Willis says.

"Don't touch it," I tell her. "Do you remember what florist company delivered it?"

"No, but the delivery person was a blonde-haired woman. She was driving a blue delivery van."

"Dani, do not touch that card," I shout over my shoulder going across the hall to the security room. "Tony go back to sixteen hundred hours on the front door camera."

He taps the monitor, then swipes it with his finger a couple of times and taps the monitor again. A blue delivery van pulls up in front and a blonde- haired female climbs out with the plant in her hands and a clipboard.

She keeps her head down as she walks up to the steps, ringing the doorbell.

Willis opens the door.

"I have a delivery for Danielle Hawk."

"I'll sign for it." Willis takes the clipboard, signing the paper on top, then handing it back. The woman hands him the plant and the card.

"Show your face," Tony growls.

As if she heard him, the woman lifts her head before climbing back into the van, driving off.

Her features are familiar, but I don't recall ever seeing her up close.

Tony goes back to the part when she looks up. He freezes the picture and taps the monitor sending a copy to Fontenot with instructions.

Swiping the monitor, he goes back to the beginning. Then slows down the video frame by frame. The delivery van pulls up. He freezes the frame. "No plates."

I sit down in front of the monitors simultaneously tapping them, pulling up the cameras facing opposite directions that record activity on the street, poring through the footage for the same timeframe until I find what I'm looking for.

"Look." I replay the footage frame by frame.

On one monitor, my Silverado is backing down the driveway; the camera captures it turning left at the stop sign.

On the other monitor, a blue van pulls away from the curb when the truck makes the turn.

"She waited until Dani left the house to make the delivery," Tony says.

My cell phone beeps. I open the message. Riley was able to extract an image from the video. I nudge Tony to change the screen on the monitor he's sitting in front of and I go through the security codes to open the image so he can see it too. It's grainy and the person is in the shadows, but there's no mistaking who's standing on the side of a building holding the rifle. She knew enough to stay out of view of the cameras in the courtyard, but she didn't factor in the adjacent business having an old security system. "That's the second shooter."

"Is that—"

"Yes," I interrupt him. "I'm taking the plant to Ig, then I'm going to have a final conversation with that woman. Can you—"

"With my life and even then, I'll keep fighting."

I know he means every word of his vow.

I go in search of Dani. She and Willis are bagging up the plant, the holder, and soil in plastic bags. She hands them to me. The card is put in a separate bag.

I pull her into my arms, lift her chin with my fingers, and kiss my wife. "I love you, Dani, and I'm coming home to you guys. *Tony's* got eyes on you until I get back." That last part was more for Willis.

My movements are on autopilot while my mind sorts through what's going on. I pull into a stall in front of Ig's building, grab the zip lock bags, and climb out of the truck.

First I clear security to get to his section, then place the bags in a specimen box. In the locker room, I strip down and go through the decontamination shower. Ig is anal about the controlled environment of his facility. I change into a Level C hazmat one-piece jumper, and step into Major Ignacio Acosta Jr.'s very sterile laboratory.

He's already pulled the plastic bags out of the box and is taking samples of the card. At another table, I put samples of the soil, leaves, and doggie treats on slides and get them ready for him to go through the process of analyzing.

Ig loves all this stuff. He's in his element. He'll let us in the operating room, but his laboratory is different. Ig has a creative mind. Medical personnel dream of having space and endless funding to make medical history. Ig has it right here.

After I finish my part, I get out of his way and watch the medical genius at work.

At zero four hundred hours, I get a text from Vin: Trevor is going to pull through. I pass the message on to Dani.

At zero six hundred hours, Ig reads the lab results.

"The leaves of the Peace Lily have traces of raw beef on them. The meat-flavored dog treats didn't have any substance added to them. The card is covered with a low LD50 of altered snake venom that is absorbed through the skin and fast acting. The venom attacks the major organs of the body causing them to shut down. The victim goes into organ failure within twenty-four hours of coming in contact. Did you read the handwritten message?"

"No."

"It says, 'You should have died in that courtyard.'"

———◆———

My fingers keep up with the ideas flowing through my mind.

"Sir?" Porter stands in the doorway, waiting for permission to enter.

I nod.

The frown on his face and the hesitant steps across the threshold of the door are enough to make me stop typing.

Porter stares me in the eyes. "I showed the photo of the delivery person to Edwards. He confirmed it to be Deidra Billups. I went to Malinda Williamson's residence to bring her in like you requested, but her place has been cleared out. Her car is in the garage. I found the body of Tristan Banks in the trunk. Preliminary report indicates he's been dead for twenty-four hours. I searched his pockets and found a paper that was three-quarters of the way burned. The only thing salvageable was the copy of the seal from the state of Arizona. I went to his office at the county registrar's office and wiped his computer clean."

The strength of my fingers tries to burrow ten holes into my skull. Time's run out. She knows about Kourtney.

I stand and present my hand for a handshake. "Get your house in order. Riley will be in contact."

"Roger that, sir."

I watch him leave the room.

———◆———

"Daddy," Kourtney sings, jumping into my arms the minute I close the door.

"Hi, baby girl." I kiss her cheek and carry her into the family room.

"Trevor ate a plant that made him sick, but Uncle Vinny said he's going to be okay."

"I'm happy Trevor's okay."

She jumps out of my arms and reclaims her spot on the floor next to her dog. She rubs his head. "I'm going to take good care of you, boy."

"Hi, Emma." She's sitting on the sofa. Worry lines on her forehead. "Why the long face?"

"I don't want anything to happen to Mommy."

"Nothing's going to happen to Mommy. I'll make sure of it. Where is she?"

"Aunt Jessi made her go lie down because she's been up all night."

"Where's Aunt Jessica?"

"She went to the hospital."

I kiss her cheek, then leave them in the family room.

The minute I open the door, I hear Danielle's recorded voice. She's sitting on the couch with a note pad in her hand. "I thought you were supposed to be resting."

She picks up the digital recorder, turning it off. "I can't rest knowing some woman used our daughter to threaten me."

"Deidra Billups."

"What?"

"The woman's name is Deidra Billups. Right now, I need to close my eyes for a minute. Come lie with me." I take her hand pulling her off the couch.

We kick off our shoes and climb into bed.

"I'm sending you and the girls out of the country."

She yawns. "I will do whatever you ask me to do."

"Right now, I'm asking you to close your eyes and go to sleep."

"You know what I meant."

"You should have been more specific."

She grunts and wiggles and squirms until she finds a comfortable position. It's not long before her breathing pattern starts to slow to that of slumber. I hold her close and her body completely relaxes. A few more minutes, she's snoring.

My calm demeanor is successfully masking the turmoil deep within. I close my eyes and mentally run through the details for Plan C.

Never have we had to go this far, but the situation calls for it. RAGS's leader knows more about our operation than any other adversary.

My mind is on elimination overload. Every thought is about how I'm going to take these people down. If I'm to stay on top of the game, I need to get back to the office. My cell phone vibrates in my pocket. Without disturbing Danielle, I pull out it and read look at the ninja cartoon character Max sent.

I slip out of the bed and go downstairs to my home office. Tony packed up my confidential files and moved them and my weapons into the security room under the stairs before he left. It killed me to tell him to leave, but every move we make from now on has to be well thought out. We can't tip Langford off until he's staring down the barrel of my gun right before I pull the trigger.

I look around to make sure nothing looks out of place. I access our home security system and change the list of people authorized to bypass security measures and have access to the security room.

Marie is in the kitchen. I count to three, deep exhale, and step in the doorway. "I'm going back to the office to for a couple of hours. Dani is finally asleep."

"Okay, Bryan. I'll keep an eye on the girls and make sure they don't disturb her. Do you want me to put a plate in the oven for you?"

"Yes, please. It smells good." Langford has had many opportunities to harm Dani and Kourt. I'm trusting he won't do anything to them in the next few hours.

———◆———

Max and I pull into the garage of the office building at the same time.

"Ready to get dropped on your ass?" He loves to talk trash when we spar.

I shove him into the elevator's cab. "When have you ever been able to drop me on my ass?"

"Your memory is failing in your old age, Bry."

"Aren't you knocking on fifty's door?"

He fakes indignance. "Fuck you, I just turned forty-five and I look damn good for my age."

"Good evening, sir. What floor?"

"Third floor." I inspect Max's face. "Didn't you just have a mug lift?"

He flips me off. "Keep it up, Bry, and you'll be my bitch by the end of this workout."

The elevator doors open; we step off and enter one of the three sparring rooms. We drop our gym bags in the corner. I change into my workout clothes and start warming up. The intimidation taunts continue. Max knows I need to do something physical so I can focus on tightening up Plan C.

I secure the strap of my headgear, put in the mouth guard, then step onto the mat and wait for the old man. Very people know this, but Maxim Li Chen is a real-life ninja.

We circle each other, then get into stance.

"I need it hard and rough, Maxie. I've got a lot of energy."

"I love giving it hard and rough. You've heard that old saying, once you let Maxim break you in, you'll never want the taco again."

"Maxie. The pussy I have at home is sweeter than you." I throw the first punch.

My body does what it is trained to do while I get into my head. I visualize each enemy. List how I'm going to take them down and why it's necessary for me to kill them.

Max and I have worked up a sweat.

At one point, I'm so focused on what's in my head, Max backhands me across the face.

I freeze.

"Don't go pea in a pocket on me now. I bitch slapped that Horny Toad harder than that."

"That's her!" I throw off the headgear, run out of the room to the stairway, take them three at a time to the fourth floor.

I burst into Porter's office. "Pull up that image of Deidra."

Max comes through the door behind me. "Who's her?"

I point to the screen. "Slim down her face a bit. Give her green eyes, red hair, a mole on the right side of her mouth, collagen lips and a spray tan." The image changes several times.

"That's Madelyn Brooks," Max shouts.

"Deidra Madelyn Billups-Brooks," I correct him.

I tap my pants looking for my phone. "Fuck, I left it in my gym bag."

Porter takes a shaky breath. "I solved the anagram and created an account. I know what the haunted house is for." He turns his monitor around for us to see. "It's the contract to kill Phantom's Elite Special Operations Team. RAGS need you guys out of the way because of this." The satellite photos are of surface-to-air missiles attached to transporter erector launcher and radar vehicles traveling through Yemen under the cover of darkness.

"Colonel Hawk," Riley's voice carries throughout the building.

I push the button for the speaker phone and dial Riley's number.

"A lock down has been initiated at nine, seven, three, three, one, Canyon Road."

My house.

"Initiated by whom?"

"Danielle Lauren Hawk."

Dani and the girls are in trouble.

"Lock it down. No one in, no one out. Block all Wi-Fi and cell phone towers in a thirty-mile radius. Block all satellite signals in the area. Keep Hawk emergency signal open." I turn to Porter. "Have Delta Team on standby for backup. We're going in, in thirty minutes."

"Roger that, sir."

My superpowers kick in. I fly to my office, pack up all my weapons, the two military briefcases, and Edwards's laptop. Next, I fly down to the garage. Max is gearing up, standing by my truck with my gym bag at his feet.

"You retired from the field," I remind him as I open the storage unit in the floorboards to take out my military duffle bag.

"If someone is fucking with them, I'm in on the kill."

I change into my special ops gear right there in the garage.

Max dumps his bags on the backseat and climb into the front. "What's the plan?"

"Rescue my wife and children. Evacuate the Vice President, and the people on our lists. Attract the enemy. Destroy the real leaders of RAGS."

"No survivors," Max vows.

I put in a call to the President of the United States while I race to my house.

DANIELLE'S INTERLUDE

I DON'T KNOW HOW LONG I'VE been asleep; Kourtney is shaking my shoulder. "Mommy, Mrs. Brooks is here to see you."

Why would Madelyn come to see me? I haven't seen or heard from her since her son was expelled from the school. "Where's Dad?"

"He went to the office."

"Where's Marie?" I sit up in the bed and look at the time on the clock. It's seven thirty in the evening.

"I don't know. She was in the kitchen."

Marie usually has dinner on the table by now. "Have you guys had dinner yet?"

"No, and we're hungry."

"Who let Mrs. Brooks in the house?"

"I don't know. She just walked into the family room and started talking."

"Where's Emma?"

"She's in the family room. Mrs. Brooks told me to come wake you." The tone of my daughter's voice motivates me to get out of bed. I slide my feet into flip flops, I go to the bathroom, wash the sleep out of my eyes, and rinse my mouth.

Kourtney and I hold hands walking down the stairs.

Painting a fake smile on my face, I walk with my daughter into the family room. "Hello, Madelyn."

She's standing in front of the mantel leering at our family photos. As usual, she's inappropriately dressed. Revealing blouse. Jeans so tight they look like they are cutting off the circulation to her lower half. Big hooped earrings. Designer stiletto heels.

"Hi, Danielle," she ribbits as she turns to face me with a fake gasp. "Tsk! Tsk! Sweetie-pie. You are so fat." She smirks. "Don't you think you need to push away from the table? If you aren't careful Bryan might stray, if he already hasn't."

I glare at her. "Why are you here?"

"Didn't your babysitters teach you better manners? Invite me to sit. Offer me a glass of wine. That is the hospitable thing to do."

My automatic reaction is to roll my eyes. "Have a seat Madelyn and tell me why you're here." To hell with the glass of wine. She won't be staying long.

She sashays to a chair, eases down, and crosses her legs.

I sit on the sofa in between the girls. Emma climbs onto my lap straddling me, her arms wrap around my neck. I look over her shoulder at Madelyn with a raised eyebrow, rubbing my daughter's back.

"How are you? I heard about your tumble down the stairs."

"I'm fine."

"You really should be more careful. You could have died and I wouldn't have made money…"

Emma shifts, like she's shielding me. Her arms squeeze me tighter. She's holding me so close I feel her rapid heartbeats.

Trevor whines. He slowly rises on wobbly legs and turtle walks to the doorway. His head twists as he looks toward the kitchen. The front of my leggings feels warm all of a sudden. I pull Emma back, staring at her.

She just peed on me!

Madelyn continues to talk, but her words are not registering. Emma is shaking like a leaf. Her eyes are wide and glossy. She's looks like she's choking. My daughter is in full panic mode.

I've got to call Bryan. Damn, I left my phone upstairs. Where is Marie? Let me get my children out of here, then I'll call Bryan.

"Will you excuse me, Trevor needs his pain medication, that's why he's whining." I grab Kourtney's hand and stand, shifting Emma to my hip. I don't give Madelyn the chance to reply. "Come help me, girls. Come, Trevor," I command.

Kourtney can barely keep up with my pace as I fast walk down the hall to the kitchen. I'm determined to get to Marie.

"You're okay, baby," I whisper in Emm's ear. "Mommy needs you to breathe, sweetie." The hallway seems fuzzy the closer we get to the kitchen. *It's smoke!*

"Marie?" I try not to sound panicked. We tear through the kitchen door. She's not in here, but pots are on the fire and smoke billows from the oven door. "Why didn't the smoke alarms go off?" I look up. Something is covering them.

I sit Emma in a chair and rush over, turning off the burners and pushing the off button for the oven. "Stay here." I run to the laundry room and call for Marie. She's not in there.

Trevor whines and paces in front of the walk-in pantry. Something thick and red is seeping from under the door. I tiptoe over and open the door.

My hands cover my mouth to stifle the scream. Marie lies lifeless on the floor. I can't see where the blood is coming from.

I grab my girls' hands and get them out of the kitchen. We go to Bryan's office and close the door behind us after Trevor turtle walks in.

The girls look terrified and Trevor's ears are standing up.

"Jacob's mom is the lady who said you're going to die and not be my mommy anymore," Emma whispers. "But she looked different."

"Okay, baby. It's going to be okay." I go into protective mode. I place my hand on the desk sensor. "Riley?"

"Yes, ma'am."

"Lock down the house."

"Identification please."

"Delta. Lima. Hotel. Nine. Zero. Five. Eight."

"Lock down commence in ten, nine, eight, seven, six, five, four, three, two, one." I hear the motor on the shutters rolling down over the windows and doors. The house grows dark. My eyes quickly adjust to the darkness.

The firecracker-sounding pop from a bullet leaving a gun travels through the house.

The girls start to scream, but I cover their mouths with my hand.

"You're only going to piss me off, Danielle," Madelyn shouts from the family room. "Let's not play hide and seek. I wouldn't want to accidently shoot Kourtney. I just learned how valuable she is. Bryan can't get to her fast enough to save the day. When I left him, he was fucking Amelia anyway." Madelyn's voice is coming from the hallway between the family room and Bryan's office.

Trevor whines. I push my daughters under the desk. "Hush, boy,"

I command and push him under the desk too. I grab the desk lamp, yank the cord out of the socket, kick off my flip flops and tiptoe to the door.

"You remember Tristan Banks, don't you? Stephanie Banks's husband. Our kids got kicked out of the school for calling Kourtney those names. Guess what Tristan does for a living? I'll give you a hint. I know your and Bryan's secret. Have you told her yet?"

I look toward the desk and pray our girls don't understand.

"Of course, I had to kill him because he suddenly grew a conscience and wouldn't give me a copy so I thought I'd get yours and show it to my people."

Her footsteps move past the office door heading toward the kitchen.

I tiptoe back to the desk. "Come on," I tell them and help them to their feet.

We tiptoe to the door. Trevor's nails tick-tack on the hardwood floors. Madelyn will hear us if Trevor follows, but I'm not leaving him behind.

"Girls, take off your shoes and give me your socks."

They do not hesitate to do as I tell them. I set the lamp on the floor and, one paw at a time, I slip the socks on Trevor.

He tilts his head to the side and stares at me like I'm insane.

"Don't judge me." I pat his head. Then turn to the girls. "We need to get somewhere safe. Grab hold of his collar and help me pull him to the wall under the stairs. Do not stop pulling no matter what happens. If she comes out of the kitchen, don't stop pulling." We ease him to the door. Trevor does not resist. "Kourt, open the door with your other hand." She turns the knob and slowly pulls the door open. I check the hallway. Madelyn's footsteps are coming from the formal dining room. "Quickly," I whisper. The girls and I pull Trevor by his collar to the wall under the stairs. My hand gropes and slides and feels along the wall. I try to find the sensor in the dark. Just as I'm about to give up, my hand slides over something small, flat, and cool. The panel slides open. We drag Trevor in by his collar. I place my right hand on the inside sensor to close the door.

An automatic light turns on in the security room and the monitors turn on.

Madelyn is still in the kitchen. She's pushing and pulling on the windows and doors, a gun in her hand.

"Riley."

"Yes, ma'am."

"Get a message to Colonel Hawk."

"Identification code for Hawk signal."

"Delta. Lima. Hotel. Nine. Zero. Five. Eight."

"Incorrect identification code."

"What the hell?! How do I get in touch with Bryan?" My fingers twist the wedding and engagement rings around my finger. First I need to go upstairs to get a couple of things, then I'm getting us out of this house. "You guys stay in here with Trevor. Do not come out for anyone but Dad, your uncles, or myself. Do you understand me?"

"Yes," Emma cries.

"I mean it, Kourtney. Do not come out for anyone other than us."

"I promise I won't come out for anyone but *you*." There's sadness in Kourtney's teary eyes that tug at my heart.

"You girls know what to do if someone approaches you?"

They nod.

Madelyn is in Bryan's office using her cell phone as a flashlight. She's trying to open the file cabinets. Someone is outside the backdoor typing on a laptop. I can't see their face. It could be Willis.

I open the storage cabinet and search for things I can use. It's full of weapons, equipment, gear, and emergency supplies. I pick up a pair of sweat pants and underwear for Emma, then open a package of wipes. I get her out of the wet clothes and clean her up. She dresses herself while I look through the cabinet for something for me to wear.

My stomach is too big for the clothes Bryan put in here for me. The only other choice I have are men's cargo pants and a sweatshirt. I'm not going to complain. He at least chose the right size panties.

I slip the sweatshirt over my head. It stops midway over my thighs. I reach underneath, peel off the wet leggings and panties, wipe myself down, and get dressed. I roll the pant legs up to my ankles.

Next, I snap a utility belt around my waist under my baby bump.

The gun holster clips onto the belt. I test out the weight of the guns and how quickly I can disengage the magazine and slap a new one in before I slip one in the holster and put two magazines in the thigh pocket.

Kourtney raises a questioning eyebrow at me.

I smile. "Dad taught me."

"Why would Bryan do that?"

"I'll explain later." I sit on the floor and cover each foot with three socks. Bryan didn't put any sneakers in here for me so I have to go with the smallest pair of military boots I can find. I tie the laces as tight as I can.

"Mommy, what are you doing?" Emma asks.

"Getting us out of here, sweetie."

"Don't you think we should wait for Daddy to come home?"

"I can't get in touch with Daddy to let him know what's going on and we need to get out of here." I peek over their shoulders at the monitors. Five people in black clothes are on the roof over the garage.

I take off the sweatshirt. Put on the biggest armor vest, then cover it with the sweatshirt. From the medical supplies, I put two elastic bandages in a pocket.

Madelyn is creeping along the hallway, her froggy voice coming over the sound system in the security room. "Danielle, why prolong this? RAGS don't want Bryan anymore. The billion is for his death. I just need to use his daughter as bait to get him to the warehouse. If Emma hadn't peed on you, you would already be dead. Come on out. Take the bullet that's coming to you and I'll be on my way."

I need to turn this into a game so my daughters don't get scared by the threats that Horny Toad is making. I pick up three walkie-talkies, handing one to each girl. The other one I keep for myself and attach an earpiece. "You guys remember how to use these, right?"

They nod.

"I'm going to play hide and seek with Mrs. Brooks and I want you two to help me cheat." I turn off the monitors to the outside cameras and lower the volume on the speakers in the room. "Don't pay attention to what she's saying. Mrs. Brooks likes to trash talk when she plays games."

I put on a pair of night vision sunglasses and play with the small buttons on the frame until I figure out how they work.

"Kourtney, where did you put the old wedding ring I gave you?"

"In my jewelry box."

I smile at my daughter and kiss her on the cheek. "You have a creative mind. Do you think you can find a way to get in touch with Dad? Tell him I'm playing hide and seek with Mrs. Brooks."

"For you I will try."

"Sweet Pea, I want you to keep your eyes on the monitors and tell me where Mrs. Brooks is, okay?"

"Okay."

"Do not be afraid. We will get out of here. Where is she, Sweet Pea?"

"She's going to the garage."

I move to the wall. "Riley, play audio in my earpiece and turn down the lights in here."

The lights dim. I place my hand on the sensor and quickly slip out when the panel opens. I close it and turn on the night vision glasses. The hallway is vacant. My steps are awkward in the boots, but I creep my way to the stairs.

"Mommy, she's coming back."

Just as I take the first step up, a shot breaks the silence through-out the house. The wood of the banister near my hand vibrates as splinters fly from the impact.

She blindly fires shots as I charge up the stairs. Madelyn trips over the first stair in her pursuit. I make it to the landing and look back. With the help from the night vision sunglasses, I see her crawling on all fours. Her hands sweeping the floor. I mimic her sarcastic smirk and run for our bedroom.

"You must be really good on your back. I've been trying to ride Bryan's pony for nine years. How did you do it?" Even without the earpiece I can hear Madelyn talking. The house has never been this quiet.

"Daddy has a pony?" Emma's voice whispers in my ear.

I press the button on the cord to reply. "No, honey."

"Then what pony is Mrs. Brooks trying to ride?"

"I'll explain later. Where is she?" I'm not about to tell my eight-year-old daughter that Mrs. Brooks wants to screw her dad.

"She's touching the wall."

"We don't have time for this, *Danielle*," she says my name like it's a filthy word. "I know my way around."

In our room, I go to the closet, turn on the keychain flashlight and open my safe. The envelope I need is hidden at the bottom. I dump out the other files to get to it. I fold the envelope and tuck it in a deep pocket.

From my jewelry box, I get my mother's wedding ring. It is the only other piece of jewelry that holds sentimental value. I pick up my phone and key in the code to unlock it, then try to call Bryan. The phone isn't getting cell service.

"Emma, come out from hiding. I won't hurt you. I'll take you with me."

"Is she really going to take me?" Emma's panicked cries fill my ear.

A disgruntled *hmph* makes its way through the earpiece.

"No, baby, she cannot get in the security room and I'm not letting anyone take you guys."

"Mommy, she's walking up the stairs."

I quickly leave our room and run toward the other side of the house. As I'm passing the landing, Madelyn raises her hand firing shots left and right. Bullets hit the wall beside me.

"I have plenty of bullets for this gun. If I'd been the one across the street from the theater you'd be dead."

I tiptoe down the hall into Kourtney's room and lock the door behind me.

"What the fuck are you doing, Danielle?" Bryan's angry voice comes in loud and clear in my ear.

"First, stop cussing. Madelyn is doing enough of that and the girls can hear you. Second, I know what the key is and I'm upstairs getting it."

"Danielle, we're coming in shooting anyone *not* in an ESO combat uniform. Get back to the security room and stay there!"

I search Kourtney's jewelry box. "Cuddles, the ring isn't in your jewelry box."

"Oh yeah, I hooked it around Uncle Vinny Bear's paw."

I turn on the tiny flashlight and hunt for the grizzly bear cub. "Where is he, Cuddles?"

Alpha male growls in my ear. "Fuck that fucking bear! Downstairs. Now!"

"Daddy!" Emma chastens.

I check the closet, around the toy chest, under her bed.

"She just went in your room, Mommy."

"Thank you, Sweet Pea. Cuddles, I still can't find him."

"He's there, I played with him last night before I went to sleep."

"Danielle, I swear, if you're still in Kourtney's room when I get in that house, you'll regret it." That was no idle threat and I dare not give a flippant response. Bryan is in Deathly-Dangerous-Alpha-Male mode right now. I know I'm pushing a button, but I keep searching for the ring anyway.

"Mommy, she's standing at the stairs."

"Stay still! She's listening for your movements," Deathly-Dangerous-Alpha-Male commands.

"She's walking toward our rooms."

"When Brooks go into Jessica's room, haul ass down the stairs and back to that security room and stay there until I come for you," he orders.

I tiptoe to Kourtney's bathroom searching for Uncle Vinny Bear.

"Do you understand me, Danielle?"

"Yes, Bryan. I read you loud and clear," I whisper.

"Mommy, she's not going to Aunt Jessi's room."

"Find somewhere to hide, now!" Bryan screams in my ear.

"Danielle, I'm tired of this game."

Emma's bedroom door creaks as it opens. If she tries Kourtney's door, she'll know I'm in here because it's locked. I channel my inner weightless body and tiptoe to the door, disengage the lock, then dash for the pile of teddy bears in the corner of the room. I bump into Uncle Vinny Bear. He shields me. I pile the other bears around us as best I can and take the glasses off.

"Was James lying when he said you guys weren't fucking? Is Bryan the first to stroke your kitty? You got pregnant on purpose like Amelia, didn't you?" Madelyn's right outside Kourtney's room.

"Mommy, you have a kitten?" Emma asks. "Where is it?"

"Not now, Emma," Deathly-Dangerous-Alpha-Male barks.

Kourtney's room door opens. "You must realize by now he's a professional liar. It's all about the victory for him. You're just another one he fucked. He didn't want Kourtney. It's a shame he has to die though. Amelia says Bryan's a hanging man. But a cut of a billion dollars will satisfy me more than Bryan can."

"What do you hang on, Daddy?"

"Not now, Emma," Bryan snaps.

She's moving around Kourtney's room.

"Why would you want to be with a man who hates his own kid?"

Bryan's not denying any of this! Kourtney can hear everything this woman is saying. I know it's not true, but our daughter may not.

The sniffs and heavy breathing in my ears are from Kourtney's tears. I can't say anything to reassure her that her dad loves her without jeopardizing my hiding spot.

Madelyn is in the room.

I turn off the walkie talkie so I can concentrate. It's pitch black. I can't see anything. I must rely on my sense of sound and smell to tell me where she is.

A tickle of spent gunpowder reminds me of Vin's shooting range. This scent isn't as strong, but I know she still has the gun in her hand. The heel of her shoes is slowly coming down on the hard-wood floors approaching the bears' corner.

I hold my breath.

The bear next to my hand moves, then falls to the floor. Something brushes my shoulder. Another bear falls.

"You're smart, Danielle. Instead of fighting, you and I should join forces. Slay some ghosts. Collect the pay. Run RAGS together." Her coffee-stale breath is right in my face.

The sound of her footsteps moves past me.

"I'll wait for you by the stairs," she says.

Her footsteps move further away.

I exhale and put the night vision sunglasses back on.

The gold chain is around the bear's paw like Kourtney said. I unhook it and slide on the other ring, then clasp it around my neck.

If Madelyn is really waiting for me by the stairs, then I'll have to fight my way past her. It's not my first choice considering I'm pregnant, but when that's the only course of action to get me back to the security room before Phantom burst through the walls, then I'll beat the hell out of that Horny Toad blocking my exit.

I go to the bathroom, close the door, and get out the tiny flash-light. What I need is on the vanity tray. I pop open the container of petroleum jelly and spread some on my face. Mrs. Franklin once told me it's an old trick she and her friends used to do before fighting a rival. She also said they put their hair in a bun and hid razor blades in it so when the hair pulling started their opponents cut their fingers. There are no razors in here, but I do bun-up my hair.

From the pocket of the cargo pants I get out the elastic bandages and remove them from their packaging.

I wrap my wrists and hands.

I tread out of the room and tiptoe down the hall.

Madelyn Brooks is feeling her way along the banister. The opening to the stairs unblocked. If I'm real quiet and take my time, I can ease by her and run down the stairs.

I visualize a mouse, make myself small, and creep forward.

Midway to the first stair, the motor on the shutters hums. The windows and doors will no longer be blocked. Sunlight and Phantom ghosts will be spilling in soon. I pick up speed.

"Grr…" Madelyn charges. She forces me against the banister. The unforgiving wood pressing into my back. We're inches from the opening.

I capture the wrist of her gun hand with my left and force it and the barrel to point away from me. My right arm struggles to maintain distance between her and my stomach.

The goggles fly off my face.

Tiny slits of setting sunlight shine through the upstairs windows. Madelyn can see me as clearly as I can see her.

When you're up against the ropes, free your mind and look for your opponent's weak spot, then go in for the kill.

Madelyn's other hand is trapped between me and the banister. I lean back more. The fingers of my right hand strain and stretch and hook through her big hooped earrings. A slight outward twist and a forceful downward tug at the same time I head butt her nose.

"Oww!" Madelyn drops the gun.

She stumbles back. I drop her earring and keep her moving. My feet kick at legs and knees. We half circle the landing. Madelyn steps back to protect herself. Glass breaks downstairs. Her reflexes are quick. She catches my booted foot. My fingers strangle the banister to keep balance. I draw my knee in; she stumbles forward in her heels. I kick out. Madelyn wobbles and windmills with one hand, the heels of her stilettos hang off the top step.

Eyes cold, Madelyn Brooks's smile sends a chill across the nape of my neck. She grips my foot with both hands and leans back, pulling me forward.

My son survived one tumble down a flight of stairs. He won't survive another.

Quickly, I drop to my butt, hook my arm around a wood post. I use my upper body strength to keep from tumbling down the stairs, while my free foot kicks her fingers.

She's not giving up.

I anchor the tip of the boot to the heel of the other, use it as leverage to slide my foot out of the boot she's holding.

Madelyn's face freezes in horror. I'm easing back from the stairs. She falls backward.

Bump!

Thump!

Crack! The sickening crunch sound of her neck breaking echoes in the house.

I reach down and turn on the walkie talkie. The shutters are a quarter of the way up.

From the earpiece dangling around my neck, I hear Bryan yelling my name. I put it back in. "I'm okay. Sweet Pea, how many people are in the house?"

"Five. They came out the garage."

I jump over Madelyn's body at the bottom of the stairs. The shadow of the person in the hallway stretches toward me. I change direction and run to the sitting room, heading toward the formal dining room.

"Dani, we're coming through all ground floor entrances in sixty—"

"I'm trying," I interrupt him. I toe-off the other boot and quietly move to the door leading to the kitchen.

The room is clear. I make my way over to the counter, grabbing two knives out of the block. In the doorway to the hall, the person's back is to me. The distance is further than what I practiced with Max.

I hold the tip of the knife's blade. Raise my arm, keeping it straight. Reach back, snap my arm forward and throw the knife.

Glass breaks throughout the house. I don't wait around to see if the knife hit its mark. I run back through the formal dining room.

"Where is she?" an angry male calls out. More shots fired.

Heavy footfalls pound the floor. I run through the sitting room to the front of the house. I get to the wall under the stairs. My hand swipes the sensor. The security room door slides open. Glass shatters in the family room. The front door slams into the wall. My sock-covered feet slide inside. My hand reaches for the sensor.

"Get down!"

The girls drop to the floor, I drop in front of them, shielding my daughters with my body. The glass of one of the monitors shatters. They scream and Trevor growls.

I turn over, panting.

A male wearing dark-colored jeans and shirt stands in the doorway pointing a gun at me.

Trevor steps in front of me. Chest out, teeth bared, he growls and barks. *Thank you, Dad for bringing this dog into our lives.*

The man lowers his gun, aiming at Trevor. I grip the blade of the knife in my hand, aim for the man's chest and throw.

He stumbles back. The security door slides close.

I check the girls to make sure they're okay, then hug and kiss Trevor. "You're such a good boy."

He whines and falls to the floor. It took a lot of energy for him to do what he did. I rub his stomach.

"Mom, someone is at the door," Kourtney says.

I peek at the monitor. A muscular male in jeans and a jacket slides his hand over the sensor.

"Get under the desk," I command and climb to my feet.

I shed the sweatshirt. Slide the gun from the holster. Take the safety off. Rack the slide. Gun pointed downward, trigger finger alongside the barrel. I face the door.

Never point your weapon at anyone or anything unless you are absolutely sure you're going to fire it. Know who or what you intend to shoot; and what's beyond it or them.

Feet apart, I calm my body and mind just like Bryan taught me at the shooting range.

"He used his elbow to break the glass, Mom. He's pulling out wires."

"Thank you, Cuddles. Now I want you guys to get under the desk. Close your eyes and cover your ears." I don't take my eyes off the door.

"Trevor, come," Kourtney commands.

He crawls toward her as the door slides open.

My arms rise. Finger on the trigger. Site lined up, I address the man in front of me. "Keep your hands where I can see them."

He surrenders with both hands and takes three steps back. "Ma'am, remember me? I'm Ross. Colonel Hawk sent me to extract the girl and move her to a safe location."

"This is where you and I have our second problem. The girls have strict orders to stay in this room until Colonel Hawk comes for them. Since you're not him they're not going with you."

"What's our first problem, ma'am?"

"You aren't part of the plan."

His nose wrinkles. An eyebrow arches. It appears Ross doesn't understand what I'm saying.

"There is no plan, Dr. Edwards. Colonel Hawk gave me orders to move you and the girls to the warehouse." Subconsciously, his eyes look up and to the left before settling back on me and the gun.

"I take it you haven't been trained in the art of lying; otherwise you wouldn't have broken eye contact. Plus, you called me Dr. Edwards."

"Ma'am, everyone on the Elite team is dead including the Colonel." Ross steps forward.

I aim lower and fire a warning shot near his foot, then quickly point the gun at his forehead.

He hops back. "What the fuck, bitch!"

"The next one will be in your head if you call me bitch again or take another step toward this room."

Ross sneers. He makes a move for his weapon, but he's tackled to the floor by two men dressed in black and wearing ski masks. The larger man stands over Ross and fires two silent shots. Ross's body jerks from the impact, and the light in his eyes goes out.

I aim my weapon at them.

"Maxim," the smaller one says, then removes his mask so I can see his face.

"Vincenzo." His mask is already in his hand.

I exhale and lower the weapon, put the safety on. I gaze over my shoulder. The girls are still huddled under the desk. Eyes closed.

Hands over their ears.

The gunfire around the house stops. I step out of the security room as Bryan steps in the doorway.

He's breathing heavy. Fire in his hazel eyes. The skin along his jawline is tight. "We taught you kill shots, not warning shots."

"Marie."

"She's alive and on her way to the hospital. Willis and Ignacio are riding with her."

I hand the gun to Vin and wrap my arms around Bryan. My forehead rests on his hard chest and I let the tears flow.

His shoulders relax a bit. "I'm proud of you. Except the part when you left the security room. And when you turned off the walkie. And for not thinking about taking the hidden stairs down to the garage so you wouldn't have to fight your way past Brooks. And for not putting a bullet in Ross's head..."

"I'm starting to think you're not proud of me."

"You didn't panic, Dani. You handled the gun safely and correctly. I am proud of you. I'm pissed off that you didn't follow the emergency plan."

I take the envelope out of my pocket. "I couldn't let her walk out of here with this. Plus, you told me the minute I realize what the key is, I should get it."

He presses his lips into mine. "That ring you risked your life for is a replica. I've had the real one since the new year."

"What?"

"I'll explain later." He kisses me.

"She's the one who told Emm I was going to die."

"I know."

"We need to talk to Kourtney."

"If you'd kept your walkie on, you would have heard me tell Kourt Madelyn is lying." He unsnaps the armored vest and helps me out of it. "Can I go check my daughters now? Make sure they're okay?"

I step aside.

"It's safe, girls," he says.

Emma runs out. Bryan bends down scooping her in one arm and reaches for Kourtney. She scuttles away from him and wraps her arms around me. Burying her face in my back.

"Cuddles, I need to make sure you're not hurt."

JACKI RENÉE

She doesn't budge. Her hold around my waist tightens.

"Bryan, they've seen and heard so much. We need to get them out of here. Take them somewhere quiet where we can talk about what happened."

"I'll meet you in the Range Rover." He sets Emma on her feet. I coax Kourtney out from behind my back.

She bends down, removing the socks off Trevor's paws. "Thank you for protecting us, boy." She kisses his head. "Come, Trevor." Kourtney follows me to the door to the garage.

There are people being carried out of the garage by men in camouflage when I open the door. I use my body to block the girls' view. When last person is carried out, I lead the girls to my truck and open the back door for them.

Our emergency backpacks are in a locked storage cabinet. I get the key out of the glove compartment and go get them. Even Trevor has a backpack. I rummage through them and find shoes and socks for us.

Once I settle in the front seat I exhale and rest my hand on my stomach. The baby kicks and punches and shadow boxes. I close my eyes and wait for Bryan.

CHAPTER TWENTY-ONE

"DANIKINS TOOK DOWN THREE OF the eight people," Max says.

Vin whistles. "Did you see her throw those knives?"

Max pats his chest. "She's a fast learner."

We're viewing the security footage to get a full assessment of how my home was infiltrated.

Marie had no chance to protect herself. She was caught off guard when Madelyn Brooks strolled into the kitchen unannounced. She didn't see Ross come out of the laundry room. He hit her in the head with the butt of a gun. The knife in her hand sliced through her arm as she fell to the floor unconscious. Ross dragged her body into the pantry.

As acting onsite Watcher, Ross had access to the layout of my house. I'm happy I didn't give him full access to the blueprints of the property. He must have coached Madelyn on how to navigate the house in the dark. That's the only way she would know her way around without running into walls or bumping into furniture.

Tony walks in. "I know for sure the one Dani got in the back is from ILA. I sent photos of the others to Riley for identification since dead men can't talk." He peers over our shoulders at the monitors. "Langford is a cold piece of work. His day is coming though."

I check my watch and stand up. I need to get Dani to the hospital so Jessi can check her. All that running and tussling couldn't have been good for her or my son. "Are we all clear on what happens next?"

No one replies. They don't even look my way.

"I know you guys don't like the plan—we always stick together, but this time we have to change up. The enemy *knows* us. We have to come at them with something different."

"You're right, man." Tony turns around for a bro-hug.

I slap him on the back a couple times, then hold him by the shoulders so he can see my face. "You got this, Paul." Normally he's the one who pushes us to be our best, now it's time for me to return the favor.

Chen stands, followed by Ricci. We form a triangle of support around our friend.

"Is Fontenot ready for the bunker?" Paul asks.

Ricci nods.

"Lock up my wife's house when you're done," I say and leave them in the security room.

I don't dare look at the destruction as I walk to the garage. If I do I will chuck the plan and murder Langford the minute I see him.

Dani cocks a questioning eyebrow when I open the driver's door and slide in behind the wheel. I start the truck. "Girls, our house is safe." I back out of the garage and down the driveway onto the street. "Mommy and I practiced what to do in case of an emergency and she did everything she was supposed to do to keep you safe until your uncles and I could get here." I reach over for my wife's hand as I drive my family away from our home.

She twines her fingers with mine. "Dad and I realize you heard and saw a lot of things that you don't understand. Let's talk about how you're feeling. It's okay to ask questions."

"I feel fine, Mommy," Emm says. "Mrs. Brooks can't take you away from me. I was scared at first because she told me her friends were there to make sure you aren't my mommy anymore."

"I will *always* be your mom, Emm."

We wait for our other daughter to say something.

"Kourt, how are you feeling?" Dani finally asks.

"I'm okay, Mom," she replies softly.

"Where are the cameras in our rooms?" Emm asks.

"They are in the ceiling."

"Why do we have cameras in our rooms?" she asks.

I look at Dani for help with this one.

"Daddy has a very important job. There are cameras all around the house so he or one of your uncles knows where everybody is in case of an emergency. Like today."

"At the stables, Mrs. Brooks told me I already have a mother." My fingers tighten on the steering wheel. "Is that true?"

"Emma, the woman who gave birth to you was Mrs. Brooks's friend. Danielle's name is on your birth certificate. She is your mother. Mommy legally adopted you. Do you understand what that means?"

Kourty mumbles something incoherent. I glance at her in the rearview mirror.

"I think so. Do you love Mommy and Kourty?"

"Of course, I do. I love Mommy, you, Kourt and the baby. I will always love you guys."

"Humph," Kourt grunts.

"Do you want to ask something, Kourt?"

"Who is Riley?" Emm asks.

She's full of questions. I guess that's a good thing. "Riley is a computer that helps me do my job."

"If I put my hand on the wall will the door to that room open for me?"

"No, sweetie, only grownups can open the door to that room," Dani answers.

"Are there any more secret rooms in our house?"

I look at Dani for help.

"There are some things Dad can't tell us, but he did tell me about the security room because it's one of the safest places in the house to hide."

"Dad, can you *really* tell a lie?" I'm not exactly sure how to answer this. I don't want my girls not to trust me.

"Some things I can lie about and some things I can't." I'm trying to be as honest as I can. "I don't lie to you guys."

Dani squeezes my fingers.

Kourt smacks her lips.

I look in the rearview mirror in time to read her lips saying, *"That's a lie."* She's shaking her head.

I turn onto the highway, and press on the gas.

The miles go by and Kourt still hasn't asked a question or said anything.

"Where is your pony and why are you the only one who can play with Mommy's kitty?" Emm asks out of nowhere.

I bite my cheek to keep from laughing and throw a raised eyebrow at Dani.

She shakes her head.

I nod.

She mouths, *no!*

I poke my lip out and mouth, *please!*

"Sweetie, Mrs. Brooks was being very inappropriate when she was saying those things." Dani narrows her eyes at me. "Do you have any other questions?"

"No, that's it," Emm tells her.

"What about you, Cuddles? Is there anything you want us to explain?" Dani asks.

"No," she whispers.

Dani shifts in her seat to look at our unusually quiet daughter. "When you're ready to talk, Dad and I will listen."

"Okay."

Dani gasps and presses her hand into her stomach. I noticed the periodic sudden movements when we first got on the highway, but I didn't say anything.

I squeeze her fingers, *are you okay?*

She squeezes twice, *I'm okay.*

Exiting the freeway, I drive the three miles to the hospital and pull around to the back. Hawkeye PPOs are waiting for us.

I lead my family to the service elevator. Kourt avoids making eye contact and coming near me. Trevor licks her hand like he's asking what's wrong. She pats his head.

We go up to the fifth floor. Dani wants to check on Marie before she goes to the room I had set up for her and the girls.

I open the door and let them walk in ahead of me. Willis sits on the couch with tears in his eyes. This bastard is pushing it with his fake concern for his wife.

Dani rushes to the bed. She brushes Marie's hair off her face and kisses her forehead. "Is she okay?"

"She lost a lot of blood. Ignacio had to put nine stitches in her arm. He said she's going to be okay." The bastard wipes his eyes with a white handkerchief. He's probably sorry his wife didn't bleed to death.

Okay, enough of his bullshit. "Danielle, until I can secure a place to take you and the girls for a couple days, we're staying here. Jessica is in the room next door. There's food and beds for you guys.

I'll go down and get the backpacks in a minute." I know she's wondering why I have my chest puffed out. Thankfully she recognizes I'm in combat mode and doesn't challenge me.

"Do you want to see what your brother looks like in my tummy?" she asks the girls.

I hold the door open for them and close it when they walk out.

"Ross and Mills were behind that little stunt?" Willis asks. "Did you know about Brooks?"

The old man doesn't realize he's giving himself away. Mills wasn't there.

Keep it together, Hawk. Let him continue to hang himself.

"Of course, you knew. You shut me out of the department."

"As the former Second Command, you know I can't discuss alternative security measures with anyone other than POTUS and the ESO team."

"I'm not the enemy. I gently pointed you in your enemy's direction."

"That makes me question your truths after reading what your daughter, Elizabeth, stole from you." There's no need for me to hide that little bit of information. I want it known that I *know* the real story now and have the proof to back it up.

"You can't take me in without jeopardizing the safety of the American people. You've always needed me."

"I've outgrown you, Langford. Federal Agents are on their way to take you into custody."

"Do you complete your mission and protect the American people? Or do you turn your back on your country and save the woman you love? I told you—you can't do both."

"The difference between you and me is I have a strong, wise, and hardworking woman by my side who helped me find the balance, so I do have it all."

The sarcastic chuckle and the dismissive wave of his hand mocks my relationship with my wife. His gaze shifts to the bed.

Marie is awake and listening to us.

"The woman by my side is far from weak as you imply. And she's a better liar. Aren't you, Antoinette?" Willis blows a kiss to his wife.

"Va lamèd!" Marie growls.

"Gònn a lenfè."

"Vou prèmiyè."

"Salops parèy to sé dèt li mourí. Par jou–limé mo va dèt kouri RAGS avèk Phantom.

"Bèt. Embété. Kwa mò, vou va pa viv lon asé a vu solèy–lévé. Mò mær pou bon di mò a gaddé un ti des quoi fouré pou sériyé."

I leave them to hash that out in their language. They can't leave the floor anyway. From the sounds of things, I may have to send someone in to make sure Marie doesn't get out of the bed and kill Willis.

I hold my mic sleeve up to my mouth. "Did you hear that?"

"Yes, I did," Fontenot's voice comes through the earpiece in my ear.

"What did they say?"

"She yelled, 'Fuck off.' He to her, 'Go to hell.' She said, 'You first.' He told her, 'Whores like you should be dead. By daybreak I will be running RAGS and Phantom.' She called him a stupid, stupid fool. Then said, 'Believe me, you will not live long enough to see the sun rise. My mama told me to keep a little something put away for emergencies.'"

"Good job, Fontenot."

"Thank you, sir."

The two PPOs step aside so I can enter the room next door.

Danielle is on the bed and Jessica is pointing to the monitor. The girls *ooh* at the view of their baby brother.

"You guys, the men outside of the room are here to protect you. Please do whatever they tell you to do."

Everyone except Kourtney responds. She doesn't even turn around to acknowledge me.

"How are they?" I ask my sister.

She turns the monitor. "He's very active right now, but no contractions."

I kiss Emm on the top of her head, then reach for Kourt. She scurries away, crawling under the bed to the other side. She buries her face in her mother's chest. Trevor lifts his head, watching her.

"Cuddles…"

Dani raises her finger interrupting me.

"Honey, what's wrong?" She rubs our daughter's head. "You were quiet the whole ride here. Can you tell us how you're feeling?"

She sniffs. "Mad. I feel really—really mad."

"What's making you mad?"

"Bryan never wanted me."

She hasn't called me Bryan since I let them in on their mother's birthday surprise.

"Cuddles, you are my daughter. Remember we had the ceremony and Judge Humphrey said I was your dad. Your last name was changed to Hawk. If I didn't want you, none of those things would have happened."

Her head snaps up, eyes flare with anger. "That. Day. Was. For. Emmy. Not. Me." She enunciates each word.

"No, baby girl. That day was for all of us."

"Honey, your dad supports you the way dads should. He does things with you that dads do for their daughters. Bryan loves you like a father should."

"Do fathers always leave their daughters? He didn't leave Emmy. Are dads supposed to *lie* to their daughters? Cause he hasn't told the truth yet!"

"What truth do you need to hear, Kourt? Mrs. Brooks said those things to make you mad at me."

She lifts her head again. I recognize the glare and brace myself. She's looking at me the way Dani looked at me when she wanted answers.

"I was mad at you before *she* said anything."

Dani sits up higher in the bed redirecting our daughter's attention on her. "Okay, Kourtney. I need you to take a breath. You have been angry for a while now. It's time to tell Dad and me why."

Jessica turns off the ultrasound machine and quietly leaves the room before the storm hits.

"Dad, what is Kourty talking about?" Emm's soft curious voice breaks the silence in the room.

Kourt smacks her lips. "You are so dumb sometimes, Emmy. Bryan never loved me. James gave my mom some kind of key a long time ago. *Your* dad wants it, so he's been *pretending* to love me and Mom to get it."

My airways become blocked. I force the words through. "Cuddles, it's not like that…"

"Don't call me Cuddles!"

"It's okay to feel sad and hurt and to be angry," Dani says. "But we need to talk about this calmly. You may not yell at your dad like that again. You can tell us why you've been angry."

She's points an angry finger at me. "That man is not my dad. I don't have one." She looks at her mom. "I only have you."

Her words are a knife piercing my heart.

Dani reaches out to her, holding her cheek, giving our daughter a minute to calm down.

Kourt slides the ring off her finger, holding it out to me. "You don't want me. Well, I don't want you either."

I open my hand. The warmth of the thin platinum ring brands the palm of my hand.

"That's how I'm feeling," she whispers, then runs to a bed, lies facedown and cries. Trevor whines. He lumbers to his feet, then jumps onto the bed with Kourt. She reaches out, throwing her arm around him while her sobs make her body convulse.

I storm out of the room slamming the door behind me.

"Arrgh!" My fist tries to redecorate the wall. I'm trapped in another cage, its walls strengthened by more separation and unforgiveness.

With my back against the wall, I slide down until I'm sitting on the cold tile floor, Kourt's ring pressing into the palm of my hand. My head rocks back against the solid white wall. I keep my eyes closed to hold the tears in. My worst fears stare back at me behind my closed eyes. She'll never understand the sacrifice Dani and I made. In her eyes, I will always pick her sister.

"Bryan?" Dani whispers. "We need to talk to them about this, calmly and honestly. She'll understand. She's hurting and we have to keep that in mind. It's up to us. The secret has to come out tonight." Dani holds her hand out to me. "Please come back in the room. We can't keep this from them any longer."

"I…" My voice cracks as I try to talk around the lump lodged in my throat. I'm completely lost. "My… my daughter will think… my daughter thinks I don't love or want her," I stutter. "How do I… She'll never under… What do I say?" I close my eyes.

I need to get out of here.

I need air!

I jump to my feet and run to the elevator, but it will take too long. Dani calls my name. I run for the stairs and kick the door open, my legs and feet flying down five floors to the lobby then out the back door to the parking lot.

I run to Dani's Range Rover and jump in—"*Arrgh!*"—punching the interior roof of the truck until my knuckles are numb.

My head drops to the steering wheel and I let my tears roll down my cheeks.

My chest burns.

Unbearable pain is what I feel throughout my body.

"She's my daughter," I yell to the world.

Learning to withstand hours of interrogation is a walk in the park compared to the pain of losing the love and trust of my baby girl. I made her feel unwanted and unloved.

This pain is not a weakness leaving my body. This pain is my body. It is me.

How do I make this right?

I hear someone sobbing.

Is that me?

Is that sound coming from me?

My pain escapes and I stop fighting against it, letting my emotions take over. Allowing myself to cry it out until I'm numb all over. Then I wipe my face, put the key in the ignition and start the Range Rover.

I do well past the speed limit on the highway to get to my office.

I go down to the first floor and run to the facility.

Edwards is asleep when I walk into his room. I drag him out of bed.

"What the fuck, Hawk?! What are you doing?"

I turn on the lamp. He looks at me.

"Is it my wife and son?"

"Do you really think I'd fucking cry over your family?"

"Did something happen to Danielle?"

"What changed, Edwards?"

"What are you talking about?"

"You and Jamal were on your way to ruling RAGS. What changed the course of action?"

"I didn't know I had a twin brother until senior year of high school. I mean I always knew I was being trained to pair with someone in the future. I didn't know who until I overheard Danielle's foster dad arguing with Hopper about the Edwards boys. Jamal and I were never meant to run RAGS, we were being trained to get close enough to kill the leaders."

"Did you always know it was Willis and Marie you were supposed to kill?"

"No, not until I met up with Hopper here in Boulder."

"Is that when you learned Danielle's connection to them?"

"Yes."

"How did you get the gun that killed Dani's parents?"

"I stole it from Hopper. I didn't know the history behind the gun until you told me."

"Do you have the information for the offshore account?"

He nods. "Jamal and I memorized it, then burned the paperwork."

"Why didn't you tell us Hopper is one of the good guys?"

"He's so deep undercover, you wouldn't have believed me without proof, which I didn't have. It's on that laptop."

My phone vibrates. It's a message from Paul. I type out a long reply, then turn the screen so Edwards can read it.

James stares me in the eyes. "How can I help?"

———◆———

In my office I access the information stored on Riley. Images transfer from the files to apps I'm creating.

I send and receive secured messages. When I finish, I make a phone call to my Commander in Chief. "Sir, to get our house cleaned top to bottom, we have to let it play out."

"I trust your judgment," he says.

"Thank you, sir."

"Twenty-four hours, Colonel."

I set my watch. "Affirmative, sir."

I drive back to the hospital. The back parking lot is empty except for a red Chevy sedan. I kiss the photo one last time. I grab the backpacks from the back and go to the service elevator.

Focused on my mission, I step out of the cab onto the unsecured fifth floor.

CHAPTER TWENTY-TWO

MARIE IS WATCHING TV WHEN I walk into the room. It's on a news channel that's about to go off. Danielle's sitting on the couch with Willis. Marie gasps, pointing to the television and turning up the volume.

On the screen is the live video of a car engulfed in flames along with Tony's press photo.

"It's been confirmed that local ex-sheriff officer, Anthony Paul, was killed in this fiery crash caused by a suspected drunk driver. Paul was traveling south on Thirtieth Street. The unidentified drunk driver traveling northbound at speeds upwards of ninety-five, veered into oncoming traffic at the intersection of Thirtieth and Valmont Road and hit Paul's Chevy Camaro head-on. According to eyewitnesses, both cars exploded on impact. Firefighters are on the scene trying to gain control of the flames, but it's obvious from the intensity of the blaze, there are no survivors." The reporter presses his finger to his ear, his gaze drops to the desk, and he nods his head. "I've just been informed that the suspected drunk driver has been identified as twenty-three-year-old, Yang Ma-han. His father is the owner of one of China's biggest telecommunications corporations."

Willis stands. "Isn't that the young man who tried to run into Danielle back in December but Porter blocked him?"

I go to Danielle, pulling her up off the couch, wrapping my arms around her. "I have to go." My voice is void of any emotion.

"We have another late breaking news story," the anchorman announces.

We look up at the screen again. "At approximately ten fifteen this evening, two men were gunned down in the driveway of the home of global business owner Bryan Hawk. Mr. Hawk and his family were not at home at the time of the shooting." My press photo comes up on the screen. "Preliminary reports indicate that the two men were leaving Mr. Hawk's residence when a silver late model four-door car stopped in the middle of the street, the gunman opened fire, striking both men in the head and chest areas, then drove away. We have reporters en route to the scene. We will continue to broadcast live."

I pull away from Danielle. All color has drained from her face.

Acosta bursts into the room. "You heard?"

I nod.

"Don't go, Bryan. Please don't leave," she cries grabbing my hands.

"I have to."

"No, you don't. Choose us, Bryan. Stay here with me. Choose *me* this time."

I rub her back as I address Acosta. "Assemble Delta Team. Meeting in fifteen minutes."

"Roger that, sir." He rushes out of the room.

Dani shoves me away. "So, what I want doesn't matter to you? If you leave this hospital, that's it. I'm done. We're done."

"Please don't do this, Danielle. I have to go. This is my job, you know this."

"What I know is that if you go out there you will die. Did you see what just happened? Someone is systematically eliminating you guys and you want to step out into the open for them to take a shot at you? Are you ready to die, Bryan?"

"No one knows when or how they're going to die. That's life. I have a job to do."

She storms out. I follow her to the other room.

"A little overdramatic, but you did good. Here's your backpack. Do not tell Willis or Marie anything. The situation is bigger than what we planned for. There are some things I need to tell you, but first go get dressed."

Danielle takes the backpack and walks into the bathroom, closing the door behind her.

Moving fast, I get out my laptop and the girls' iPads. I connect them via USB and download the individual apps I created onto each tablet, then put them back where I found them.

Trevor raises his head when I approach Kourtney's bed. Her eyes are puffy and her cheeks are red. I use the back of my hand to make sure she isn't running a fever. An illness will cause a glitch in the plan.

The dinner I ordered sits uneaten on the mobile bedside table next to her bed.

I take her ring out of my pocket and carefully slip it back on her finger. It has a tracking chip on the underside of the band. I'll know where she is at all times. There's one in Emma's ring too.

I lean over and kiss my baby girl's cheek. "You have always been Kourtney Allison Hawk and I love you more than you will ever know." I scratch Trevor behind the ears. "Take care of my girls."

He whines and licks my hand, and I can almost hear him say, *With my life and even then, I'll keep on fighting.*

I go to the next bed. "I love you so much Emma Rose Hawk. You and your sister stick together no matter what."

Danielle steps out of the restroom dressed in maternity jeans, a sweater, cross-trainers, and a headband that pushes the hair off her face, but covers her ears.

I open my arms and she steps into them. "President Hart will be our go between." I hand her a cell phone. "This phone is your direct connection to him. Do not make any other calls from this cell phone. I'm going to give Riley the command to self-destruct once I get to my office."

"Bryan…" She squeezes me tight.

"If it comes down to it, I want you to do whatever you have to—to keep yourself and our children alive." I look over at my baby girl sleeping. My heart already misses her. "I need you to promise me one thing." I raise my pinkie finger and wait for her to hook hers. "If I die, promise me you'll make her understand my decisions were never meant to hurt her."

"We will tell her together, Bryan."

I link our fingers. "Walk me down."

Two PPOs follow us to the elevator. In the cab, I kiss Danielle with everything I am, willing her to be strong, to remember what is real. The next twenty-four hours are uncertain for both of us. If I die, I want to die knowing I did everything in my power to right my wrongs with this woman.

Getting off the elevator, we walk into the lobby where Ignacio is waiting. "I'll meet you at the office," he says as we walk out the lobby doors.

He goes to the physician's parking stalls in front of the hospital. "Take care, Danielle." He waves getting into his orange Camaro.

I cup my wife's cheeks and stare into her eyes. "Danielle Lauren Hawk, if these are my last minutes with you, I want you to know everything. If I had known how deeply rooted you were in this, I would never have moved you and Kourtney to Boulder."

I lean in and whisper all my secrets in her ear. When she tries to pull away, I hold her close and continue. Once the web of lies starts to unravel there is no way to stop its momentum until the truth is all revealed.

I press my lips to hers to keep her from asking questions.

The engine in Ignacio's car roars, making the lobby's windows and the ground tremble. He pulls out of the parking stall and creeps to the driveway. The brake lights shine bright at the stop sign. He makes a slow right turn. The bushes block my view.

I lean away from Dani. "I love you..."

BOOM!

A ball of fire and metal sails into the air. I push Danielle into the arms of the PPOs ordering them to get her back upstairs. She holds onto my hand. I tug and look over my shoulder. "Baby, let me go." I yank my hand from her grasp and run toward my friend's car.

"Nooo!" Dani shouts. "Come back, Bryan! Please don't leave me and..."

I can feel the heat from the flames before I round the bushes.

BOOM!

———◆———

Trevor whines and barks. He nudges me with his nose, then runs to the window. He whines and pants and looks over his shoulder, twists his head.

Mommy and Bryan didn't know I was awake when they were talking. Why it is okay for grownups to keep secrets and tell lies, but when kids do it we get punished?

I wish we never left Arizona. Why did her stupid job have to let her go? Mom could've found another job at a different hospital or somewhere else besides here. We had our own house. I wonder if we can get it back. I'm going to tell Mom I don't want to live in Boulder anymore.

If she has to stay here because of that baby, then I'll go back to Arizona by myself. I wish I never found that picture in Mommy's closet.

Cry baby Emmy sits up in bed, looking around the room. "Where's Mommy?"

I make my eyes squint at her and make a fist with my fingers. "Why didn't you tell me about Mrs. Brooks?"

"She said if I told anyone they would get hurt too."

"I'm your best friend. I told *you* when Marie said those funny words to me."

"But Mrs. Brooks promised people would hurt anyone I told. You saw those bruises on Mommy."

Trevor runs to the bed, licks my hand, and runs back to the window. He barks.

This time I get up and follow him. Something is making him excited. He's supposed to be lying down.

It's dark outside. You can't see the mountains. You can't see anything except for the flowerbeds under the light poles and the red lights on the back of a car stopped in the driveway. I reach out and scratch my dog's head. "What is it?"

The windows rattle. A red and orange fireball shoots up to the sky. I scream and duck down beside Trevor. He howls.

"What was that?" Emmy is on the floor, under the bed.

"Something exploded."

I wait to see if anything happens. When I stand, I press my face on the cold glass of the window to see what's going on. "Someone's running up the driveway and I see a ball of fire by some bushes."

The person turns and this time the explosion makes the building shakes.

I scream again, drop to the floor and fast crawl to hide under the bed with my sister. Trevor is crawling too, but he's slow. He stops when he's next to me.

Emmy starts to cry. "I want Mommy."

"Me too."

The room door opens real quick. Two men run in. One is blond and one is bald. They look around then come over to the bed where me and Emmy are hiding.

The baldheaded man grabs my foot. I scream and try to scoot back more and use my other foot to kick his hand.

Emmy's on her stomach screaming and holding onto the wheel of the bed. The blond-haired man has both her feet.

Trevor growls and barks and snaps at the man pulling my leg. My dog bites down on the man's hand. Baldy yells and drops my foot. I get on my hands and knees and crawl to the other side.

The blond-haired man is picking up my sister off the floor. She's kicking his legs and reaching back, over her head, pulling his hair. He turns around and starts walking toward the door.

Mommy told us to always look out for each other. I put my foot on the rail of the bed to help me get up on the mattress. I run then jump on the man's back. I hit him as hard as I can with one my left hand and hold on with the other.

Blondy lets go of my sister. She falls to her feet. "Run, Emmy." I jump off his back, grab my sister's hand and we run for the door. "Let's go, Trevor," I yell. I hear the jingle of his collar from him running.

"*Banati,*" one man yells.

We stop running. It's the safe word Bryan told Mommy to teach us. It means *my daughters* in Arabic. Trevor stands in front of us. Chest out. Ears back. He's on alert. The bald man says the safe word again, this time with both hands in the air. The sleeve of his jacket is torn.

Trevor sits. His ears relax. He whines.

"I'm Bond. That's Gipson," the blond man says. "We have to get you guys out of here?"

"Where's my mom?" Emmy asks.

"Someone else is bringing her. We have to go. Now." Gipson picks up my backpack and the one for Trevor. Bond grabs Emmy's.

Gipson takes my hand and rushes me to the elevator. Trevor is keeping up. I look over my shoulder to make sure my sister is behind me.

Bond pushes the up button on the elevator. When the door opens two more men are waiting, their hands behind their backs, but in the reflection, I see black guns in their hands.

Gipson inserts a key in the lock on the elevator panel and the doors close. My stomach drops as we go up. The light on the sign flashes as we reach each floor. After the ninth floor the doors open.

We're on the roof.

A big helicopter is waiting with the doors open. Red lights run around the circle on the platform. A red light on the tail of the black sky bird blinks.

Gipson bends, then tells me to stay low. He leads the way against the wind of the blades. It's loud. I can't hear anything.

On the helmet of the man sitting in the front is a silver hawk. It sparkles in the moving red lights. He's watching us.

I'm lifted into the helicopter and told to scoot to the middle seat. Gipson straps me in a seat belt that goes over both shoulders. Headphones are placed over my ears. I adjust the microphone over my mouth.

Emmy is across from me. There's even a seat belt for Trevor.

Gipson sits in the seat next to me. Bond is next to my sister. One man from the elevator gets up front with the pilot; the other is on the other side of Emmy.

The doors close. In the headphone, I hear a man talking.

"Is that you, Dr. Barrett?"

"Yes, it's me. Your dad sent me to get you and your sister out of here."

Someone says we're clear for takeoff, then the helicopter is lifting up.

I lean as much as I can to see the view. The circling lights on the platform are green. The fireball is still burning. I see the red and white flashing lights of fire trucks getting closer.

We get higher in the dark sky. The hospital gets smaller. We move away from the building in the opposite direction of Boulder.

The men are talking.

Emmy looks scared. I'm not, riding in a helicopter is cool.

The hospital gets farther and farther away. "Excuse me, Dr. Barrett. Where are we going?"

"To the airport. A plane is waiting for us."

"Will Mommy and Daddy be there?" Emmy asks.

"They will meet up with you but not at the airport."

Emmy looks like she's about to throw up. Mommy told her to be brave and not make herself sick. I nudge her with my foot and squint my eyes. She nods and wipes her tears away.

Trevor lies on the seat with his head on my lap. I hope this excitement doesn't make him sicker. The veterinarian said he needs lots of rest. I scratch him behind the ear and rub his back. He's a good dog. I'm happy I picked him.

———◆———

The elevator doors open on the fifth floor. I jerk away from the men who stopped me from following Bryan. How dare he tell me that last bit of information then run toward a burning car. You don't tell somebody that kind of news without explaining yourself.

Stay focused Danielle. He told you to stick to the plan, no matter what.

I fast walk around the nurse's station and rush to Marie's room. Willis stands at the window looking out. Marie is sitting up as high as she can in the hospital bed.

"Bryan's dead," I say with no emotion whatsoever in my tone. My gaze is set on Marie, but I don't see her.

Willis flies out of the room, his baritone voice barking orders.

"Come, Dani," Marie says. "Get off your feet. You're in shock."

I blink and then focus on her.

Fine wrinkle lines and teary eyes stare back at me. Marie motions for me to sit in the chair by the bed.

I sit down and take her hand in mine. It's feels like I'm holding an ice cube. She's shaking.

"I need to tell you something." Her voice is weak, but determined. "I need to tell you a story. It's a story I've wanted to tell you since the first day you and Kourtney came to the house." Marie pauses. "Bryan and Willis never wanted me to tell you this."

Unsure of what she's waiting for, I say, "Okay."

"Willis and I were married ten years before I got pregnant. He was constantly out of the country. We had little time to—" Blood rushes to her cheeks. "Once he was discharged he came home and started a landscaping business. I got pregnant right away. We were blessed with a daughter in 1969. We tried to have more children, but it didn't happen. Our only child was a true daddy's girl. At sixteen, she started seeing a nice young man. They were the same age. He was a year ahead of her in school. Good kid. A smart kid. Valedictorian of his class. Willis had a fit when he found out about their relationship. No boy was good enough for his baby girl. The young man worked part-time at the movie theater. I thought he was good for our daughter. She was rebellious and struggled in school. It was a good day if I only got one call from the teachers. There was one teacher though who never called. Her chemistry teacher."

Her hands are beginning to warm up in between mine.

"School was almost over. My daughter told me about their plans to spend their precious summer days together. He was going off to college. It took some convincing, but Willis finally agreed to let her go to the boy's graduation. When she didn't come home by dinnertime, Willis was livid. He was about to go looking for her. At the same time, the boy's parents came knocking on our door looking for their son. He disappeared after the graduation. A verbal disagreement broke out. His parents blamed us. Willis blamed their son. I tried to convince them the kids were just spending as much time together as they could. The neighbors called the police. It was a big to-do on our street. The officers made the boy's parents leave. Willis called his Army buddies to get help with searching for our daughter. I went to her room to look for clues and prayed she'd come home. The days turned to weeks. Weeks to months. Months to nineteen years. I never gave up hope for our daughter. She would never just run away. I knew something terrible had to have happened to them."

I pull a couple tissues from the box on the tray and hand them to her. Marie nods her gratitude and wipes her eyes.

"Early one morning, Willis got a call. After a short conversation, he hightailed it out of the house. I thought it strange he would leave so suddenly and not tell me where he was going. I got worried when he didn't come home before I went to bed. He wasn't there when I woke the next morning. I paced the floor all day. Called everyone I knew. Late that evening, the phone rang. It was Bryan. He said Willis was injured and was asking for me. He said he was sending someone to the house to take me to the airport. I needed my passport and Mil ID and he'd explain everything once I got to my destination. I rushed around the house to be ready on time. Tony knocked on the door exactly one hour after the phone call. When we got to the airport, Tony made sure I boarded my flight, then rushed off for his flight to Arizona. Bryan met me at the gate at the airport in Zweibruken, Germany. He drove me to a military medical center."

Tissues forgotten, grief-stricken tears roll down her cheeks.

"It frightened me to see men holding guns and standing in front of a hospital room door. After going through an identity verification, I was allowed inside. Willis looked pale and weak. He was hooked up to machines. A bloody gauze pad taped over his stomach. *I know what happened to our daughter,*" he struggled to say, but then a machine started to beep and they rushed him off to surgery. Bryan stayed by my side and was back and forth on the phone with Tony making sure someone was protected. I had no clue as to what was happening. I kept asking myself, who are these people? Who is my husband? I wanted to know where our daughter had been for nineteen years and why she never came home. I wanted to know why Willis was in a military hospital in Germany with a life-threatening injury when he'd been discharged from the Army for over thirty years. The surgery took hours. Once Willis was out of recovery and conscious, they let me see him. I had questions that he needed to answer. I remember being furious with him. Willis told me about being Second Command of Phantom. He said our daughter and her boyfriend ran away to California and she was pregnant when they left home. Then he told me…" She pauses to catch her breath. "He told me our daughter was dead. She and her boyfriend were victims of a drive-by shooting. Her boyfriend died instantly. Our daughter died at the hospital, but her baby survived and was raised in foster care."

Hold your breath.

"Bryan got a phone call and left Germany to get back to the States. I stayed with Willis until he was strong enough to be transferred to the military hospital here in Colorado. He stepped down from his position. Bryan was the youngest man to be appointed Second Command. Twenty-six years old and in charge of a secret military branch. Willis was so proud of him. It took months for Willis to fully recover. Then we went to Tucson, Arizona to see our granddaughter."

Tingles ripple up my spine. Marie's Southern drawl is more pronounced.

"Willis and I were there when our granddaughter graduated, with honors, with a Master's in Psychology at age twenty."

Snatch away from her. Sit up straight in the chair. Begin to shake your head. Let tears pool in your eyes.

"We clapped proudly when you, our granddaughter, graduated

with honors with a Doctorate in Clinical Psychology." Marie's eyes plead for understanding. "Before your grandfather gave your hand away in marriage, he warned Bryan, to take care of our granddaughter or there will be hell to pay."

Let your emotions make your body quiver. Slowly shake your head like you don't believe her.

"What's... your daughter's... name?" I stutter.

"On your birth certificate, her name is Antoinette Beaudry-Tatum. But your mother's real name is Elizabeth Elaine Langford. Your father was Daniel Lawrence Tatum. You have his brown eyes."

Cover your mouth with your hands. Eyes bugged out and scream like your life depends on it.

"Arété ça, manmzèl. Mo fini ki bezin a dèt fini fé. Lála alé prepare la-yé fiy a parti. Dépéshé, piti. Nô proménné va gin isit banbay."

"She said: 'Stop it, young lady. I done what needed to be done. Now go prepare the girls to leave. Hurry now, child. Our ride will be here soon.'

"Answer: Yes, grandmother. "Wé, granmé."

**Bryan and Danielle's Story
Concludes
In the Third Novel
in the**

MEN OF PHANTOM SERIES

SECRETS AND LIES
Coming October 2017

———◆———

CHAPTER ONE

"HI, YOU MUST BE HAWK," Danielle says. She opens the screen door. "James left me a message. I could barely understand it because of the background noise, but I did make out to expect you." She steps back and gestures for me to come in.

I walk into the living room. The first thing I notice is the scent of flowers. I don't see any around the living room, but there are petals in a glass container on the coffee table.

"You must be Danielle, his girlfriend." I hold out my hand.

Her gaze drops to my feet and travels up, pausing for a second on my thighs then the fly of my jeans. The fingers of her left hand tug her earlobe.

Danielle stares into my eyes. Her lips part, and I witness the slow escape of her exhaling. My body reacts.

It's one thing to view her through a camera lens; up close can't compare. Something about seeing Danielle in person. Being this close to her. Gives me a different perspective on how I should approach this case. I feel this— pull toward her.

She blinks then shakes her head. The connection is broken, but not the gravity between us. She shakes my hand and holds up her left to show off the gold band around her finger. "I'm his wife."

The thought of her with that traitor makes me angry. My grip on her hand tightens. "What?! Edwards never said anything about… are you old enough to be married?"

Danielle snatches her hand back. Her eyes go from welcoming to frosty in a matter of seconds. "Since yesterday evening. And I'm of consensual age, Mr. Hawk."

The way she said my name makes me sound like an old man. Judging by her body language, I'm guessing that's exactly what she intended.

I raise my hands, surrendering. "I'm sorry, that came out wrong."

Her shoulders relax. "I apologize as well. I'm used to being questioned about my age. Today I have a massive headache and my temper is quick. And I'm taking my last final in an hour."

I walk around the back of the loveseat, drop my duffle bag and sit. On the coffee table is an empty bottle of expensive champagne. No glasses.

My arms rest along the back of the loveseat as my right ankle rest on my left knee. I make myself at home. I look around the room, spotting the hidden surveillance cameras Tony and I installed a few weeks back.

Two opened shiny black foil packages under the sofa across from me catch my eye. I try not to let it show on my face how much the condom packages make my gut churn. The thought of her screwing Edwards is sickening.

I concentrate on her pretty brown eyes. "Where's your husband? I thought he'd be home from the base by now."

"James deployed this morning for a tour in Iraq."

My arms drop and I plant both feet on the carpet. "He's where?"

"On his way to the Middle East."

"Edwards didn't say anything about a tour when I called."

"He asked me to apologize and for me to let you crash on the couch for a few days."

I get to my feet and reach for the handles of my duffle bag. "Thanks, but I can't stay here if Edwards isn't here. I'll find a motel for the night, then hop on the bus to go visit my parents in Colorado Springs." Why did I just tell her where my parents live?

"It's graduation season. All the decent hotels and motels are booked up."

"I slept in a six by six hole in the ground for three months. I'm sure I can handle one night in a less-than-stellar motel." Okay, Hawk. Get your shit together. You do not tell the object of your assignment anything personal!

"James wouldn't say to let you stay if he didn't think he could trust you. Besides, I will be in and out most of the week anyway. I picked up some extra hours at work. We need the money."

"Let me pay you for the…"

"That wasn't a hint about you paying to stay here." She stops me. "I wouldn't feel comfortable charging you. You are too tall for the sofa so I doubt you'll get much rest." Her eyes travel my body again.

I leave my bag where it is and resume my relaxed posture on the sofa. The corner of my mouth turns up. I lick my lips. "I'm good with my hands *and* I can cook. If you won't let me pay for my stay, the least I can do is earn my keep in other ways."

Danielle's thighs press together and her nipples draw an outline in her shirt. I hold her gaze for a minute longer than what is considered friendly.

A mischievous smirk forms within the smile on her face. "The handle on the toilet is broken and the garbage disposal isn't working in the kitchen. Are you DIY or the type to call the manager? I guess I'll know the answer when I get back." She picks up her backpack off the counter that separates the living room from the tiny kitchen. "There is a spare key in the cabinet over the sink in case you need to go out for anything. I'll see you around eleven. There isn't much to eat in the fridge." Danielle walks out the door before I can respond.

The hawk stirs. I sit, staring at the closed door. The vibrations of my cell phone in my pocket breaks the trance.

"How long we got?" Tony asks.

I check my watch. "Roughly seven hours. Six just in case she leaves work early. Do you know how to fix a toilet handle?"

"No."

"What about a garbage disposal?"

"Dawg, what were you guys talking about?"

"Never mind. Find a hardware store and buy new ones and ask how to install 'em. I'm going to start removing the cameras."

"Hey, call Amelia. Ig said she's been blowing up your desk phone.

Oh, and Langford wants you to report in once you get set up."

"Okay, thanks." I end the call.

Before I get started, I go over and retrieve the condom packets from under the sofa, pick up the champagne bottle off the coffee table, and dump them in the trash. Next I go around the apartment and dump all the waste baskets. Not that I want to find the used condoms, that thought of them being in here makes me want to hurl.

The last trash I empty is the one in the bathroom. I frown when I see tampon wrappers. I don't know too many females who are into period sex.

I tie up the garbage bag and take it down to the dumpster in the back. Now I can concentrate on finding the faulty cameras.

By the time Tony gets here, I have everything ready for us to install the replacements. "We staying the week or heading back tonight?"

"You can head back once we're done. I know Charly's pissed that you canceled on her again."

He hands me a camera after I get up on the stepladder. "Nah, she was chill when I talked to her this morning. I told her I have training all week."

I secure it in place, turn it on, and put the cover over it. "Is she the one you'll tell about Phantom?"

"One day. But definitely not now. Maybe after we're married." He unpacks another camera and gets it ready.

I climb down the ladder and move it to the next spot. "You really want to be tied to one woman?"

"Charly's my do right girl."

"What's a do right girl?"

"The one girl who makes you want to do right. The one who is different from all the others. The only one you can be real around."

"Man, where you get that sappy shit from? A female I bet. Love is just a word people use to explain that animalistic need to fuck all day and all night." I shove him toward the ladder while I turn on Danielle's computer and log on to the site to access the camera.

"First, my dad is the one who told me about do right girls. Second, you have a twisted view about love considering how long your parents have been together. And third, I hope I'm around when you meet that one girl who knocks you on yo ass."

"Whatever," I say. "Angle it a little more to the right."

Tony makes the adjustment and secures the camera.

It takes us an hour to finish with the installation. Tony questions me about what Danielle looks like in person. We've been friends long enough to know when someone is holding back information. He doesn't push, but the jokes and innuendos are rolling off his tongue.

When we're done, we search the apartment for stolen information. Edwards wouldn't take everything with him. He's been cautious with each transaction.

We find a stack of letters in the back of the closet under the floorboards. Edwards and his twin brother knew enough about the worldwide web to use an antiquated way to correspond. This must be how they exchanged classified information and communicated where and when transactions would go down.

By seven thirty, we have the letters copied and put away. Tony reads the instructions on how to change the toilet handle while I do the work. The garbage disposal was easier. All I had to do was push a button.

I check the refrigerator and cabinets for food. As much money as Edwards was raking in, I can't believe his meager lifestyle. The fact that his wife feels she needs to take on extra hours at work just to make ends meet tells me he's stacking his cash and she knows nothing about it.

I have Tony take me to the store before he heads back to the hotel. I tell him to go home to his girl before she dumps him. He says he's staying.

When Danielle walks through the door, twenty minutes after eleven, she looks like she's ready to fall on her face. I take her backpack and guide her to the sofa.

"Still have a headache?" I ask.

She nods. Her eyes close and her head drops back.

Feeling sorry for Danielle, I unlace her shoes and slip them off her feet.

"Thank you," she says and tucks her feet under her butt.

"Have you eaten today?"

She shakes her head. "My stomach's been queasy all day."

Can a woman be pregnant and on their period? I'll call my sister when Danielle goes to sleep. "I'll make you some soup and crackers. You need food in your stomach before you take something for the headache."

"We don't have any in the house."

"I went to the store earlier." I stand. "And I fixed the toilet and the disposal. *And*—I straightened up the living room."

Danielle smiles with her eyes closed. Without thinking, I lean over about to kiss her forehead, then stop myself. I go to the kitchen and grab a can of soup out of the cabinet.

"How much did you have to drink last night?"

"Not even half a glass of champagne."

"You had to have had more than that. The bottle was empty. Did you guys have friends over to help you celebrate?"

"Nope. I remember feeling sleepy after a few sips so I stopped drinking it. James woke me this morning before he left. I'd fallen asleep on the loveseat. He finished the bottle."

I pause. He had sex with her while she was asleep? That dirty bastard! I'll kill him.

Danielle yawns. "We didn't consummate our marriage."

What?! But I found two condom packets under the sofa. Somebody was fucking last night. If it wasn't her and Edwards, then who? I make a mental note to go get the bag out of the dumpster and have Tony sort through it. Whatever he finds we'll give to Ig. I'm guessing Danielle was drugged last night and whatever was used didn't set well with her stomach.

I find a pot and turn on the stove. I keep an eye on her while I warm up the soup and put crackers on a plate. When it's done, I carry it to the living room and set it on the coffee table.

Danielle cracks an eye open, then closes it. I pick up the bowl and sit next to her. I scoop up a spoonful and hold it up to her lips. "Open."

Her lips part and I tip the spoon so the liquid dish pours into her mouth. She chews and swallows. "Yuck, canned soup."

I laugh and offer her another spoonful. She takes it without complaint. *This isn't so bad.* I switch up and hold a cracker up to her lips. This makes her smile. My eyes become fixated on her mouth. Danielle is blindly allowing me to take care of her in this moment of illness. I'm a stranger. It would be wrong to take advantage of the trust she's giving me.

She finishes the soup and is munching on the last cracker. I take the bowl back to the kitchen and go to the bathroom and get the bottle of pain reliever I saw in the medicine cabinet earlier today.

Again, with her eyes closed, Danielle opens her mouth and I slip two white pills past her lips and hold up the glass of water.

She swallows. "Thank you, Bryan."

I settle next to her on the sofa and guide her head to my shoulder. "It's my pleasure, Dani."

I pick up the TV remote, prop my feet up on the coffee table, and turn down the volume. She cuddles into my side and gets comfortable. My cell phone buzzes. I ease it out of my pocket and read the text from Tony. I look straight into the camera. Smile. And flip him off.

———◆———

What is that smell?! Why is it so hot?

I open my eyes and look around. Oh yeah, Ig's Camaro is on fire. The second blast knocked me against the brick wall. I fell behind the bushes. I exhale and roll onto my stomach and military crawl to the edge of the scrubs to peek down the driveway in front of the lobby. Dani and the PPOs are not out here.

The loud sound of a helicopter's blades slicing the night air on the rooftop mixes with the sirens and horns of the fire engines racing through the street toward the hospital.

I check my watch, then look up again. Hawkeye Personal Protection's helicopter is hovering over the hospital's helipad. It flies off with my girls onboard. I'm on blackout. No communications with anyone. Yes, I'm scared for my family.

I do a visual check of the area, then climb to my feet and jog down the driveway, sticking to the shadows, to the back of the building. I hide and wait for the next round of people to drive away. Dani is one of them. I need to see for myself that she is okay. That last confession was a complete shock, but I needed her to know everything just in case.

BOOKS BY JACKI RENÉE

MEN OF PHANTOM SERIES

Necessary Lies – Book One of Lies Trilogy
Lies You Tell – Book Two of Lies Trilogy

Be a part of an exclusive club, join the Men of Phantom Street
Team. For more details visit **www.iamjackirenee.com**.

Connect with me on:
twitter @iamjackirenee
facebook /iamjackirenee
instagram /iamjackirenee
goodreads /goodreadscomJacki_Renee

www.ingramcontent.com/pod-product-compliance
Lightning Source LLC
Chambersburg PA
CBHW060954120726
47910CB00002B/626